After O'Connor

After O'Connor

STORIES FROM CONTEMPORARY GEORGIA

Edited by Hugh Ruppersburg

The University of Georgia Press · *Athens and London*

Published in cooperation with the Georgia Humanities Council

This publication was supported in part by the
Georgia Humanities Council.

Acknowledgments for previously published work
appear on pages 373–375, which constitute an
extension of the copyright page.

Library of Congress Cataloging-in-Publication Data
After O'Connor : stories from contemporary
Georgia / edited by Hugh Ruppersburg.
    p. cm.
    ISBN 0-8203-2556-2 (alk. paper) — ISBN 0-8203-2557-0
(pbk. : alk. paper)
    1. Short stories, American—Georgia. 2. Georgia—
Social life and customs—Fiction. I. Ruppersburg, Hugh.
PS558.G4 A35 2003
813'.01089758—dc21   2003005060

British Library Cataloging-in-Publication Data available

Contents

Acknowledgments

I am grateful to a number of individuals for their help with this anthology: Nancy Grayson, associate director and editor-in-chief of the University of Georgia Press, who provided support, direction, and encouragement from the start; Nicole Mitchell, director of the Press, for her endorsement of this project; Erin McElroy, assistant editor, and Ben Emanuel, editorial assistant, for their work on editorial matters and permissions; Wyatt Anderson, dean of the Franklin College of Arts and Sciences at the University of Georgia, for material and moral support; Sam Prestridge, for assistance and advice, for library work, proofreading, and editing, and for the Elvis lawn ornament in my front yard; Kristen Griffin, for her proofreading and clerical skills; and Stephen Corey, Michael Bishop, T. R. Hummer, and Judith Cofer, for advice and information along the way. And most especially I thank my wife, Patricia, and our sons, Michael, Charles, and Max.

This volume is dedicated to my friends and colleagues Wyatt and Margaret, Clif and Sylvia.

Introduction

Flannery O'Connor's death in 1964 marked the end of an era in Georgia writing. One of O'Connor's central themes was the modern world and its corrupting influences. In story after story, from "The River" to "A Good Man Is Hard to Find" to "The Enduring Chill" to her novel *Wise Blood,* she pondered the menace of modernity. One of her symbols of the modern world was Atlanta, a twentieth-century infernal city that is never far off in her fiction—if it is not physically near, it is close by metaphorically. Characters who come from Atlanta invariably are pernicious influences (the parents in "The River") or are doomed (the family in "A Good Man Is Hard to Find"). Given her portrayal of the modern world and its inhabitants, we can conclude that O'Connor was not optimistic about Georgia's future.

Had she lived past the age of thirty-nine, O'Connor probably would not have changed her mind about modern Georgia, though Atlanta itself has greatly changed. The city she described in some of her stories of the 1950s and 1960s barely resembles the international Atlanta of the twenty-first century, with its population in the millions, expressways and perpetual clogs of traffic, skyscrapers, sports teams, MARTA, CNN, and Centennial Olympic Park. Set against what it has become, the Atlanta of O'Connor's lifetime seems quaint and parochial. She would hardly recognize modern Atlanta, and she clearly wouldn't like it.

O'Connor belonged to a generation of writers defined by the first half of the twentieth century and by the Second World War, the central event of their lives. The dawning of the nuclear age, the revelations about the Holocaust, the Cold War, the growth of the American interstate system, improvements in transportation and communication, and the rapid development of computers and other forms of technology all gave a new character to modern Georgia and the rest of the nation. Although many of the best known of Georgia writers from the middle decades of the century—O'Connor, Carson McCullers, Byron Herbert Reece, Margaret Mitchell, Conrad Aiken, Frank Yerby, and others—may have believed that they lived in a modern world, their world is nearly as remote from the present day as the nineteenth-century world of A. B. Longstreet and Joel Chandler Harris was from theirs. The writers of the last several decades in Georgia—the writers of contemporary Georgia—thus merit consideration on their own distinctive ground.

All of the writers in this collection have written and lived in Georgia for a significant period of time. Some were born in the state and lived out their lives here; others have simply passed through. We no longer live in an age when we can expect people to stay in one place for the main part of their lives. The 2000 census of Georgia shows that a majority of the people now living in the Atlanta area were born outside the state, and a significant percentage were born outside the United States—many of them in Latin America and Asia. Nearly 45 percent of the state's residents, or more than 3.36 million people, were born outside the state, and more than half a million of these outside the United States. By 2010, a majority of people living in the state will have been born somewhere else. These figures only hint at the changes in Georgia since the end of the Second World War, changes that continue to occur today. The 2000 census revealed a state more diverse than Zell Miller ever imagined when he first used the term "two Georgias."

These demographic shifts in Georgia's population are bringing about a significant change in Georgia's culture. We cannot assume—if we ever could—that being from Georgia means sharing in a common set of values and beliefs. A modern citizen of Georgia is as likely to be from San Francisco or Baltimore as from Atlanta or Valdosta or Brunswick. One might argue that there are different cultural areas in Georgia, that the culture of Atlanta is distinct from the culture of the north Georgia mountains or the wiregrass region of southwest Georgia. Though there is merit to this argument, even within specific areas such as Atlanta there is radical variation. What it means to be a "regional" writer, or a writer from Georgia or from any other state, has changed fundamentally. While it is clear that in the more rural areas of Georgia the ideas of place and a regional heritage may remain important, it is also clear that for many writers they no longer are relevant.

Although O'Connor used regional characters and settings in her work and explored themes that might be identified as "southern," she also wrote about subjects fundamental to the human condition. Her writing was known throughout the world, and she was widely respected as one of the great practitioners of the short story form. Her concern with subjects not limited by region links her to many writers of the present day. At the time of her death more than thirty-five years ago, however, only a few of the writers in this volume had reached adulthood, and a few hadn't even been born. For some of these writers—Bailey White, Lynna Williams, Pam Durban, and Ferrol Sams, for instance—O'Connor was a grand and imposing monument in an old southern literary tradition which they wished (consciously or not) to join. William Faulkner, Eudora Welty, and Katherine Anne Porter were among the other members of this tradition, and they were imposing role models. (Speaking of Faulkner's iconic status and influence, O'Connor once quipped, "Nobody wants his mule and wagon stalled on the same track the Dixie Limited is roaring down.")[1] Other writers rejected the tradition and its influence. They might recognize its vitality and its accomplishments, but they did not feel a part of it, perhaps did not want to belong to it, and meant to follow their own paths. Some were quite insistent in doing so.

Alice Walker has eloquently expressed her admiration for O'Connor in her essay "Beyond the Peacock: The Reconstruction of Flannery O'Connor," in which she wrote that "O'Connor's characters—whose humanity if not their sanity is taken for granted, and who are miserable, ugly, narrow-minded, atheistic, and of intense racial smugness and arrogance, with not a graceful, pretty one anywhere who is not, at the same time, a joke—shocked and delighted me. . . . She was for me the first great modern writer from the South."[2] Walker makes clear that her admiration for O'Connor does not automatically extend to other white writers in the southern literary tradition, such as Faulkner and Welty, and that it is the individual qualities of O'Connor's fiction she admires, rather than the tradition O'Connor was a part of.

For a number of contemporary writers in Georgia, especially African American writers, the white southern literary tradition looms as an oppressive force, and they have looked elsewhere for material, values, and inspiration. Shay Youngblood's *Big Mama Stories,* with its narration through African American English and its emphasis on family and neighborly kinships in the African American community, seems deliberately to use the conventions of her own culture. Tina McElroy Ansa's story "Willie Bea and Jaybird" evokes the work of Zora Neale Hurston so strongly that it is no surprise to learn that Ansa acknowledges Hurston as a major influence. Pearl Cleage's story "Four from That Summer: Atlanta, 1981," written as a kind of personal memoir about the serial murders of African American children during the early 1980s in Atlanta, combines letters and narrative to evoke the horror that many Georgians felt about what was happening that summer. Anthony Grooms in his story "Negro Progress" describes a young man caught up in the turmoil of the civil rights movement in Birmingham, Alabama. His character wants a conventional life of marriage and affluence but finds himself drawn into the crisis of the moment. The specific dilemma of a young black man trying to decide whether to commit to the civil rights movement is one perhaps faced by many young African Americans in the 1950s and 1960s. Though this subject lies at the heart of the African American experience in the twentieth century, in a more general sense the story is about any young man trying to choose the course he will follow in life. Thus though the story might be the product of African American concerns and traditions, it also speaks to a wider audience.

For a few writers, the literary traditions of American writers mean little—an example is Ha Jin, a native of mainland China, where he lived until he moved to the United States in 1985. And for many, perhaps most, of the writers in this volume, the literary traditions of the South are not all-powerful forces. They are as much a matter of literary style as they are a set of geographically based themes, values, and beliefs. They are employed by choice and will, not as an inescapable fact of existence. In this sense, the notion of regional traditions no longer has the meaning it once did.

The typical writer in this anthology was either born somewhere else and then moved to Georgia or was born in Georgia and moved away. The exceptions are the native-born Georgians who have lived all their years in the state and who will in all likelihood die here, Ferrol Sams, Bailey White, and Mary Hood among them. Many of the stories included here are set in Georgia, but their settings are as likely to be small towns and large cities (such as Atlanta) as the rural parts of the state. Others are set outside the state—in Mississippi, California, Alabama, or China. Many are marked by the southern literary traditions out of which they were written; others show the mark of other literary influences, or reveal no recognizable influences at all.

A good example of a traditional southern story is James Kilgo's "The Resurrection of George T. Sutton." Kilgo, born and raised in South Carolina, moved to Georgia in 1967 and lived here until his death in 2002. Though his 1998 novel *Daughter of My People* chronicles events from his family past in the South Carolina low country, his story in this volume, "The Resurrection of George T. Sutton," is informed by his experiences in both South Carolina and Georgia. Details of geography aside, the attitudes it expresses about place, family, and tradition are familiar in both states. It is a traditional southern story in its concern with a community heritage and its use of oral narrative. It is a story about a story, about a rumor that has circulated in the town for years. The story's narrator finally realizes he must track the rumor down, not out of mere curiosity, but because it is a part of the community that gave him his identity. He finally must invent portions of the story when he fails to tease out all the facts. In this sense it is a story about how writers write, merging fact and fantasy with the purpose of arriving at some image of reality that is true despite its half-imagined, half-real origins. Readers will recognize that Kilgo was working the same veins of oral narrative and community talk mined by William Faulkner in such novels as *Absalom, Absalom!* and *The Hamlet,* though Kilgo had a different style and perspective.

Pam Durban's story "Soon" is written in a similar tradition, though her writing bears the influence of such southern literary ancestors as Eudora Welty and Elizabeth Spencer (and also of Virginia Woolf, a British literary ancestor).

Durban was born in South Carolina. She lived much of her adult life in Georgia but now resides in North Carolina. Her fiction draws on traditions from all the places she has lived, and she belongs to Georgia as much as to South and North Carolina. "Soon" is about three generations of women struggling with their heritage and the region in which they live. In Bailey White's "An Unsuitable Attachment" and Lynna Williams's "Comparative Religion" we encounter the kind of eccentric humor and bizarre characters made popular in the fiction of Eudora Welty (both these writers work in her shadow, though they step outside it as well). Janice Daugharty's "You're No Angel Yourself," whose narrator recalls the characters in Welty's "The Petrified Man," describes in comical yet empathetic terms the efforts of a recently widowed fifty-two-year-old woman to find a man at a country music bar.

Other stories may have a regional setting but in fact concern issues that are of general importance in the contemporary world, issues for which setting is merely an incidental context. If family can represent tradition, it sometimes proves a not entirely happy burden for the characters who shoulder it. We see this clearly in Sheri Joseph's "The Waiting Room," where family members must decide whether to end life support after a brother's suicide attempt (this story recalls Katherine Anne Porter's "He"). The story's main character must make the difficult decision when no one else is able. A similar burden weighs on the dutiful daughter in Lynna Williams's "Comparative Religion," who must drive the countryside with her addled mother while her father is away. It is perhaps no surprise that Williams has chafed at the label of southern writer, though in some ways it fits her well. Cynthia Shearer's "Flight Patterns" and its treatment of a daughter's problematic relationship with her errant father is another story about the burdens of living in a family. Greg Johnson, in "Crazy Ladies," illuminates a critical moment in a family's existence and the forces that form the personalities of the women who belong to it. Philip Lee Williams's "An Early Snow" is set in north Georgia, but the setting has little to do with the basic concerns of the story: an old woman who has wandered away from home and the unhappy daughter who takes care of her. The concerns of Judson Mitcham's "The Light," which explores the narrator's grief and guilt over a dead friend, also grow out of a human situation rather than the region in which characters live. The story could take place anywhere, and the setting simply provides a context for the events that occur.

Other writers in this anthology may examine similar issues but abandon a regional setting entirely. Carol Lee Lorenzo's "Nervous Dancer" and John Holman's "Rita's Mystery" focus on marriages in crisis. Charlotte Holmes's "Gifts," set in California and written in the style of Raymond Carver, describes a woman scarred by substance abuse struggling to hold on to a personal relationship that she is unwilling to believe she might have earned. Scott Ely's "The Lady of the Lake" illuminates a crucial moment in the lives of two friends whose paths are about to diverge forever. Although this story takes place in Mississippi, the setting is entirely incidental. Charlie Smith's stark "Park Diary" is best described as set in the mind of its narrator.

A few of the stories in this volume look sharply at the burden of place and associated traditions. This may be one of the themes of Pam Durban's "Soon." Another example is Melanie Sumner's "The Guide," about a young woman traveling alone in the Sahara. Culturally and personally, the woman has lost her bearings, and the "guide" who leads her serves only to confirm to her the depth of her plight. The rejection of one's own region may be a basic theme for Sumner, whose stories in her collection *Polite Society* by their very subject—a young woman who joins the Peace Corps and goes to teach in Africa—exemplify a desire to move as far away from one's native region as possible. Sumner's recent novel, *The School of Beauty and Charm,* about a rebellious girl chafing against the constraints of family life in a small southern town, continues the pattern. Frank Manley in his story "Chickamauga" offers a different take on the subject of region and tradition. A man scarred by his experience in the Vietnam War visits a Civil War battlefield and encounters a mentally deficient character named Sonny Hightower who can neither read the historical markers nor understand what they signify. He is tempted to believe that they signify nothing: "There are no mistakes. Invisible pathways lead through the earth, currents of the air and sea beyond our means of comprehension. It all made sense now, just for a moment, until he looked at Sonny Hightower and realized there was no message. He was a moron. That was the message." Ultimately, however, he arrives at a different conclusion.

A writer who moves easily from one kind of writing to another is Michael Bishop, who is well known nationally for his science fiction stories and novels. He writes more conventional fiction as well, as "The Road Leads Back," about a famous Georgia writer and her friend, demonstrates. This story considers issues of friendship and faith, and of how friendship can be tested when one friend is an ardent believer and the other a skeptic. Despite the clearly identifiable southern style of this story, an element of fantasy does creep in. Dramatist Jim Grimsley provides another example of a writer who moves in and out of styles and modes of writing. He has written in several genres—drama, southern stories, novels concerned with gay sexuality, and science fiction. In "New Jerusalem" he works in the O'Connor tradition. This excellent but traditional story—with its use of dialect, rural characters, and a spiritual theme—is increasingly rare in contemporary southern fiction. Toni Cade Bambara, well known as an

African American writer of novels, stories, and plays, in "Going Critical" writes about an African American mother and daughter confronting issues of disease and morality that have little to do with race.

Among the writers whose stories seem to exist entirely outside the context of Georgia and the American South, Ha Jin immediately comes to mind. So too does Judith Ortiz Cofer, though she has written a number of essays and poems with southern settings and themes. Their stories in this volume at first glance may seem so divergent from the others that they hardly seem to belong. Yet they do belong, and in the most fundamental of ways.

Cofer's "Nada," set in New Jersey, on the surface seems to be about a culture unfamiliar to many Georgians. It describes an older immigrant woman who has lost her husband to a heart attack and her son to the war in Vietnam, where he was fighting along with other Americans. Doña Ernestina stands as an emblem of what it means to move from one place and culture to another. The first sentence of the story reveals that "Almost as soon as Doña Ernestina got the telegram about her son's having been killed in Vietnam, she started giving her possessions away." Her loss of husband and son is the loss of her last link with the land of her birth. "Nada" illustrates what it means to have and then to lose an identity based on the culture of one's birth. What Doña Ernestina experiences is hardly unique to people who have moved to the American mainland from the island of Puerto Rico; it is in fact a theme of importance in traditional southern writing, and to the experiences of people who have come to Georgia from other parts of the world. Flannery O'Connor would have appreciated the story for its demonstration of the impact of the loss of one's past and culture— a theme she wrote about in her own way in "A Late Encounter with the Enemy" and "The Displaced Person."

Ha Jin's "Too Late," like most of his fiction, is set in mainland China and displays the mark of his experiences during the Cultural Revolution. The story, about a soldier named Kong Kai who is consorting with a young woman from a local village, at first seems to have little to do with the Georgia writing elsewhere in this collection. Jin wrote it, we can assume, without the slightest regard for the place where he happened to be writing it: the place that mattered to him was clearly the one in which the story was set. The subject at first seems to be the Chinese army's wish to control the behavior of its recruits. Yet the story fits well with others in this Georgia volume. It is first of all about people in love, a subject that extends beyond borders of place and language. The theme of two young people who seek to be together in spite of the forces against them is in fact quite familiar in the literature of America and the South. There is even a faint echo of John Keats's "The Eve of St. Agnes" in the end of this story, whose young lovers flee into the night and are lost forever, except for the brief note

Kong sends to his commanding officer a year later. The tale of the army's failure to deny the happiness of these young lovers is passed from one person to another and becomes something akin to legend. We then begin to see in Ha Jin's story a kinship with Jim Kilgo's "The Resurrection of George T. Sutton," Tina Ansa's "Willie Bea and Jaybird," Charlotte Holmes's "Gifts," and others.

In general, the stories in this collection demonstrate that writers and writing in contemporary Georgia continue a vital and living literary tradition. Yet it is a tradition that is constantly redefining and reinventing itself, and that grows increasingly broad and encompassing as the years pass. Certain facts of the state's geography—and its people, culture, politics, and economy—may help form the tradition, but it is also the product of numerous influences from outside the state and its region. We sense the looming and inescapable past in some of these stories, but we sense as well its powerful absence, either through the deliberate way writers contrive to leave out the past or through their indifference to it. And many of these stories, unwilling to embrace any sense of a tradition linked to some fleeting and receding sense of the past, clearly look forward to the future.

The literary tradition these stories represent is so fluid and diverse that it transcends the conventional meaning of the word *tradition.* Rather, it is a continuum that extends beyond the boundaries of the state to embrace the rest of the nation and the world.

Notes

1. "The Grotesque in Southern Fiction," in *Mystery and Manners,* ed. Sally Fitzgerald and Robert Fitzgerald (New York: Farrar, Straus, and Giroux, 1974), p. 45.
2. Alice Walker, *In Search of Our Mothers' Gardens: Womanist Prose* (New York: Harcourt Brace, 1975), p. 52.

Tina McElroy Ansa

Tina Ansa's portrayal of characters in "Willie Bea and Jaybird" recalls Zora Neale Hurston in such stories as "The Gilded Six Bits" and her novel *Their Eyes Are Watching God*. Though relatively brief, her story succinctly captures Willie Bea's character and the arc of her relationship with her husband Jaybird. "When I read Zora Neale Hurston's *Their Eyes Were Watching God* and *Mules and Men*," Ansa has said, "I thought to myself, 'You mean I can write about my people, the way we walk and talk, how we live and love, and it can be literature?!'" Ansa was born in Macon and educated at Spelman College in Atlanta. After working as a newspaper reporter for the *Atlanta Constitution* and the *Charlotte Observer* and as a correspondent for CBS Sunday Morning, she moved with her husband to St. Simons Island on the Georgia coast, where she continues to live. Her first novel, *Baby of the Family* (1989), was cited by the Georgia Center for the Book as one of the "Top 25 Books Every Georgian Should Read." Her other novels include *Ugly Ways* (1993), *The Hand I Fan With* (1996), and *You Know Better* (2002). Ansa has twice received the Georgia Authors Series Award.

Willie Bea and Jaybird

When Willie Bea first saw Jaybird in The Place, she couldn't help herself. She wanted him so bad she sucked in her bottom lip, cracked with the cold, then she ran her tongue so slowly over her top lip that she could taste the red Maybelline lipstick she had put on hours before. He looked like something that would be good to eat, like peach cobbler or a hot piece of buttered cornbread.

She had just entered the bar clutching her black purse under her arm and smiling to try to make herself look attractive among the six o'clock crowd of drinkers and dancers and socializers, every one of them glad to be done with work for the day. He was there at the end of the bar in his golden Schlitz uniform sharing a quart of Miller High Life beer with a buddy. Willie Bea noticed right away how he leaned his long frame clear across the bar, bent at the waist, his elbows resting easily on the Formica counter. There didn't seem to be a tense bone in his lean, efficient body.

He look like he could go anywhere in the world, Willie Bea thought as she followed her big-butt friend Patricia as she weaved her way to a nearby table already jammed with four of her friends, two men, two women. "If somebody put him in a white jacket and a flower in his buttonhole, he could pass for an actor in a Technicolor movie."

As the jukebox started up again, playing a driving Sam and Dave number, he looked around the bar, picked up his glass of beer, and headed toward her table with his chin held high over the other patrons. When he smoothly pulled up a chair to her table and straddled it backwards, Willie Bea crossed her stick legs and pinched her friend Pat's thigh under the table to give her some Sen-Sen for her breath.

"Hey, Little Mama, you got time for a tired working man?"

She had to remember to wipe the uncomfortable moisture from the corners of her mouth with her fingertips before she could respond to him.

She still felt that way, four years after they had started going together, when she looked at him.

Nothing gave her more pleasure than to be asked her marital status with Jaybird around.

"Willie Bea, girl, where you been keeping yourself?" some big-mouthed woman would shout at her over the din of the jukebox at The Place. "I ain't seen you in a month of Sundays. You still living with your aunt, ain't you?" This last expectantly with pity.

Willie Bea would roll her shoulders and dip her ears from side to side a couple of times in feigned modesty.

"Naw, girl, I *been* moved out of my aunt's," Willie Bea would answer. "I'm married now. I live with my . . . *husband.*"

The old horse's big mouth would fall open, then close, then open as if she were having trouble chewing this information.

"Husband? Married??!!"

"Uh-huh. That's my husband over there by the jukebox. Naw, not him. My Jay is the tall light-skinned one, the one with the head full of curly hair."

Willie Bea never even bothered to look at her inquisitor when she pointed out Jay. She could hear the effect the weight of the revelation had had on the woman. And Willie Bea only glanced smugly at the old cow as she raced around the bar nearly knocking over a chair to ask her friends and companions why no one told her that skinny little shiny-faced Willie Bea had a man.

"I thought she was sitting there mighty sassy-looking."

Even Willie Bea would have admitted it. Most days, she did feel sassy, and it was Jaybird who made her so. He burst into the bathroom while she was in the bathtub and pretended to take pictures of her with an imaginary camera. He teased her about flirting with Mr. Maurice, who owned the store on the corner near their boardinghouse, when the merchant sliced her baloney especially thin, the way she liked it.

Now, she really thought she was cute, with her little square monkey face and eager-to-please grin, a cheap jet-black Prince Valiant wig set on the top of her head like a wool cap with her short hair plaited underneath and a pair of black eyeglasses so thick that her eyes looked as if they were in fish bowls.

Jaybird had done that to her. He even called her "fine," an appellation that actually brought tears to her eyes, made huge and outlandish by the Coke-bottle-thick glasses.

"Fine." It was the one thing in life Willie Bea longed to be. She had no shape to speak of. She was just five feet tall and weighed about ninety pounds. But she did her best to throw that thing even though she had very little to throw.

"If I had me a big old butt like you, Pat," she would say to her friend, "y'all couldn't stand me."

The pitiful little knot of an ass that she had was her sorrow, especially after noticing from Jaybird's gaze that he appreciated a full ass. His favorite seemed to be the big heart-shaped ones that started real low and hung and swayed like a bustle when the woman walked. Many mornings, Jay lay in bed watching Bea move around the room getting dressed and thought, Her behind ain't no bigger than my fist. But he didn't dare say anything, even as a joke. He knew it would break her heart.

But since she knew she didn't have a big ass, she did what she had done since she was a child when someone told her what she was lacking: She pretended she did and acted as if her ass was the prize one in town. The one men in juke joints talked about.

Wherever she went—to the market, to work cleaning houses, to The Place, downtown to shop—she dressed as if she had that ass to show off.

She wore tight little straight skirts that she made herself on her landlady's sewing machine. Skirts of cotton or wool or taffeta no wider than twelve inches across. Not that wide, really, because she wanted the skirt to "cup," if possible, under the pones of her behind and to wrinkle across her crotch in front. Using less than a yard of material and a Simplicity quickie pattern she had bought years before and worked away to tatters, she took no more than an hour to produce one of her miniature skirts.

On Sundays, when the house was empty of other boarders or quiet from their sleep, Willie Bea used her landlady's sewing machine that she kept in the parlor. The steady growl of the old foot-pedal-run Singer disturbed no one. In fact, on those Sundays she and Jaybird went out and she did no sewing, the other tenants of the large white wooden house felt an unidentified longing and found themselves on the verge of complaining about the silence.

Willie Bea looked on the ancient sewing machine, kept in mint condition by the genial landlady who always wore plaid housedresses and her thin crimpy red hair in six skinny braids, as a blessing. She didn't mind that the machine was a foot-propelled model rather than an electric one. It never occurred to her to expect anything as extravagant as that. For her, the old machine was a step up from the tedious hand-sewing that she had learned and relied on as a child. With the waistbands neatly attached and the short zippers eased into place by machine, her skirts had a finished look that would have taken her all night to accomplish by hand.

Many times, she felt herself rocking gently to the rhythm she set with her bare feet on the cold iron treadle to ease a crick in her stiff back before she realized that she had been at the job nonstop all afternoon. Just using the machine made her happy, made her think of men watching her at the bus stops in her new tight skirt and later, maybe, these same men letting some sly comment drop in front of Jaybird about her shore looking good.

She imagined Jaybird jumping in the men's faces, half angry, half proud, to let them know that was his *wife* they were talking about. Just thinking of Jaybird saying "my wife" made her almost as happy as her being able to say "my husband."

She loved to go over in her head how it had come to pass, their marriage. They had been living together in one room of the boardinghouse at the top of Pleasant Hill for nearly three years, with him seeming to take for granted that they would be together for eternity and with her hardly daring to believe that he really wanted her, afraid to ask him why he picked her to love.

As with most of his decisions, movements, he surprised her.

One evening in August, he walked into their room and said, "Let's get married." As if the idea had just come to him, his and original. She responded in kind.

"Married? Married, Jay?" she said, pretending to roll the idea around in her head awhile. Then, "Okay, if you want."

It was her heart's desire, the play-pretty of her dreams, being this man's wife.

She bought stiff white lace from Newberry's department store to make a loose cropped sleeveless overblouse and a yard of white polished cotton and sewed a tight straight skirt for the ceremony at the courthouse.

When they returned to their room for the honeymoon, Willie Bea thought as she watched him take off his wedding suit that no other man could be so handsome, so charming, so full of self-assured cockiness . . . and still love her.

He was tall and slender in that way that made her know that he would be lean all his life, never going sway-backed and to fat around his middle like a pregnant woman. He was lithe and strong from lifting cases and kegs of Schlitz beer all day long, graceful from leaping on and off the running board of the moving delivery truck as it made its rounds of bars and stores.

Once when he had not seen her, Willie Bea had spied him hanging fearlessly off the back of the beer truck like a prince, face directly into the wind, his eyes blinking back the wind tears, a vacant look on his face. His head full of curly hair quivering in the wind. The setting sunlight gleamed off the chrome and steel of the truck, giving a golden-orange color to the aura that Willie Bea felt surrounded him all the time.

Overcome by the sight, Willie Bea had had to turn away into an empty doorway to silently weep over the beauty of her Jaybird.

Jaybird even made love the way she knew this man would—sweet and demanding. When her friend Pat complained about her own man's harsh, unfeeling fucking, Willie Bea joined in and talked about men like dogs. But first, in her own mind, she placed Jaybird outside the dog pack.

"Girl, just thank your lucky stars that you ain't hooked up with a man like Henry," Pat told her. "Although God knows they all alike. You may as well put 'em all in a croker sack and pick one out. They all the same. One just as good as the other. Just take your pick."

"Uh-huh, girl, you know you telling the truth," Willie Bea would answer.

"Why, that old dog of mine will just wake any time of the night and go to grabbing me and sticking his hand up my nightdress. He don't say nothing, just grunt. He just goes and do his business. I could be anything, a sack of flour, that chair you sitting on."

"What you be doing?" Willie Bea asked in her soft singsong voice, even though she already knew because Pat always complained about the same thing. But she asked because she and Pat had grown up together, she had been Pat's friend longer than anyone outside of her family. And Willie Bea knew what a friend was for.

"Shoot, sometimes I just lay there like I *am* a sack of flour. I thought that would make him see I wasn't getting nothing out of his humping. Then I saw it didn't make no difference to him whether I was having a good time or not. So, now, sometimes I push him off me just before he come. That makes him real mad. Or I tell him I got my period.

"Some nights, we just lay there jostling each other like little children jostling over a ball. I won't turn over or open up my legs and he won't stop tugging on me."

"Girl, both of y'all crazy. That way, don't neither of you get a piece. That's too hard," Willie Bea said sincerely.

"Shoot, girl, some nights we tussle all night." Pat gave a hot dry laugh. "Henry thinks too much of hisself to fight me for it, really hit me upside my head or yell and scream, 'cause with those little paper-sheer walls, everybody next door would know our business. So while we fighting, it's real quiet except for some grunts and the bed squeaking."

Then, she laughed again.

"I guess that's all you'd be hearing anyway."

Willie Bea tried to laugh in acknowledgment. Once Pat told her, "Shoot, girl, I've gotten to liking the scuffling we do in bed better than I ever liked the screwing."

That made Willie Bea feel cold all over.

"It's like it make it more important," Pat continued. "Something worth fighting for. Some nights when he just reach for me like that, it's like he calling me out my name. And I turn over ready to fight.

"I would get somebody else, but they all the same, you may as well pick one from the sack as another. But look at you, Bea. You just agreeing to be nice. You don't believe that, do you?"

"I didn't say nothing," Willie Bea would rush to say. "I believe what you say about you and Henry. I believe you."

"That ain't what I mean and you know it. I'm talking about mens period."

"I know what you saying about men."

"Yeah, but you don't think they all alike, do you?" Pat asked.

Willie Bea would start dipping her head from side to side and grinning her sheepish closed-mouth grin.

"Go on and admit it, girl," Pat would prod.

After a moment, Willie Bea would admit it. "I don't know why he love me so good."

Then, Pat would sigh and urge her friend to tell her how sweet Jay was to her . . . in bed, at the table, after work. Especially in bed.

Willie Bea balked at first, each time the subject came up. But she always gave in, too. She was just dying to talk about Jaybird.

Most women she knew held the same beliefs that Pat did about men. They sure as hell didn't want to hear about her and the bliss her man brought her. She had found they may want to hear about "you can't do with him and can't do without him" or how bad he treat you and you still can't let him go. All of that. But don't be coming around them with those thick windowpane eyes of hers all bright and enlarged with stories of happiness and fulfillment. Those stories cut her other girlfriends and their lives to the quick.

But her friend Pat, big-butt Pat, urged Bea to share her stories with her. Sometimes, these reminiscences made Pat smile and glow as if she were there in Willie Bea's place. But sometimes they left her morose.

Willie Bea, noticing this at first, began leaving out details that she thought made Pat's love pale in comparison. But Pat, alert to nuances in the tales, caught on and insisted that Willie Bea never leave stuff out again if she was going to tell it.

And Willie Bea, eager to tell it all, felt as if she were pleasing her friend as much as herself. So she continued telling stories of love and dipping her ear down toward her shoulder in a gay little shy gesture.

"When Jaybird and me doing it, he has this little grufflike voice he uses when he talks to me."

"Talk to you? What ya'll be doing, screwing or talking?" Pat would interrupt, but not seriously.

"He says things like, 'Is that all? That ain't all. I want it all. Uh-huh.'"

At first, Willie Bea was embarrassed disclosing these secrets of her and Jaybird's passionate and tender lovemaking. But Pat seemed so enthralled by her stories that Willie Bea finally stopped fighting it and gave herself over to the joy of recounting how Jaybird loved her.

Pat never told Willie Bea that many of the women at The Place talked under their breaths when Jaybird and Willie Bea came in together.

"He may sleep in the same bed with her, but I heard he put an ironing board between 'em first," some said.

"He can't really want that little old black gal. He just like her worshiping the ground he walk on," another would add.

Pat knew Willie Bea would have tried to kill whoever said such things. But even Pat found it hard to believe sometimes that her little friend had attracted Jaybird.

Mornings, Pat watched Willie Bea step off the city bus they both took to their jobs, her too-pale dime-store stockings shining in the early light, her narrow shoulders rotating like bicycle pedals in the direction opposite the one she sent her snake hips inside her straight skirt, and thought how changed her friend was by the love of Jaybird. Now, that walk is something new, Pat thought, as the bus pulled away from the curb.

Willie Bea, who lived two blocks above Pat, got on the bus first, then alit first when she got near the white woman's house she cleaned five days a week. Pat stayed on until the bus reached downtown near the box factory where she worked. They rode to and from work together nearly every day.

So, one evening when Pat wasn't on the bus when she got on returning home, Willie Bea began to worry about her. All that one of Pat's coworkers on the bus said when Willie Bea asked was, "She left work early."

I wonder if she's sick, Willie Bea thought.

She was still thinking about her friend when the bus began making its climb up Pleasant Hill. I better stop and see 'bout her, Willie Bea thought.

She was still standing with her hand near the signal wire when the bus slowed to a stop in front of the cinder-block duplex where Pat lived, and Willie Bea saw the gold of a Schlitz beer uniform slip back inside the dusty screen door of her friend's house.

The bus driver paused a good while with the bus door open waiting for Willie Bea to leave. Then he finally hollered toward the back of the bus, "You getting off or not?"

Willie Bea turned around to the driver's back and tried to smile as she took her regular seat again. When she reached her boardinghouse, she was anxious to see Jaybird and ask him who the new man was working on the beer truck. But he wasn't home.

She sat up alone on the bed in the boardinghouse room long after it grew dark.

Willie Bea didn't know how long she had been asleep when she heard the rusty doorknob turn and felt a sliver of light from the hall fall across her face. Jaybird almost never stayed out late without her or telling her beforehand.

"You okay, Jay?" she asked sleepily.

He only grunted and rubbed her back softly. "Go back to sleep, Bea," he said. "I'm coming to bed now."

Willie Bea lay waiting for Jaybird to say something more, to say where he had been, to say he saw her friend Pat that day. But he said nothing.

And when he did finally slip into bed, it felt as if an ironing board was between them.

Toni Cade Bambara

Several years after Toni Cade Bambara's death, "Going Critical" was published in a volume of her unpublished writings edited by Toni Morrison. Its concern with the impact of terminal illness on a mother and daughter's difficult relationship has clear autobiographical elements. An important figure in the Black Arts Movement of the 1960s and 1970s, Bambara was a prolific writer and editor. In addition to her novels and short story collections, she also wrote plays, screenplays, and essays. Born in New York in 1936, she earned a B.A. from Queens College and an M.A. from the City College of the City University of New York. In the late 1970s she moved to Atlanta and joined the faculty of Spelman College. Bambara's important books are *Gorilla, My Love* (short stories, 1972), *The Sea Birds Are Still Alive* (stories, 1977), *The Salt Eaters* (novel, 1980, for which she won the National Book Award), and *Those Bones Are Not My Child* (1999), a novel about the serial killings of black children in Atlanta during 1979–1980. Bambara died in 1995 of cancer.

Going Critical

One minute, Clara was standing on a wet stone slab slanting over the drop, a breaker coming at her, the tension tingling up the back of her legs as though it were years ago and she would dive from the rocks to meet it. And in the next minute, the picture coming again, brushing behind her eye, insistent since morning but still incomplete. Then the breaker struck the rocks, the icy cold wash lifting her up on her toes, and the picture flashing, still faint, indistinct. Teeth chattering, she flowed with it, tried not to understand it and blur the edges, but understood it beneath words, beneath thought. The brushing as of a feather, the wing-tip arrival of the childhood sea god who had buoyed her up from the deep when she'd been young and reckless in the waters. A feather brushing in the right side of the brain, dulled by three centuries of God-slight neglect, awakened in Clara at the moment of her daughter's conception.

Nineteen eighty, middle-aged woman in dated swimsuit and loose flesh, sliding perilously on moss slime stone, image clustering behind right eye, image-idea emerging from the void, a heresy in one era, a truth in the next, decaying into superstition, then splashing its message before returning to the void. The water sucking at the soles of her feet before sliding out again to sea, she saw it and shivered.

And then she was running, forgetting all her daughter had taught her about jogging. Running, she pushed her chilled body through an opening in the bushes as though heading toward a remembered site—a clearing, a desert nearly, where the bomb test was to be conducted. They'd been told through memos, at briefings, and over the PA system that they were in no danger providing, so long as, on the condition that, and if. No special uniforms or equipment had been issued, not even a shard of smoked glass. They were simply to take up their positions in the designated spots where the NCO rec hall was to be built. Line up, shut up, close the eyes—that was all, once the incomprehensible waivers had been signed.

Cold and damp, Clara plunged through the green, seeing in memory remnants of the ghost bush, seeing the open-mouth Lieutenant Reed, a gospel singer in civilian life, crash through the bush at the last minute, leaving a gaping wound. The twigs and leaves trying to squeeze to, trying to knit closed, trying to lock up before the blast. Their straining prying Clara's eyes open. And in that moment, the deep muffled thunder of the detonation. And the ground broke and the light flared and her teeth shook in the jellied sockets of her gums. Her heart stopped, but her eyes kept on seeing—Lieutenant Bernice Reed a shadow, an X-ray, the twigs and leaves transparent too, showing their bones.

Clara passed through the bushes out of breath and exchanged her swimsuit for a towel, wondering if the bush still quaked on the flats in Utah. Had it ever closed, had it ever healed? And did Bernice Reed still sing in the choir in Moultrie, Georgia, or had she left her voice there in the wounded green?

II

"Ya know, Mama, the really hip part of the fish and loaves miracle?"

Clara watched her daughter squat-walk across the sandy blanket, thinking fishes and loaves, the Piscean age, Golden Calf, the Taurean. Wondering too, would the girl ever get it together and apply her gift in useful ways in the time of the Emptying Vessel?

"There were no dishes to wash, no bottles to sterilize or nipples to scrub. And no garbage to put out, Mama. That was the miracle. Hell, feeding the multitudes ain't no big thing. You and Aunt Ludie and women before and mamas since been doing that season in and season out."

Season in and season out. To feed the people, Clara muttered, pulling her overall strap over her shoulder and hooking it. What crops would be harvested from the contaminated earth?

"But of course, it was probably a classic case of the women doing the cleaning up. So quite naturally all that non–high drama escaped the chronicler's jaundiced eye."

"I knew you were going to say that," Clara said. She stumbled into her clogs, watching Honey bury a lump of potato salad in the sand.

Honey shrugged. "How boring it must be for you to always know what I'm going to say."

"Not always. I don't always know, I mean."

Clara stuffed garbage into a plastic sack while her daughter gathered up the casting stones. The bone white agate Honey always used as the control was slipped into the leather pouch she wore around her neck. The two pebbles she'd found on the beach, the yes and no for the impromptu reading, Honey tossed into the picnic hamper.

"You were able to help them?" Clara knew Honey would merely glance toward the couple she'd read and shrug. The arguments over the proper use of Honey's gifts had been too frequent and too heated of late. Honey could not be lured into a discussion just like that. Clara ignored the press of time and softened her voice all the more. "You saw something for them?"

They had walked right up, the couple, tracking sand onto the blanket, ig-nored Clara altogether as though she were already gone, and said to Honey that they'd recognized her from the Center and would she read their cards, or read their palms, or throw the cowries, or "Give us some money," the woman had joked not joking, "Cash money in the hand," karate-chopping the air and bar-ing her teeth. And Clara had done a quick aura-scan, first of the couple, swarmy and sparkish, then of her daughter, a steady glow.

"They seemed bad news to me," Clara said, still not expecting an answer, but searching for a point of entry. And saying it for the sake of the phrase "bad news," in preparation for the talk they'd come to the old neighborhood beach for but thus far had skirted. "Vampires," Clara said flatly. Honey did not take up the challenge, but went right on gathering up their things, her beaded braids clinking against her earrings.

Clara squatted down and folded the towels, wondering if Honey'd had a chance to rest, to recharge after the command-performance reading. She leaned over to dump the towels in the hamper and too to place her hand on her daughter's nerve center.

"Was there anything helpful you could tell them, Honey, about, say, budget-ing for the future?" Clara heard it catch in her throat, "the future," and felt Honey hearing it in the small of her back.

They both sat silent for a moment, gazing off in the direction of the couple arguing and wrassling their beach chairs as far from the water's edge as they could get.

"But then, what could you tell them? Hard to make ends meet when you've got your ass on your shoulders," Clara said, and was immediately sorry.

"Mama," Honey made no effort to disguise her annoyance, "I will gladly pay you back for the wedding. I will tell Curtis not to bug you any further about a loan. And damnit, I will pay for the parking."

"I didn't mean . . ." Clara didn't bother to say the rest of it, that she was only trying her hand at a joke. Her ears, her tongue, her heart were stinging.

III

They shook the sand out, then began folding the blanket, remembering how they used to do the laundry together, each backing up till the bedspread or sheet pulled taut—the signal to begin. Sometimes, flapping it flat, they'd dance to meet in the center, doing precise minuet steps, their noses pointed toward the basement ceiling, their lips pursed in imitation of a neighbor lady who complained of their incense, candles, gatherings, "strange" ways. Or, clicking across the ceramic tile of the laundry room, grimacing in tortured Flamenco postures, they'd olé olé till Jake, overhead in his den, hollered down the heat duct to lighten up and hurry up with supper. Sometimes, as part of their put-down of the school PE program, they'd clog, doing the squarest square dance steps they could muster. Yodeling, they'd bring each other the corners of the sheet, their knuckles knocking softly when they met, blind, each hiding behind her side of the raised-high fabric to prepare a face to shock the other with, once Clara, clasping all the corners and twanging in a hillbilly soprano, or Honey, nesting her hands in the folds to get the edges aligned, signaled the other to lower the covers in the laundry basket, their howls drawing stomps from over-head.

In those free times before the lumps appeared and the nightmare hauntings began, Clara would hold on to a funny face remembered from a Galveston car-nival mask, while Honey, bending, would smooth the bedspreads down her mother's body to save her time at the ironing board. But then came the days when their signals went awry, when Clara, breathless with worry and impo-tence, and Honey, not yet reading the streaks in her mother's aura or the netted chains in her palm's mercury line, were both distracted, and the neatly folded tablecloth would wind up a heap on the basement floor. "I thought you had it, damnit. I thought you were going to take it. Shit." And Jake, husband/father, would avoid the loyalty trap by giving both bristling women wide berth for the course of the day.

There were the hot, silent times too, Clara racing feverishly through lists of healers yet to be seen, Honey searching for some kind thing to say now that ra-dium and chemotherapy had snatched huge patches out of Clara's hair and softened her gums, ruining a once handsome jawline. The covers between would get ironed flat by the heat of mother and daughter clinging to the spread, touching through terry cloth or wool or chenille, neither letting go. Overhead, Jake, his face pressed against cold iron, breathing in burnt dust from the grate and cat hairs in the carpet, weeping into the ashes, would pray they'd let go of each other before the time.

"I've got it," Clara said finally, when she could bear it no longer, neither the strain of the silence, the memories, nor her daughter's presence too close and too intense. "Let go, Honey," as though the sun that Honey's young body had soaked up all day were searing her now through the wool. "Let go."

Clara draped the blanket over Honey's outstretched arm, dropped it really, as though it had singed her, as though she wanted to be done with blankets and outings and Honey and all of it quickly and get away, race back to the rocks, to the ice-cold waters that had known her young and fit and with a future.

"Mama, are you alright?"

Her daughter whispering as in a sickroom with shades drawn and carpets muffling; Honey slow-motion bending to lay the blanket in the hamper, slow and quiet as in the presence of the dying. Clara grabbed up one handle of the wicker hamper, and Honey took up her end. And now they could go. There was nothing to keep them there except what was keeping them there. But how to begin? Honey, your ole mama's on her last leg and needs to know, you won't be silly . . . My darling, please promise not to abuse your gifts . . . Before I kick off, Sweetie, one last request. . . ? Words tumbled moist and clumsily in Clara's mouth, and she rejected them. For now she wanted to speak of other things— of life, food, fun—wanted to invite her daughter, her friend, for a promenade along the boardwalk on the hunt for shrimp and beer, or quiche and a nice white wine.

"The lunch was lovely, Honey, but I'm hungry for more. For more," she said, veering closer to the subject that held them on the sand. But she could get no further into it and was grateful that Honey chose that moment to turn aside and hook-shoot the garbage sack into the dumpster some three feet away from the arguesome couple. Clara longed to touch her again, to trace with the tip of one finger the part in the back of Honey's head, knowing the scalp would be warm, hot even. Hot Head. Jake had nicknamed her when she was just an in-fant. And Curtis had revived it of late, preferring it to Khufu, the name his wife was known by at the Center, to Vera, the name on the birth certificate, and to Honey, the name she'd given her daughter to offset the effects of "Hot Head." Honey, a name she gave to give her daughter options.

"Starved? Say no more," Honey said, walking off and yanking Clara along at the other end of the hamper. "Aunt Ludie swears she's going to put her extramean gumbo together tonight. Needless to say, I told her to put our names in the pot."

"We're not staying for the fireworks?" Clara pulled on the handle to make Honey slow up. "I thought we'd eat around here and then see the fireworks. I thought that was the whole point of parking in the lot instead of on the street, so we'd have access to the dunes and . . ." She felt panic welling up, time running away from her. "Five damn dollars to park just so we'd have a pass to the dunes, Honey."

"Whatchu care about five damn dollars, Mama? You a rich lady," Honey said over her shoulder with a smile Clara knew was not a smile at all. If Honey's lackadaisical attitude at the Center was a hot issue, then the money was a scorcher. Her daughter had married into a family on Striver's Row, had in-laws with little patience for "community," "the people," "development," and even less tolerance for how their son's mother-in-law, Clara, dispersed her funds and spent her time and tried to influence their son's wife.

"Not yet, I'm not rich. Not yet." Clara stumbled along in the sand and won-dered if she'd live long enough to see the money, at least to sign it over to the

Center and its works. The suit the former GIs had brought against the Army had dragged on for years. And though the medical reports had grown sharper from "radiation exposure a high-probability factor in the development of malignancies," to "disabilities a direct result of the veterans' involvement with the nuclear test program"—and though the lawyers for the National Association of Atomic Vets were optimistic despite the sorry box score of twenty recognized suits out of hundreds of claims, and though the Board of Veterans' Appeals had overturned earlier VA rulings, the Army was still appealing, denying, holding out.

"It's easier walking along the beach," Honey was saying, shifting direction sharply and wrenching Clara's arm, her thoughts. "And maybe we can find some sandblasted bottles for Daddy's collection."

Nineteen eighty, deadline for probable-future choice imminent, people collecting shells, beer cans, stamps, rally buttons, posters, statistics, snapshots. Middle-aged woman in loose flesh and tight overalls pulled past old men sissy-fishing along sandbar in rolled-up pants. Tips of rods quivering like thin silver needles the Chinese doctor placed along meridian, electricity turned on, mother prayers turned up drowning Muzak out. Line pulled in, fish flopping its last, hook through gills, tail fin lashing at fisherman who's wrecked its life. Life already ruined. Woman on leave from Department of Wildlife recites fish kills typed up daily. Agriculture—insecticides, pesticides; industrial mining, paper, food, metallurgy, petroleum, chemical plants, municipal sewerage system, refuse disposal, swimming pool agents.

"Remember the church fish fries here when I was little? You'd leave me with Aunt Ludie to go visit the tearoom. Remember, Mama?"

Dog River, Alabama; Santa Barbara Harbor, California; Anacostia River, D.C.; Mulatto Bayou, Florida; Salt Bayou, Louisiana.

"Mama, you look beat. Wanna rest?"

Slocum Creek, North Carolina; Radar Creek, Ohio; San Jacinto River, Texas; Snake River, Washington.

"Why don't you sit down on the rocks while I put this stuff in the car."

"Girl, don't you know my sitting days are over? And there's work to do and we need to talk." But she let Honey take the whole of the hamper onto her shoulder and march off with it. So there was nothing for Clara to do but find a dry rock not too far out on the breakwater wall and sit down, be still, be available, wait. She slumped. The weight of the day, of unhealth, relationships, trying to organize for the end, pressed her down onto the rocks, her body yearning to return to the earth—disoriented, detached and unobliged. And then the picture flashed. The bush. A maze of overgrown hedges and thickets, prickly to the eye. She, looking for a path and it suddenly there, bones at the mouth of the passage. On her knees inching through briars. Inching forward to the edge. And nothing there at the drop. No matter which way she turned, the view the same. The world an egg blown clean.

IV

"They say, Honey, that cancer is the disease of new beginnings, the result of a few cells trying to start things up again."

"Your point being?" Honey was picking her teeth, weaving in and out of boardwalk traffic, deliberately allowing, it seemed to Clara, cyclists, skaters, parents pushing baby strollers, to come between them.

"That it's characteristic of these times, Honey. It signals the beginning of the new age. There'll be epidemics. And folks, you know it, are not prepared."

"And so?"

They were side by side now, veering around a "sidewalk" artist down on his knees, pushing a plate of colored chalks along the boards, drawing rapidly fantastic figures that stumped those strollers who paused to look, dripping the ice cream or sweaty cups of beer on the artwork. Together, they walked briskly past the restaurants and bars, the kiddie park, the wax museum, the horror house, finally talking. But Clara was still dissatisfied, had still not gotten said what she'd come to the beach to say to her only child. And she still did not altogether know what it was. When my time comes, Honey, release me 'cause I've work to do yet? Watch yourself and try not to be pulled off of the path by your in-laws? Develop the gifts, girl, and try to push at least one life in the direction of resurrection?

"You do understand about the money?" Clara was hugging close as marines, couples, teenagers walking four and five abreast, threatened to shove between them. She felt Honey's arm stiffen as though she meant to pull away.

"Money, money, money. I'm sick of the subject. Curtis, his mother . . . And his father, you know, has his eye on a liquor store and keeps asking me if . . ."

An elderly couple clumping along in rubber-tipped walkers separated them. Then an Asian-American family Clara dimly recalled from the old neighborhood streamed between them, the mother spitting watermelon seeds expertly through the cracks in the boardwalk, the father popping kernels from what was evidently a very hot cob of corn, one youngster cracking into a sugar-glazed apple, the other absentmindedly plucking tufts of cotton candy from a paper cone as though it were a petaled daisy.

Liquor store. Clara frowned, her face contorted from the effort to salute her old neighbors, answer Honey, and continue the dialogue on the inside all at the same time. And so she almost missed it, not the Fotomat Honey was pointing toward where summers before they'd horsed around, meeting up with odd characters they never told Jake and, later, Curtis about; posing as sisters or actresses fresh back from madcap adventures on the Orient Express, they would give each other fanciful names and outlandish histories to flirt with. She almost missed the tearoom. Jammed between the tattoo parlor and the bingo hall, looking tinier and tackier than she remembered it, was the tearoom where Clara had watched, under the steady gaze of Great Ma Drew, her work emerge clear and sharp from the dense fog of the crystal ball that good sense had taught her to scoff at till something more powerful than skepticism and something more potent than the markings on her calendar forced Clara's eyes to acknowledge two events: motherhood, and soon (despite all the doctors had had to say about Jake's sluggish sperm and her tilted uterus), and a gift unfolding right now, a gift that would enable Clara to train the child.

Clara linked arms with Honey and steered her toward the tearoom with her hips. The woman, though, lounging against the Madame Lazar Tearoom sign was neither the seer Drew, nor any of the gypsified Gypsies or non-Gypsies that had taken over the business during Honey's growing-up days. She was a young, mariny woman in a Donna Summer do—a weave job, Clara's expert eye noted—wearing exactly the kind of jewelry and flouncy dress, vèvè-encrusted hem and metallic smocking in the bodice, that Clara always associated with the Ioa Urzulie Frieda. Clara felt Honey resisting, her hard bone pushing through flesh against her.

"Sistuh, are you gifted?" Honey challenged, before Clara could speak, could get her balance, Honey still steeling herself against her.

The woman's eyes slid insolently over them. Clara was about to give in and let Honey steer along to the dunes, but the woman flashed, and Clara felt a reaching-out come in her direction, and then a mind probe, bold, prickly, and not at all gentle.

"She's telepathic," Clara whispered, pulling Honey up short. "But can she see, I wonder. Can she see around the bend and probe the future?" Honey sucked her teeth and stood her ground between the two women. And now the woman smiled and Clara dropped Honey's arm and dropped, too, her shield. At this point in time, Clara mused, I can afford to be open to anything and everything.

"How far can you see?" Clara asked, setting up a chain reaction of questions on the inside for the woman to touch upon. She waited. In an open-bodied position, Clara invited the woman to move in.

"Mama, come on, damnit."

And then Clara felt the woman withdraw. And it was Honey's turn to smile. She was gifted, this new Madame Lazar. She was simpatico. But business is business, no freebies here. The woman slid her eyes over Honey in dismissal, and to

Clara she jerked her chin in the direction of the incense-fragrant interior and passed, sashaying in her noisy crinolines and taffetas, through the curtain.

"Oh no, you don't," Honey said, linking arms and shoving her hip hard against Clara's, almost knocking her out of her clogs. "She has a gift alright, Mama, but no principles. Liable to put a hex on you," she grinned, "plus take all your money. Let's go."

"Now wait a minute." Clara tried to disengage her arm and back up for a moment to get her thoughts lined up, but Honey was pulling her along like an irritated parent with an aggravating child. Hex, Clara thought, trying to get it organized. UF_6, the gaseous form of uranium, was called hex and that was something to talk about. Gifts and principles—exactly the topic to get to an appraisal of the Center's work. Money perfect. But Honey would not give her a moment. Who was the mother here anyway? Clara squinched up her toes, trying for traction, trying to dig in. She yanked hard on her daughter.

"Whatcha so mad about, Mama?"

"Well, damnit, what are you so angry about, and all week long too?" They were falling over the chalk artist, causing a pileup in front of the tattoo parlor. "You're mad because I'm leaving you?" She was clutching the lapels of her daughter's shirt, breathing hot breath into her face, her body shuddering. "Oh, girl, don't you know it's the way of things for children to bury their elders?" She barely had the strength to hold on as Honey dropped her face into her shoulders, pressing her beaded braids into Clara's skin. They stood in the throng, getting bumped and jostled by sailors coming out of the parlor displaying their arms and banging each other on the back in congratulations.

"Please, Honey, you say the words over me, hear? No high-falutin eulogies, OK? Don't let them lie me into the past tense and try to palm me off on God as somebody I'm not, OK? And don't let anybody insult my work by grieving and carrying on, OK? Cause I'm not at all unhappy, and Jake's come to terms with it. I've still my work to do, whatever shape I'm in. I mean whatever form I'm in, you know? So OK, Honey? And don't mess up, damnit."

"You and your precious work," Honey hissed, catching Clara off-balance. And then a smile broke up her frown, the sun coming out, and Clara could bear the pain of the beads' imprint. "Fess up, Mama," grinning mischievously, "you're mostly pissed about the five dollars for parking, aincha?"

Someone on the dunes was singing, the music muted at first by the dark and the ocean breeze. Clara leaned back against Honey's knees and issued progress reports on the boat. Decked out in banners and streamers for the occasion, flying its colors on the mast overhead, it was easing its cargo of fireworks out to the raft where T-shirted lifeguards and parkees in orange safety harnesses and bright helmets waited, eager to begin.

She could feel Honey behind her—her knees softening at intervals, then jerking awake as the singer modulated—going to sleep.

"Take care, Honey, that you keep your eyes sharp and spirit alert," she instructed, her voice sounding to her already flat, lifeless, as if it traveled from a great distance and through a veil, vibrancy gone, her self removed to the very outskirts of her being, suspended over her flesh, over the sand, on the high note now sounding while the slap of the waves, a baby's ball, buffeted by the waters, was being sucked under the rocks of the breakwater wall, and bits of conversation from blankets around them and from the boardwalk overhead, and then even the high notes, churned below her.

She was hanging in the music, in the swoop of the notes across the humps of the dunes so like beings rising from the sand, dipping down in sound between the childrens' pail-castles and grown-ups' plumped pillows, buoyed up again toward the moon, full, red and heavy, till the wail of a child and Honey's jerking pulled her back again inside her skin. Being dragged past them by a mother determined to ignore her son's bedtime tactic, a young child in a Hank Aaron shirt was trickling sand across Clara's toes and bawling, his tiny hand digging up another fistful from a bulging pocket to trail sand across the tufts of dune grass and up the steps to the boardwalk gate, people shoving over as though they recognized this tribal wiseman spreading the time-running-fast message to the heedless, then making sand-paintings on the boards, chalkings, the ritual cure for sleepwalkers.

"It begins," Clara said. But still Honey did not sit up to appreciate the view. The fisherfolk had parked their poles and taken up their perch on the rocks, couples on blankets propped each other up, the boardwalk crowd bunched along the railing, the overflow packed on the top steps, leaning into the mesh of the gate—the vista was wide open for the first whoosh of yellow and pink that careened across the night sky. The ahhhhh from the crowd harmonizing with the singer climbing an octave and the bedtime boy still wailing and wheeling around in the chalk drawings, smearing and stamping. A rocket shot out across the waters and exploded into a shower of red, white and blue that fountained down at the far end of the breakwater wall.

"Don't miss this," she said, her voice hollow again, drawn into the music, into the next burst of colors, pulses of energy like the frenzy of atoms like the buzzing of bees like the comings and goings of innumerable souls immeasurably old and in infinite forms and numerous colors. She was floating up, her edges blurring, her flesh falling away, the high note reachable now coming at her from nine different directions, sailing out with her past the boat's flag, echoing through blue through time. And she was a point of light, a point of consciousness in the dark, looking down on her body accusingly—how could it let her go like that?—but ready to be gone and wanting too to go back and nestle inside her old self intimate and warm, skin holding her in, bone holding her up, blood flowing. Her body summoning not yet. Her daughter a magnet, drawing her back.

A cluster of pinwheels came spinning from the boat deck, and the bedtime boy seemed content to whimper between wails. But the singer held on, leaning into the music, pressing sound into the colors. A salvo of sparklers shot out, streaking across the pinwheel's paths, sizzling.

She'd put sparklers on Honey's birthday cake the year Alvin Ailey's company came into town. Had thought it a brilliant change from pastel candles, but the children were frightened, leapt from the table, overturned the benches, dragged half of the tablecloth away in tatters, knocked over the ruffled cups of raisins and nuts, and the punch bowl too. She tried, as they scooted away bursting balloons which only made it worse, tried to explain, as they tripped entangled in crepe paper streamers and string, taking off to the woods before she could assure them, those children of the old neighborhood who'd never seen Chinese New Year, who'd never celebrated the Fourth of July with anything louder than an elder's grunt "Independence for whom?" or "Freedom, my ass!" or anything noisier than a greasepopping what-the-hell barbecue, who'd never seen a comet or heard the planetarium's version of asteroid, the running children who'd never been ushered from bed to watch the street rebellions on TV or through the window and have explained why things were so—doing the hundred-yard dash to the woods fleeing sparklers, Honey right along with them, leaving her with frosting on her chin and hundreds of lessons still to teach.

"You chuckling, coughing, crying, or what?" Honey's voice was drowsy. And Clara didn't know the answer, but remembered the twenty-five dollars' worth of box-seat tickets to see the Ailey dancers, and the exhausted birthday sprinter falling asleep in the middle of *Revelations,* Jake shaking her by the shoulders to at least watch a few dollars' worth.

"That a human voice or what?" Honey sounded neither irritated nor curious, her way, Clara supposed, of letting her know she was still available for talk. The boy was still crying and the note was still holding as firecrackers went off, sounding powerful enough to launch a getaway spaceship. "Ain't it the way," Jake had said just that morning, huddled over the pale, "they mess up, then cut out to new frontiers to mess up again." The singer climbing over the thundering, holding out past the crowd's applause, past the crowd's demand for release, past endurance for even extraordinary lungs, the note drawn thin and taut now like a wire, a siren, the parkees, looking now like civil defense wardens sending up flares from the shoot machines, cannons. And still the singer persisted, piercing, an alarm, step-sitters twisting round in annoyance now, the first wave of anger shaking through the crowd at the railing, a big man shoving through to the gate and to hell with a dune pass, heroic, on the hunt for the irritant to silence it. Then a barrage of firecrackers heading straight across the water caused many to duck before reminding themselves, embarrassed, that this was Sunday at the beach, holiday entertainment and all's well.

"A jug of wine, a crust of pizza and thou for Crissake," someone was saying. Then the note shuddered to a gasping halt and the bedtime boy's wail was cut short by a resounding slap heard on the dunes. After a faint ripple of applause, attention turned fully to the lifeguards prying open the last crate, the parkees spinning out the remaining pinwheels to hold the audience until the specialty works that would spell out a message, the final event, could be crammed into the cannons and fired off.

"Girl, wake up and watch my money."

Honey, knees wobbled against Clara's back, glanced round and smiled at her efforts to come awake and keep her mother company.

There was no way she could carry her child to the car anymore, lay her down gently in the back seat, cover her over with a dry towel, and depend on tomorrow for what went undone today. Clara turned toward the water and joined the people, attentive to the final event about to light up the sky.

Michael Bishop

Although Michael Bishop is one of the nation's leading science fiction writers, he writes in other genres as well. His story "The Road Leads Back" portrays the relationship between a famous southern writer and her friend from Atlanta. With elements of faith, comedy, and fantasy, the story pays both skeptical and genuine tribute to one of the most famous writers from the state (most readers will easily recognize her). Born in Lincoln, Nebraska, in 1945 and educated at the University of Georgia, Bishop taught briefly in Colorado and in Georgia before deciding to become a full-time writer. His science fiction has been widely recognized, and he has received numerous awards, including several Nebula Awards from the Science Fiction and Fantasy Writers of America. The *Washington Post Book World* has called Bishop "an unusually literate writer . . . among the most interesting and resourceful writers of short fiction today, inside the sf field or beyond." He lives in Pine Mountain, Georgia.

The Road Leads Back

I am really only interested
in a fiction of miracles.
—Flannery O'Connor

Flora Marie did not want to visit the Benedictine monastery in Alabama. Back in April, at the insistence of Aunt Claire, who had paid for the pilgrimage, she had made a fatiguing round-trip journey by air to Lourdes. Aunt Claire had believed that a reverent dip in the shrine's waters would enable Flora Marie to throw away her crutches and live again as a "normal person."

Today, viewing herself in the rippled mirror on her bedroom door, Flora Marie still wore her crutches like jai alai baskets, their metal armlets pinching her biceps, her fingers clutching the padded grips. She wanted to pivot about and stump over to the paper-strewn desk visible in the murky glass—to settle in and work for an hour—but her unflagging encourager from Atlanta, Hetty Bestwick, had slain that option a week ago. Peeved, Flora Marie tried to resign herself to a long, dusty car ride in the bludgeoning July heat. It was plaguesome. If her mother and her aunt had had a nit's worth of sense, they would have sent her to Cullman, Alabama, two hundred miles away, *before* flying her to France and the overcrowded shrine of St. Bernadette.

Flora Marie closed her eyes. She knew what she looked like. "Not a beauty," her mama said. "Not even groundhog cute. But you have this quirk—almost a dignity—that may rescue you from spinsterhood."

But Flora Marie did not expect or even desire rescue from spinsterhood. She hoped instead for rescue from the inherited disease—systemic lupus erythematosus—gnawing at her connective tissue and periodically adorning her face with a rash like small red butterflies basking in the sun. This morning one such butterfly had alit in the valley between her nose and her left eye socket. It did not pain or even tickle her, but it seemed a malign rather than a healthy omen. Shoo enough of these critters into the morning and they would whelm the eye of day with blood . . .

Flora Marie opened her eyes and her bedroom door and stumped into the gloomy hallway. Characters in her stories never stood in front of mirrors as a pretext for physical descriptions. Only creative-writing students and Saturday-evening poetasters resorted to that gimmick, the former from ignorance, the latter from laziness. Anyway, this damned trip to the abbey was interrupting her writing, and who knew how long she had left, for writing or anything else? Seventeen years ago, while still a young man, her daddy had died of lupus.

In the hall, Mama Craft grabbed her by the shoulders, tugged at a pleat, grimaced at her hair. Flora Marie bore the insult. After all, she did not look like a woman to whom miracles happen. Sparse henna bangs stuck to her brow, while the rest of her hair stood out in frowsy Bozo-the-Clown tufts. Pressing down on them had no effect; they sprang out again, like packets of cotton batting or fiberglass insulation. A dress of blue polyester with a strand of pearls at the neck, almost a choker, rescued Flora Marie—that word again—from utter risibility. Or, going by Mama Craft's sour moue, maybe not. Who but a lupus patient or a hypothermia victim wore long sleeves in July?

From the parlor Bestwick shouted, "Come on, Rima! Unless you want to spend an extra night in a motel, we need to hit the road!"

"Rima?" Mama Craft said in a stage whisper.

"It's one of Bestwick's jokes, Mama. You call me Flit, she calls me Rima."

"I don't get it."

"*Green Mansions* by W. H. Hudson. I'm the bird-girl."

"I still don't get it."

Frowning, Flora Marie kissed Mama Craft on the forehead. "Innocence becomes you, Mama—as does your total absence of irony."

Mama Craft frowned just like her thirty-some-odd daughter, who clanked into the parlor like a tipsy Frankenstein's monster.

Bestwick strode forward in a loud floral-patterned skirt and a blouse of such sheer white muslin that her bra showed through like a Mafioso's gat. She kissed Flora Marie on the brow, as Flora Marie had kissed her mama. Her lips tarried, though, as if distilling nectar from the other woman's sweat.

"Hey, Rima, you look tip-top. I mean it. You'll come back ready to knock out a thousand pages."

"I look like a wounded pterodactyl. Half a page knocks *me* out." She leaned back from Bestwick's kiss.

"You ready? You look ready."

"My death on the road is on your shoulders, Bestwick. Find an old Negro man to dig me a hole and dump me into it. Then tamp down enough red clay to keep the hounds from clawing me back out."

Mama Craft took Bestwick's arm. "Forgive her. Flora Marie's always preferred sarcasm to sentiment, crassness to courtesy."

"Plain talk to alliteration. What's happened to you today, Mama? Did you drip vinegar into your egg-poaching water?"

"See? If Flit does die on the road, she'll slide straight to hell—with no layover in purgatory."

Flora Marie said, "With Mama around, God need never send me demons."

"You two." Bestwick seized the lumpy suitcase near the door, a TWA tag still on its handle, and swung it outside to her ivory, postwar Packard—in Flora Marie's eyes the automotive equivalent of a dromedary. Three peahens scratched in the driveway dust, and a black-and-white cow with enormous eyes ogled the house, its lips scrubbing each other like suede castanets.

Refusing help, Flora Marie slapped on a wide straw hat with a green plastic window in its brim and made her way outside to the Packard. She shoved her crutches through the back window and assumed the shotgun post with a gaze of stoic martyrdom. Let's get this over with, she thought. Once she had, no one—not even Bestwick—would impose again on either her fear or her tractability.

Driving northwest on Georgia 212, Hetty Bestwick steered as if the edges of the blacktop kept shifting, as if each dip in the road had the depth of a gulch. She sang torch songs like "Stormy Weather," "The Man Who Got Away," and "Some Other Spring," not kiddy crap like "This Old Man" or "She'll Be Comin' Round the Mountain." For this blessing, Flora Marie lifted thanks to the archangel Raphael, St. Christopher, St. Nick, and Anthony of Padua.

She and Hetty Bestwick had met in person only twice before this road trip to the Ave Maria Grotto at St. Bernard Abbey—once at the Crafts' homeplace, Blue Peacock Pastures, and once in Atlanta when Flora Marie spent a week in Piedmont Hospital. Otherwise they knew each other only through correspondence, which Bestwick had initiated by writing a letter, at once approving and critical, about a story of Flora Marie's, "The Feast of Perpetua," in an issue of the *Okefinokee Quarterly*. Few people read the literary journals in which Flora Marie published under the pseudonym "F. M. Throne," and fewer still wrote letters to their contributors. The letters that did come sounded like either the praise of doting parents or the ravings of psychopaths.

Hetty Bestwick had written, *"Did you have Wm. Faulkner's* The Town *in mind when you wrote this story? Not as a model, of course, or even as an anti-model, but as a satiric riposte to its romantic satire of idiot country lust. If so, Mr. Throne, you probably should have made Perpetua a little more self-aware."*

The critique went on—intelligently—for three more single-spaced typed pages. Flora Marie replied as earnestly as Bestwick had addressed her, confessing her true identity and divulging her real name. Soon, they were avid typewriter-pals, discussing—debating, in fact—everything from the writings of Dietrich Bonhoeffer to the novels of Iris Murdoch to the probability of miracles in a secular age. Flora Marie did not care to imagine the vast hole that would open in her life if Bestwick—cheerleader, kibitzer, and pest—ever withdrew from their friendship.

"Roll up your window, Rima," Bestwick said as they bumped past a tumbledown strip mall on Atlanta's outskirts.

"Why? You figger to get rich off your otter-graphed F. M. Throne first editions if I have a heat stroke 'n die?"

"Come on," Bestwick said. "Roll it up."

Flora Marie cranked the handle. Squeaking, a pane of glass hitched upward in the opening. Like the visor in her hat brim, this pane must have originated in a factory in the Emerald City of Oz. It filtered the world into her vision in kaleidoscopic shades of green, as if through the bottom of a Co' Cola bottle, bathing her in fake forest coolness.

"Criminy," Flora Marie said.

"I meant to have green in every window, but couldn't afford it. So I put it there." Bestwick shrugged.

"Thanks." A doctor had told Mama Craft that Flora Marie's sensitivity to light, a feature of her lupus, required special measures—a hat, stockings, and long sleeves in summer. They should also put tinted glass in their car windows. Taking these measures made every trip outdoors a complex safari. "For a two-day trip, Bestwick, you shouldn't have bothered."

"Sue me."

"For what? Signed copies of my own books?"

"And of a hundred other, even better, writers."

Bestwick had a library, all right. She wrote reviews for the Atlanta newspapers and a Catholic publication, the *Bulletin*, to which F. M. Throne also contributed. She spent most of the money she made as a civilian office grub at Dobbins Air Force Base on novels, biographies, philosophy texts, and periodicals. According to her letters, books insulated her sitting-room apartment. They held up tabletops, spilled from her closet, smoldered on stove eyes. She slept on them. She traded them for others and used them as barter bait. The clothes she had on today she had swapped for a review copy of a new book by a notorious southern female novelist.

"You sure made out on that deal," Flora Marie said.

"Amen." Bestwick guffawed, and the Packard chugged along with three of its windows open, like a blast furnace on Firestones. Soon they struck U.S. 278, which angled up to Cedartown, down to Piedmont, Alabama, up again to Gadsden, and up and across to Cullman, their destination. Despite the Andrew Marvell shade of her green window, Flora Marie's dress stuck to the upholstery. Sweat pooled in the toes of her low-heeled pumps. Her joints burned like sulfur pits.

Still, they halted only for fuel and bathroom breaks. Motoring westward, they ate Mama Craft's tomato-and-mayo sandwiches, guzzled ice water from cheesecloth-draped Ball jars, and wrangled like sisters.

Why couldn't they have waited for cooler weather? Lourdes hadn't really had time to kick in yet. Bestwick said, "Some folks have bosses and can't pick their vacation times." Flora Marie said, "Anyway, St. Bernard Abbey has no *reputation* for healing the blind and the crippled. It's just a monastery with a bunch of tiny buildings as a tourist attraction. I might as well dip in Lake Lanier." Bestwick said that a "woman of faith"—this was a dig, for Bestwick seemed always on the edge of losing hers or tossing it aside like a prolapsed girdle—could turn a pig-sty into a shrine, a whorehouse into a hospital. A monastery clearly offered better source material for a positive transformation than *those* "building blocks." "But *you* don't credit miracles," Flora Marie said. "You thought my pilgrimage to Lourdes a—a 'superstitious farce.' That's a quote, Bestwick." "And an accurate one," Bestwick said. "But I have more faith in you than I do in God, and more love for you than for Yahweh in his guise as Cosmic Bully." In spite of herself, Flora Marie flinched. "Easy," Bestwick said. "God ain't gonna chunk a thunderbolt through our engine block."

Ahead of them, an Alabama State Trooper in a fawn-colored uniform, a Smokey Bear hat, and glossy boots stood in the highway, his hand extended like a halfback stiff-arming a defender. An eight- or nine-year-old boy in blue jeans, sneakers, and a T-shirt with a big zigzag across it—like Charlie Brown's in the *Atlanta Constitution* funnies—squatted on the shoulder, his eyes on the ground. Bestwick cried, "Holy Jeez!" and hit the brakes. Envisioning a collision, Flora Marie shut her eyes. The Packard screeched to a shuddering stop.

Thankfully, they had *not* steamrollered the trooper, who squinted at them out of a horsey face twitching madly. He reminded Flora Marie of a cowboy actor over whom she had once swooned in serials at the Pix Theater downtown.

"What did I *do?*" Bestwick said. Despite her skeptical adult conversion to the Catholic Church, she had an ineradicable streak of guilty Calvinism in her makeup. That streak sometimes mixed with a severe blue nihilist tendency that caused her to pale about the dewlaps, as she had now.

"Howdy, ladies," the trooper said. "I need to borrow your car."

"Where's yours?" Bestwick asked.

"A fella faking a accident right there," nodding toward the boy, "tricked me into playing Good Samaritan. Then the sneaky sumbitch—pardon my French—grabbed my pistol and stole my patrol car."

"That *child* grabbed your gun?"

"Nome," said the trooper. "That's my boy Wallace. A perpetrator unknown

hoodwinked us. If you won't give up your Packard, mam, I'll have to expropri-
ate it."

The boy piped, "He didn't hoodwink *me*! That red-checkered rag over his
face told me straight off he was a sneaky sumbitch!"

"Watch your language, Wallace," the trooper said.

Bestwick told Officer Stagger that he and Wallace could ride with them to
Hokes Bluff or the nearest Alabama patrol station, but she had no intention of
giving her car to anybody without legal title to it. Officer Stagger could try to
make her, but lacking a gun, he would have to compel two law-abiding
women—one on crutches—with his fists or his wits, and Bestwick doubted the
efficacy of the latter.

"We'll ride." Officer Stagger beckoned the boy over, and they climbed into
the backseat.

Wallace hugged his door and refused to look at his daddy. He mumbled,
"This is fur shit." The patrolman flushed like a Baptist at a beatnik poetry festival. Flora Marie feared that he would lean over and strangle his son.

"Sir," Bestwick said, "why'd you bring Wallace out here with you?"

"For two months he begged me to. This morning, I truckled and did it."

"I never figgered *this*'d happen," Wallace said.

Flora Marie asked, "Is it legal to take your kid on patrol?"

"Nome. I broke the rules for the ungrateful little squeak. I may've lost my
job." His he-man voice had a tremolo in it.

"Why don't I drop you at the next phone?" Bestwick said. "We'll carry
Wallace home while you get right with your bosses. No need at all to mention
the boy rode with you this morning."

"I appreciate that," the trooper said. "I still may get canned, but I appreciate
that a almighty lot."

Wallace snorted.

They did what Bestwick had suggested, dropping Stagger at a farmhouse to
use the telephone and then transporting Wallace to a wood-frame bungalow
outside Gadsden. Their good deed did not divert them from their own route
even so much as a mile. But as he got out, Wallace told them that because his
mama worked, he would have to spend the afternoon alone, watching sunlight
crawl across their pine-plank floor.

"Do something useful for your folks," Bestwick said. "Wash some dishes.
Make a bed. Get dinner ready."

"Read a book," Flora Marie said to his back.

On the front porch Wallace turned and shouted, "I'm probably adopted!
Think I'll jest haul ass to Alaska!" He jumped off the porch and darted into a
forbidding copse of sycamores.

"He's running away," Flora Marie said mildly, for the boy had an impressive dearth of charm.

"The little heathen's snapping your garters. Don't worry about him. It's time you worried about yourself."

They drove on past walls of pines and blackjack oaks, past cow pastures and huge tree-festooning veils of kudzu.

By the time they reached Cullman, Flora Marie could not even think about visiting its outlying monastery. The torrid backblasts of eighteen-wheelers had rocked a hot ache into her bones and scoured her of strength. Their whole on-the-road adventure had set a lupine beast loose inside her, and the beast was rampaging, tearing up the place. Aloud, she confessed only to travel fatigue.

Bestwick found a motel, Osterreider's Slumber Shacks, a village of twelve log cabins with blinding white seams, as if someone had caulked them from giant toothpaste tubes. The Shacks sat two miles from St. Bernard Abbey, in a pine glade, with a totem pole in front of each cabin and a placard on the pole to name the cabin: Sequoyah, Black Elk, Pontiac, and so on. Both women burst out laughing when Mr. Osterreider assigned them to cabin Rain-in-the-Face.

The shower in Rain-in-the-Face barely worked. Water leaked from it in echoey drips. There was a clock radio but no television set, and every station—as they searched for an accurate time report—had a gargling announcer or a rushing avalanche of static. Silverfish infested the wallpaper. Palmetto bugs scurried from the radiator to the shade of their spavined double bed. Without warning, Flora Marie stabbed one of the scuttling critters with a crutch tip.

"Now I know why your mama calls you Flit," Bestwick said. "You're flat-out lethal to insects."

"Actually, Bestwick, she calls me Flit because I don't. It's her only gallop into facetiousness."

"You don't what?"

"Flit about. I stay the course. I have the patience of Job. Except when I get to thinking that pretty darn soon I might cease to be—here, anyway—and leave an irksome lot of work undone."

"So why not get good and Catholic and pray?"

"I ain't a good prayer, Bestwick. My type of spirituality is almost completely shut-mouth."

Like ten-year-olds in a summer-camp cabin, they talked long after darkness had fallen. They traded gibes, secrets, jokes, philosophies, literary likes and dislikes, and chunks of family history. Flora Marie learned that, from the age of ten, Hetty Bestwick had stayed her own course as an orphan.

"I saw my mother hang herself," Bestwick said. "When I came in the front door, she kicked over the stool she'd climbed and began to strangle. I grabbed her feet to pull her down, but that just made it worse."

"Oh honey."

"Do you suppose she went to Hell?"

"For killing herself?"

"For letting me see her do it."

Flora Marie had no answer for that. She had no answer for a lot of things. She understood the impetus to apostasy, though. Prostrate, she had crawled to its brink once a week for the past eight years.

"I don't think Lourdes worked," she said. "I'm afraid this won't either."

"Hey, Flit, maybe you haven't given Lourdes enough time. Put on the patience of Job. Some miracles have to gestate."

"If you believed that, why'd you bring me here? It steps all over the miracle that Aunt Claire tried to give me."

"Insurance," Bestwick said.

Flora Marie stayed mute. She considered faith not insurance but a response to love. It wavered only when you saw no clear evidence of the love that had triggered it. Disease, betrayal, and suicide could strike you with spiritual cataracts more surely, and much more quickly, than could either age or rationalism.

"What's the matter?" Bestwick said. "Didn't you pay your premiums?"

"Probably not. It ain't my policy."

Bestwick walked over to Flora Marie, lifted her pointed chin, and kissed her on the mouth. Flora Marie stared at her in frank perplexity.

On Tuesday morning, the ivory Packard cruised onto the grounds of St. Bernard Abbey, past the small monastic cemetery and into the parking area near the entrance to Little Jerusalem and Ave Maria Grotto. They had come so early that they had first choice of the tourist slots, so Bestwick parked in front of the gift shop by which visitors stepped down into Brother Joseph Zoettl's one-of-a-kind garden of miniature basilicas, churches, and statues, "The Scenic Shrine of the South."

A man in a coarse white habit—the monks in the distance wore *black* robes—met them at the car. Construction noises issued from the deeper grounds, methodical work on a huge stone abbey church. Wielding her crutches, Flora Marie saw them now as flying buttresses—the architecture of man versus the architecture of God. Obviously, the new abbey church would last longer.

"Pardon," the monk in white said, "but no one may enter the garden until noon." Brother Joseph, he added, was installing a new replica, and the abbot wanted no mishaps as the old man pursued his special calling.

Bestwick protested. She recounted all their reasons for visiting and cataloged their travel hardships. "This is F. M. Throne," she said, nodding at Flora Marie. "For eight straight days her mother has recited novenas to heal her of her lupus. At nine A.M. today, Mrs. Throne will recite the final novena as her daughter genuflects before the Virgin in Ave Maria Grotto. Miss Throne's cure, her mother believes, hinges on the *simultaneity* of these two faith events."

The white-clad monk did not even blink.

A regular pillar of salt, Flora Marie thought.

"Miss Throne writes reviews for the *Bulletin,*" Bestwick said. "Her story 'The Feast of Perpetua' appeared in last fall's issue of the *Okefinokee Quarterly.*"

The monk turned to Flora Marie. "I've *read* that story." His pupils contracted. "It was wonderful—excellent, in fact. Come." He led them around the gift shop, so that Flora Marie would not have to negotiate the stairs, and introduced them into the garden by a gate reserved for monks and postulants. Then he vanished.

"Our first miracle," Bestwick said.

"Yeah. A monk who reads the *Okefinokee Quarterly.*"

Flora Marie looked about. An asphalt path made a circuit among the garden's trees. On each side Lilliputian structures arose, entire cityscapes alternating with isolated caves, towers, and statues. You could not help feeling like a clumsy ogre here, especially if you lurched past the displays on crutches. She and Bestwick proceeded inward.

Still no sign of Brother Joseph, the hunchback Benedictine who had created the miniatures and laid out the garden showcasing them. The women strained to see farther down the path, to hear some noise betraying Brother Joseph's work at a site beyond the main grotto and the hillside Holy Land replicas. Despite the patchy shade, heat seethed from the stones of the low retaining walls.

"My God," Bestwick said. "This place is bizarre."

Brother Joseph had based his models of the Statue of Liberty, St. Peter's Basilica, the Alamo, the Hanging Gardens of Babylon, Noah's ark, and every other structure on postcard images. He had shaped them from marbles, seashells, cold cream jars, green-glass fishing-net floats, birdcages, broken glass, paste jewelry, sequins, and concrete. For the twin domes of the Immaculate Conception Cathedral in Mobile, he had used old toilet-bowl floats. Every structure had something cockeyed about it, for Brother Joseph had gathered his materials at random and guessed at the architectural features not visible on his postcards. This asymmetry, along with a childlike disregard for scale, blessed the whole garden with the waking irreality of a fever dream. Except for the sincerity, it all hinted at something akin to satire.

"I like it," Flora Marie said. She approved of distortion. Abstraction, on the other hand, irked her.

"You would," Bestwick said.

They hiked past a Roman aqueduct, the Coliseum, the Leaning Tower of Pisa, and an effigy of St. Frances Cabrini. At the Ave Maria Grotto they halted so that Flora Marie could hang her head—in worship or shame?—before a standing Virgin Mary, baby Jesus in her arms, at the center of a cave at least thirty feet tall. They did this for the white-clad monk's sake, in case he was spying on them from a gift-shop window.

Bestwick whispered, "Feeling any stronger?"

Flora Marie lifted her gaze to the Virgin's chalky face, then fixed it on Bestwick. "I'm ready to go, Hetty."

"You only call me Hetty when you're irritated."

"I'm ready to go, Bestwick."

Bestwick's upper lip glistened with sweat. "You're the one who buys into this miracle stuff. Work with me a little." She nodded at the Virgin Mary among the shell-encrusted stalactites. "Work with *her*."

"It doesn't want work. It wants submission."

"Then sub*mit*, goddamn it. I didn't drive across parts of two states just for you to tighten your jaw."

Flora Marie looked down the path, which, just beyond the hillside of Holy Land miniatures, circled back to the gift shop. She clanked off toward those scenes.

"Work does enter into it," Bestwick said, following her. "*Ora et labora*—work and prayer. That's the Benedictine motto."

"I work better at home."

"You're deliberately misconstruing me."

Around the Holy Land diorama, clanking uphill for a change, Flora Marie spotted the creator of the miniatures. Near the end of the path, Brother Joseph Zoettl, a miniature himself, stooped over a fairy-tale structure with a central bell tower and a pair of flanking turrets. He wore the black Benedictine habit, which stressed rather than softened his hunchback, and he probed with a putty knife at the tiny steps climbing to the model's turret level. Beside him, a fidgety weasel of a man in overalls and ragged tennis shoes held out a palette of soupy cement.

"Hold still, Norbert," Brother Joseph said.

"*Finally*," Bestwick said. "Behold your miracle worker. Looks less than god-like to me."

"He's an artist, not a miracle worker," Flora Marie said. "You only get them mixed up if you mistake talent and craft for omnipotence."

Bestwick sucked her teeth. "Let's cut the sniping, Marie, and see what the little bugger can do for you."

Brother Joseph looked up, squinting out of a thin gnomish face. His putty knife sliced the air anxiously. He smiled with puzzling tentativeness. The man whom he had called Norbert scowled as if his belly ached and stared at the two oncoming women with evident distaste. Neither man had expected visitors.

Bestwick took charge. She escorted Flora Marie up to Brother Joseph and told him the same story—minus the novena business—that she had laid on the monk in white. She said that the white-robed monk had let them into the garden so that Brother Joseph could speak an intercessory prayer for Miss Throne and heal her once and for all of her potentially fatal disease. Flora Marie turned tomato red, but *not* from a rash of epidermal butterflies.

"I make little buildings." Brother Joseph tapped his current project. "For healing prayers you should go to Abbot Luibel or Brother Rotkopf." The skin on Flora Marie's arms began to itch. Brother Joseph's project was a model of the basilica-shrine at Lourdes. An image of the original shrine flickered in her mind's eye atop this detailed, but bent and askew, copy.

"Oh," Brother Joseph said. "Meet Norbert Grimes, postulancy candidate. Only yesterday he came—again. Already I have put him to work."

Norbert Grimes spat a sullen "Hullo." A glob of cement plopped from the palette onto one of his sneakers.

"So you hope to find God here, Mr. Grimes?" Bestwick said.

"No, mam—just to get lost from whole damned herds of hell-bound women."

"Norbert," Brother Joseph chided him.

"Until y'all take me in, call me Ishmael," Grimes said. "My mama kicked me out, my grandma dumped me on strangers, and three ungrateful bitches divorced my ass." He laid his palette aside, pulled a reddish rag from his pocket, and wiped his ferret face.

"Maybe they didn't like the way you talked," Bestwick said.

"So far as my blood kin goes, I doubt hit," Grimes said. "They unloaded me before I'd said word one, much less pea-turkey. My exes I won't assume to speak for."

"Good for you," Flora Marie said, registering both his handkerchief and the hate in his eyes with a tingle of near recognition.

Bestwick turned to Brother Joseph. "We believe in *you*," she said. "And in God, of course, and we've driven two hundred miles. You must pray for Flora Marie and lift the curse of her lupus."

Brother Joseph shook his head.

"How hard is it to say an intercessory prayer? It can't be as hard as making these buildings."

"I am better with my hands than with words, Miss Bestwick."

"How old are you?"

"Eighty. Eighty this year."

"Miss Throne is thirty-three and an artist like you. Do you want her life snuffed out before she can complete even *half* her life's work?"

"Don't blackmail the poor man," Flora Marie said.

Brother Joseph frowned. Gently gripping Flora Marie's left arm, he laid his free hand on his Lourdes replica. "Can you stand without crutches, young woman?" Flora Marie nodded. "Then hand them to Norbert."

Grimes took them as if receiving a pair of aluminized rattlesnakes.

"O Raphael," the old man said, "lead this woman to the country of transfiguration. Heal her so that she may not be as a stranger in the province of joy. Remember her, you who are strong, you whose home lies beyond the region of thunder."

He neglected to say *Amen,* but Flora Marie, who intuited that Brother Joseph had never spoken so many words at one time in his life, felt a charge in her blood, a fresh elasticity in her joints. When he released her arm, she half believed that she could walk unassisted back around the Ave Maria Grotto to the garden gate and Bestwick's car. She resolved to try.

Grimes's arms leapt spastically. "*What 'n hell!*" he shouted.

Flora Marie's crutches broke free of his hands and stepped out onto the path *by themselves.* They scissors-hiked in mechanical cahoots along the route that she had just contemplated. Looking at once snake-bit and spite-driven, Grimes dragged a pistol from his bib pocket and fired away at them. These shots reverberated like sonic booms. Even the blue jays fell silent.

"*Damnation!*" Grimes cried in fury.

Flora Marie's legs failed her, and she dropped amid her skirts like a cut-loose marionette. Brother Joseph crouched beneath his lopsided hump, leaning away from his fake Lourdes and grasping his head like a kid in a Civil Defense drill.

Bestwick said, "Holy Jeez," and knelt beside Flora Marie. "Holy Jeez, are you okay?" She glared at Grimes with thermonuclear hostility.

"Please don't fret," Flora Marie said. "I'm fine—no different than before."

"No thanks to Ishmael there." Bestwick stood and faced the alleged postulant. "You crazy bastard. It's no damned mystery why all your women cast you out."

"Shut up," Grimes said. He turned his pistol on the miniature Lourdes and blew away a turret. Concrete shrapnel jumped, striking both Brother Joseph and Bestwick, and grazing the brim of Flora Marie's hat. "If I want comments from a high-horse lezbo, I'll ask for 'em." He leveled the barrel at Bestwick.

"Take him at his word," Flora Marie advised.

Bestwick put her hands on her hips. "Like you'd *really* shoot, you two-bit make-believe Capone." Cuts on her forearm oozed long red freckles.

Grimes thrust the pistol forward and squeezed the trigger, which *click-click-clicked* like the switch on a dead car battery. Bestwick stooped, crossed her arms over her bosoms, and screamed in terror. From everywhere around the grotto, monks came running, including the monk in white, all lifting their skirts like belles at a cotillion. "You lucky bitch!" Grimes threw his gun at Bestwick's feet. Then he zigzagged up the slope on which Brother Joseph had built his own Lourdes, vaulted a wrought-iron picket fence, and ran like sixty. His red-checkered rag fluttered atop the turret fragments on the shrine's upper court.

The white-robed monk called after him, "Norbert, you can't keep coming and going! One day you must make your profession! One day you'll have to *stick!*" Grimes yelled an obscenity over his shoulder. Some young Benedictines pursued him out of sight, hearing, and bounds—whereupon Flora Marie's crutches scissored back around the pathway, climbed the slope, leapt the fence, and, clanking almost melodically, joined the implausible chase.

Bestwick recovered her wits. She seized fistfuls of Brother Joseph's habit and twisted them cruelly. "I didn't want you to make the *crutches* walk! You were supposed to help *Flora Marie!* Can't you do a simple miracle right?"

"Stop it," Flora Marie said.

Brother Joseph had gone as white as a bleached camisole. He leaned away from Bestwick's frenzy. "I tink everyting I try comes out a smidgen crooked. Maybe—maybe you haff come to the wrong man."

"You did fine," Flora Marie said. "You sure knocked the props out from under *me*. The real miracle is, you kept us from getting killed."

"Poppycock!" Bestwick blurted. "*Poppycock!*"

The white-clad monk helped Flora Marie up. Brother Joseph knelt before his shattered facsimile of Lourdes as a penitent. He sifted its turret fragments through his fingers, appearing to ponder the task of restoring what Grimes had ruined. Flora Marie regarded him with clinical rue. It wasn't every day that you witnessed a miracle, even a splendidly bungled one.

Bestwick turned on the monk in white. "That man stole a state trooper's pistol and patrol car!" She flung her hand after the absconding culprit. "He shot up that toy building. He nigh-on to murdered *me,* and you're worried about him making a *profession of faith?*"

The white-robed monk thought a moment. "Even if the brothers fail to catch him, he'll be back. He shows up here three or four times a year. The next time he does we'll give him over to the proper authorities, the unhappy fellow."

Bestwick raged at this offhand expression of sympathy. How many innocents would Grimes maim or kill before he returned to St. Bernard Abbey?

Flora Marie dialed this rant out. Grimes longed for commerce with humanity, solace in the company of men. His inability to stick surely had something to do with the fact that these men wore habiliments reminiscent of the raiment of women. Flora Marie felt woozy again. How long would her crutches run before they collapsed, and would they ever return to buttress the remainder of her problematic walk?

A month later Hetty Bestwick telephoned Flora Marie from Atlanta to announce—as a courtesy to Flora Marie, given her sisterly interest in her soul—that she had decided to leave the church. The events at the abbey had forced her to an irrefutable conclusion, that the patriarchal God who had effected the "miracle" of the crutches would rather play the fool than the physician.

Distressed, Flora Marie said, "What about the fact that Grimes's pistol jammed when he tried to shoot you?"

"That was no miracle," Bestwick said. "That was shoddy firearm manufacture." Anyway, she no longer believed in a God who would pull such a pair of grotesque stunts. She would certainly never renounce her painstakingly arrived-at disavowal of an antique communal superstition.

"I ache for you," Flora Marie said.

"Rejoice for me," Bestwick said, and soon rang off.

Two days later Flora Marie posted a letter in which she harangued her apostate friend: *"Faith is a gift but the will has a great deal to do with it. . . . Subtlety is the curse of man. It is not found in the deity."* Their friendship endured for several years, but nothing Flora Marie ever wrote or said turned Bestwick back.

And when Flora Marie died at age thirty-nine, devastating Mama Craft, Hetty Bestwick, and a vast cloud of admirers, butterflies rose from Blue Peacock Pastures and whelmed the eye of day with blood.

Pearl Cleage

Known primarily as a dramatist, Pearl Cleage also writes poetry and fiction. Born in Springfield, Massachusetts, in 1948, she studied at Howard University and Yale before completing her studies at Spelman College, where she graduated in 1971. Cleage has worked in journalism and education positions, but she has enjoyed her greatest success as a writer, playwright, and director. She has been playwright-in-residence at Spelman College and is an active leader in the Atlanta arts scene. Her dramatic work has been performed in Atlanta, New York, and Chicago. Her published writings include *One for the Brothers* (short fiction, 1983), *We Don't Need No Music* (poetry, 1971), *The Brass Bed and Other Stories* (fiction and poetry, 1991), *Deals with the Devil and Other Reasons to Riot* (essays, 1993), *Flyin' West* (drama, 1995), and *What Looks Like Crazy on an Ordinary Day* (novel, 1997).

Four from That Summer: Atlanta, 1981

One: May

My daughter is six and knows the words to songs by Kool and the Gang and the pledge of allegiance to the flag. My daughter has a closely cropped afro like mine, filigreed golden earrings from South America, and makes collages with me on Sunday afternoons. She wears blue jeans with patches, light blue jogging shoes, pleated skirts and button-up sweaters, and, every Tuesday afternoon, a Brownie uniform with a cap that matches.

My daughter can read, write, do simple subtraction and speak a few words of Spanish. With no attempt at objectivity, I would describe her as an almost perfect child. She is also a *black* child, and at the present time, she is living under a state of siege in the City of Atlanta.

Since July 1979, when the first body was found, until last week, when the seventeenth was confirmed, the mystery and horror surrounding the murders of black Atlanta children have been mounting. Adults feel outraged, frightened, incredulous, angry, suspicious. Kids feel surprised.

"Why are they killing kids?" my daughter says, and it is impossible to answer. Explanations center on a sick mind. Someone who doesn't know what they are doing. Can't help it. Someone driven and desperate.

My daughter's eyes fight against the words. She is unwilling to admit to adult madness or to her own vulnerability. There is nothing in her six year old child's consciousness to account for random, calculated violence against her peers. It is like being a woman and first understanding what rape is.

A few days later, my daughter and I are deciding between hash browns and pancakes at the McDonald's drive-in window and she says, "What if we could carry guns?" "What?" I say. "Guns," she says, "kids could all have guns and then if somebody tries to make us get in a car, we could whip out the guns and say no! Leave us alone or we'll shoot you!"

A few days after that, she says: "We run home from the bus now." She is talking about herself and the children she walks home from school with: another little black girl, also age six, and two little black boys, ages eight and ten. They used to walk the block from the bus stop, examining dead possums in the street, singing the chants they learn on the bus to pass the distance, chasing each other, whispering and giggling and kicking rocks.

Now when they get off the bus, they join hands and run the block, arriving at home out of breath, panting, looking over their shoulders, poking each other, and feeling foolish at being so frightened of something they can't see or understand.

Being a black child in Atlanta now must be a little like being a Northern black person watching Bull Connor at work during the Sixties. We would sit in Detroit, or Chicago, or Philadelphia, and watch the Alabama police cracking heads, and feel for the first time a kind of vulnerability that settled on our chests like witch-trial stones and stayed there.

Except then we could do something. We could send money to Civil Rights groups, or march in the street, or read books about the "Revolution" and refuse to accept our second-classness by confronting those who would deny us.

My daughter has no money to send to anyone. The marches begin nowhere and end nowhere. There are no books about organizing to fight people who murder small children and there is no way she can possibly refuse to accept her childness.

"I don't think it's a good idea for kids to carry guns," I tell my daughter. "Guns are very complicated and kids might shoot each other by mistake."

My daughter considers this and then speaks without looking up from her lap. "Well," she says softly, "we wouldn't have to use the bullets. Maybe we could just scare the people away from us. We would promise to be real careful," she says.

And it is my turn to look away.

Two: June

(Letter to a friend just back from a bad month in New Orleans)

what price cynicism?
in love and too jaded to write a love poem.
all victories difficult.
all gains constantly under threat of erosion.
everybody has a hungry heart.
dear kay:
my life in the bush of ghosts:
lunch at gabriel's restaurant with a political operative.
what do you hear, he says. politically, i mean.
adjusting glasses. smoking dark brown cigarettes
without inhaling.
scrambled tofu, i say, with green peppers and onions.

and white wine, i add, knowing he can afford it. this
is a campaign lunch after all.
well, not much, i say.
i don't do politics anymore.
i don't read the paper.
i don't go to city hall.
i hardly vote.
and if i can manage, i just generally don't give a damn.
see?

my life in the bush of ghosts:
New Orleans always seems like refuge until you turn on the t.v. in the motel where Mark Essex went up on the roof and demanded his stuff back and they are showing *Vixens* in living color. Or until the junebugs walk up your arm while you sit hunched over your typewriter as if the only difference between flesh and furniture is temporary, with the distinction so tenuous as to be inconsequential.

James Caan told *Rolling Stone* that he had lunch with Marlon Brando and Brando said, Jim, whattya want more than anything else in the world? And Caan reports that his answer was, I'd like to be in love. And Brando said, yeah, me too.

my life in the bush of ghosts:
A midnight phone call from L.A. tells me that Bob Marley's cancer has spread everywhere and he has no more locks and no more chances. My mother writes one page of determined cheerfulness to tell me the new medication isn't working and she will start chemotherapy in two weeks and even though my stepfather won't let her smoke dope, I consider asking a friend to get me a couple of ounces of the best Hawaiian for old times' sake in case she needs it.

the bushes are full of ghosts:
The wind is up outside and Peachtree Street traffic snakes toward a disco called "Animal Crackers" and they're pulling bodies from the river so fast my friends call from California/Indiana/Detroit/Mississippi and demand answers from *me*. They are incredulous/angry/frightened. My daughter suggests that maybe I should let my hair grow since some of the children are bigger than I am and she is afraid someone will think I am a boy.

the bushes are always full of ghosts:
New Orleans is a dream.

The wind makes Peachtree feel like a moor and I crane my neck, strain my eyes, searching for Heathcliff in the darkness.

Soon come.
Love,
P.

Three: July

It is billed as a benefit for the children's fund, but it's Michael Jackson at the Omni and the only relevant question is: how can one little Negro be so fine? He is beautiful and young and glitter pants and silver shoes and my daughter in my arms, eyes as round as the moon, holding her hands over her ears against the roaring of the crowd.

"This is the loudest noise I've ever heard," she says to me, cuddling closer. And I hold her and we sway and laugh and scream.

"Michael!" we say. "Oh, Michael!"

Now half past midnight, and home. Exhausted, I tack up the poster we have bought of the five Jackson brothers gazing at the camera with shirts open to the waist and hands on hips and tight jeans and they seem alive in our small room. They are a tangible presence with *heat*. I talk to the poster.

"Hi guys," I say. "Good concert!"

"Mom!" my daughter says, and laughs a little.

"Put on your nightgown," I say, but she stands still. Shy. Embarrassed. Eyes riveted to toenails.

"What's wrong," I say. Confused.

She looks up, flushed, and when I see her face, I know what it is. She cannot change in front of the poster boys. They are too real. Too present. Too wide-eyed and staring.

"Not in front of them?" I say, and she grins, sheepish and relieved, hiding her head against my stomach. "Yeah," she says. "They keep lookin' at me!"

"Want me to take them down?"

"Put them on another wall," she says.

I take them down, apologizing. "Sorry about this, Mike, but you guys gotta lighten up just a little bit okay? The kid is only seven!" And she laughs.

We tack them up over the ironing board, neutral territory, and tell them good night. She is yawning now, curled up in her Jacksons' tee shirt instead of a nightgown, and we laugh and she says, "I love you," and I say, "I love you too."

And she smiles again, asleep before she can reply.

Four: August

Twenty-eight dead and we began to share the same pictures. Explore the same theories. We decided it was genocide.

Drooling rednecks, consumed by hatred and evil.

Plotting in the hills. Stashing rifles in the trunks of their cars. Transporting ammunition in the backs of dirty pick-up trucks. Travelling in packs like mad dogs.

Sneaking into our community. Spying on us. Isolating our children. Waiting until they are vulnerable. Snatching them off the street. Snuffing the life out of them. Throwing their bodies in the woods. Sliding them into the river with a splash where they turn up downstream days later, swollen and stinking.

We wanted it to be one of Them. One of those we already know is after us. One of the ones we have already learned to watch out for.

We are not prepared for the Suspect—the Accused—to be one of our own. We are not ready to gaze at his picture on the front page and look into our own eyes, the eyes of our brothers/husbands/fathers/lovers/sons. We are not prepared for the madness to show itself this way. Not prepared for the hatred to turn inward, gnawing on itself as if it was possible to eat its way out, and still survive.

The arrest of the Suspect does not comfort or reassure us. "A scapegoat," we say to each other. "Pressure from the White House." "The governor made them do it, man. Don't you know anything?" We become investigators, dismissing publicized evidence as inconclusive, circumstantial, unconvincing.

We still admonish our children to travel in groups and not to go with strangers. We still share the vision of the carload of Klansmen cruising our street, tracking our young manhood as if they were rabbits. We still close our eyes and shake our heads and look away from each other's faces when they flash the Suspect's picture on the nightly news.

It's just too close. Too familiar a face to be the Danger . . . to be the fear made flesh . . . and the flesh made fear . . . beating among us like a telltale heart.

Judith Ortiz Cofer

Judith Cofer was born in Puerto Rico in 1952 and at the age of eight moved with her family to Patterson, New Jersey, an experience in the background of her 1989 novel *The Line of the Sun*. When she was fifteen, her family moved to Augusta, Georgia; she has lived in Georgia ever since. Cofer writes both as a Puerto Rican immigrant and as an American. Although many of her poems and stories describe life in Puerto Rico or the challenges of moving from the Island to the American mainland, she explores other subjects as well. Cofer's other works include *Peregrina* (poetry, 1986), *Terms of Survival* (poetry, 1987), *Silent Dancing* (essays and poems, 1990), *The Latin Deli* (essays and poems, 1993), *An Island Like You: Stories of the Barrio* (1995), and *The Meaning of Consuelo* (novel, 2003). A Franklin Professor of English at the University of Georgia, Cofer is the recipient of the O. Henry Prize for Short Fiction, the Anisfield-Wolf Book Award, the Pushcart Prize, and many other awards and grants.

Nada

Almost as soon as Doña Ernestina got the telegram about her son's having been killed in Vietnam, she started giving her possessions away. At first we didn't realize what she was doing. By the time we did, it was too late.

The army people had comforted Doña Ernestina with the news that her son's "remains" would have to be "collected and shipped" back to New Jersey at some later date, since other "personnel" had also been lost on the same day. In other words, she would have to wait until Tony's body could be processed.

Processed. Doña Ernestina spoke that word like a curse when she told us. We were all down in El Basement—that's what we called the cellar of our apartment building: no windows for light, boilers making such a racket that you could scream and almost no one would hear you. Some of us had started meeting here on Saturday mornings—as much to talk as to wash our clothes—and over the years it became a sort of women's club where we could catch up on a week's worth of gossip. That Saturday, however, I had dreaded going down the cement steps. All of us had just heard the news about Tony the night before.

I should have known the minute I saw her, holding court in her widow's costume, that something had cracked inside Doña Ernestina. She was in full luto—black from head to toe, including a mantilla. In contrast, Lydia and Isabelita were both in rollers and bathrobes: our customary uniform for these Saturday morning gatherings—maybe our way of saying "No Men Allowed." As I approached them, Lydia stared at me with a scared-rabbit look in her eyes.

Doña Ernestina simply waited for me to join the other two leaning against the machines before she continued explaining what had happened when the news of Tony had arrived at her door the day before.

She spoke calmly, a haughty expression on her face, looking like an offended duchess in her beautiful black dress. She was pale, pale, but she had a wild look in her eyes. The officer had told her that—when the time came—they would bury Tony with "full military honors"; for now they were sending her the medal and a flag. But she had said, "No, *gracias*," to the funeral, and she sent the flag and medals back marked *Ya no vive aquí:* Does not live here anymore. "Tell the Mr. President of the United States what I say: No, gracias."

Then she waited for our response.

Lydia shook her head, indicating that she was speechless. And Isabelita looked pointedly at me, forcing me to be the one to speak the words of sympathy for all of us, to reassure Doña Ernestina that she had done exactly what any of us would have done in her place: yes, we would have all said *No, gracias,* to any president who had actually tried to pay for a son's life with a few trinkets and a folded flag.

Doña Ernestina nodded gravely. Then she picked up the stack of neatly folded men's shirts from the sofa (a discard we had salvaged from the sidewalk) and walked regally out of El Basement.

Lydia, who had gone to high school with Tony, burst into tears as soon as Doña Ernestina was out of sight. Isabelita and I sat her down between us on the sofa and held her until she had let most of it out. Lydia is still young—a woman who has not yet been visited too often by *la muerte.* Her husband of six months has just gotten his draft notice, and they have been trying for a baby—trying very hard. The walls of El Building are thin enough so that it has become a secret joke (kept only from Lydia and Roberto) that he is far more likely to escape the draft due to acute exhaustion than by becoming a father.

"Doesn't Doña Ernestina feel *anything*?" Lydia asked in between sobs. "Did you see her, dressed up like an actress in a play—and not one tear for her son?"

"We all have different ways of grieving," I said, though I couldn't help thinking that there *was* a strangeness to Doña Ernestina and that Lydia was right when she said that the woman seemed to be acting out a part. "I think we should wait and see what she is going to do."

"Maybe," said Isabelita. "Did you get a visit from *el padre* yesterday?"

We nodded, not surprised to learn that all of us had gotten personal calls from Padre Álvaro, our painfully shy priest, after Doña Ernestina had frightened him away. Apparently el padre had come to her apartment immediately after hearing about Tony, expecting to comfort the woman as he had when Don Antonio died suddenly a year ago. Her grief then had been understandable in its immensity, for she had been burying not only her husband but also the dream shared by many of the barrio women her age—that of returning with her man to the Island after retirement, of buying a *casita* in the old pueblo, and of being buried on native ground alongside *la familia.* People *my* age—those of us born or raised here—have had our mothers drill this fantasy into our brains all of our lives. So when Don Antonio dropped his head on the domino table, scattering the ivory pieces of the best game of the year, and when he was laid out in his best black suit at Ramírez's Funeral Home, all of us knew how to talk to the grieving widow.

That was the last time we saw both her men. Tony was there, too—home on a two-day pass from basic training—and he cried like a little boy over his father's handsome face, calling him Papi, Papi. Doña Ernestina had had a full mother's duty then, taking care of the hysterical boy. It was a normal chain of grief, the strongest taking care of the weakest. We buried Don Antonio at Garden State Memorial Park, where there are probably more Puerto Ricans than on the Island. Padre Álvaro said his sermon in a soft, trembling voice that was barely audible over the cries of the boy being supported on one side by his mother, impressive in her quiet strength and dignity, and on the other by Cheo, owner of the bodega where Don Antonio had played dominoes with other barrio men of his age for over twenty years.

Just about everyone from El Building had attended that funeral, and it had been done right. Doña Ernestina had sent her son off to fight for America and then had started collecting her widow's pension. Some of us asked Doña Iris (who knew how to read cards) about Doña Ernestina's future, and Doña Iris had said: "A long journey within a year"—which fit with what we had thought would happen next: Doña Ernestina would move back to the Island and wait with her relatives for Tony to come home from the war. Some older women actually went home when they started collecting social security or pensions, but that was rare. Usually, it seemed to me, somebody had to die before the Island dream would come true for women like Doña Ernestina. As for my friends and me, we talked about "vacations" in the Caribbean. But we knew that if life was hard for us in this barrio, it would be worse in a pueblo where no one knew us (and had maybe only heard of our parents before they came to *Los Estados Unidos de América,* where most of us had been brought as children).

When Padre Álvaro had knocked softly on my door, I had yanked it open, thinking it was that ex-husband of mine asking for a second chance again. (That's just the way Miguel knocks when he's sorry for leaving me—about once a week—when he wants a loan.) So I was wearing my go-to-hell face when I threw open the door, and the poor priest nearly jumped out of his skin. I saw him take a couple of deep breaths before he asked me in his slow way—he tries to hide his stutter by dragging out his words—if I knew whether or not Doña Ernestina was ill. After I said, "No, not that I know," Padre Álvaro just stood there, looking pitiful, until I asked him if he cared to come in. I had been sleeping on the sofa and watching TV all afternoon, and I really didn't want him to see the mess, but I had nothing to fear. The poor man actually took one step back at my invitation. No, he was in a hurry, he had a few other parishioners to visit, etc. These were difficult times, he said, so-so-so many young people lost to drugs or dying in the wa-wa-war. I asked him if *he* thought Doña Ernestina was sick, but he just shook his head. The man looked like an orphan at my door with those sad, brown eyes. He was actually appealing in a homely way: that long nose nearly touched the tip of his chin when he smiled, and his big crooked teeth broke my heart.

"She does not want to speak to me," Padre Álvaro said as he caressed a large silver crucifix that hung on a thick chain around his neck. He seemed to be dragged down by its weight, stoop-shouldered and skinny as he was.

I felt a strong impulse to feed him some of my chicken soup, still warm on the stove from my supper. Contrary to what Lydia says about me behind my back, I like living by myself. And I could not have been happier to have that mama's boy Miguel back where he belonged—with his mother, who thought that he was still her baby. But this scraggly thing at my door needed home cooking and maybe even something more than a hot meal to bring a little spark into his life. (I mentally asked God to forgive me for having thoughts like these about one of his priests. *Ay bendito,* but they too are made of flesh and blood.)

"Maybe she just needs a little more time, Padre," I said in as comforting a voice as I could manage. Unlike the other women in El Building, I am not convinced that priests are truly necessary—or even much help—in times of crisis.

"Sí, Hija, perhaps you're right," he muttered sadly—calling me "daughter" even though I'm pretty sure I'm five or six years older. (Padre Álvaro seems so "untouched" that it's hard to tell his age. I mean, when you live, it shows. He looks hungry for love, starving himself by choice.) I promised him that I would look in on Doña Ernestina. Without another word, he made the sign of the cross in the air between us and turned away. As I heard his slow steps descending the creaky stairs, I asked myself: what do priests dream about?

When el padre's name came up again during that Saturday meeting in El Basement, I asked my friends what *they* thought a priest dreamed about. It was a fertile subject, so much so that we spent the rest of our laundry time coming up with scenarios. Before the last dryer stopped, we all agreed that we could not receive communion the next day at mass unless we went to confession that afternoon and told another priest, not Álvaro, about our "unclean thoughts."

As for Doña Ernestina's situation, we agreed that we should be there for her if she called, but the decent thing to do, we decided, was give her a little more time alone. Lydia kept repeating, in that childish way of hers, "Something is wrong with the woman," but she didn't volunteer to go see what it was that was making Doña Ernestina act so strangely. Instead she complained that she and Roberto had heard pots and pans banging and things being moved around for hours in 4-D last night—they had hardly been able to sleep. Isabelita winked at me behind Lydia's back. Lydia and Roberto still had not caught on: if they could hear what was going on in 4-D, the rest of us could also get an earful of what went on in 4-A. They were just kids who thought they had invented sex: I tell you, a telenovela could be made from the stories in El Building.

On Sunday Doña Ernestina was not at the Spanish mass and I avoided Padre Álvaro so he would not ask me about her. But I was worried. Doña Ernestina was a church cucaracha—a devout Catholic who, like many of us, did not always do what the priests and the Pope ordered but who knew where God lived. Only a serious illness or tragedy could keep her from attending mass, so afterward I went straight to her apartment and knocked on her door. There was no answer, although I had heard scraping and dragging noises, like furniture being moved around. At least she was on her feet and active. Maybe housework was what she needed to snap out of her shock. I decided to try again the next day.

As I went by Lydia's apartment, the young woman opened her door—I knew she had been watching me through the peephole—to tell me about more noises from across the hall during the night. Lydia was in her baby-doll pajamas. Although she stuck only her nose out, I could see Roberto in his jockey underwear doing something in the kitchen. I couldn't help thinking about Miguel and me when we had first gotten together. We were an explosive combination. After a night of passionate lovemaking, I would walk around thinking: Do not light cigarettes around me. No open flames. Highly combustible materials being transported. But when his mama showed up at our door, the man of fire turned into a heap of ashes at her feet.

"Let's wait and see what happens," I told Lydia again.

We did not have to wait for long. On Monday Doña Ernestina called to invite us to a wake for Tony, a *velorio*, in her apartment. The word spread fast. Everyone wanted to do something for her. Cheo donated fresh chickens and Island produce of all kinds. Several of us got together and made arroz con pollo, also flan for dessert. And Doña Iris made two dozen *pasteles* and wrapped the meat pies in banana leaves that she had been saving in her freezer for her famous Christmas parties. We women carried in our steaming plates, while the men brought in their bottles of Palo Viejo rum for themselves and candy-sweet Manischewitz wine for us. We came ready to spend the night saying our rosaries and praying for Tony's soul.

Doña Ernestina met us at the door and led us into her living room, where the lights were off. A photograph of Tony and one of her deceased husband Don Antonio were sitting on top of a table, surrounded by at least a dozen candles. It was a spooky sight that caused several of the older women to cross themselves. Doña Ernestina had arranged folding chairs in front of this table and told us to sit down. She did not ask us to take our food and drinks to the kitchen. She just looked at each of us individually, as if she were taking attendance in a class, and then said: "I have asked you here to say good-bye to my husband Antonio and my son Tony. You have been my friends and neighbors for twenty years, but they were my life. Now that they are gone, I have nada. Nada. Nada."

I tell you, that word is like a drain that sucks everything down. Hearing her say *nada* over and over made me feel as if I were being yanked into a dark pit. I could feel the others getting nervous around me too, but here was a woman deep into her pain: we had to give her a little space. She looked around the room, then walked out without saying another word.

As we sat there in silence, stealing looks at each other, we began to hear the sounds of things being moved around in other rooms. One of the older women took charge then, and soon the drinks were poured, the food served—all this while the strange sounds kept coming from different rooms in the apartment. Nobody said much, except once when we heard something like a dish fall and break. Doña Iris pointed her index finger at her ear and made a couple of circles—and out of nervousness, I guess, some of us giggled like schoolchildren.

It was a long while before Doña Ernestina came back out to us. By then we were gathering our dishes and purses, having come to the conclusion that it was time to leave. Holding two huge Sears shopping bags, one in each hand, Doña Ernestina took her place at the front door as if she were a society hostess in a receiving line. Some of us women hung back to see what was going on. But Tito, the building's super, had had enough and tried to get past her. She took his hand, putting in it a small ceramic poodle with a gold chain around its neck. Tito gave the poodle a funny look, then glanced at Doña Ernestina as though he were scared and hurried away with the dog in his hand.

We were let out of her place one by one but not until she had forced one of her possessions on each of us. She grabbed without looking from her bags. Out came her prized *miniaturas,* knickknacks that take a woman a lifetime to collect. Out came ceramic and porcelain items of all kinds, including vases and ashtrays; out came kitchen utensils, dishes, forks, knives, spoons; out came old calendars and every small item that she had touched or been touched by in the last twenty years. Out came a bronzed baby shoe—and I got that.

As we left the apartment, Doña Iris said "Psst" to some of us, so we followed her down the hallway. "Doña Ernestina's faculties are temporarily out of order," she said very seriously. "It is due to the shock of her son's death."

We all said "Sí" and nodded our heads.

"But what can we do?" Lydia said, her voice cracking a little. "What should I do with this?" She was holding one of Tony's baseball trophies in her hand: 1968 Most Valuable Player, for the Pocos Locos, our barrio's team.

Doña Iris said, "Let us keep her things safe for her until she recovers her senses. And let her mourn in peace. These things take time. If she needs us, she will call us." Doña Iris shrugged her shoulders. "*Así es la vida, hijas:* that's the way life is."

As I passed Tito on the stairs, he shook his head while looking up at Doña

Ernestina's door: "I say she needs a shrink. I think somebody should call the social worker." He did not look at me when he mumbled these things. By "somebody" he meant one of us women. He didn't want trouble in his building, and he expected one of us to get rid of the problems. I just ignored him.

In my bed I prayed to the Holy Mother that she would find peace for Doña Ernestina's troubled spirit, but things got worse. All that week Lydia saw strange things happening through the peephole on her door. Every time people came to Doña Ernestina's apartment—to deliver flowers, or telegrams from the Island, or anything—the woman would force something on them. She pleaded with them to take this or that; if they hesitated, she commanded them with those tragic eyes to accept a token of her life.

And they did, walking out of our apartment building, carrying cushions, lamps, doilies, clothing, shoes, umbrellas, wastebaskets, schoolbooks, and notebooks: things of value and things of no worth at all to anyone but the person who had owned them. Eventually winos and street people got the news of the great giveaway in 4-D, and soon there was a line down the stairs and out the door. Nobody went home empty-handed; it was like a soup kitchen. Lydia was afraid to step out of her place because of all the dangerous-looking characters hanging out on that floor. And the smell! Entering our building was like coming into a cheap bar and public urinal combined.

Isabelita, living alone with her two little children and fearing for their safety, was the one who finally called a meeting of the residents. Only the women attended, since the men were truly afraid of Doña Ernestina. It isn't unusual for men to be frightened when they see a woman go crazy. If they are not the cause of her madness, then they act as if they don't understand it and usually leave us alone to deal with our "woman's problems." This is just as well.

Maybe I *am* just bitter because of Miguel—I know what is said behind my back. But this is a fact: when a woman is in trouble, a man calls in her mama, her sisters, or her friends, and then he makes himself scarce until it's all over. This happens again and again. At how many bedsides of women have I sat? How many times have I made the doctor's appointment, taken care of the children, and fed the husbands of my friends in the barrio? It is not that the men can't do these things; it's just that they know how much women help each other. Maybe the men even suspect that we know one another better than they know their own wives. As I said, it is just as well that they stay out of our way when there is trouble. It makes things simpler for us.

At the meeting, Isabelita said right away that we should go up to 4-D and try to reason with *la pobre* Doña Ernestina. Maybe we could get her to give us a relative's address in Puerto Rico—the woman obviously needed to be taken care of. What she was doing was putting us all in a very difficult situation. There were no dissenters this time. We voted to go as a group to talk to Doña Ernestina the next morning.

But that night we were all awakened by crashing noises on the street. In the light of the full moon, I could see that the air was raining household goods: kitchen chairs, stools, a small TV, a nightstand, pieces of a bed frame. Everything was splintering as it landed on the pavement. People were running for cover and yelling up at our building. The problem, I knew instantly, was in apartment 4-D.

Putting on my bathrobe and slippers, I stepped out into the hallway. Lydia and Roberto were rushing down the stairs, but on the flight above my landing, I caught up with Doña Iris and Isabelita, heading toward 4-D. Out of breath, we stood in the fourth-floor hallway, listening to police sirens approaching our building in front. We could hear the slamming of car doors and yelling—in both Spanish and English. Then we tried the door to 4-D. It was unlocked. We came into a room virtually empty. Even the pictures had been taken down from the walls; all that was left were the nail holes and the lighter places on the paint where the framed photographs had been for years. We took a few seconds to spot Doña Ernestina: she was curled up in the farthest corner of the living room, naked.

"Cómo salió a este mundo," said Doña Iris, crossing herself.

Just as she had come into the world. Wearing nothing. Nothing around her except a clean, empty room. Nada. She had left nothing behind—except the bottles of pills, the ones the doctors give to ease the pain, to numb you, to make you feel nothing when someone dies.

The bottles were empty too, and the policemen took them. But we didn't let them take Doña Ernestina until we each had brought up some of our own best clothes and dressed her like the decent woman that she was. *La decencia.* Nothing can ever change that—not even la muerte. This is the way life is. *Así es la vida.*

Janice Daugharty

Janice Daugharty was born in Valdosta, Georgia, in 1944. She married soon after she graduated from high school, and though she attended college for two years at Valdosta State, she devoted most of her energy to running her family. She began writing at thirty-nine, and after ten years of seeking publication, she saw her first novel, *Dark of the Moon*, published in 1994. A succession of books quickly followed: the story collection *Going through the Change* (1994) and the novels *Necessary Lies* (1995), *Pawpaw Patch* (1996), *Earl in the Yellow Shirt* (1997), *Whistle* (1998), and *Like a Sister* (1999). Daugharty has commented on her career: "After ten years of writing apprenticeship, my publishing success came suddenly—one, two, three books sold in 1993. Then I took time to stand aside and ponder the journey, that fog of living through my fictional characters, and I was sad. But when I searched for alternatives, I found none."

You're No Angel Yourself

Lyneice has about decided that she'll be sitting at the same table by herself every Saturday night at Mama Mia's from now till the Rapture when up walks a shaggy-headed hunk—no Theodore Bundy, granted, but good-looking enough—and asks her to dance.

And then it takes all she can do to rise from the round table without her gold sandal heels setting on their sides. A fast dance that, for the love of God, gives even the drummer trouble. Little chunky fellow, trying hard to keep up the beat. Lyneice feels that she knows the drummer, she's sat so many weekend nights close to the smoke-riddled bandstand. But now here she is on the dance floor and looks like this could be it, what she's come for, what she's been coming for since her husband Son died with cancer two months ago. God forgive her, it'd been a pleasure to see him go, and not just because he suffered so.

This could be it.

She settles into moving her feet to every other beat—she's seen that done, though on her it feels like the slowing down of old age. She turned fifty-two, last birthday. No hag since she's started taking care of herself: she has cut and frizzed her skimpy red hair, naturally red, so that it appears teased rather than thin; she's bought a denim skirt and hemmed it—twice, as courage dictated—and a couple of loose, knit turquoise and magenta shirts that hide her barrel body. Her legs are long and, though shapeless, they are slim. She doesn't have much going for her, but she has slim legs. At least *one* of the things men go for.

Her dance partner is working up a rhythm by pumping his arms; his round thighs, under new blue jeans, move in jerks, his feet are practically still. He has a far-off look, dark panicky eyes, and his slick brown hair splays in bangs on his deep forehead. And he is younger than Lyneice—what she's always looked for in a man—yet no boy. He's hardly glanced at her twice.

She has to make good of this opportunity. So when the steel guitar, tortured by a sullen man under a dove felt cowboy hat, cries its last note, she slings her head and laughs and takes hold of her partner's hard tanned arm (everybody looks tan at Mama Mia's in the murky smoked-orange light).

He stares her square in the eyes with a cast-iron where-the-hell-did-you-come-from look, and she knows he's drunk. They all are.

Racket picks up from the pool room in the brighter alcove off the dance hall, and then the band strikes into another country tune, a slow worrisome crooning by the girl singer with long full hair: *Satin sheets to lie on, satin pillows to cry on* . . . And Lyneice more or less leans into the fellow, rocking and dozing him back onto the floor.

She could swear he's glad to have somebody to prop on. He hunkers low and breathes into her neck, clutching her hand through a twist of arms. His beery breath sends white-hot streaks from her brain to her toes.

A tall handsome man in a white T-shirt and jeans is dancing snug with a small woman in a short white pleated skirt. She looks like an old cheerleader. She has a smirky pug face that, at first glance, makes you think she's crying. Latching onto each other, they keep bumping into Lyneice, upsetting the suction of her man's mouth on her neck. Each time the two couples make contact, the man in the white T-shirt eyes Lyneice and her new man threateningly, as if it's their fault. His all-purpose gaze drills through the smoke and beer fumes. For a while, Lyneice's fellow seems not to notice, keeps up his safe cozy cuddling, but as the other couple circles behind and hips him from the rear, his head jerks up and his hand lets go of Lyneice's hand. "Watchit, bud!" Lyneice's man says, narrowing in on the other man.

> Satin sheets to lie on,
> satin pillows to cry on . . .

Lyneice two-steps her man toward the bandstand railing, behind several other cuddling couples, but the pressure of her leaning partner sends her back-trotting to the end of the dance floor, just off the pool room, two couples away from the couple who has bumped them.

The man in the white T-shirt spies them and dances the old cheerleader in their direction and rumps Lyneice, driving her into her slack partner like a brad on a shoe. He comes alive, like a mad man waking from a coma, and seizes the man by the shoulders of his white T-shirt, shoving him back. Scattering grumbling couples on the dance floor and skittering tables all the way to the bar, in the rear of the room.

The old cheerleader, in white canvas shoes and socks, squeals and hops up on one of the round tables, walking table to table to the bar. Legs so shapely and spry they don't go with the raddled, made-up face.

Half the crowd funnels toward the door and out with spirits of smoke; the other half follows the fight toward the bar, some urging the men on and others trying to break them up.

Lyneice, on the floor, trails the cheerleader, on the tables, toward the elled bar, knowing she should head out the front and home, a thirty-minute drive any way you cut it, to Cornerville. But the excitement of the fight carries her on. Besides . . .

The two men, tussling more than socking one another, have cramped up like wrestlers, both cursing and mumbling in contradicting low tones. Beer bottles on the bar slide and collide, popping on the floor.

Lyneice, behind the crowd, can see that her man is wedged against the bar, back bent and head lolled, the man in the white T-shirt welded to him, both sliding with the collecting beer bottles.

The old cheerleader now stands on the table behind Lyneice, holding to her shoulders and yelling, "Git him, git him, git him!" Lyneice whirls around, glaring into the smirky crying face with caulked wrinkles. She has to be at least forty-five, Lyneice decides.

Night after night, she has watched the old cheerleader sit perched on a bar stool, swigging from bottles of Bud held by the neck. And when the "last call for alcohol" comes at midnight on Saturday, she'll order a whole six-pack to carry her over till two A.M. when the band breaks. She always has some fellow picked out to go home with or to take home with her. Someone different, though the same crowd of maybe thirty, or fifty on a good night, comes back each week. Lyneice has been coming to Mama Mia's long enough to witness the rotation of the old cheerleader's men.

Lyneice hates to admit it but she's been jealous. And now she finally snags a man of her own, and what does this old cheerleader do but spoil the whole affair—well, relationship, same thing—by bumping into them.

"Get off my shoulder," says Lyneice and shrugs, tipping the old cheerleader to the floor, where she lands like a lizard.

Lyneice peeps between two men in the double line of bar-dwellers, who are egging the fight on, and sees that her fellow is up from the bar, straightening his blue velour shirt and mumbling. Looking around. And all at once, she feels a tight clutch of arms around her waist and glances down as she skids back into a table to see the little sagged, squinty-eyed face of the old cheerleader, walking on her knees and snarling up like a fice dog.

The back of Lyneice's head whacks the edge of the table as it slides away and banks with the others in an ongoing series of thunks and clacks, like freight cars coupling, and she goes down on her butt, the gold straps of her sandals spiking light from the sputtering candles. The crowd turns and closes in on Lyneice and the woman, their faces glowing orange in a semicircle of roundmouthed OOOOOOOOOOOOOs.

The old cheerleader scrambles on top of Lyneice like a playful child and grapples for her hair. Lyneice dodges, crawling on her spine beneath the table, and humps the back of the old girl on the underside of the top. She can see the legs of the table lift, hears the feet clank on the tacky floor.

The old cheerleader still scrabbles up Lyneice's long body. Lyneice stretches away as the woman makes for her hair, long pink nails raking Lyneice's arms, her neck, while cursing in a tight seething voice—"Bitch, bitch, double-bitch, whore." Her brown ponytail swishes, and with each swish comes the spot-cleaner odor of hair spray.

With Lyneice's head now stuck out the other side of the table, she glimpses her man, still squaring his shirt on his broad shoulders as he heads for the front door, or what she thinks is the front door. Maybe the bar. She is turned around, confused.

Arms finally freed from the old cheerleader's grasp, though her legs still bracket Lyneice's waist, Lyneice could now pry her loose, could pick her up and toss her aside, but she stays, craning away to save her hair, eyes on the circle of men, lusting for a female fight.

"Y'all start playing," Mama Mia calls from the bar in a quelled desperate voice. The band picks up loosely, as in the middle of a song, and the female singer with the rich raspy voice starts singing:

> Satin sheets to lie on,
> satin pillows to cry on . . .

Lyneice wallows her way to an opening between tables, with the girl still astride and still cursing, but in a tone without *oomph*, like an actress alone going over her lines. Her pale squinty eyes shine as the men skiffle about the table and yell, "Go to it, bitches, git it!"

The old cheerleader's stiff brown ponytail switches Lyneice's face as she lunges and kisses her on the mouth, wet and sweet-beery. The men whoop and clap. Lyneice yanks her head to the side and handles the old cheerleader around the waist and stands her on the floor on her knees. Her slack rucked lips form into a smirk.

Hand covering her mouth, Lyneice rolls over and scrambles up and lopes across the dance hall like she's walking against the wind. Through the pool room and along the musty dim hall, to the rest room.

The raw light of the bare bulb overhead shines down on the desilvering mirror and shoots back a reflection of Lyneice's blown-up hair, only slightly ruffed, and her smeary lips, like red rickrack on white cotton. She turns on the warty spigot, cups her hands and sucks water into her mouth, swirling it cold around her teeth till they ache. When she looks up in the mirror, she spots the old cheerleader behind her.

"Don't you come near me, girl," Lyneice says, wringing the knob of the spigot and slinging her hands.

The woman, whose face is now crying more than smirky, her pink lipstick streaked across her fine fallen features, backs to the beige cracked plaster wall.

Her hands are clasped behind, small pointed breasts making anthill shadows on the wall by the john, which is jammed with tissue, yellow water. "You're no angel yourself," she says.

"I ain't said I was." Lyneice can see that there is no fighting or loving left in the woman and she feels relieved, bold. Mad. But she fears turning and looking and maybe finding that the woman out of the mirror might be the same woman who'd latched onto her. She can still feel the tight legs around her waist. The warm mouth on hers. She cups more water and swishes it around in her mouth, and when she looks up again the woman is gone.

Sunday morning, Lyneice's only day off from Wrangler's, where she sets in hip pockets on jeans—she could do it in her sleep and seldom anymore stitches down the pocket openings—she wakes at seven and can't fall back asleep.

Robins outside the sunny window of her bedroom are threshing in her flower beds, bordering the concrete walk, and she sits up to watch the chesty rust birds hop and flip flakes of cypress mulch to the dead brown grass. She knuckles the window to chase them away, but they don't even flinch. Two more hop across the grass between the front of the house and the dirt road and start scratching the mulch side to side, speckling the walk. She'll have to sweep up the mess today.

Since Son died, she finds herself keeping up the small relocated, renovated mill house that used to sit with fifty others like it on the Sampson Powder Camp, just up the dirt road and across Highway 129, north of Cornerville. The house had been white then, with Sampson-red trim, the brownish-red color of apples gone bad. But she'd painted the clapboards blue, and though the color turned out a shade brighter than she'd have liked, at least the house looked new. New to her anyway.

In the bathroom, she brushes her teeth while looking in the mirror of the medicine cabinet she bought from Kmart last month. A chromy bright inset chest with a glaring white fluorescent bulb across the top that brings out her freckles. Bending down to rinse her mouth, she thinks about the old cheerleader with the smirky crying face and is afraid to look up in the mirror again.

On her way to the kitchen, at the back of the house, she decides to go to church, maybe even Sunday school. She is up in plenty of time and can't use sleeping late as an excuse.

Look for a man in church, that's what she'll do, like her Uncle B.F. and Aunt Mae have been after her to do. But unless Lyneice is willing to commit adultery—and she's finally got up the nerve to tell them that—she's not likely to find a man. They're all married or widowed, and the widowers are so old they can barely creep into church.

Enough of that from living with Son, twenty years older, and taking care of her drunk daddy and brother in the falling-down cabin across the Alapaha River (her mama had left home with another man when Lyneice was three). Not to mention taking care of four head of stepchildren and two of her own.

For the first time in her life she is free. Free to come and go and sit around watching TV till she feels like going to bed. Nobody—Son, for instance—to make her feel guilty for watching The Late-Night Movie.

She remembers that the special on Theodore Bundy, Florida Serial Killer, will be on TV tonight and makes a mental note to check the listings in the *Valdosta Daily Times*. A good-looking man like that, a murderer. She can't believe it, and if he did kill all those women, he must have had a good reason. But she knows better; she's just looking for an excuse to ogle him without guilt of lust. Lust in the heart, she's been told, is the same as lust of the flesh. She doesn't believe that. And judging by what goes on these days, lust is no biggie anyway.

When she was a girl—always her opening line to bring up the past—people were lusty enough, just didn't go around and about it out in the open, like now. She and Son certainly didn't, hardly looked at one another in the last few years, except for her to wait on him, but she knew he'd been messing around with other women. Fine by her. Actually, when he did have sex with her, she'd pretend to be on the verge of a climax—a sure-fire way to get him to wrap it up quick.

When he'd come courting her at the cabin across the river, he never made any bones about loving her, or even lusting after her: he needed a woman to look after his four small children, and stingy as he was, he wasn't about to hire someone after his wife had left him for another man. Same situation as her daddy and mama. And that's how come Lyneice to volunteer as mama to Son's children. That and desperation to get out of the woods and away from her daddy. She'd like to say that her reason was solely for the purpose of mamaing Son's children, but that would be a lie. She'd raised them well enough with what she had to raise them with—sent them to school, clean and neat and fed, till they got grown. But never really mamaed them.

Now, the three stepgirls and their brother call once in a while, maybe drop by if they need a babysitter. Lyneice tries to be gone. And generally is—another benefit to working at Wrangler's.

She's made friends at work too, though most of the women are married and settled or have boyfriends. A few play the field, like Lyneice—she loves to think of herself as "playing the field."

She gets dressed for church, wearing her respectable long print skirt and white blouse with the Peter Pan collar. Then she goes outside to sweep the walk where the robins have scattered the expensive cypress mulch.

While she's out, she decides to sweep the concrete around her blue Fairlane, under the carport. She always loves sweeping the concrete slabs, feels almost rich: before, she has had to contend with dirt paths and mud holes at the back door; and before that, palmettoes and gallberries a step off the doorsteps of the old cabin across the river. A few pitcher plants the only out-of-the-ordinary thing on the place to take pride in.

She backs the Fairlane out to the dirt road that ends at her yard, the start of woods, a wall of pines on three sides, and on the other a house nearly identical to hers. Ginnah Ruth, her neighbor, has stuck colored cups from styrofoam egg cartons on each blade point of her Spanish bayonets. Looks just like flowers to nearsighted Lyneice.

A quarter mile into Cornerville, and when she dips at Troublesome Creek, nearing the blinking red light at the crossing, she can see from the flat red brick courthouse a couple of slow cars turning in at the white Baptist church. And suddenly she cannot fight back feelings of lack of interest—simple lack of interest—a dull drain on her conscience that makes her eyes draw. Like springs pulling toward the back of her head.

She yawns and idles off on the gravel road between the churchyard and the small aqua cafe that's been recently switched to a feed store. A prime site, being the only rotating vacancy in the little town, for the dream ventures of the would-be businessmen. So many in Swanoochee County, like Son, found themselves out of work when the Sampson Company closed, some twenty-odd years ago. The company men dug and hauled fat litard stumps to be shipped to a mill that ground them for dynamite. And when the job went, Son's dynamite-making skills were spent on Lyneice.

Gazing straight ahead, as though to keep from being recognized, she shortcuts along the other side of the church and behind the courthouse square, headed home.

After eating a whole can of Sweet Sue chicken and dumplings, during which she kept feeling glad she didn't go to church, she feels guilty on her full stomach, lazy really, too lazy even to cook a decent pot of the homemade kind. And wasteful. Every other Christian woman in Cornerville had probably cooked chicken and dumplings earlier in the morning and then gone to church, just as Lyneice had before Son died.

She feels misplaced.

But as she starts to lie down for a nap—and doesn't she deserve it, after working all week?—she feels itchy and eager to be up and dressed in one of her new short skirts—more denim—and doing something. What?

She could go visit Uncle B.F. and Aunt Mae, a routine she's followed all her life. See if the routine still pleases her, if routine still brings on feelings of peace. Doing what she should be doing and not what she feels like doing. She should have learned a lesson last night, but truth be told, if juke joints were open on Sundays, she'd go.

Well, maybe not on Sundays . . . she's not *that* liberated yet.

She doesn't get good inside Uncle B.F.'s housetrailer door before he starts harping on her skirt.

"Mae," he says, scooting his stocky pulpwood body to the edge of his recliner, "I want you to look a-there. I be-dogged if Lyneice ain't hemmed up her skirttail again." He laughs, lacing his stuffed fingers. His feet in dusty black Sunday shoes are crossed, laid over on the sides.

Lyneice cackles—"Uncle B.F.!"—and tugs down her skirt to cover her knees as she sits on the couch.

Aunt Mae, crocheting in her recliner next to his, smiles, rocks and stares down at her twisting fingers. One she's lost after a catfish finned her.

A slow fire ticks in the bulky Buckstove, which has scorched sunflower designs in the Celo-tex tiles above. An armload of split oak has been tumbled next to the heater with raw fat-litard splinters and siftings of bark and dirt. Around the mess, the blue linoleum floor is swept clean.

The narrow room is otherwise tidy, though crowded: a brown couch with a parrot motif, and three Lazy-boy recliners. The "his and hers" recliners facing the couch, and the one not sat in touching arms with the couch. The unused chair is piled high with quilting scraps and stacks of Aunt Mae's sewing customers' clothes and folded squares of fabric. A couple of pillows made from cut-on-the-line-and-stitch kits.

At the other end of the living room/kitchen, a long table covers half the space, and a doll-house range on the facing wall sends a smell of eggy warmth. A clock ticks somewhere.

Uncle B.F. stares out the off-track sliding glass door at his mixed herd of cattle, browsing the winter rye pasture—an odd enamel green against the woods line of spiky gray blackgums behind the field. He's a man out of place in a mobile home, a man you can tell has lived in a house; he cuts all his firewood and even sells some. "You landed you a man yet?" he says.

"Uncle B.F., I declare!" snickers Lyneice. Around him she always feels like a homely little girl, a naughty one lately. She used to stay with him and Aunt Mae when she was growing up, *when* she could. And they were good to her, in their way. But Uncle B.F. is bad to joke—bad jokes, to which there is no right response. So she laughs.

Aunt Mae holds her swarthy stout face down to keep her bun of coarse brown hair from wallowing against the recliner back. Making sure it is neat for night church, coming up. Deftly with her four-fingered hand, she turns the start of a white star doily, while unraveling the roll of crochet thread in the seat beside with a flap of her elbows. "You mean you ain't cornered you a man up there." She nods west, the direction of Valdosta—up there.

"Ain't run up on the right one yet." In a way Lyneice enjoys their picking, and especially Aunt Mae's curiosity, which places Lyneice in a different category— devil, not angel—from the homely homebody she used to be. Feels like she's loosened a tight bra. Actually, they make her feel downright exciting. She decides to go a bit farther.

"I tell you what, Aunt Mae, if I could find me a fellow looks like that Theodore Bundy, I'd grab him."

"Bundy!" hoots Uncle B.F., his thin lips curling out. He had dozed back in his chair; now he sits up. "You mean that *killer*?"

Aunt Mae quits crocheting and stares at Lyneice above the Lifesaver-orange plastic frames of her glasses.

"You ain't got a lick of sense," Uncle B.F. hollers. "That man's kilt I don't know how many people. Girls—girls like you."

"Uncle B.F.!" Lyneice titters and sits back, daring to cross her freckled legs. One foot swinging in a black pump.

"You see that scandal on TV?" His green eyes pop in his square red face. "Claiming to be a Christian, pshaw!"

"Way I see it, Uncle B.F., the thief on the cross stood a chance of heaven."

"Hush yo mouth! That rascal's just putting on, trying to keep from going to the chair."

"Murderers shall not enter the kingdom of heaven," pipes Aunt Mae with a satisfied smile. She flips her star doily.

Lyneice can offer up no defense for Bundy, so she says, "Well, what I mean is, he ain't bad-looking."

Uncle B.F. sits back and considers the source: he knows how silly a silly woman can be. "I tell you what, gal. You keep on hanging around *them places* and first'n last you gone run up on you a Bundy. Ain't that right, Mae?"

Mae nods, satisfied.

By the end of the week, Lyneice has settled back into her Wrangler pocket-stitching swing, till her hands feel as if they're moving, even still. And come Friday night she feels sure that if she doesn't make the effort to go to Mama Mia's, she'll spend the rest of her life getting up, going to work, coming home, watching TV and going to bed. Church on Sunday. Strange how she'll be so tired, then get to Mama Mia's and, hearing the razzy whang of the mixed country and rock band, feel completely rested, locked into a wild world with time on hold.

She doesn't drink, never has, and doesn't smoke, but the smoky reek of the bar doesn't faze her; it is part of the atmosphere. The "dim lights, thick smoke and wild wild music" atmosphere that the girl in the band often sings about.

Around nine, Lyneice eases in, wearing her shortened denim skirt and gold sandals, and sits at her usual table. The waitress, a bow-chested woman with a bony body, gapped teeth and white cotton-candy hair, smiles as she twitches past with a high tray of drinks. "Be with you in a minute, hon. Coke, right?"

Lyneice shakes her head and laughs, squinting through the orange haze at the same old crowd: two women at the jukebox about her age; a crowd of men around the pool table behind the lattice partition laced with green plastic vines; the familiar band members babying guitars and drums, while the girl singer frams out a melody on the keyboard; and at the bar, the usual stool-perchers, a few men and women; and the old cheerleader in her pleated white skirt and canvas shoes, holding a Bud by the neck. Men hanging on her like coats on a rack.

Lyneice gets her foot swinging good as the band lights into "Old-timey Rock & Roll," but has to hold it steady for the bar crowd passing to the dance floor. For the old cheerleader, snapping her fingers and jigging, as she lures one of the men along the alley of smoke.

On the dance floor, her brown ponytail swings side to side as she twists her head and slides side to side, up and away from her partner. Her smirky crying face faded as a doll's left out in the weather.

Lyneice can feel someone behind her before the man nudges her shoulder. She turns and one of the regulars—a young man with a dark drawn face and sharp black eyes—nods toward the floor. She follows. All during the dance he motions with a goody-goody finger for her to come closer. She smiles and keeps dancing, hitting every other beat, at a loss for what to do with her hands. They sling at her sides.

When the dance ends, he goes back to her table and sits in the other chair. The waitress with the gapped teeth brings Lyneice's partner a Busch in the can and he whacks her on the rump. She does a bow-bellied sprint toward the bar, laughing back. The man yells after her, "Bring one for the lady here," through a megaphone of hands.

"I don't drink," Lyneice admits through snickers, but the band has cranked up on the intro to another number. Drowns her out.

Her partner cups his ear, dirty in the dirty bar light, but gives it up and swigs from the can, each swallow telling in the sliding knot on his throat.

Young, she thinks, but not my type.

She feels someone rub against her left shoulder. Another man leans down, breathing in her face. "Daince?"

She giggles, gets up.

A slow dance, his hard body pressed close, she keeps her eyes wide, mind on her big toes, which his boots keep cracking like pecans. He fixes that: he presses one knee between her legs, straddling her thigh like a fence.

By the time the dance ends, Lyneice is panting; sweat trickles from her scalp, dampening her bangs. She blows at her forehead and fans with her hand, settling in for a rest just as another fellow happens out of nowhere—this one *really* young, with a thin face and clear blond hair. She laughs and shrugs and gets up to dance, a tune that starts out slow but ends in a medley of dirty dancing numbers.

Another man has joined the one at her table, with another chair drawn for Lyneice when she gets there, and two cans of Busch and a bottle of Bud at her place. To be polite, Lyneice sips from the bottle of Bud, being careful to grip it around the body, not the neck—her Coke is gone anyway—and it turns her mouth like a dose of baking soda.

As the band breaks, the first fellow, who looks strange now after so much time and men have passed, reaches across the table and places his rough hand on hers. Dead weight. No message in it. The new fellow puts his arm around the top of her chair and scratches her back with his thumbnail. Makes her drowsy.

She needs to go to the rest room but is afraid if she leaves, they'll be gone when she gets back. She can hold it.

The two men spew smoke, swig beer and sing along with the jukebox during band break, but when the band members straggle back, setting drinks on the rail and self-consciously taking their places, both men scrape their chairs around to dance with Lyneice. But another has already caught her hand and is leading her off to the dance floor.

Though Lyneice has sipped only a little beer, it makes her feel woozy, light and framed into her own head, and she has to really deliberate over whether this is the same fellow who danced with her the weekend before. After a few turns around the floor, with his mouth sucking her neck, she knows it's him. Though not as limp drunk as last Saturday, he's on his way.

She wants to ask him why he left her in that predicament with the old cheerleader, but she's too self-conscious, questioning is not her way, the music is too loud.

After the dance, in a fool's imitation of acting the gentleman, he guides her back to the table with her arm twined through his, hand resting across his waist. He deposits her in the chair and drifts off toward the bar.

Next dance he's with the cheerleader, who pokes out her butt and pushes against his chest with both hands; dancing pigeontoed, she pulls close as if he's her new lover.

No longer giddy but dazed and set apart, like a bad case of flu, Lyneice is still dancing with different and same men. And between dances starts checking everybody out, leaving the men to focus on their beers. Four men now at her table.

At the bar, the old cheerleader swivels away with her bald tan legs crossed, twitching a stark white tennis shoe, elbows back on the bar. Men prop beside her, left and right, and three meander in front, nursing beers. The later it gets— it's twelve-twenty now—the thicker they flock. When the music starts, she hops down, springing as she walks to the snap of her own fingers, small round butt stuck out. On her way to the dance floor with a pack of men.

Slow-dancing again with the man from the night before, Lyneice snags eyes with the old cheerleader during a turn: the woman's head on her partner's shoulder, Lyneice peeping around the sunken head of her partner, well on his way to limp drunk.

During the next break, Lyneice takes a chance on losing her men—seven, now, all told—and goes to the rest room. There's always more anyway. As she passes through the pool room, two men at the table stop spiking balls to stare at her. She follows the narrow hall, a tunnel of smoke, and hears them talking. She knows it's about her though she can't make out a single word.

Squatting over the john and feeling the burning pressure of her bladder let go with a horsey guttering, she watches the latched brown door, the cracked beige wall where the old cheerleader stood last night. She doesn't quite finish— usually she tries to pee twice, keep from getting bladder infections—but her legs are quaking too badly. She doesn't even wash her hands—she's held hands with half the maybe-diseased men in the place anyhow—and starts out.

Like an accident that can't happen because you've just thought about it, the old cheerleader's face pops around the door, white in the raw wash of light from the rest room.

"Oh!" says Lyneice, snickering, "you scared me."

"You're no doll yourself," says the other woman, pushing past without touching. She pulls up her skirt and squats over the toilet, her white lace bikini panties fastened around her boxy tan knees.

Lyneice starts to shut the door.

"Ain't none of us nothing but a joke," the woman says like a friend—no, a sister. A little sister you've slept with all your life who can say anything because she knows you so well. Nothing tells as much about a person as sleeping with them.

Her weak, socketed eyes are sad and sincere, her face your own when your make-up's off and your hair's wet.

By two A.M., Lyneice knows she'll take one of her men home, she knows he'll go, and she knows he'll be her last. She closes her eyes and picks one.

Pam Durban

Pam Durban is one of the most accomplished short story writers in the modern South. A writer in the style of Eudora Welty, she skillfully evokes the inner lives of her characters without losing touch with the outer world they inhabit. Durban was born in Aiken, South Carolina, and studied creative writing at the University of North Carolina at Greensboro. After teaching at a succession of schools, she joined the creative writing faculty at Georgia State University in 1986 and taught there for the next fifteen years. With David Bottoms she founded *Five Points* literary magazine. In 2001 she moved on to the University of North Carolina at Chapel Hill as Doris Betts Professor of Creative Writing. Her books include *All Set About with Fever Trees, and Other Stories* (1985), *The Laughing Place* (novel, 1993), and *So Far Back* (novel, 2000). Her story "Soon," first published in the *Southern Review* in 1996, is a multigenerational chronicle of women struggling to break free from the bonds of a tradition and heritage that they cannot and finally do not want to escape.

Soon

Martha's mother, Elizabeth Long Crawford, had been born with a lazy eye, and one morning when she was twelve her father and the doctor sat her down in the dining room at Marlcrest, the Longs' place near Augusta, Georgia, and told her they were going to fix her so that a man would want to marry her someday. Her father held her on his lap while the doctor pressed a handkerchief soaked with chloroform over her nose and mouth, and she went under, dreaming of the beauty she would be. But the doctor's hand slipped, and when Elizabeth came to, she was blind in her right eye. For the rest of her life what she remembered of that morning were the last sights she'd seen through two eyes: the shadows of leaves on the sunny floor, the hair on the backs of her father's hands, the stripe on the doctor's trousers, the handkerchief coming down. Then blindness. The rise and the downfall of hope, one complete revolution of the wheel that turned the world, that's what she'd lived through.

Marlcrest was a hard name to pronounce. The first syllable sprawled, it wouldn't be hurried; the last climbed a height and looked down on the rest of the world the way Martha's mother had done all her life. It had been a hard place to live, too. One hundred acres of level, sandy land on a bluff above the Savannah River, and a house raised high on brick pillars to offer the people of the house a view of the river, a chance at the river breezes. When Elizabeth married Perry Crawford, he agreed to live there, too. *She* wasn't leaving. In the family cemetery on the bluff stood the Long tomb and the graves of the children who'd died at birth, who had fallen or been trampled by horses or killed by cholera or yellow fever during the two hundred years the Longs had lived at Marlcrest. Before the Civil War, slaves hauled muck up from the river—the *marl* of which the *crest* was made—to spread on the fields. Many died there: smothered in the mud, collapsed in the heat, snakebit, drowned. They were buried in a corner of a distant field that the pine woods had taken back years before Martha was born, though even in Martha's time a person could still find pieces of broken dishes, shells, empty brown medicine bottles under the pine needles, as if the people buried there had been carried out and lowered down by others who believed that the dead could be quieted and fed.

After the botched operation, Martha's mother lived where the wheel had stopped and she'd stepped off. The blind eye that the doctor had closed gave her a proud, divided look, as though half her face slept while the other stayed fiercely alert, on the lookout for the next betrayal. It was how she'd looked at seventy-five—disfigured and ferocious—when she'd summoned Martha and her brother, Perry Jr., to the nursing home in Augusta where they'd put her after a series of small strokes had made it dangerous for her to live alone at Marlcrest any longer. For six months before they'd put her in the home, there'd been trouble after trouble. She'd stopped payment on every check she wrote. The doors of the house, inside and out, had filled up with locks. Every night her calls to her children were packed with complaint. The woman they'd hired to stay with her was a thief, a drunk. Someone was downstairs picking the locks. It was that Herbert Long from up the road. He and his family, descendants of the slaves who'd once lived on the place. For a hundred years they'd bided their time; now they'd come to steal from her.

At the nursing home that day, Martha and Perry Jr. found their mother in her wheelchair in the sun by the window. She was dressed in beige linen, her best earrings, heirloom pearls. Her hair had been freshly restored to a cresting silver wave, and she was draped in Arpège perfume, as she had been in all her finest hours. "Well, don't you look nice, Mother. What's the occasion?" Martha asked, kissing her mother's sweet, powdered cheek.

Some papers their mother had in her purse, that was the occasion. Notarized contracts. Smiling brilliantly, she handed over the documents, one by one, to Martha and Perry Jr. She'd sold Marlcrest—the whole kit and caboodle—to a developer who planned to bulldoze the house, clear the land, build a subdivision there. Plantation Oaks, he'd call it. "Here is a copy of the title deed," she said, passing it to Perry Jr. "As you will see, it is properly signed and notarized." He turned it over, held it up to the light, looking for the error that would void the contract. As for the family records and belongings—the *contents* of the house, she said, leaning toward them from her wheelchair with her hands folded in her lap and high color in her cheeks, savoring (Martha saw) the vengeful triumph of this theft—she'd sold them all to a young man from a southern history museum in Atlanta. *Smack,* she struck the wheelchair's armrest. *Done.* He'd been coming to visit her in the nursing home since Martha and Perry Jr. had put her there—it had been almost exactly one year now. He'd even driven her out to Marlcrest a time or two to pick up something she'd forgotten. The Long family had many possessions of historical interest; already the museum people were calling their belongings the most important collection of southern artifacts ever acquired in Georgia. Fine linen shirts and baby gowns sewn by slave seamstresses. Diaries and ledgers and sharecropper contracts. Tools, portraits. A complete record of plantation life. The young man had been so sweet to her. He had all the time in the world to sit and talk. He never sneaked looks at his watch or found some excuse to jump up and rush off five minutes after he'd sat down.

Not that Martha and Perry Jr. hadn't been expecting it somehow. What has been lived will be handed on. Throughout their childhoods their mother had told them she lived by *high ideals,* which meant that everything had to be right—but since nothing ever was right, she was constantly, deeply, and bitterly disappointed by every person and every circumstance. *Horsy* had been her word for Martha, and in it were catalogued all of Martha's lacks. A long face, big teeth, lank hair, eyes that shone with dark, equine clarity. Yes, and Martha was also too *big,* too meaty. She sweated in the summer heat, and in winter her fingertips stayed cold. Perry Jr. was never more than an adequate student, a lukewarm son. Even her husband, Perry Sr., had failed her. When Martha was sixteen and Perry Jr. eighteen, their father sneaked off early one October morning to go duck hunting alone in the swamp below the old slave burying ground and was struck dead by a heart attack. After dark the sheriff found him up in the duck blind, still seated on his camp stool with his gun across his knees, looking out the little window hole in the sidewall of the blind, as though he were watching the mallards flash and preen in the dark water below.

His death made their mother furious; afterward she widened her search for the thief who'd robbed her. And yet, though Martha and Perry Jr. had both expected that someday their mother would get to their names on her long list of suspects in the crimes against her, neither was prepared for it. Is anyone *prepared* for the actuality of life, which is always more surprising or horrifying or sweet than we could ever have imagined? Not at all. We dream and wish and plan, but something more subtle, more generous and devious, arranges reality for us.

After they'd heard all their mother had to say about what she'd taken from them, after she'd leaned back, satisfied, and looked from one to the other of them with that brilliant and terrible *any questions?* look on her face, Martha had closed her eyes. She saw the bulldozer push the house. It swayed, cracked, fell, carrying beds, tables, chairs, the smell of closets, her grandmother's round hatboxes and furs, the river's wide curve that she could see from her bedroom window in winter when the leaves had fallen and the trees along the banks were bare. Carrying even the slave cemetery, where, in the spring just past, Martha had found weeded ground, plastic lilies in a Mason jar. Propped against a pine tree. In the nursing home that day, Martha felt the world fail and move away from her for the first time; fail and move away the way her mother had taught her it would, not with words exactly, though Elizabeth had certainly given her children enough of those, but with her footsteps walking away from them, her closed face, her fury.

Their mother died within a year of that day. A stroke, of a magnitude even *she* would have approved—maybe—as the cause of death in a person of her stature, knocked her out of her wheelchair in the nursing home dining room one Saturday evening and killed her before the first hand touched her. In her coffin, Martha was startled to discover, her mother looked different than she had in life. The perfect wave of silver hair was intact, as were the long, elegant fingers, and yet, lacking the ferocious hauteur that had been its life, her face looked wasted and starved, as if under the rage a ravenous sadness had been at work. Not even the undertaker's crafted composure, the small rueful smile he'd shaped on her mouth, or the benign glow of the pink light bulbs in the funeral home lamps could soften the face she would wear now into eternity.

2

What do you do with what you've been handed? Martha would not have her children saying *poor Mother* over her coffin. She went back to the life she wanted, a calm and common life, firmly planted. As Martha saw it, her mother's bitterness and rage were exactly as large and violent as her hopes and her longings, and so it was these longings that Martha would uproot in herself. That's why she'd married Raymond Maitland in the first place (against her mother's wishes), a decent man from a decent family, a big, careful, sober man with jug ears who wanted what she wanted. They lived in the country outside Augusta, and Raymond, a salesman, traveled up and down the coast, only he called it the *eastern seaboard*, because he believed the high-minded sound of those words gave him a competitive edge over his coarser peers. His territory stretched from Myrtle Beach, South Carolina, to Jacksonville, Florida, and at one time or another, he sold insurance, encyclopedias, building materials, pharmaceuticals, vending machine snacks, and office supplies. The drawers in their kitchen and den filled up with pencils, ballpoint pens, rulers, rubber jar-lid openers, key chains, thermometers, and spatulas, all printed with the names and slogans of companies he'd represented.

In the spring, summer, and early fall, he drove with the windows rolled down (this was in the fifties, before air conditioners were standard in most cars), his left arm resting on the window ledge, so that his arm was always sunburned when he returned from a sales trip. At home, it was one of their pleasures for him to shower, lie on their bed in his undershorts, and doze, with the fan blowing across him and the radio tuned to the light classics station, while she rubbed Solarcaine on his sunburned arm as gently and patiently as if his skin were her skin, so that he imagined sometimes that the spreading cool relief came from her fingertips, their delicate, swirling touch.

Then one day in late July, the summer he was fifty-eight and Martha had just turned fifty-six, the summer Raymond Jr. finished graduate school at Georgia Tech and their daughter, Louise, had her second baby, Raymond returned from a week-long trip up the coast. He traveled for Tom's Peanut Company then. He threw his car keys onto the kitchen counter and fell into her arms, groaning about the six hundred miles he'd just driven through the *goddamn* heat, and at his age, too. He smelled of fry grease and cigarette smoke overlaid subtly with sweat and metal, the smell of the road. Someday they'd find him dead of a heart attack, slumped over the steering wheel on the shoulder of some sweltering back road in the Pee Dee swamp. A desk job, that's what he wanted now. To keep him closer to home, closer to *her,* that was the ticket. "Take a shower," she said. "Come lie down."

While she rubbed the cream into his arm, she felt the silky slackness of aging flesh under her hands; she saw that his muscles were starting to droop, go ropy. His chest had begun to sag, too. And as she tenderly catalogued the marks of time on her husband's body, she noticed that his left arm was as pale as the rest of him. She looked at the small, pleased, and peaceful smile on his mouth. She sat on the edge of the bed with the fan blowing across them, the Solarcaine squeezed onto her fingers, and a picture rose up to meet her as though his skin had released it, like a smell: a woman in green shorts lounging in a white wicker chair, her big tanned legs crossed, smoking a cigarette and laughing.

She rubbed the Solarcaine into his pale arm. Next day she went through the phone bills for the last six months, found call after call to a number in Little River, South Carolina. The voice that answered when Martha called matched the thick legs, the cigarettes, the indolence of the woman whose image had wormed its way into her mind. That night, when she showed him the phone bills, Raymond put his hands over his face and cried. It was true, he said, it was true, he'd gotten in over his head. He would break off with her, her name was— "Don't you dare speak her name in my house," Martha shouted—if Martha would just be patient and give him time. If she would just forgive him.

Patience she had, and time. Plenty of both, and also the will to forgive. For six months they tried, but it had gone too far with the other woman. The story came out in pieces: the things he'd given her—jewelry and cash, a semester's tuition for her son at the University of South Carolina—the promises he'd made. She was a widow, twenty years younger than Martha. It almost drove Martha crazy. Just when she thought she'd heard the whole story, he'd choke out more until it seemed there was no end to the future he'd planned with this woman.

When Raymond left to go live with his big-legged woman in Little River, Martha told him she wanted two things—no, three, she wanted three things:

she wanted the house in Augusta, and she wanted the house in Scaly Mountain. Louise and Raymond Jr. had been in grade school when Raymond and Martha had bought a beat-up old white clapboard house two stories tall and one room wide, roofed with tin, that sat on a foundation of stacked stones in a valley at the foot of Scaly Mountain, North Carolina; they went there every summer and at Thanksgiving, too, if they could manage it. Always, when they got there, Raymond had to be first out of the car. "Let Daddy have his minute," she'd say to the children, holding them back. He'd make a big show of stretching and breathing, as if he couldn't get enough of that air. Then he'd stand with his hands on his hips, his chest thrown out, king of the hill. Next he'd lean his elbows on the car door, push his wide, smiling face through the open window, squeeze her arm and say, "We're fifty-cent millionaires, Martha, sure enough," as if this discovery were new to him every time, meaning it didn't take much to make him feel rich. Meaning that what he had was all of what he wanted. Then he'd kiss her richly on the mouth, and they had arrived.

The third thing she wanted from Raymond was never to hear from him again. She meant it, too, about cutting him out of her life for good. She knew the way to the cold, bare space inside herself where she could live by the absolutes she declared. Goodbye, Raymond. "I thank my mother for the strength she instilled in me," she told Louise during the divorce. "No, really. She's the one who gave me the backbone for this." Finishing cleanly, she meant, cutting the cord.

3

Five years after the divorce, Martha announced that she was moving to the house in Scaly Mountain. "My thermostat must be broken, I can't take this heat any longer," she told Louise, who was frantic about her mother's moving so far away, and all alone, too. "What if you fall?" Louise asked. "What if you have a stroke or a heart attack?"

"Friend, come up higher," Martha joked with her friends from the Episcopal church when they asked her if she'd thought through what she was doing. She told others that she was retiring. From what? they demanded to know. From what? From canasta on Monday and bridge on Tuesday (she did not say), from standing in the vestibule before Sunday morning services, alert for a new face. ("Welcome to All Saints'. Are you visiting with us this morning? Would you please fill out this card and drop it in the collection basket? We're glad to have you.") From taping books for the blind and pushing the book cart around the hospital corridors, intruding on the desperately ill, challenging them with her smile to cheer up. From muffins and casseroles and sympathy calls and notes of congratulation or consolation. From rushing to church every time the doors swung open or having to explain her absence to some anxious friend. Goodbye to all that.

She did not speak to anyone of the solitude she craved: to be alone, with new vistas in front of her eyes and unfamiliar, rocky ground below her feet. She did not tell anyone how she wanted to be rid of Raymond, whose cigarette smoke clung to the paneling in the den and lingered in the closets of the Augusta house. The week before she decided to move, she'd come across a moldy package of Tom's cheese crackers way in the back of a kitchen drawer, and she'd known then that this house would always push reminders of Raymond up to the surface, no matter how hard she scrubbed and bleached and aired. He rested more lightly on the mountain house. There she would lift Raymond's few T-shirts out of the bottom drawer of the dresser in their bedroom and tear them into rags; she would take down his coffee mug from a kitchen shelf, tear his meticulous handwritten instructions off the wall between the water heater and furnace and be finished with him for good. Then he would be gone the way her mother was gone. The mother whose grave she still visited dutifully twice a year, carrying a poinsettia at Christmas, a lily at Eastertime, standing with head bowed, her heart empty of any longing to see her mother, of any wish to speak.

But a person can't just do *nothing*, can she? Can't sit all day with her hands folded or a game of solitaire spread out on the kitchen table. Can't not talk to other people without beginning to hear strange echoes in the conversation she's carrying on with herself. So she went to work. She had the pasture behind the house cleared, she put in a pond. She added two rooms and a porch onto the back of the house, and she lengthened the kitchen until the house looked like a white, wooden shirt with outstretched arms. Over the mountain, to Highlands, twice a week she drove her white Dodge Dart to the senior citizens' center for canasta and talk.

Every week she wrote to her children, letters full of questions and advice. "Have Sarah Lynn's teeth shown any signs of straightening?" she asked her daughter. "If not, do *please* take her to the orthodontist." And "Those old linen napkins I gave you are to be used as *tea towels*," she wrote after she'd visited Louise and found the napkins balled up in the rag basket under the kitchen sink. Her daughter's letters were long and chatty, with fabric swatches stapled to them or pictures of the children enclosed. Raymond Jr. wrote his full-speed-ahead notes on "Memo from Raymond Maitland Jr." paper. He was big in Coca-Cola down in Atlanta, she told her friends over the canasta table. Very big, she'd repeat, arching her eyebrows to show that words simply could not map the circumference of his orbit.

Without fail she wrote a weekly letter to her brother, Perry Jr. After his wife died, he'd drifted into mysticism, joined the Rosicrucians. His letters were about the migration of souls, the power of the spirit to transcend time and space, to enter that place where there was no death, no beginning or end, only a current that carried you up and up, endlessly spiraling toward fulfillment, completion, bliss. He wanted to join his wife, he wrote. He could hardly wait for that day.

Martha sat in her bedroom in the mountain house she had made her own— no trace left of her traitor husband or her bitter black wind of a mother, not so much as a photograph of either of them—a plain, tall woman in a sleeveless blouse and a full skirt made of a coarse woven material like burlap. Her braids were crossed and pinned over the top of her head; she wore orthopedic sandals with wool socks and sat with her ankles crossed, her back very straight in a high-backed chair pulled up to a white wooden table. One must be *realistic,* she wrote to her brother, apply the styptic pencil to one's scratches, pour iodine into the deeper wounds, get on with life in *this* world. Reality (she underlined it twice) was a constant and trustworthy companion who, once befriended, never let one down or walked away and loved someone else. A person must not wear himself out with wanting what it is impossible to have. What was finished must be done with and put away. "False hopes are cruel, Perry," she wrote. "We must not exhaust ourselves waiting for what will never happen. I speak from experience when I say this. As you well know, I have suffered indignities at the hands of life, we all have, but the longer I live the surer I become that the consolations of life—if any—must be sought and found in facing it squarely, as it is. The mind must not be allowed to wander where it wants, else it might end up lost in a wilderness of longing and regret. This I believe."

And then, late one September afternoon, when she'd lived in Scaly Mountain for a year, when the pond was full, the meadow fenced, the hay rolled and drying in the field she leased to a neighbor, as she sat on the porch after supper, watching the evening light flood into her valley and spread across the foot of her meadow, something changed in her. She felt it catch and roll over the way tumblers move inside a big lock. Maybe it was the gold light slanting across the fat rolls of hay that invited the change. Maybe it was the chore she'd finished—writing her mother's name and the date of her death in the Long family Bible—or the way she sat with the book open on her lap, watching the ink dry on the page.

Now this was no modest Sunday school Bible with a white pebbled cover and gold-leaf pages, a tiny gold cross dangling from a red-ribbon marker. It was the original family Bible in which the record of Long births, weddings, and deaths had been written since 1825. A serious and heavy book with a tooled leather cover, a lock and key. It smelled of the smoke of many fires, and its registry pages were stained and soft as cloth. When her father had opened it for family devotions, Martha used to imagine thunder rolling off its pages. She had gone to Marlcrest after her mother had sold everything; without hesitation and without guilt, she'd lifted the Bible off the carved wooden stand next to the fireplace in the downstairs parlor, where it had rested throughout her life and her mother's life and her mother's and her mother's lives, and taken it home. For a year, the museum wrote to her about the Bible. They were tentative, respectful letters at first. Later, letters from lawyers began to arrive. She'd ignored them all. Now, looking from her mother's name out to the hay drying in her meadow, she felt herself lifted, carried, and then set down one place closer to the head of the line her mother had vacated.

That's when the idea of the reunion came to her. She would gather what was left of the Long clan around her, here, in this place. The next morning she drove into Highlands and ordered stationery printed up with *Long Family Reunion* embossed across the top. She set the date for the following summer: July 6–9, 1969. All winter she wrote letters and logged in the answers, then sent back diagrams of the house with rooms and beds assigned.

Give Martha time, her brother used to say, and she could plan anything. Perry Jr. had landed with the Allies on D-Day; he always said that Martha could have planned the Normandy landing. She'd certainly planned *this*. Collected promises from twenty-five far-flung Longs, then stood in the parking lot she'd leveled in her meadow and waved them to their designated spaces with a flashlight, like a state trooper at a football game. She carried their suitcases and marched them up to the house and directed them to their rooms.

For the children there were relay races and treasure hunts and nature hikes down the valley with Martha at the head of the column, like the Scout leader she'd been when Louise was growing up, a walking catalogue of the lore of trees, reptiles, and stones. The girls in her troop had nicknamed her Skink, the lizard, for her bright-eyed, darting restlessness. For the grownups there was plenty of food, plenty of talk; the family Bible and photographs traveled from hand to hand. There was the Long family tree, a scroll as big as a blueprint, on which their genealogist had mapped every twig and root. At night there were games and prizes. A prize for the oldest Long, a dim old uncle, ninety-three that summer, who sat patiently wherever he was put until someone came back for him. And for the youngest, a son born in June to Lamar Long, who'd been promoted that summer to foreman of the weave room at the Bibb Mill in Porterdale, Georgia. A blue baby, they called him, born with a defective valve in his heart. A good baby, all eyes, who lay quietly in his basket studying the faces that followed each other like clouds across his sky.

Bossiest woman in the world, they whispered among themselves. Exactly like her mother, poor soul, some of the other ones said. Even her own brother had butted heads with her in the kitchen over something silly, over cream. One morning he came whistling into the kitchen, intending to skim a dollop of cream for his coffee from the top of one of the bottles of raw milk that Martha had bought from a neighbor. Right behind him came Martha, who plucked the bottle out of his hand before he could shut the refrigerator door. "I am saving this, Perry," she told him, "to go on top of the blackberry pie I shall make for the farewell dinner."

"Oh, come on, Martha, I only want a teaspoon," he said.

"No, I cannot spare that much." For half an hour it went on this way.

Then Perry tried for the last word. "I want some of that cream, Martha," he said, holding out his cup to her. It trembled in his hand. "Just a smidgen to put in my damn coffee."

"Well, you can't have it, Perry," she said. "I told you, it's for the pie. I need it all." She held the bottle out to show him—not the thick yellow clot in the neck of the bottle, but the cream, the *cream* whipped into high, stiff points and her pie, warm and rich beneath that sweet, smothering layer. Couldn't he see it? She could, and the thought of that cream-to-be made tears stand in her eyes. Then the thought of herself crying over *whipped cream* made her furious. She who'd written to her brother about dignity and the pitfalls of looking too far into future or past for happiness or consolation, who had thrown all the force of her considerable will into living in the world as it *is*. Finally Perry Jr. slammed his coffee cup down onto the kitchen counter and walked out. That night he said to one of the other men, "I had to lock horns with Martha today." And a child who overheard the remark and the laughter that followed pictured two warring moose in a mountain meadow, their enormous racks locked, shoving each other until they fell from exhaustion and died. Then the passing seasons, then the bones covered with hide, the bleached antlers still entangled.

On the last day of the reunion, as she'd planned, Martha climbed the rickety wooden stepladder, shooed away helpers, and strung Japanese paper lanterns between the big silver maple beside the road and the cedar nearest the house. At six-fifteen they would eat, followed at seven by speeches, testimonials, recollections, a song or two, and a final word from the genealogist, who'd traced the family back to England and tonight would name for them the place from which the first Longs had set out for the New World hundreds of years before. Exactly at six, Martha struck a small silver bell with a silver fork and waited until its clear note had died away, then invited everyone to line up, which they did, oldest to youngest, as she'd planned. Then they filed past the tables made of sawhorses and planks and covered with white cloths and filled their plates. Chicken and corn and beans—they heaped it on—banana pudding and coconut cake and, of course, Martha's blackberry pie topped with a mountain range of whipped cream.

They'd just settled down to eat when she heard Abel Rankin coming down the road. He was her neighbor, the one who sold her the raw milk out of cans he carried in the back of his wagon, that wholesome milk from his own cows from which she'd salvaged *all* the cream. When she heard the clink of the cans, the jolting rattle of the wagon, the jingle of Sawdust the mule's bridle and the stumbling crack of his hooves on the rocky road, she dished up a plate—chicken and beans and coconut cake—and walked out to the edge of the yard to wait for him. When Abel Rankin saw her, he reined in the dun-colored mule and said, "Evening" (never quite meeting her eyes), touched the brim of his brown felt hat, and took the plate of food she held up to him. "Eat this, Mr. Rankin," she said.

He ate quickly, hunched over on the wagon seat as though eating were a chore he had to finish before nightfall, while she held Sawdust's bridle, patted his face, felt the bony plank of his nose, his breath on her hands. When the children came running to pat the mule, she took charge. She made them line up and listen to her. "Now, stroke his nose lightly," she said. "You must stroke an animal as lightly as you'd stroke a hummingbird. You want him to remember you?" she asked. "Blow into his nostrils. Gently, gently, like this, you hear me talking to you?"

Those were her mother's teachings, her mother's actual *words*. As soon as they'd left her mouth, she felt her mother walk up and stand behind her, listening, to hear if she'd gotten it right, how to treat an animal. Her mother had always kept a reservoir of tenderness toward animals unpolluted by her general disappointment and bitterness. No animal had ever betrayed her. Oh, no. When Martha was a child, there had always been a pack of half-starved stray dogs skulking around the back steps at Marlcrest, waiting for her mother to feed them. There had always been a shoebox on top of the stove full of baby squirrels rescued from a fallen pine, tenderly wrapped in flannel and bottle-fed into independence.

Her mother had owned a Tennessee walking horse, a flashy bay named Jimbo, whose black mane and tail she'd braided with red ribbons before she rode him in shows. She used to nuzzle, stroke, pat the horse, bury her face in his mane, while Martha hung on the paddock fence, listening to the dark-gold and fluid warmth that filled her mother's voice when she talked to him, waiting for that warm and liquid love to overflow the dam in her mother's heart and pour over her. Waiting, still waiting. And now her mother had come and stood so close that Martha imagined she heard her mother's breath whistling down the bony narrows of her imperial nose. Her mother, who'd traveled this long way to find Martha and withhold her love again, just to remind her daughter, as a good mother should, that her love might still be won if Martha would just be patient and not lose heart, if she would just get it right for once.

Martha held her breath, then shook her head to clear it and turned to see if anyone had noticed her standing there like a fool with her eyes squeezed shut and her fists clenched at her sides, swept away in a fit of hope. Up on the wagon seat, Abel Rankin worked steadily at his supper; the children cooed and stroked Sawdust's nose and laid their cheeks against his whiskery muzzle. Back in the yard, people sat on the green grass and on the porch, enjoying their food. They circled the table and filled their plates a second time, a third; they lifted thick slabs from her beautiful pie. What a ridiculous old woman you are, she thought. Standing there waiting for your dead mother to touch you. But there it was again, percolating up through the layers of years, bubbling out at Martha's feet like a perverse spring. This sly and relentless force that moved through the world, this patient and brutal something that people called hope, which would not be stopped, ever, in its work of knitting and piecing and binding, recovering, reclaiming, making whole. Which formed from the stuff of your present life a future where you would be healed or loved and sent you running forward while it dissolved and remade itself ahead of you, so that you lived always with the feeling, so necessary to survival in this world, that you were not just trudging along but moving *toward* something.

She guessed that if you could just give up hope, your time on earth would be free of longing and its disfigurements. God knows she'd tried. But you couldn't. Not even her mother had done that, finally. Even after she'd sold Marlcrest out from under them and momentarily righted the wrong of her life by taking from someone else what she felt had been taken from her, she hadn't been satisfied. Instead, she'd begun to pine and grieve over her old poodle.

Rowdy was his name, Martha's only inheritance. She'd taken him to her house when she and Perry Jr. had put their mother in the nursing home. He was thirteen years old then, morose and incontinent, a trembler, a fear-biter. Nothing left of him but gluey old eyes, a curly coat, and bones. On a Saturday morning soon after he came to live with her, he turned over her garbage while she was at the grocery store and ate rancid bacon drippings out of a small Crisco can. She found him on her kitchen floor, greasy and struggling to breathe, and rushed him to the vet's, where he died two hours later, his blood so clogged with fat his old heart just choked on it.

Until her dying day their mother had been greedy for news of Rowdy, details of his diet, the consistency of his stools, and Martha and Perry Jr. had given them to her. They'd even pretended to be passing Rowdy back and forth between them, sharing the wealth. On one visit, Perry Jr. would tell their mother how on cool fall mornings Rowdy had enough spark to chase squirrels around Perry's back yard. On the next visit, Martha would continue the story, say that Rowdy still enjoyed his dog biscuits even though he gummed them now and it took him forever to eat one. He's a little constipated, she would say, but he's fine. "Well, then, you're not feeding him enough roughage," their mother would say. "Feed him apples. I must have told you that a thousand times, don't you listen when I talk to you?" she would say, the old fierceness darkening her good eye. Then she would smile. Toward the end, when she smiled at them, it was her skull that smiled; then the weeping would begin, the longing, the sorrow. "Why don't you bring my little dog to see me?" she would sob. "Soon, Mother," they would promise, patting her hand, smoothing back her hair. "Next time."

4

Now it is August, twenty-five years past the summer of the reunion. Olivia Hudson, one of Martha's grandnieces, is driving through the mountains with her husband and small son when they pass a road that runs up a narrow valley, and she says, "That looks like the road to my great-aunt Martha's house, the one where we had the family reunion, remember my telling you about that?" She had been seven that summer, the blue baby was her brother; in photographs she stands protectively close, her hand always resting near him, on the side of bed or blanket. Now they turn back and head up the valley, and as they drive Olivia studies the landscape, looking for clues. She cannot imagine that the house is still standing, but she hopes that some arrangement of trees and pastures and fences will rebuild it in her mind's eye and set it down on its lost foundation. She hopes for sheets of roofing tin, a standing chimney, steps leading up to an overgrown field. Anything.

Instead, they drive around a curve and she sees the house, the *house* itself, rising out of a jungle of saplings and shaggy cedars. Silver maple saplings, hundreds of them, Olivia sees as they drive closer. The leaves flash and flutter in the breeze. A realtor's sign lies on its side in the grass, near the stump of the big silver maple that has spawned the little trees, the one that threw its wide shade across the front lawn the summer of the reunion. And what Olivia feels as they wade and push toward the house through the thick grass and saplings is an emotion so quick and powerful it takes her by surprise. It is as potent as love *recovered*, the feeling itself, not the memory of the feeling—an urge to laugh out loud and also a dragging sadness, and a longing for no particular person or thing, a longing to *know* what the longing is for.

And Olivia thinks that if the house had been sold, had become someone else's house, unpainted, the screens kicked out, the yard full of junk cars, or if a picket fence had been thrown around it, a straw hat with flowers in the band hung on the door, its power to move her would have dissolved into its new life. As it is, its power is original, strong. She feels as if she could look in and find them all at dinner, Martha circling the long table, pouring raw milk into the children's glasses, and the mothers following her, pouring it out, refilling their children's glasses with the store-bought, pasteurized kind.

Of course, what she sees when they've waded through the grass and stepped over the rotten place on the porch and looked in through the cloudy glass of the narrow window beside the door is the front room of an abandoned and neglected house. Bloated chairs, scattered papers, white droppings everywhere, a cardboard box packed with blue bottles. She *has* to get inside.

Down the mountain they find the realtor. Billie is her name. She has diamonds on the wings of her glasses, jewels on her long black T-shirt, ragged black hair and Cherokee-dark eyes, Cherokee cheekbones. She is so heavy and short of breath that Olivia's husband has to boost her up the broken front steps, but when they get inside the house, she turns brisk, businesslike. Martha's children still own the place, but they're so busy they never come here. That's why they've put it up for sale. Someone is about to buy this place and turn it into a bed-and-breakfast inn, take advantage of the business from the new ski slope over at Scaly Mountain. Since Olivia is kin (now that she's been around Olivia for a while, Billie can see the resemblance, yes: "You favor your aunt Martha," she says), wouldn't she be interested in buying it? Of course, Olivia would have to make an offer right away, today in fact. Billie checks her watch. She's expecting an offer any minute from the bed-and-breakfast people.

Books lie scattered on the floor of every room; faded curtains sag from bowed rods; blackberry vines tap against the glass in the kitchen door. "You know, people around here say this place is haunted," Billie calls to Olivia as Olivia starts up the stairs to the second floor. "Your great-aunt Martha died in this house, and they say she came back as a cat to haunt it."

Olivia laughs. "If anyone would haunt a place, it would be Martha," she calls down the stairs, thinking of the grizzled tabby with the shredded ear and stony face that had been sitting on the porch when they'd driven up, that had dissolved like smoke between the foundation stones when they'd stepped out of the car. Thinking of Martha's tenacity. The famous struggle with her brother over the cream. She thinks of Martha fighting battles, righting wrongs, the clean, bleached smell of her clothes. Martha had wanted something out of life that couldn't be found in one lifetime, no doubt about it. Naturally, her spirit would go on poking and probing and quarreling here, striding, big nose first, into a room.

Remembering all that, Olivia comes into the long room under the eaves where the women and girls slept during the reunion. Now it is full of rusty file cabinets and busted-open suitcases and, strangest of all, in a closet, a wedding dress and veil, vacuum packed in a white box under a clear plastic window, without a date to place it in time or a name to connect it with anyone's life. Outside the window that's set so low in the wall she has to stoop to look through it, she sees her husband following their son through tall grass behind the house, and beyond him, a dip in the overgrown meadow where Martha's pond once lay, that shallow, cold, muddy pond that never cleared except where it ran over the spillway.

Olivia opens a drawer in one of the file cabinets—she has to yank it because of the rust—and flips through crumbling file folders stuffed with brown and brittle papers. Real estate forms, a Rosicrucian newsletter, yellowed stationery with *Long Family Reunion* printed across the top. She thinks of the week she spent in this room, The Henhouse, the men had named it. All that clucking, fussing, preening, a bunch of broody hens. Her father, who loved jokes, had lettered the name on a piece of cardboard, along with a drawing of a plump hen with a big behind and long eyelashes looking coyly over her shoulder, and tacked it onto the door. Olivia had never before been included among the women nor surrounded by so many of them. They slept under starched sheets and thin blankets on old camp beds set in rows. She'd pulled her bed over near the window, next to her mother's bed and the baby's basket. From there she'd watched the moon rise, the constellations wheel up from behind the mountain, the morning light fill the valley. The month before she died, so Olivia has heard, Martha added a sunroom onto the south side of the house. And now this house and all its rooms have been died out of, left and locked away, abandoned, begun again and never finished.

"Your aunt Martha really knew her way around these mountains," Billie calls up from the bottom of the stairs. "One time she went to a neighbor's funeral at the Church of God up the road there and another woman went with her who wasn't from around here either. But that other woman, she dressed up in high heels, a nice navy dress, a mink stole, and a hat. You know those Church of God people are *strict*. They don't allow any fancy show in their churches. They say that when that woman came in dressed in her finery and took a seat, everybody turned and stared until she got up and left their church. But your aunt Martha now, she wore a plain black cardigan sweater over a dark dress. She wore low-heeled shoes. She came in and sat in a back pew, quiet as a mouse. They accepted her just like she was one of their own kind."

Olivia is pleased to hear about Martha's dignity for a change. Billie's story restores height and luster to the foolish and shopworn figure her aunt has become over time, handed down through the family. All over that part of the mountains, Billie says, people had talked about Martha at the funeral as though she'd done something remarkable by going there properly dressed. But when the story got back to Martha, she didn't see what all the fuss was about. It didn't surprise her that she'd done the right thing. Dressing for the funeral that morning, she hadn't given a thought to what she should wear: everyone knows what to wear to a *funeral*. She'd just reached into her closet and pulled out a black dress. Since it was a cool fall morning, she'd added a black sweater. At the last minute she'd even slipped off her wristwatch and left it in a drawer to keep its gold band from offending the eye of any member of that stern congregation. The watch had been a birthday gift from her children one year, and looking at it reminded her of their faces—small and clear and full of light—when they were young and the days ahead seemed numberless.

She'd gone into the crowded, chilly church and sat in the back pew and listened to the congregation sing a hymn. Harsh, unaccompanied, the singing had reminded her of a creekbed in a drought with the sun beating down on dry stones, but that dry creek had carried her anyway, back to the summer of the reunion and the walk she'd taken with her grandchildren to see the orchard. The haunted orchard, the children had called it, where a blight had killed the trees and withered apples had clung to the branches through a whole year of seasons. Standing there with the children, she'd turned to her daughter's oldest boy. "And what do you intend to make of yourself when you grow up, Mr. Albert Redmond?" she'd asked.

He'd looked up at her out of pale blue eyes as he pivoted on his heels, inscribing circles in the dirt of the road. He was ten, beginning to fizz. He wore red high-tops, a whistle on a lumpy purple-and-orange lanyard that he'd made at Boy Scout camp earlier that summer. "A fifty-cent millionaire," he'd answered her, grinning.

Hearing Raymond's words in the child's mouth had made her heart pound, her cheeks flush. And just like that, Raymond had joined them. Uninvited, unwelcome, he'd come back with his gosh-and-golly face, his pale traitor's arm, all the things she'd made herself cold and deaf and blind to years ago. "Well, son-of-a-gun," she'd heard him whisper warmly in her ear, insinuating more, "how about them apples?"

"Well, I hope you won't waste too much of your valuable time pursuing that course," she'd said to the boy that day, staring at the orchard, dizzy, suddenly, as though she'd waked up to the earth's circling, the endless motion of return that had brought her here, where it had seemed for a moment that the stubborn and contradictory truths of those trees had merged with the warring truths of her own life: the trees had died, but the fruit would not fall. Hope could cling to nothing, and a shriveled apple was all it took to coax love to come slinking back into this world. Inside the fruit she saw seeds; inside the seeds, more fruit. In this motion she saw the turning shadow that eternity throws across this world and also the current that carries us there. She had not forgotten.

When the hymn was done, the preacher told the story of the narrow gate, the strict accounting, the raked, leveled, and weeded ground of the promised land toward which they traveled in sure and certain hope of the resurrection. And when the service was over, she stood outside the church and greeted those harsh and unblinking souls as if they were kin.

Scott Ely

A native of Atlanta, Georgia, where he was born in 1944, Scott Ely grew up in Mississippi. He earned B.A. and M.A. degrees at the University of Mississippi and an M.F.A. in creative writing at the University of Arkansas. He served a tour of duty in Vietnam from 1969 to 1970, an experience he considers the "most important event of [his] life" and one that figures prominently in his writing. Ely has taught English and creative writing at Winthrop University in South Carolina since 1986. He is the author of two short story collections, *Overgrown with Love* (1993) and *The Angel of the Garden* (1999), and two novels, *Starlight* (1987) and *Pit Bull* (1988). He is married to the poet Susan Ludvigson.

The Lady of the Lake

Even when I was a kid I wondered how those little towns in Alabama and Mississippi got their names, how someone who lived in a house without windowpanes could muster up the nerve to name a town Athens or Florence or Paris, and that, too, when what they were naming was no more than an empty space, or at the most a single store and a few houses with the hogs wallowing in the street. So when Defoe Michaels said there was a party at Como, a picture of a villa perched on a mountain above a blue lake came into my mind. That spring I'd studied the Italian Renaissance in my art history course at Ole Miss.

"We could go in your car," Defoe said.

He was leaning against the doorway of the Texaco station watching his father pump gas into my car, which I had bought after a summer spent planting pine trees. I'd been stung by hornets, struck at by more than one rattlesnake, and had my skin frescoed by poison ivy. The car was a 1956 Oldsmobile in almost perfect condition, its chrome bumpers spotless, the silver rocket hood ornament reflected in the wax job I'd spent the morning giving it. Because my father had said he was not going to pay for a degree in art history after I dropped out of pharmacy school, I was going in the Marines in October. Once I finished my tour in Vietnam my plan was to take my combat pay and go to Italy. After that I'd return to college on the G.I. Bill and study art history. At the time I had not thought at all about dying.

I never saw Defoe work in that filling station a single time. He was a gambler, not more than ten years older than me. Defoe was a beautiful man, the proportions of his body perfect, as if he had been chiseled out of dark-veined marble by Michelangelo. His face stood out among those lean, patchy red and white hill faces of the townspeople, and some said there was some Indian thrown in and others claimed some Negro too, which I tried not even to think about when I was around him because he was the kind of man who could tell what you were thinking. Maybe that was what made him such a good poker player. When he looked hard at you, the muscles in his face twitched like they were receiving signals.

"Your daddy let you go?" Defoe asked.

Defoe never drove. I might see him come home on a visit driving around the courthouse square with some woman at the wheel of a big car. The women were all pretty, and I never saw him with the same one twice. No one knew why he didn't drive.

"I go where I please," I said, trying to act casual.

He laughed and stepped off the raised curb, crossing the ten or twelve feet to where I was standing. He was wearing a beautiful summer-weight wool suit, which anyone could see had been made by some New York tailor, and a pair of pointed shoes that you probably couldn't even buy in Memphis. The suit clung to his body like no department store suit ever would, so you could see and almost feel the smooth flex of muscles and bone and skin. Old Mr. Michaels went around to check the oil.

Defoe looked the car over.

"Nice," he said. "But runs a little rough."

"Carburetor needs rebuilding," I said.

"You come get me at six," he said.

I wondered where the woman was who had brought him. I'd seen her standing with him in front of the drugstore, a pretty woman like all the others.

I paid old Mr. Michaels for the gas.

"You been back to the Tallahatchie?" Defoe asked.

And I could see him, standing naked on the rust-stained bridge girder while I waited my turn beside him, my eyes on the long scar which ran from his right nipple to his shoulder blade. He'd come home with that the first time he left town. Then he dived, his compact dark-skinned body disappearing into the brown water.

I'd been twelve at the time and too scared to follow.

"Plenty of times," I said. "It's easy."

He grinned and said nothing. Mr. Michaels handed me my change. When I got in the car and started it, Defoe bent down and leaned his arm on the paint-chipped windowsill, careless of the rich fabric of his jacket.

"Don't you be late," he said.

We drove toward Como, the setting sun fat and swollen over the hills. Defoe was dressed in a white linen suit with a blue tie. When he pulled a silver pocket flask out of his pocket and took a drink, I thought of what my father would say if he knew I was on the road with Defoe Michaels. But that was one reason I had joined the Marines, to keep from becoming like my father. When I told him I'd joined up, he yelled and called me stupid. Mother cried. I told him I wasn't going to lead a comfortable, safe life. I wasn't going to work in a pharmacy every day.

Defoe handed me the flask, and I took a drink. I'd already sweated through my yellow button-down shirt and had loosened my striped tie, once knotted in a neat Windsor. These were the kind of clothes I'd learned to wear that first year at Ole Miss. It was one of those real hot days and wasn't going to get much cooler when it turned dark. Defoe looked like he was sitting on a cake of ice, that suit perfectly white and unrumpled, his hair slicked down so the wind didn't toss it around like it was blowing mine. His pink silk shirt had a big "D.M." in baroque white stitching over one pocket.

"You up at the university?" Defoe asked.

"Not anymore," I said.

Then I told him about the Marines.

Defoe grinned and took another sip from the flask. That big swollen sun was now directly over the road, looking like when we topped the next hill we were going to drive right into it.

"Going to Vietnam?" he asked.

"I guess," I said.

I took another drink, the whiskey burning as it went down in a way I was trying to learn to like.

"I lost the station," Defoe said.

I looked over at him but didn't say anything.

"It was in Memphis," he said. "Just got outplayed. That's all."

I thought of old Mr. Michaels pumping gas and never saying much. But he'd lent me tools and given me parts on credit to get the first car I bought running. His wife had Defoe when she was almost forty. Now they both were old. I imagined Defoe telling them as they sat around the dinner table and how they had stopped eating in amazement, their jaws moving slowly on the okra or ham, as Defoe explained in his soft voice how in a card game he had destroyed their lives.

"You bet the station?" I asked.

He looked at me, the muscles in his face twitching.

"I bet money I didn't have," he said.

I concentrated on the road.

"We'll find us a couple of women in Como," he said. "Have us a good time."

"That's right," I said.

I was wondering whether the Michaelses would go live with relatives. The station was probably the old couple's retirement, and Defoe had gambled it away. He didn't even seem sorry and that made me mad. It was no more to him than if he had pawned his watch to pay a debt.

I looked at him out of the corner of my eye while pretending to be studying a kudzu-filled ravine.

"Don't you judge me," Defoe said.

"It's none of my business," I said.

"That's right."

I turned off the highway and drove a twisting road that finally dropped down to the lake. It wasn't a real lake. The Corps of Engineers had dammed up the Tallahatchie River, and now the town of Como had a lake not five miles from the city limits. Below us were the lights around the spillway, the road running right across the top of the huge, earth-filled dam.

"I felt bad after I lost the station," he said. "Nothing has ever made me feel that bad."

Neither one of us said anything for a long time. I was eager to reach Como and get out of the car. Then Defoe spoke again.

"I lost it and went up to my room and got me a blow job. She wouldn't let me have her car. I could have won it all back with the car."

I thought of the woman in front of the drugstore. She had long dark hair and wore a blue summery dress with white sandals. I thought of her bending over him, Defoe's body stiff with the tension of the loss and then him coming, momentarily free from all of it. While she still had the taste of him in her mouth, he had asked her for the car keys so he could go back to the table. Now I knew why he didn't own a car.

"You could have done it," I said.

And there was a part of me that believed he could. He looked that confident, sitting there next to me in his white suit, his hand around the silver flask, the other arm propped on the car window.

"Well, it don't matter now," he said. "We'll drink some whiskey. Chase some women."

He laughed and I joined him as we drove across the dam, the lights of Como sparkling in the distance.

The dance, held at the National Guard Armory, was part of the town's annual Lake Como Festival. They had a fish fry, a parade, and a beauty contest. I had been the year before and had a good time.

Inside the barnlike building, Defoe and I went our separate ways across the concrete floor. Every now and then we'd meet and share the flask. I noticed he wasn't dancing but standing here and there in the crowd watching the dancers. It was hot in the building, the flashing lights from the bandstand making his white suit look purple.

Then I finally got a chance to dance with the Lady of the Lake, the winner of the beauty contest. She was dressed in white and wore a pasteboard crown decorated with glitter. Her long blond hair, so straight I could imagine her mother ironing it before the dance, swung loose down her back. The strapless evening dress she wore was staying up fine all by itself. She was barefoot, and since it was a slow dance, I was worried about stepping on her feet.

"I've seen you at school," she said.

Penelope was a year ahead of me. She felt light in my arms as we moved across the floor, cigarette smoke hanging in blue clouds above our heads, her face with those high cheekbones looking up at me. I didn't ever want to stop dancing with her. Just as I was telling her about my going in the Marines, someone cut in. I looked up and saw Defoe with a grin on his face.

"Go find you somebody else," he said.

I stood by the wall and watched them dance. They looked good together, both dressed in white. Defoe was smooth, very smooth, and I didn't care for the way he pulled her close to him like they were already lovers. When the music was fast, Defoe stood almost completely still, just moving his hands while she danced around him. Nobody cut in.

Then I found another girl to dance with and kept looking for Penelope but didn't see her again. When the band took a break I looked for Defoe. I went out to the car, expecting to see him filling up the flask from the bottle under the seat. He was there all right, and Penelope was with him. Defoe was kissing her, their mouths glued together, he standing up tall and straight and she kind of clinging to him.

They heard my feet on the gravel. She stooped down and picked up her crown. He took it from her.

"Her daddy's got a cabin out on the lake," Defoe said. "Let's go out there. She'll fix us something to eat."

We all got in the car, she between us in the front seat. He still held her crown. We passed the flask around.

"Aren't you supposed to stay at the dance?" I asked. "You're the Lady of the Lake."

She laughed.

"Not anymore," she said. "Defoe's got my crown. This is my first and last contest. I'm not spending my life dieting myself into pageant dresses. I'm not going to be Miss Mississippi."

Defoe tossed the crown out the window.

"Honey, you already are Miss Mississippi," he said.

I wished I'd said it first and thought of Defoe kissing her by the car. That should have been me. He would drift off and maybe never come back to Como. After the Marines I was coming home. She would still be here, teaching school in one of the nearby towns.

"Drive out to the lake," she said. "We'll dance all night in the cabin. I'll fix y'all breakfast."

I was drunk, but the whiskey didn't seem to have affected Defoe at all. She was just as drunk as me.

She had told me to watch for a turn onto a gravel road just before the road that led to the dam. I'd found the turn and was starting to make it when she put her hand on my shoulder.

"I want to go swimming first," she said. "You drive on up to the dam."

"We'll swim at the cabin," Defoe said.

"No, in the spillway," she said.

I knew she didn't mean the real spillway but the emergency spillway, built to deal with a deluge that would overwhelm the spillway and threaten the dam. The spillway was simply a concrete pathway over the western end of the dam which dropped into a channel that led to the river. The channel had filled with rainwater and was a deep clear pool perhaps five hundred yards long.

"I left my swimming trunks at home," Defoe said.

"We won't need 'em," she said.

At the spillway we stood off behind the car while she undressed. Defoe smoked a cigarette as we listened to the rustle of that gown coming off and then the sound of her wading into the water. He didn't seem to be interested, and I tried to act the same. As we stripped down to our underwear, she swam around treading water and yelling at us to hurry up. He folded the white suit neatly and placed the silk shirt and blue tie on top of it.

"You watch her," I said. "She could drown."

"Come on," she shouted.

Then we waded into the water which in the shallows was as warm as the air but turned cool as it got deeper. I had left the car running, and we swam around in the beams from the headlights.

"Let's swim to the dam," she said.

"It's too far for you, honey," Defoe said.

"Someone could get a cramp," I said.

"I might as well have stayed at the dance and become Miss Mississippi," she said.

She started swimming, a smooth crawl, and we followed. As soon as we swam out of the lights and the darkness closed in, I got scared. On both sides rose the walls of the channel, made where the engineers had cut through a hill. I began to feel as if we were swimming in the bottom of a well or a cistern, doomed to swim round and round with no way out. She was much faster than either of us. When I turned over on my back to rest and looked up at the stars, I heard her steady kick in the distance. Defoe floated by me.

"She's a banker's daughter," he said.

Then, out there in the darkness, wondering whether I was going to make it to the safety of the spillway, I saw it all.

"It won't work," I said. "She'll never do it."

"But she'd marry you, college boy," he said.

He was treading water now, and I did the same.

"I'm a Marine," I said.

"You'll always be a college boy. You'll come home and finish your college and take over your daddy's drugstore. I'll be out there with nothing."

It crossed my mind that Defoe might try to hurt me. But I was a little taller and heavier than he and those days of diving contests off the bridge were long gone.

"Nobody forced you to gamble," I said.

"Everybody gambles," he said. "Her daddy the banker gambles. He just calls it something else."

Penelope was calling to us to catch up.

"You swim on back to the car," he said.

Just then I heard the engine begin to run rough. It gave a couple of coughs and died.

"You go," he said. "Battery'll run down."

He was beginning to gasp for breath. Playing cards is not a good way for a man to stay in shape.

I turned away from him and swam for the spillway, swimming a slow crawl because I had a long way to go. When I reached it, Penelope was sitting on the lip at the bottom dressed only in a merry-widow bra and panties.

"Where is he?" she asked.

There was a faint splashing sound from the channel. I guessed he was floating on his back and resting and told her not to worry. I hoped he'd turn back to the car and leave us alone to talk. I'd tell her about Defoe, how she couldn't depend on him. I'd tell her about all those women. But instead we heard the steady sound of his swimming coming closer and closer until finally he pulled himself up out of the water and lay on the lip breathing hard. When she helped him to his feet, he put his arms around her. I turned my head away and looked at the headlights which I already imagined were growing dimmer.

"What were y'all talking about out there?" she asked.

"Gambling," he said.

I thought of her winning the Miss Mississippi contest. She could do it. She was even more perfect than Defoe. And then the Miss America title in Atlantic City. Soon the accent would be gone. She'd be in Italy long before me.

"I'm going on the road with Defoe," she said.

I wanted to scream, *No, you can't.* Only through a great effort did I keep my mouth shut. Defoe was looking at me; he knew what I was thinking. I could imagine what she thought the road was going to be like—she standing with her hand on his shoulder while he sat at a poker table. But really what was going to happen was that he would take everything from her, and not just money. I noticed the headlights were now definitely fading. The battery was not a good one.

"You better go swim back to the car," Defoe said.

"You go," I said.

"We'll draw for it," Defoe said. "Honey, you get a couple of sticks. Long stick wins."

I heard a snap as she broke a stick in half. Then a couple more as she trimmed them to size.

"You draw first," he said.

I could barely see the sticks in her closed fist, a thin one and a fat one. I chose the thin one, the stick slick and waterlogged, bits of it crumbling against my fingers as I pulled it out of her hand. She handed the other to Defoe. We compared sticks, holding them up against the lighter darkness of the sky.

"They're the same," I said.

She started to laugh and then we were all laughing, laughing so hard that we all sat down on the lip, the sound of our voices echoing off the walls of the channel.

"Both of you go," she said, "case somebody gets a cramp."

Defoe had a hard time with the swim, having to stop and float on his back several times. Neither of us did any talking. When we got close to shore, I picked up my stroke and swam on ahead. As I started the engine, I watched him stagger out of the water, his underwear hanging loose about his thighs. It was clear that he was not going to be able to make the swim again.

"We'll let the battery charge a few minutes," I said. "Then we'll swim back."

Defoe was still breathing hard. He got out the flask and took another drink. Then he offered it to me. I refused. My head was clear from the swim, and I wanted to keep it that way.

"You think I'm doing wrong?" Defoe said.

"It's not for me to say," I said.

"My daddy's gonna lose everything. It's my fault. I've got to do something. You know he's gonna take a job at the chicken plant. He'll never last out there. I get to wear a suit and tie doing what I do. It makes me no different from those lawyers at the courthouse. I dress better than them."

I took the flask out of his hand and drank.

"She'll marry me," he said. "I'll treat her good. She don't want to be a beauty queen. She don't want to go back to the university and make a schoolteacher."

"Her daddy won't give you a dime."

"He might."

So no matter what, he couldn't stop being the gambler.

"You take the car," I said.

He took another drink from the flask and gave me a long look as if he were trying to figure out what the catch was.

"I'm leaving in two months," I said. "You can sell it. Stake yourself to a game. You can pay me back with your winnings."

He laughed.

"I'll sit right here and wait for her to swim back," he said.

"Won't be much attraction for her in that," I said.

He knew I was right. Defoe dressed slowly and carefully. I gathered Penelope's gown and my clothes and put them in a pile on the grass.

"You doing this for her?" he asked.

"No, for you," I said. "For your daddy."

Then I realized that was not true at all.

"I better see that money when I come home," I said.

I tried to sound tough, but I knew it was still the voice of a boy. Defoe was not going to be impressed.

"I pay my debts," he said.

I was thankful that he didn't laugh at me.

"But you got to remember. I'm not as good a gambler as you think. I lose more than I win. It's doing it that attracts the women, not the winning."

It occurred to me that maybe when I returned nothing would be changed: Defoe riding into town in a car driven by some pretty woman and his laconic father pumping gas at the station and my father standing behind the counter at the pharmacy.

For a moment I thought he was going to reach out and take my hand, but we just stood there, our arms at our sides. Then he got in the car.

Instead of driving off he hesitated, his face, illuminated by the dashboard lights, turned toward me.

"You watch yourself in them swamps and jungles," he said.

I started to speak but then he was gone, the taillights glowing red in the darkness. I waded into the water and started my swim to the spillway. Penelope and I would swim back and then—if her father's cabin were not too far—we would walk through the early morning darkness to it. And after dancing the night away on its polished heart of pine floor, we'd sit in canvas chairs on the porch, the sweat cooling on our faces, her hand in mine, and watch the sun rise over the lake.

Starkey Flythe

    Starkey Flythe is a native of Augusta, Georgia, who has worked as a lawyer, freelance writer, poet, and editor. While employed by the Curtis Publishing Company, he was executive editor of the *Saturday Evening Post* from 1974 to 1976 and managing editor of *Country Gentleman.* His story collection *Lent, the Slow Fast* (1990), where "cv10" appeared, won the 1989 Iowa Short Fiction Award. Flythe's story is about an elderly man coming to terms with his memories of the Second World War. It is a story of memory, of friendship, and of aloneness. With his wife dead, his daughter unsure what to make of him, and his friends all dead or beyond reach, he discovers in the hulking body of the aircraft carrier where he served during the war the only way he has of defining himself, of finding meaning in his life.

CV10

Walter could almost feel the rush of breath, hear the women roaring, mothers, girlfriends, sisters, sweeping up toward the flight deck, the warm fall day, San Francisco, 1945. A couple chasing a blue-jump-suited baby girl just beginning to walk wobbled by him in exaggerated pursuit. He had been alone that day. Hadn't wanted to get off the ship or sleep anywhere but the chain-hung bunks inches above and inches below two other men whose smells and habits he knew better than his own.

He had been seventeen, eighteen the next week. Lt. (jg) Stinson was dead. Three thousand men ("officers and men," they always said in casualty lists as if they died differently) yelled down at thirty thousand skirts, and nobody said anything to him. Buddies he'd held when they were bleeding, buddies who'd cried, told him heart secrets, secrets that still made his cheeks red, buddies had their sea-bags on their shoulders. They'd said good-bye the night before, at the party in the mess, and later in the hangar deck, the warm Pacific melting by, gold in the moonlight, peace, relief a kamikaze wasn't spiraling toward them overwhelming. There would be peace. Friends always. They would remember the dead. In the morning, they'd forgotten all about it.

There had been a telegram for him in the USO clearing station from his uncle and aunt—they lived outside Indianapolis—his mother had died while he was at Marcus Bay and he hadn't known about it for three weeks. The telegram sounded like a message from the president. "Congratulations on a job well done. You are welcome to stop by here a day or so in the absence of other plans." He had wondered, never found out, whether his father was still alive. His father had left his mother when Walter was eleven. A sailor. That was why Walter had wanted to join. Quit high school. Find his father. Or be like him.

Walter's legs trembled walking up the wood steps to the ship's entrance. He remembered the gangways. He'd paid $6.00 to get in, didn't want to ask if there was a discount for veterans who'd served on the ship. The woman ticket seller was in a glass box with a pass-through slot like a drive-in bank teller. "World's largest ship museum."

The hangar deck had been painted a sort of aqua. Walter felt he was in a place he'd lived in his whole life and never been. The first day at sea he'd had to go all the way forward with a stack of flight logs and he'd hugged the wall he was so frightened by motion, huge engines being wheeled along to mechanics' stations, the men in forklifts avoiding collisions only by the roll of the ship as it steamed south, going nobody knew where. The ceiling opened up then and a tennis-court-size elevator descended, two F4Us, their wings folded like obedient insects, waiting to be worked on, huge in proximity though Walter had seen them tiny in the sky. This ship was the war. He might be killed. Wounded. That was worse, fliers said who'd already been in the Pacific theater and had come back through Norfolk for rehab or mustering out if they'd been hurt bad—some said "good"—enough.

"Where the hell have you been?" the petty officer who took the logs from him said. "I called you down here forty-five minutes ago!"

Then he got to know people. Men called out to him, "Ears!" Everybody had nicknames, Annapolis custom filtering down to enlisted men. He had mess mates, bunk mates, sick bay where he worked, a plane he was assigned to. When sorties were run, every man had a top-deck station except the engine room crew, and Walter had Stinson's. Walter had a job, a war to win, the scrambled-egg hats kept saying. Not a day went by, not one, not a single solitary day, that he didn't say Stinson's name. "Hey, Buddy," Stinson, officer, gentleman, pilot, told him. "I'll stand up with you when we get back and you head down the aisle."

"Married?" Walter asked. "I might not . . ."

"Hoo! Everybody's going to. And I'll invite you to mine. I'm going to drink so much champagne my blood'll run clear. Hooo!"

Then Stinson, Lt. (jg) Wallace "Whippet" Stinson lifted off the flight deck on his first mission and the flight officer worried the propellers wouldn't catch, the air was so humid: Stinson came back seven pounds lighter. Not one man had been lost; they'd hit Marcus, hit the Japanese planes on the ground, the fueling depot, the port. And Stinson said he was so scared he was sitting in a pool of water in the cockpit and it wasn't sweat. Walter pulled him out of the plane; Stinson turned his face aside so nobody could see his eyes. Only Walter saw them: blank, dead.

The officers were snooty the first weeks out until proximity, dependence, and fear closed the social gap. Stinson was friendly. Walter remembered the eyes: warm, coffee-colored, not so dark they didn't catch the light when he smiled. He told Walter to call him "Whip"—"They'll think you're saying Skip."

"Don't tell anybody!" Stinson gripped Walter's arm so hard Walter thought the young lieutenant's hand—he would always be young in Walter's mind, though he'd been four years older than Walter—would draw blood. Stalking along the flight deck, parts of it covered with linoleum squares now and colored arrows so people wouldn't lose their way on the "museum" tour, Walter felt the wattle under his chin.

"Tell anybody what?" Walter had asked.

"That I'm afraid. That I'm scared. The sky's a poison lake. Every tracer you see means three you don't. You won't even know when you won't even know." Walter thought he was joking, this man, boy, now, who'd been to college, had a girl he was going to marry back home, a boy whose parents sent him money even over his navy officer's pay. "I mean it!" He said he was afraid as much of the other men on the ship as he was of the sky.

"So am I," Walter whispered, but the hours of clamor, the turbines, antiaircraft aak-aak, the earphones, the awful fear of not being able to pick out the sound that would kill you, deafened them. That was their friendship; they could not hear each other, but they talked to each other.

"God, Ears! I can't keep going up the rear end." That was his expression for night flights. "They want you to fly in formation. I'm supposed to be two inches off the wing—worse, *between*—the wing tips of two jerks who're myopic grain-alcohol drinkers. How do they get the stuff? You're not supposed to let it out of the dispensary."

"The head surgeon . . ."

Walter began to find his way, the ladders he'd gone up and down, a monkey, nearly three years, the passage to the lavatory where he'd sat, exposed to the rest of the crew; he saw a couple, their whole appearance a Hawaiian shirt, focusing on a Corsair set up for display, and just as Walter looked at them, simultaneously they touched their crotches, she to brush some ash from his cigarette— think of letting them smoke, here—and he for heaven only knew what reason—and Walter remembered the cook'd put something in the food to keep that part of the body out of the ship's mind.

"I don't want to get you in trouble," Walter had said. "You're not supposed to fraternize." The bronze plaques on the top deck, the "Hall of Fame" that only included officers and industrialists, war fat cats, made Walter furious.

Nobody had ever liked Walter before. He had been the wrong size all the wrong years. Too small for B-team in eighth grade. Too big for Midgets in seventh. The difference between not being popular and not being liked hadn't occurred to him until he got on "The Fighting Lady"—the expressions they had—"So-and-so is still on patrol"—"So-and-so made the supreme sacrifice."

Coming here—the South—was wrong, he thought, the first night. He had walked along the streets and walked, walked, been glad in a way his wife had died; she wouldn't have liked the idea of a pilgrimage to an aircraft carrier. She was younger, too young to remember the war, much else. Stinson hadn't been able to "stand up for him at his wedding." Walter remembered the day. Carlice, his wife, had a bad complexion. She cried and cried the day of the wedding because two big places erupted on her cheek and chin. She put some sort of cover makeup on the spots that only accentuated them. He didn't know how to say that night, as she lay crying beside him in the bed they would share thirty-five years, that it didn't matter. That the heart was somewhere underneath the skin. He had walked, thinking of that, of his daughter who tried to be dutiful though she was, he knew, slightly embarrassed by him. His ears? Job—learned in the navy—male nurse—the years before female telephone linemen, male steward-esses. He kept walking, as if he weren't getting anyplace and yet felt he could go on and on, passing little southern city-gardens. Stinson had had a farm. "Country place. When I fly over these tropical plants I wonder if they'd grow back in the states."

"You better keep your mind on your tail," Walter told him. "You thinking about daffodils."

"Every gunner, every cook, every medic, every clerk-typist is assigned to a pilot and a plane. That's *your* baby! You'll serve that knight like the squires of old! He won't—can't—go into battle without you!" Walter could hear the deck officer lecturing them.

"Kids on the living room floor," Stinson said, "running toy airplanes around on the rug. Varoom, varrooom!"

Walter would wind up the prop on the fighter, thinking any second he was going to get his skull sliced. He wouldn't be the first. Then he'd crouch by the side, or down in the gunneries while the navy-blue plane, wings unfolded, varoomed, varrooomed, Whip standing on the brakes, the other planes beating behind him, Walter hoping the engine was warmed up enough though God knew, in the heat, Alaska should've been ready. Then Walter would watch, his ears stinging, heart banging against his T-shirt, Stinson bump, bump, bump down the deck, over the great number cv10 painted near the end, and hobble off into the sky, the other planes screaming down the line seconds later.

The mission was not a success: the Japanese knew where the fleet was now; hiding behind atolls and steaming zigzag all over the Coral Sea didn't work any-more. Kamikazes were bouncing off every carrier and cruiser. One—a near miss—had been fished out of the water on the starboard: the cockpit had been bolted down from the outside and the dead Japanese pilot's controls had been wired on. "Dumb sucker," Stinson said.

There was a big brouhaha over whether—he looked like a bee with his goggles, helmet, earflaps tight around his chin—the Japanese should be given Christian burial. "Oh, Jesus," Stinson said. "Shoot the works! Who knows who's next?"

He was. Fewer fighters were getting back; those who made it had been through the wringer. The seaman artist who rated a cheer whenever he appeared topside with his rising-sun template to paint Zeros and sunken ships on the quarterdeck vanished. The sick bay was packed. Walter knew the navy hymn by heart from funerals. "Remember the first word in that event," Stinson said.

When Stinson hit the flight deck, it was moments after the Japanese had rained phosphorus over the ship. When you stepped on a piece it burst into flame. Nobody could get to the planes to pull the pilots out of the way. The stop straps were burned through. Walter was helping put a cast on a boy with a broken hip. They had him up on a winch. The cook was painting thick layers of plaster over the body. Walter would've laughed if he hadn't seen the boy's face. The smell of bloodsoaked flight jackets cut off bodies mixed with sweat and nausea, the jerk and sway of the carrier as the skipper tried to outmaneuver the fire bombers. People were being sick and nobody had time to mop.

"No, he ain't in yet, Stinson," two medics said who'd brought another body—they thought he was alive—how could you fly in, make a perfect landing, and be dead? "And he probably won't be in. You hear the reports?" He got in. Seventy-eight wounds on his chest, back, legs. Flak. How could he talk? Walter wondered, much less upset than he thought he would be; working, patching up bodies made him think he could save anybody. The chief surgeon took a piece of metal half the size of a bicycle rim out of Whip's face.

"Don't worry," Walter said.

"We weren't the only ones," Stinson said, naked, his body like an ocean with whitecaps only red.

"The only ones?"

"Who were scared."

"Shut up a minute," the surgeon said, and took another metal rim out of his cheek.

"How do I look?" Whip asked.

"Leslie Howard." When Whip tried to smile, Walter saw half his teeth were gone. His face twisted the way a tree turned in strong wind.

He hung on. Walter wrote letters for him, read to him from Saroyan books. Running his hand over the names of the commemorative tablets now—Walter wasn't able to find anything, his battle station, the places he thought he could never forget—he thought those had been the happiest days of his life. Somebody was dependent on him. Somebody spoke to him without saying a word. That sound—the noise between the noises—answered practically every question for him. The present. The war. Friendship. The rest of life. The name finally under his fingers, the block letters pressing into his knuckles, was more painful than any of the past. If the war had ended a different way, Stinson alive, Walter, they'd never have seen each other again. This way they would always be friends. Some men's lives never ended; they kept wandering around thinking something else was coming.

Walter knew it before Stinson. His color. The chief took in Stinson's appearance sideways. The ship news, a legal-size sheet whose inanity was undimmed by casualties, told of more and more victories. The Japanese were "broken" but didn't seem to know it.

The flag didn't go into the water. He knew sometimes parents didn't get the exact flag. Walter thought how hard getting food out to the carrier was, mail off, on, keeping ammunition, parts coming.

The hot wind that boiled the stomach mixed the words: Walter had never liked the chaplain though he'd dragged ten men out of a bulkhead fire, and never, Stinson said, let you forget.

> ... the Lord,
> who opened ...
> a path through mighty waters,
> drew on chariot and horse to their destruction,
> a whole army, men of valour ...
> never to rise again.

They always read that at the dumps. Walter's duties now included, if there was a moment in the bleeding, hauling out the prayer books. The white edges were dirty along the funeral service pages.

> they were crushed, snuffed out like a wick:
> ...
> Here and now I will do a new thing:
> ... Can you perceive it?

Walter stuck books—they were always flying off over the rail—in as many hands as could hold them. Four other packages. Whip would've said, "Odd man out." They began with him. Walter couldn't see the splash, to mark the spot in his mind.

The body there, a picture, stayed, a cage like the sunken ships and plane skeletons fish swam through. The boatswain's pipe—Walter didn't know whether he was here or there, now, then—keened. "Now hear this." They were showing a movie forward.

Walter went in, sat down. The dark slowly gave way around him. He remembered going to a show with Whip—one of the things officers, men could do together.

"Nothing makes you forget quicker than a flicker. Well, we can't get a pint." Stinson's voice was right there, next to him. In the images rolling, in competition with the waves, Stinson whispered, surprised, "I know I'm still on a ship."

Walter stared at the few tourists in the seats. Bored. Squirming. Whispering. They had brought children. The film was a documentary—had won an Academy award. How phony the narrator's voice sounded, false the sailors' smiles, passing down the mess line. He recognized no one though the film was made when he was on the ship. It went on. Walter felt proud, more like these people than the boys who'd squeezed into the theater then, lined the walls, hung from the girders, stuffed the aisles until the fire officer said they had to clear out and a roar of protest sounded to panicky sailors like the air raid warning.

Slowly, Walter took in the steel beams, the X-girders, the superstructure of the flight deck above. He would wait till the end of the movie though he might be the only one left in the theater. He didn't feel as alone, as afraid as he had the day, those years gone, when the carrier docked. He'd go back to the motel— think of having someplace to go—and when the rates went down he might phone his daughter and son-in-law. Or watch television. Go for a walk, see whether he could make out the ship from the other side of the bay.

Jim Grimsley

While Michael Bishop established himself as a science fiction writer before trying his hand at more conventional forms of writing, Jim Grimsley began as a writer of drama and fiction, and then science fiction. He has fared well in all three arenas. Born in Edgecombe County, North Carolina, in 1955, he moved to Atlanta after undergraduate study at University of North Carolina earned him a B.A. in 1978. Grimsley had seen his plays produced in Atlanta and off-Broadway venues before his first novel, *Winter Birds,* was published in 1994. Other novels include *Dream Boy* (1995); *My Drowning* (1997, which won a Lila Wallace–Reader's Digest Writers Award and helped Grimsley earn recognition as Georgia Author of the Year); *Comfort and Joy* (1999); *Kirith Kirin* (2000), a science fiction novel that won the Lamda Literary Award for Horror/Science Fiction/Fantasy; and *Boulevard* (2002). A selection of his plays has been published as *Mr. Universe and Other Plays* (1998). He is senior writer-in-residence at Emory University and playwright in residence at 7 Stages Theatre in Atlanta.

New Jerusalem

Lomax made Mama promise to have a picnic the first spring day that come up good and warm. Mama could devil some eggs and fry some chicken, and Alphonso could set up Lomax's easel and paints by the cow pond. They'd carry some bug spray and a fly swat. Mama fretted about when she would possibly find the time to worry about devilling eggs, with cows in calf and the help to watch every minute. "What they don't wreck they steal," Mama always said. On this occasion, she added, "But if you want a picnic I will lay aside my duties and get you one up, the next pretty day."

"It's not as if I won't be right in the kitchen with you," Lomax said.

Mama sighed and clucked her tongue. "I don't know if I would call that help."

Many dairy disasters intervened, and Lomax also sold a picture and had her final visit to the hospital. "I've about decided I know how I'm going to spend my money," Lomax announced, post recovery, on the morning Mama finally decided the weather inclined toward picnic quality.

"Leave it in the bank," Mama said.

"I'm going to buy me a trip to the moon." Lomax peeled boiled eggs and dropped the shells into a small metal pot. "If what I read here is correct the government will be offering trips up that way soon. And it would be mighty good to be up there where I wouldn't weigh but fifteen pounds. I'll buy me a one-way ticket, you watch."

"You will not do any such of a thing."

"You can come with me if you ain't dead," Lomax said. "I'll buy us two tickets."

"Listen to me Lomax Lamb," Mama said, swelling up her chest. "Nobody ain't been to the moon and nobody ain't going there."

"Mama, you saw the astronauts standing on the moon just like I did. Right on the television."

"If you believe everything you see on the silver screen you are in sad shape. Them pictures was from a t.v. studio somewhere." Mama mixed the potato salad with her hands. The wet potatoes made oceanic belches as she rolled them over the chopped celery and onion. She spied Lomax eyeing the red pepper box and said, "If you ruin them devil eggs with that cayenne pepper I will turn you across my knee big as you are. Good as I love a devil egg."

"They got to be hot," Lomax said, and devilled them just as she pleased.

Alphonso carried the painting apparatus. The color of deep tree shadow, Alphonso came up to Lomax's ribs, his body a riot of contained energy as he headed across the pasture. Lomax had to warn him not to drag the canvas through the grass. She followed behind, swinging merrily on her crutches, doing her best to keep up. A leather quiver of paints and brushes swung at her hip, weighing against her cotton dress. In the distance the small herd of Mama's cows lowed and swished flies. Mama had told the Mexican to move them to the east field but Lomax no longer trusted cows to stay where they belonged. She verified the integrity of the fence with careful inspection. Alphonso was singing about how to set his feet on higher ground, and the clear bell tone of his voice put Lomax in a good mood. Mama kept telling Alphonso to go slow and Alphonso answered he was going as slow as he could without plumb dying. Mama waddled through the high grass dragging the picnic basket and thermos full of muttering ice cubes. Once a gust of wind tore the floppy hat with the gauze band off Mama's head, and Alphonso dashed after it, dropping everything. Mama squinted helplessly, and Lomax put her own smaller hat on Mama's head. "There, there," Lomax said, gauging the damage to her canvases and paints as Alphonso leapt like a sprite through the grass.

At the cow pond, Mama told Alphonso, "Miss Lomax is going to fly to the moon. What do you think about that?"

Alphonso squinted at Lomax. He set up the low easel where she could reach it, and spread the flannel blanket for her, beating down the grass. "It's probably some snakes out here," he said.

"You don't believe me, do you?" Lomax demanded.

"How do you plan to get to the moon?" Mama tittered, which meant she had made up a joke. "You got a rocket in your room?"

"I'm buying me a ticket. You watch. I may go today." Lomax lowered herself to the blanket and arranged her paint tubes in a rainbow.

Alphonso said, "Miss Estabelle showed me on her t.v. where they ain't no moon, they just a big light, and we close to it as we going to get."

"Miss Estabelle don't have a t.v.," Lomax said.

"Estabelle certainly does have a t.v.," Mama said, unwrapping a plate of cheese crackers.

"Well it don't work," Lomax said.

"She says she can see the picture," Mama said.

"Miss Estabelle don't need no t.v. to show the moon for what it is," Alphonso said, and ran off after a dragonfly. He came back with it cupped in his palms, listening to it and letting Lomax listen too. The dragonfly hummed a popular radio tune. They, both Lomax and Alphonso, laughed at the same time in the same amazement, but the tune continued, unmistakable. "Miss Estabelle says the dragonfly is the eagle of the insect." Alphonso threw up his hands and the dragonfly burst into Lomax's face. She gasped and sat back.

Alphonso selected the wing and the short leg from the chicken plate. Mama handed Lomax a fried chicken breast, and she ate the chicken with one hand and dabbed paint onto a strip of cardboard with the other.

"I need some potato salad and saccharin tea," Lomax said.

"These eggs are seasoned just right," Mama said, "mighty good."

"I do not want one word of praise after you hollered at me like you did. This chicken is so dry it ain't even worth mentioning."

"Lomax Lamb I will knock a knot on you."

Lomax dabbed and stroked. The wind ran across the grass like something alive, and the pulse of it made her stand outside herself, listening from a great distance. The whole canvas of color seemed to arrange itself without any help from her, while she admired the taste of the chicken breast and listened to the wind. Alphonso ran off somewhere again. He might have been dancing in the grass, from the look. Far off beyond the fence, under a grove of shade trees, the cows were grazing. For a while Lomax watched them, partly to admire them and partly to make sure they were staying where they belonged. For a while she watched the frame shacks the help lived in, the Mexican woman in her yard, chickens at her feet. The water of the cow pond translated itself through Lomax's fingers into a patch of eerie aquamarine which shimmered on the canvas. She liked that blue. Pausing, she watched the color and the real water, spooning on potato salad and shoving a whole devil egg in her mouth.

"You eat like a sow," Mama said.

"You never taught me any manners that stuck, so blame yourself if you get disgraced." Lomax licked her fingers for the last bit of cayenne, and purposefully slurped her tea.

"Yonder she comes," Mama said.

Alphonso ran breathless beside Miss Estabelle along the edge of the cow-pond. Miss Estabelle carried her cane and a strand of cattail like a rod and scepter, her dress bleached grey by the sun, holes cut raggedly for her arms and legs, an ample, full garment, rippling in the breeze. Miss Estabelle, who lived in the woods beyond the pasture, had a wide, flaring nose and high, round cheeks, the skin beginning to go slack and hollow beneath. She eased herself down in the grass and folded her hands in her lap. With her calm, mild eyes she studied the picnic blanket, and then turned to Mama. "You brought your little girl into the cow pasture," she said.

Lomax, nearing thirty-four, felt uneasy being called Mama's little girl. She started to say something but Mama gave her the eye. "Yes, I brought her on a picnic out here, after she worried me for a solid month."

"The children got no patience," said Miss Estabelle.

"Is your real name Esther Belle?" Lomax asked, watching the colors of the woman's face and daubing paint with small, nearly invisible gestures.

"I ain't got no name but what the Lord call me." Miss Estabelle made circles in the air with her cane, clean blond wood worn smooth by handling. "But I wish he would call me to the Angels. I'm ready to go."

"Hush that," Mama said. "When here I have fried all this chicken."

"God bless you for a short thigh and some potato salad," said Estabelle politely.

"Mercy, you can eat more than that. Eat some of this slaw. And this ham biscuit."

"God bless you," Miss Estabelle said, "it's not every white woman can fry chicken." She dipped her thin bonnet of hair toward Mama, who gave her a plastic fork and a cup of sugar tea. A bee buzzed around their heads. Alphonso whacked it dead with Lomax's paint pallet. The dead bee stuck to the cardboard and Alphonso, fearing the sting of the bee-ghost, refused to remove it. Lomax stuck the corpse to the canvas on a white patch that had begun as a water lily, painted over the dead insect with black and red, the dry paint and sealer preserving the bee for the ages. The others ate and watched Lomax. Alphonso told Miss Estabelle that Miss Lomax was going to the moon soon. He clapped his hands and laughed. Miss Estabelle said the moon was no place to go, there was a whole sea of storms on it, and nothing would grow.

"I am not of this world," Lomax said, sitting up straight. "I would be right at home there."

"I don't know why she talks like that, I take her to church," said Mama, wiping her mouth between bites of chicken back. "Though God knows I could confess her sins for her if anybody wanted me to."

"Oh hush. Nobody wants you to."

Mama fixed her with a glare.

Miss Estabelle rapped her knuckles. "Honor thy father or thy mother."

"It is a heap easier to honor my father who is dead and gone," Lomax said, in a practical tone. She sat back and studied the canvas. Again she felt the wind come up and heard Alphonso's laugh of delight when it whipped the grass in shadows and waves. Mama and Miss Estabelle were in the midst of agreeing there was no respect left among the young. Mama said she never knew what she did to deserve such a worthless daughter, good for nothing but to dab color all over everything and dirty up the sink with paints. Lomax allowed drily that this worthless daughter presently brought in a sizable chunk of the family income with them dabs of color, whereas Mama could barely convince a cow to give milk.

Mama harrumped and bit an egg with too much cayenne.

"This picture is of the pond right here," said Miss Estabelle, pointing, while Mama hurriedly drank a glass of tea.

"How do you know what it is?"

"You got the lily and the water crocuses. You got Alphonso. Why look here. I see what you done. I bet you think that's me, don't you?"

"I don't reckon I ought to say," Lomax purred, "you might try to charge me." Turning her head this way and that. "Like a sunny day."

"It's mighty nice of you to notice. My Mama don't appreciate my art until it transfigurizes into dollars."

"You need a cow in it," Mama said. "I like a good picture of a cow."

Miss Estabelle said, "You were wicked to paint that Prophet like you did."

Lomax felt a thrill go up her spine. "When did you see my Prophet?"

"I saw him when I saw him," Miss Estabelle said. "He has been reading the writing on the wall. He has been weighed in the scale and found wanting. His days have been numbered and are brought to an end."

"Is she talking about that ugly picture you got hanging over your dresser?" Mama smeared mayonnaise onto ham biscuit. "Many's the time I've spoilt my appetite looking at that thing."

Miss Estabelle turned to Mama and asked, in a bold voice, "What would you do if you saw somebody's real face struck by the grace light?"

"It's no sense in wondering," Mama said. "Do you want some more sugar tea?"

"Thank you for some," said Miss Estabelle, extending her cup, her arm veined, the soft flesh feathering from the bone. She smiled up into Mama's face. "But you need to know, Mother Lamb. You need to know what to do when you see the Face."

"Lomax will certainly tell me what to do when she sees it," Mama said, and Miss Estabelle shook her head.

Lomax let a little smile occur but went on painting. She had rarely felt such conflagration. Afternoon light hung over the pond like liquid amber. Dragonflies swooped in curves and sang, jewelled wings flashing. Alphonso leapt in the grass, bluish light on the planes of his face, his glad self-absorption evident as a thread through a multitude of expressions. Her hand pursued each gleam, slashing with the brush, teasing it, studying the canvas like an adversary. She could hardly make a wrong brushstroke if she tried.

"The handwriting is on the wall," Miss Estabelle said, in a voice meant to reach Lomax. She sipped from her dixie cup.

The heat of the afternoon lulled them to silence for a while. Finally Lomax felt her arms get heavy, and laid down her brush.

She thought she had done it with this one: the boy leaping in cobalt explosions, the scented weight of pond lilies, cattails bending over the prophets, the white woman with the devil egg in hand and the black woman under her broad straw hat, both rooted to the earth at the edge of the water. She thought she had done a good picture but refused to look at it; she could feel the image against the lids of her eyes. At any given time the completion of a picture left her dull and spent, but today she felt electrified. Distance was what she craved, and motion. She flung down her brushes and the pallet as if it were the last time. Struggling to rise, she gathered the crutches under her arms.

"Where do you think you're going young miss?" Mama asked.

"For a cruise. Down yonder by the tractor. I been meaning to inspect it. And I don't want no company either."

"Look for the tree with the branch hanging down like two snake tongues," Miss Estabelle said.

Lomax glared at the woman and then shoved off through the grass. Alphonso stood as Lomax swung forward, and she feared he would try to accompany her; but instead of following, he sang "I Surrender All" at the top of his lungs.

By the time he finished "Near to the Heart of God," Lomax was close to the rusted-out tractor that marked the end of the pasture. Every kind of vine and wildflower had overgrown the tractor shell, and countless cattle had left deposits in regard to their passing, giving the effect of a swell of ground around the flaked, corroded wheels. The effect was as if the earth were rising up to swallow the decayed metal husk. When she turned to look at the cow pond and the picnic, the blanket dwindled to the size of a postage stamp and Mama appeared no bigger than a safety pin. Miss Estabelle sat like a spider, rubbing her front legs together. Alphonso twisted, turned, leapt, chasing a dragonfly across the meadow.

Lomax swung through the grass, the soft, sharp tips tickling her legs. When she reached the tractor she guided herself round it slowly. She memorized the colors, browns and oranges, varying greens and occasional pastels. Her arms grew tired and she wanted to sit. Out here by the tractor was no shade, but a little further, at the edge of the pine woods, she could sit on a nice cool bed of pine needles.

By the time she reached the shady woods she needed to catch her breath and rested for a moment, looking around to find a comfortable spot. The picnic and cow pond had diminished even smaller. Silent woods and pasture surrounded her. As she moved forward on her crutches, she arced through the undergrowth with conscious quiet, as if her passage might disturb the somber day.

Out of the corner of her eye she spied something reaching down from the lower branches, seeming to move toward her, and she drew in a quick breath.

Two branches forked down from the lower limbs of a tree, smooth and curved, like snakes.

In the roots of this same tree, a bed of dry leaves, pine needles and moss had formed, inviting her quietly.

She eased herself into the natural seat and studied the snake-branches, envisioning them as living, twisting serpents, this same shade of gray but oily and slick-looking, wrapping themselves round Miss Estabelle's arms. Lomax could hardly get her breath.

She had not realized she had come such a long way. When she settled down against the tree she recommenced her study of the rusted tractor, meaning to add it to her canvas. Now that she was here, she wished she could have brought canvas and paint with her, or that she could silently summon Alphonso to bring them. The rusted hulk seemed farther away than it should, colored like a piece of autumn, every brown shade of rot and decay. In the foreground, green flies buzzed around fresh cow pies, wildflowers and mushrooms growing abundantly in the ordure.

She heard something nearby, small feet treading on pine needles. When she turned to see what animal it was, the sound stopped. Lomax sat perfectly still. An image passed through her head, unexplained: bare feet treading across a bed of red flowers, the feet bruising the petals as rich scent rose.

A child emerged from behind a tree, a dirty little urchin in a tee shirt.

At first she thought it was the youngest son of the Mexican woman, a boy of about this age, and she called out to him, thinking the poor toddler had strayed into the woods. But the Mexican children were shy and hesitant. The smile that lit this young boy's face knew no fear, and his dark eyes shone like chips of earth.

He smelled like flowers. A warm breeze blew from behind him, and she closed her eyes, drinking in the warmth and scent. When she opened her eyes again, the boy had stepped closer to her, and she was startled.

The child spoke some language she did not know. "I can't understand you," she said. He smiled and pointed to the trees behind him.

A cow waited there, dappled in a fall of sunlight through upper branches. The cow swished her tail in a lazy, graceless way, chewing with a look of bland contentment. The little boy spoke again, and then began to sing in a large, clear voice. The cow heard him and her ears perked up. The boy went on singing and the cow, transfixed, trotted toward him.

The child ran to meet the cow, laughing, looking back at Lomax with eyes full of delight. When he reached the cow he gripped the curled fur of its forehead and then leapt onto the cow's generous back. Sitting there, swaying from side to side, he gazed at Lomax, his expression gradually changing. The boy wrapped his legs tight against the cow, which allowed the weight on its back without a sign of resentment. The boy studied Lomax, and finally shook his head.

Lomax dug the crutches firmly into the soft earth and struggled to her feet. "Child," she called, "come back here."

The boy blinked. He looked down at the cow, leaning to kiss her between the ears.

Lomax swung forward on her crutches. The child nudged the cow with his heels and the placid beast gradually ambled off toward the distant trees. Lomax tried to follow but couldn't keep up. The child and the cow drew farther and farther ahead of her, till finally she called out, breathless, "If you want me to follow, why won't you wait for me?"

The boy looked back at her sadly, his dark curls shining, visible till he was a long way off. Even afterward Lomax could hear him singing.

How long she stood still she could not have said. But when she turned, careful to place the crutches on firm ground, only then did she hear the commotion, the cacophany of the lowing herd that rushed toward her, feverish to reach the place into which the cow and the boy had vanished.

For a moment she was afraid. Here were the cows, as she had always expected. The whole nation of them had breached the fence and poured through, rolling toward her like a wave of water, already surrounding her. Beyond, in the meadow, her mother and Alphonso were running toward her frantically, beyond the wrecked tractor. She watched their approach with calm. Erect as a pine stood Miss Estabelle, weight on the crooked cane, her shadow tumbled over the distant picnic.

No one would reach her before the cows. She stood on the crutches feeling helpless and foolish, that she should be ending up like one of the creatures in her paintings, hopelessly trampled under the bovine of everything and laughing about it; but, finally, she turned. Heedless of her mother's voice screaming for the cows to stop right there, heedless of Alphonso who might almost have flown across their backs to rescue her, she spun round on the crutches as the first of the sad-eyed mammals nudged her thighs with a velvet muzzle. The cows hardly seemed to be hurrying. She let them carry her forward and she kept up with their progress for a long time before they carried her downward as well, weighted and rendering her into the earth, her last silent singing of color and grace.

Anthony Grooms

Anthony Grooms has written poetry (*Ice Poems*, 1988), a volume of short stories (*Trouble No More*, 1995), and a novel (*Bombingham*, 2001), which won the Lillian Smith Prize for Fiction. Born in Virginia and educated at William and Mary and at George Mason University, he has taught at a number of schools, including the University of Georgia and Kennesaw State University, where he is a professor of creative writing. Grooms has been especially active in arts administration and the promotion of creative writing. In "Negro Progress" he dramatizes a young man's struggle not to be caught up in the turmoil of the Civil Rights movement in Birmingham, Alabama. He considers running away to Paris, is tempted by his wealthy uncle's business offers, but finds himself swept up in history's inexorable force.

Negro Progress

The water hunted the boy. It chipped bark from the oaks as he darted behind the trees. It caught him in the back. His lanky legs buckled. Then, as if the fireman who directed the hose were playing a game, the boy's legs were cut from under him, and he was rolled over and over in the mud.

From the distance of half a block, Carlton Wilkes watched the white ropes of water as they played against the black trunks and lime-green leaves of the trees. In the sunlight, the streams sparkled, occasionally crisscrossed or made lazy S's.

He had been on his way to his Uncle Booker's building when he first saw the children. They were wearing school clothes. He remembered that somebody in King's organization had called for a children's crusade, placing teenagers and children as young as six on the front lines of the city's civil rights demonstrations. Even when the first fire truck skidded to a stop across the street from the park and the firemen unwound their hoses and screwed them into the hydrants, he paid little attention. Uncle Booker had quite literally ordered him downtown. "It's only your damn future that's at stake," he had said. Uncle Booker had a way of exaggerating, but when it came to business, his feet were flat on the ground. There was little Negro business that went on in the city that Uncle Booker didn't have a hand in.

Then a child's squeal, the squeal and the whoosh-and-scour of the water, made him look up at the sometimes taut, sometimes lazy ropes the firemen directed. At first, the children taunted the firemen. They danced about, darting under the arcing streams and through the mist of the pressurized water. Then the boy was tripped and rolled with such force that Carlton thought he must have been hurt. He told himself to move, to run to the boy, but this meant passing the fire trucks. Then he saw the paddy wagons and the handsome German shepherds. His legs went rubbery.

His legs seemed barely strong enough to push in the clutch as he drove to Salena's house. He and Salena Parrish had been engaged for six months but had not set a date for the wedding. She was a nurse at the city hospital, one of the first Negro nurses there. When she opened the door he saw in her expression how harried he looked.

"What happened to you?" she asked, her gray eyes growing wide for a second.

The sight of her made his heart rush. Her light skin blushed in response to his breathlessness. He stumbled across the threshold, stammering. Not until she had taken him by the shoulders did he manage to speak.

"They . . . they are *hosing* children—shooting them down like . . . like the Boston massacre."

For a moment she looked horrified, then seemed to understand him and relaxed a little. "You mean *spraying* them with water?" She tightened the belt on her robe and turned on the radio. "Just *hosing* them with water?"

There was no news on the radio. She led him to the sofa, spoke soothingly to him, and brought him a drink. It was cheap whiskey, but it calmed him. She took his hand and asked him to tell her what had happened.

"Let me get another drink." He went to the decanter in the dining room. The decanter was made of gaudy cut glass. He poured a finger, swallowed it, and poured another. The trembling stopped; he felt a little more like himself. "Doesn't your old man ever buy good liquor?"

"You know it's only for display."

He talked a moment about what he had seen, but when he got to the part about rescuing the boy, he stopped.

"Then what did you do?" She leaned toward him.

He sipped the whiskey. "I came here."

"What happened to the boy?"

"I don't know."

"Well," she said and sat back on the sofa. "Probably nothing. The radio hasn't said a thing."

The trembling came back. He paced. "I just don't know. I have a sick feeling. I can't explain it. It feels like . . . like my whole insides want to come out." He stopped while she took the curler out of her bangs. "It feels like something bad is going to happen, and if I stay here—I mean if *we*—stay here we are going to be trapped in it."

"Well, there *is* a civil rights protest."

He took a breath. "Don't be sarcastic."

"I don't mean to be sarcastic. I'm just pointing out to you that something *is* happening. You don't realize it because you don't see it every day. And, well, you have options those people don't have. Money gives you options."

"What is that supposed to mean?"

"Just an observation." Then she added quickly, "Not of you—not so much of you, sweetheart—but of my patients. You feel you may get trapped. You can afford to go to New York or California. But most of them can't. At least not in the way I'm talking about."

"What's the difference in New York?" He closed his eyes. "I wish I could really get away from here. From this city. From the whole damn country." He sat on the sofa and took her hand. "I'm serious. Why don't we get married and go overseas? We could go to Amsterdam or Paris. I hear things aren't so bad over there."

"Paris? Oh sure, *mon cher*. And just what are we going to do in *Paris*? We don't have that kind of money."

"I'll sell Dad's part of the business to Uncle Booker. He buys up everything sooner or later anyway."

"He *is* a businessman."

Carlton remembered his meeting with his uncle. "And I'm not?"

He did not go right away to meet his uncle. Salena decided to go to the hospital and asked him to make lunch for her father. Her father, Mr. Parrish, was a wiry, olive man with patchy gray fuzz on his head. He seemed agitated when he came in from his store and found Carlton in the kitchen warming up string beans and leftover turkey. "Where's Salena, Mr. Wilkes? She done got called in?"

"She went in before they called her."

"Volunteered her time? She know better'n that."

"I believe she felt they would call her anyway with the riot going on downtown."

"Riot?" He went to the washroom just off the kitchen. "I ain't hear tell of no riot. Heard they spraying them children. But spraying ain't a riot."

"No, sir. I guess not." Carlton watched Mr. Parrish's angular hips as he bent over the basin. "Anyway, Salena asked me to warm up some dinner for you." He poured the limp, sweet-smelling beans onto the plate with the turkey and candied yams. His stomach growled a little, but he decided not to eat until the old man invited him.

Mr. Parrish put the paper napkin to his collar and began his lunch. "You not in business today?"

"I had an appointment down with Uncle Booker, but . . . the disturbance was in the way."

"That's what I knew. They talk about hurtin' the white man, but they hurtin' the colored, too." Mr. Parrish sawed on his turkey. "Shuttlesworth and Walker! Call themselves preachers. Preachers ain't got no business in politics, if you ask me. Marchin' in the street ain't never got nobody into heaven." He motioned with the fork to a chair. "Help yourself, Carlton."

"I'm not very hungry."

"Can't work if you don't eat. That's what my daddy always told me. He was a farming man. Worked me sunup 'til midnight. I ain't lying. He was born a slave, you know. Had that slave working mentality. Nothing wrong with a work mentality. Two things I swore when I was a boy. One: I would get ahead any way I could—but ain't but one way—hard work. After my daddy died, Momma moved us over here to live with her brother who worked at the furnace. That when I saw how to make it: business. Momma opened the little dry goods store—just a handful of inventory—and I carried it on. My brother, Tom, he went back to farming—still farming—don't own a thing. Ain't got no pension. No nothing."

Carlton wiped sweat from his forehead back into his hair. He was wishing for a drink and the smell of the turkey was making him hungry. "What was the second thing?"

"I'll get to it." Mr. Parrish chewed. "Farming. That's what. Never gone lift another hoe in my life—unless it is to sell it. That's what your average Negro don't understand. He go out, break his back, whether it's farmin' or minin' or smeltin'—and ain't got a red cent to show for it. You got to be the middleman. The middleman or the owner. It's still hard work, but you got something in the end. Something you can sell if nothing else." He drank water. "Take yourself. You still young. You and Salena both. Well, she doing the best she can for a woman, but nursing—first colored girl or not—that's not what I want for her. She needs to settle in and raise the children and take care of the house. It's nice she got a skill and all to lean back on, in case something happens to you." He winked. "That's one thing that worries me so much about this going on. Interferes with business. White and colored, too."

"Mr. Parrish, did you *see* what was going on downtown?"

"I heard they was spraying children. Children ought to be in school, not the street—how do they ever expect to get a job out in the street? I wouldn't hire nay one of 'em—and what do they expect a white man to say if they have this on their record . . . ?"

"They were not spraying them. They were *hosing* them."

"What's the difference, Carlton?" Mr. Parrish stopped sawing the turkey with his fork. "What's the difference for us? It ain't fixin' to do nothin' but hurt us, one way or the other. Colored people too impatient. They want something and don't know what they gettin'. Now you tell me what sense it make for me to want to go all the way downtown and sit in at a white lunch counter to eat a hamburger, when my friend Harvey Brown got a rib shack not three blocks from here. And in your own business, Carlton, what good it gone be if they let us live up in Mountain Brook? You can't sell no houses in Mountain Brook, and ain't no white ever gone buy a house in Titusville. People talkin' about gettin' their freedom. Freedom ain't worth a dime if you ain't got a dime." He punched the table with his finger. "Every dollar they spend with the white man is a dollar they ain't spent with us." He pushed back from the table and folded his arms.

"We got to think this thing through. This marching business liable to drive every colored man in the city out of business."

The two men sat quietly for a moment as if considering this proclamation. Then Carlton shifted and cleared his throat. "Mr. Parrish, Salena and I have been talking. We figure if things don't get better we might go away."

The old man didn't look up. "Where to? Up North? Colored got the same trouble up North, only difference is they don't know it."

"We were thinking about Europe, maybe Paris."

"Paris, France?" Mr. Parrish looked at Carlton with incredulity. "You don't mean Paris, Kentucky? You mean Paris that in France? What the *hell* you going to do in Paris, France? You speak French? You got any family in France?" He sighed. "Son, white man own Paris just like he own Birmingham. Ain't a place in the world you can go—unlessen it's Red China—that the white man don't own. You can even go back to Africa, and you still got to deal with the white man. So you might as well save yo'self some running and deal with him right here."

Uncle Booker kept him waiting. From the window in the outer office he could see the park. It showed no evidence of the disturbance. The intercom buzzed.

"Mr. Wilkes," the secretary called to him. "He will see you now." Just before she opened the door for him, she whispered in a matronly way, "Straighten your tie."

Uncle Booker looked at his watch and shook his head. "I was here on time, Uncle Booker. But there was a riot."

"You let that foolishness stop you?"

"It was more than just a little foolishness." Carlton walked quickly to the window. "Didn't you see it from here?"

"I saw it. But I didn't let it get in the way of what I had to do." Uncle Booker packed and lit his pipe. "Have a seat, son. Believe it or not, I was young once, so I know how it is to get excited about things that don't mean a difference to you one way or the other."

"But . . ."

"I know. I know." Booker waved him silent with a chubby hand. "You're concerned about your rights—about Negro progress—I'm for all that, too. Lord, I'd be a fool not to be. And believe me, sure as the sun comes up every morning, it's coming. Maybe these schoolchildren have started something. Maybe not. Maybe we'll be singing their praises or maybe we'll be burying them. Or maybe both." He puffed and swiveled in his chair. "And you got a part in this progress too."

Carlton's stomach churned. He couldn't see himself marching.

Booker put his pipe in the pipe rest. "This will sound awful hard, but it's the truth. For someone like you, educated up North and in a white school—and got a little money behind you—the only Negro progress is to make as much money as you can. Now, before you say anything stupid, let me remind you that for three generations, even before the end of slavery, the Wilkes family has been in one business or the other. We may not have gotten our rights from the white man, and damn it, I know we didn't get his respect, but we got what we wanted because we had money."

Carlton had heard it before. Uncle Booker recounted the Wilkes businesses, from the small farm and produce store his first free ancestor had, to the white-only barbershops Carlton's grandfather had owned, to the real estate company that Carlton's father had owned, and to Booker's own insurance company. Carlton studied the short, chubby man. It was hard to believe that he was related to him.

"Now, I have a deal for you," Booker continued. "It should make you and your lady very happy—and rich. There is a man, a Northerner—and I may add, a white man—who is proposing to build some stores in various places around the city. Mountain Brook will be the first one. These are what they call *convenience* stores. They'd sell sundries and quick items. This man needs a partner—an investor. Someone who knows the area, but yet isn't exactly one of the local Okies, if you catch my drift."

After a moment, Carlton spoke. "That would take a lot of money."

"You've got it. You'll need to sell off some of those slum houses your daddy left you, and it would be tight for a few years. But you're young, and you've got your young lady to fall back on. She's Parrish's only child, and you'll have what he leaves her. But the best part," he puffed on the pipe, "the very best part will be if this civil rights thing goes through, then you'll own property in Mountain Brook and black and white alike will already be buying from you."

Uncle Booker leaned back in his swivel chair and laid his intertwined fingers across his stomach. He seemed to have been caught in a daydream. Carlton went to the window again and looked out over the park. He remembered how he felt when he had seen the dogs, and turned quickly to Uncle Booker. "I don't know about going into business with a white man. People around here wouldn't like that. It could cause trouble." The mention of "trouble" was strategic. Trouble would be bad for business.

Uncle Booker leaned forward. "Nobody will know who owns what." He leaned back in the chair and frowned. "What's the matter with you, Carlton?"

"It's just that Salena and I had been thinking of leaving Birmingham. You know, going to someplace where we could get a good start."

"Like where?"

"Like Paris."

Uncle Booker's face was still for a moment, then he laughed. "How romantic!" He leaned forward and put his thick hands on the desktop.

"Son, what do you see when you look out that window at Birmingham? Filthy smokestacks? A shabby little downtown? For certain it is not Paris. What I see is a town that black people helped to build. I see opportunity on every street corner. *Your* opportunity. You can't be afraid to claim it."

Carlton looked out the window again. In the distance he saw the columns of white smoke rising from the steel furnaces in Hueytown. Hueytown was home to the KKK. In another direction, he saw the rooftops of Titusville. Only last week bombs had been tossed into houses in Titusville. Then there was the park just in front of him. He returned to his seat. How could he make Uncle Booker understand? "Everything is changing here."

"Change can be good."

"It's just that . . . I'm afraid."

Uncle Booker leaned back again. He put the pipe in his mouth. "Of course, there is some risk. If you want to make money, you've got to take risks."

"It's not the business, Uncle Booker. I'm afraid. Afraid of what's happening here."

"Afraid?" Uncle Booker frowned and rocked forward abruptly. "Afraid? Afraid to make money?"

Carlton had started home after his talk with Uncle Booker, but the sight of the park stopped him. Close up, he could see the scars the water had left on the tree trunks and where it had stripped the leaves from shrubs. Here and there were puddles in the grass. He stood at the place where the boy had fallen. The grass was thin, and the ground had been churned up by running feet. It smelled fresh.

Remembering again what he had witnessed, he felt himself begin to shake. He looked at his hand. On the outside he was perfectly still, but on the inside everything trembled. He knew it was fear, but what did he have to fear?

Uncle Booker was right. He had nothing to lose if he played it smart. Money gave him options. He could invest and become very rich. The boycotts wouldn't hurt him. Or he could go to Europe. He couldn't live like a king in Europe, but he could live well for a long time.

He looked up from his hands and saw a police car circling the block. In the back, heads against the window, were two dogs.

No one had answered at Salena's, and he had started back to his car when he saw the men gathering on a neighbor's porch. Mr. Shannon, the neighbor, waved. He was carrying a hunting rifle. Several of the half dozen or so men carried guns. The three shots of good bourbon he had had on the way over kept Carlton's stomach still.

Mr. Shannon, a tall, brown man with a wide mouth, beckoned to him. "It's about to come on."

Carlton straightened his tie. "What's that, Mr. Shannon?"

"Walter Cronkite."

Mrs. Shannon opened the window from the inside and pushed the television to face the men. Walter Cronkite appeared inside the oval screen and spoke about Birmingham. Then pictures of the hosing came up. Carlton saw the lanky silhouettes of the children, dancing about in the white mist. A jet smacked a child and tossed her down.

"God," one of the men said.

The whole newscast was about Birmingham. No one made a sound. Even when the governor made a defiant speech no one said a thing, though Carlton could see Mr. Shannon's forearms tighten. When the newscast ended, the men looked at each other, their jaws set in anger and their fists twisted around the barrels of the guns.

"The Klan will be out tonight," one of them said.

"I'd like to see them," another said.

Mr. Shannon relaxed a little. "I don't reckon so. I reckon they're at home watching it like we are. But we'd better be on guard anyway."

"Any hooded bastard come sneaking around this neighborhood, I get me a piece of 'm," a man said.

"All you do is give Pooler a piece of mortuary business."

"Now, gentlemen," Mr. Shannon said, "we got a higher cause than to talk like that." He turned to Carlton. "Mr. Wilkes, won't you join us on watch tonight? Ever since the bombings started, we sit on different porches to see if we can't discourage whoever is doing it."

They looked like an unlikely militia—schoolteachers, millworkers, and brickmasons, fidgeting with their shotguns and hunting rifles. Someone dropped a shell and it rolled and stopped at Carlton's feet. His hand trembled as he picked it up and held it out to its owner. He worried that they would think he was afraid.

"How about it, Mr. Wilkes?" Mr. Shannon asked.

Carlton cleared his throat. "No. Not tonight."

"When?" Mr. Shannon looked directly at him but spoke softly. "Comes a time when enough's enough, and you got to do what you got to do. I say when the fire department that I pay my taxes to go and hose little colored girls, then the time's come."

"Amen," someone said.

"Shannon's the next Martin Luther King," another man said and provoked laughter from the group.

Carlton's throat was dry. "I was there this morning, Mr. Shannon. I saw it." The men grunted sympathetically. "What you saw on television, I saw face-to-face."

"Then you know what I'm talking about." Mr. Shannon held out his gun to Carlton. "I got another gun in the house. Besides, we'll take turns carrying the guns."

"No. I . . . I wouldn't know how to use a gun."

"Just carry it like you know how," someone chimed in.

Carlton backed down the stairs. "I'm sorry, gentlemen, I have an appointment—across town, and I . . ."

"He's G. W. Parrish's son-in-law," one of them said. "He's too worried about business to be free."

"No call for that," Mr. Shannon said. "If the man's got business to do, then he's got business to do. He said he would join us another night."

"May not be another night."

One of the men made a joke. "One Wilkes'll rent you a house; the other one will insure it; Parrish'll sell you your stock; and Pooler will put you under, but nay one of 'em will fight for you." A stiff laugh came from the man who said it, a big, buck-toothed man Carlton knew as a brickmason. The other men only stared at Carlton, challenging him. He fumbled for an answer but realized it was no good. He couldn't stay with them now, even if he wanted to, but to run would make him a coward or, worse, a traitor.

Then a little girl, about five, a fragile, wide-eyed child with two erect plaits, came to the screen door. "Daddy," she called in a soft, quavering voice, "Daddy, are we going to get bombed tonight?"

Mr. Shannon opened the door, took his daughter into one arm, and wedged the rifle in the crook of the other. "No, honey, we ain't gonna get bombed."

Carlton drove aimlessly until after sunset. The police were setting up checkpoints, so he drove back to Titusville and waited around the corner for Salena to get home from her shift. Soon after midnight, he saw her park her car in the driveway, nod to the men on Shannon's porch, and go quickly up the stairs. He caught up to her just before she shut the door.

"You scared me," she said. "God, Carlton, you've been drinking."

"I've been thinking."

"Come in before you wake up the neighborhood. And for God's sake, don't wake up Papa."

Carlton sat on the couch while Salena put away her things. She came back wearing her uniform and no shoes. "Listen. Maybe you should go. Daddy will have a fit if we keep him up on a work night."

A little dizzy from the drinking, Carlton stood. "I just wanted to say . . ." She pulled the pins out of her nurse's hat. In the dim overhead light her features were sullen. "I wish we could listen to music," he said.

"Papa'll . . ."

"I know what he'd do, but—don't you feel like you're between a rock and a hard place?"

She seemed to think for a moment. "No. What do you mean? I feel very lucky, altogether. Very lucky."

"You want to be more than just lucky. Never mind. I . . ."

He put his palm to his head and sighed. "I'm an ass."

She said nothing, but took his elbow and pushed him back to the sofa. "What's on your mind?"

It took him a moment to prevent his voice from cracking. "I want to get away. I'm scared this thing is going to backfire."

She folded her hands around his. "We had a fairly quiet night at the hospital. Mostly white. They were scared, too. Scared of the 'race riot.' One old woman said it was Armageddon. But when I saw those pictures of the children on the TV, I was proud. I don't know what will happen to them. I don't think it'll be good, but at least they aren't letting the white people get away with it—I mean, they are at least standing up for something." She took off her hat. Her hair fell down on her neck and she pulled it back and set it with the bobby pin.

"You weren't scared?" he whispered.

"A little. Who wouldn't be? But you've got to go on with your work."

"What about Paris?"

She sighed. "I guess I could be a nurse in Paris. The question is, what are *you* going to do?"

He took a flask from his jacket.

"Don't. It's too late. You've got to work tomorrow, don't you?"

Hearing Mr. Parrish on the stairs, Carlton put the flask away.

"Let me see if I can't send him back to bed." Salena went to the foot of the stairs and called to her father, telling him nothing was the matter. The old man complained about his interrupted sleep and kept coming down. Reluctantly, Carlton started toward the door.

"Mr. Wilkes," Mr. Parrish blurted. "What brings you around at this hour?" He was wearing a dingy sleeveless undershirt and trousers. "Something wrong downtown?"

"Everything is fine, Papa."

"Them children up to something?"

Salena tried to turn her father around at the foot of the stairs, but he brushed past her, eclipsed Carlton on the way to the door, and looked out of the sidelight. "Shannon and his crew still sittin' up. Waiting for the Ku Klux Klan!" He faced Carlton. His age showed in the bags and spots under his eyes. "Tell you one thing, the Klan ain't waitin' for them. They in bed gettin' their rest so they can put in a full day. Klan gone strike, he go 'head and strike and then go home and get a full night. Ain't that right, Mr. Wilkes?" His bare feet scuffed against the scatter rugs as he limped into the dining room. "Mr. Wilkes," he said with a certain sarcasm, "won't you join me in a taste?"

"Oh, Papa!" Salena protested.

Carlton stepped between her and her father and pulled the flask from his jacket. "I owe you one, Mr. Parrish."

"I suppose you do." Mr. Parrish took a shot glass from the sideboard and held it for Carlton to fill.

"Papa," Salena said, "Carlton was just leaving."

Motioning to the sofa, Mr. Parrish invited Carlton to sit. "I'm sure he got more gumption than to come into a man's house in the middle of the night, wake him up and then leave. Besides, this Paris thing got me so I can't sleep." He sat. "Carlton, I'm a country man and I didn't have the privilege of the education that yo' daddy give you. But I do my share of readin' and I read about these colored fellows that run off to Paris cause they can't be free in this country. But you take a look at what they do, and they all singers and horn players. That's their work. I understand that some of them make good money at it, too." He sipped the liquor. "Now you see what I'm gettin' at? I don't hear you or Salena singin' or playing no horn. Lord, the girl's momma couldn't even get her to sing in the church choir. So tell me what you gone do in Paris? You just be livin' off what yo' daddy left you—givin' it all away to another bunch of white men. Now, I know things are supposed to be better overseas, but let me tell you this. No matter how bad it gets, and it done already been a hell of a lot worse than it is now, there is no place like your home." Finishing his drink, he started back up the stairs, then stopped and looked plainly at Carlton and shook his head. "You know, Carlton, Salena my only child."

The old man went up into the darkness, and Carlton turned to Salena. "I could look into getting passports tomorrow."

Salena threw her head back and sighed. "Carlton . . . I love you, but really . . . it's a silly idea."

The sun was above the rooftops when Mr. Shannon rapped on the window of Carlton's Lincoln. "I just wanted to see if you were all right, Mr. Wilkes."

Carlton's head was cloudy, and his neck ached from having slept on the arm-rest. He mumbled a greeting to Mr. Shannon and felt in his pocket for the keys. "Excuse me, I must have fallen asleep . . ."

"Don't worry about it." Mr. Shannon winked. "I remember when my wife and I were courting—besides, it's good to be young. Why don't you come in and have a cup of coffee and some eggs? Put something solid in your stomach."

Carlton tried to beg off the invitation, but Mr. Shannon insisted, and he found himself brushing the wrinkles out of his suit and running his tongue over his stale teeth.

Inside Mrs. Shannon, her hair in rollers, was scrambling eggs. She was a tall, dark woman with genteel features. Two girls sat at the kitchen table, one the little girl Carlton had seen the day before and the other an adolescent who seemed much perturbed by his appearance.

"I'll just have coffee."

"Oh, no, you won't," said Mrs. Shannon as she scooped grits and soft scrambled eggs onto a plate with sausage patties, toast and jam. The food smelled good and Carlton was hungry; he fidgeted to prevent himself from eating until all were seated and Mr. Shannon had said the grace. The older girl, Gloria, pretended to ignore him. She ate the sausages with her fingers, pinky up. Mrs. Shannon firmly told her to use a fork, and slowly, fastidiously wiping grease from her fingers onto a paper napkin, Gloria conformed. The little girl hardly ate for staring at him. He winked at her, trying to solicit a smile, and asked her name. She turned away, but prodded by her parents she told him, "Bonita."

"That's a pretty name. Spanish, isn't it?"

"I believe so," Mrs. Shannon said. "We took it from her grandmother."

Mrs. Shannon asked about the wedding plans. "Salena tells me nothing, you know. Not that it's my business, but a neighbor would like to know."

"We haven't set them yet," Carlton said. "Maybe soon. We've been thinking about going to Europe."

"That would be a nice honeymoon." Mrs. Shannon looked impressed. "I swear, Salena doesn't tell me a thing."

"She hasn't exactly agreed yet," Carlton confessed.

"It is expensive," Mrs. Shannon said slowly. For a moment it seemed to Carlton that she would give him a sympathetic pat on the hand. "You'd better travel while you are young. Once you have your children you'll be settled for a long time."

"I did get to travel over in the Pacific during the war, or 'the conflict'—whatever they called it. Korea." Mr. Shannon piped in between bites of egg and toast. He stopped chewing and looked at Carlton. "What you think about all this mess that Shuttlesworth and King stirred up, Mr. Wilkes? You think it gonna come to something?"

This was not the conversation Carlton wanted. He wanted to ignore Mr. Shannon and to turn back to Bonita with her erect braids and tiny, square, egg-covered teeth.

"We don't need to talk about that at the table," Mrs. Shannon said. And then more softly, "It upsets the children."

"Some children are out there in jail."

Mrs. Shannon scooted back from the table, asked if Carlton wanted a second helping, and barely waiting for him to clear his mouth to reply, she put another spoonful of grits on his plate.

"Some children are in jail," Mr. Shannon repeated. "I can't say that I'm not scared for them, but there comes a time when you got to—"

"Got to do nothing." Mrs. Shannon banged the pot on the stove. "None of mine are going down there to be killed by Bull Connor."

"I'm not scared of Bull Connor," the older girl said.

"You'd better be," her mother replied. She took a breath. "We're going to upset Bonita, so just let it rest."

"It won't rest." Mr. Shannon took his plate to the sink. "Mr. Wilkes, I'm going downtown. I think a lot of us will be marching."

Mrs. Shannon cut a look at him. "You'd better be marching on to work, instead of jail. We don't have any money to get you out."

"Then I'll just stay." He went to the door. "Are you coming, Mr. Wilkes?"

Slowly, Carlton sat back from the table. He nodded toward Mrs. Shannon and stood. He felt a tremble in his knee. Gloria popped up and ran toward her father. "Can I go with you?" she asked.

The park was crowded with people of all ages. Carlton recognized no one, but Mr. Shannon, a schoolteacher, greeted many of the people, both adults and children. Policemen and firemen were gathering on three sides of them. Yet there was quiet festivity, as people greeted friends or sang hymns. Someone was singing *Gonna lay down my burden, down by the riverside. . . .* Someone else led a small group in prayer.

A bullhorn crackled, and the crowd began to shift. Carlton's mind tripped over itself as he tried to fathom everything. He couldn't understand the instructions coming from the demonstration leaders. The bullhorn seemed to be circling the park. He thought it might be coming from Bull Connor's armored car, yet he couldn't see the car. He looked for Mr. Shannon and saw the top of his curly head several yards away. He tried to follow, but the crowd pressed against him and Mr. Shannon moved even further away. It occurred to him that the people were dressed nicely, in clean dungarees and sundresses, and that the firemen were preparing to hose them as they had done to the children the day before.

Behind the fire trucks and paddy wagons he saw Uncle Booker's insurance building. He thought that if he could make it past the trucks, he might be able to take refuge in the building. What Mr. Parrish had said was evident now. How much business would the store owners along Fourth Avenue do if there were rioting in the park? They had mortgages to pay and families to feed.

The demonstrators, singing and chanting, lined up at the park's edge. Carlton was close enough to see the face of one of the firemen. He was a square-jawed young man, covered with freckles. He held the hose against his body with one arm and gripped the throat of the nozzle with his hand.

Suddenly Bull Connor's armored car rolled down the street between the crowd and the firemen. At the window sat heavy-jowled Bull Connor himself. He wiped his glasses with a white hankie and spoke into a microphone which was amplified by a speaker on the roof of the car. The demonstrators did not disband, and the car moved on. A line of helmeted policemen and their dogs moved in, cutting off Carlton's retreat to Uncle Booker's building.

The young fireman adjusted the nozzle. It seemed to have been pointed directly at Carlton, but there was some confusion. The fireman was looking back at the pumper and yelling instructions. The men at the pumper had taken out their wrenches and were tampering with the hydrant intakes. The young fireman took aim again and braced himself. Carlton saw him push down the nozzle lever.

There was still an escape route, Carlton thought, if he could get to the back of the crowd and then slip behind the fire trucks. He began to push through the crowd. Things were getting too crazy. Somebody was bound to get hurt. Negro progress was supposed to be good for Negroes; he was a Negro, but this was not good for him. He would go to Europe. He pushed faster through the crowd, not caring whom he shoved or stepped on. If Salena didn't want to go, he would go without her. Someone grabbed his shoulder. He pulled away and was grabbed again. It was Mr. Shannon. "Hold on a minute, Mr. Wilkes. We are marching on City Hall."

Carlton was still for a moment. Mr. Shannon's hand felt like a vise on his shoulder. Then he shivered, and Mr. Shannon took away his hand.

"I'm sorry," Mr. Shannon said and looked away. Carlton flushed with embarrassment. Mr. Shannon spoke again, in a steady low voice. "Won't you please walk with me, Mr. Wilkes? If you won't, I'm not sure that I can."

For a while, Carlton could not answer, and the two men stood while the crowd pushed around them. "Mr. Shannon," Carlton's voice quavered, "I'm afraid." The confession was accompanied with a great relief, but relief made him no less afraid.

"I'm afraid, too." Mr. Shannon hooked his arm in Carlton's and slowly the two got in step with the crowd. "But I feel I don't have much choice about being here. I've got my children to think about, for one thing. You're young, Mr. Wilkes. You don't have children yet, but someday you will. When you have children, then you will know that you have to make a choice to face your fears. I don't know what will happen today. We may be knocked in the head, maybe worse. Just keep thinking about the children. Think about all the children."

"All the children?"

"The children who were arrested."

Carlton tried to imagine the faces of the children. He imagined groups of children, their faces blurred by distance. He saw them as silhouettes or as flashes of color dashing in and out of the arcs of water. He saw the form of the boy who had been knocked down by the water. But he could not see the children as individuals, as people he knew. Because his father had money, he had been sent away to a boarding school in the North. Except for business, he had had only a little contact with these people, much less with their children. It had been a business errand to the hospital that had brought him and Salena together.

"Salena," he thought out loud. He had no children, but he had a future with Salena. He tried to imagine having children with Salena. How would they look? Her eyes? His nose? Her mouth and hair? Try as he might, he couldn't imagine the child's face.

Two by two, the demonstrators began to file across the street toward a gap between the police cars and the fire trucks. Secure on Mr. Shannon's arm, Carlton fell into step. They made it to where the park lawn and the pavement met before the line stopped. The demonstration leaders argued with the policemen. Again, Carlton saw the young, freckled fireman, now dragging the dead weight of his limp hose around and aiming it at the marchers. There was a murmur, and people began to kneel. Kneeling! Carlton thought. Kneeling like lambs to be slaughtered. He tried to pull away.

"Kneel and pray," someone said. "Kneel and pray."

Mr. Shannon held him tightly. "They say pray that the water won't come on, Mr. Wilkes."

Carlton shook his head.

"They are praying that the water won't come on."

They had gone crazy. It was one thing to get hosed when you were on your feet and able to run, but it was suicide to kneel down. Mr. Shannon pulled on him, his knees buckled and he landed squarely on the edge of the sidewalk.

The water didn't come.

"Oh, God. Oh, God."

People sang and prayed. Carlton dared not move. It was as if the collective will of the crowd had frozen the hydrants. If he could only stay here now. Stay. If he didn't move. If he didn't shiver. If he were as still as ice, then the water wouldn't come. Time would hold still. He caught his breath. His ears began to ring. But nothing, nothing moved. Except now, a cold molecule of sweat was slowly pushing through a pore at the base of his scalp, and swelling into a quivering bead. He must not move! "Oh, God, oh, God." He imagined the boy, rolled in the streets by the jets of white water, and the dogs—oh God, the dogs. Why was he a Negro and so scared?

The eyes of the young fireman were round, and the hose had slipped from under his arm. He was backing away from the crowd, looking over his shoulder to his colleagues for support.

Carlton saw the fireman stepping back. It confused him. His concentration slipped and he began to note his surroundings. He was kneeling in a crowd, being held by a man he barely knew, while the firemen backed away and tampered with the hydrants. He had stepped out of his life into something stranger than life. He had a comfortable home which sat on a hill above Titusville. He had a fiancée who was one of the first colored nurses at the white hospital. He had a business to run and a Lincoln Continental.

Yet he was compelled to stay where he was, on his knees, in front of Bull Connor's firemen. For if he moved, if one hair sprung up from the pomade that held it close to his skull, then the water would come on. The bead of sweat trembled and began to roll in a meandering, ticklish path over his temple and across his cheek. That wasn't his fault! He couldn't help that. He hadn't done anything to cause it to fall.

Now other beads began to roll. He felt each one individually as it prickled across his skin. Each one was a cold prod inciting his body to revolt, to shiver, to stand up and run. But if he dared, then it would be the end of him. He would be rolled in the streets, chased and bitten by the dogs. He would be no better than the others.

"Courage, Mr. Wilkes. Courage." Mr. Shannon loosened his grip, and Carlton screamed and jerked away.

"Kneel, mister," someone said, but Carlton continued stumbling through the kneeling people, stepping on them, picking a route to the rear of the park.

Then there was a whoosh. Carlton turned to see the young fireman brace himself as the hose kicked and foamed and shot water. At first the stream scoured the asphalt and sprayed up a milky, prismatic mist; then the fireman gained control of it and directed it at the kneeling demonstrators.

The jets bowled the demonstrators over and knocked them down as they tried to rise. White arcs came from every direction, and Carlton realized that he was surrounded. He pushed people aside as he ran instinctively toward Uncle Booker's building. He made it to the curb just as a column of water came at him. Diving behind a parked car, he escaped the direct force. He edged along the side of the car and peeped around the fender to see in which direction the hose was pointed.

Just inside the park, he saw a young woman in a white dress. She was bent over and stumbling as she tried to dodge the jets of water. Carlton wiped his eyes to get a better look. His heart skipped a beat. Was it Salena? He wiped his eyes again. The young woman turned in his direction, and he saw that without a doubt it was Salena. Now she had stopped running and was trying to help a heavyset man out of the mud.

Carlton ducked behind the car again. His head was spinning and the water in his eyes had broken the world into fragments. He had a clear shot to Uncle Booker's building. If he tried to reach Salena the hoses would surely catch him. He tried to convince himself that she would be all right. She was strong, stronger than himself. Maybe she was too strong for him. Maybe he couldn't imagine children with her because they had no future together. She was claiming her future, here at the park. His future was in Europe.

He tried to imagine Salena's face. He held it in his mind for a moment, but it seemed the water in his eyes was also in his head. Every time he got the image of her to stand still, it was washed away by rivulets of water. Maybe he didn't love her. If he loved her, then he would be able to see her clearly. He would be able to run to her.

He looked for her again in the crowd and in a moment found her. The white uniform was now gray with mud. She had lost her shoes. She seemed dazed, no longer crouched and running but standing and limping, an easy target. Then he saw a jet of water coming toward her. "Salena!" He stood. The scene kept spinning around him. First Uncle Booker's building, then Salena, then the fire trucks. "Run," he heard someone scream at him. "Run, run, run!" It was himself screaming. He ran. He wasn't sure in what direction. The water punched his ribs and knocked out his breath. It slammed him to the asphalt, shoved his hips against the pavement and beat on his back. He lay and caught his breath as the runoff trickled and fizzed around him. Slowly he stood and made a clumsy step toward Salena.

John Holman

John Holman was born in Durham, North Carolina, in 1951. He earned a B.A. at the University of North Carolina at Chapel Hill, an M.A. at North Carolina Central University, and a Ph.D. at the University of Southern Mississippi. After a series of teaching positions he became an associate professor of English at the University of South Florida in 1988 and then, in 1993, he became associate professor of English at Georgia State University in Atlanta. His books are *Squabble and Other Stories* (1990) and *Luminous Mysteries* (1998). "Rita's Mystery" was first published in the *Oxford American* in 1997. Its main character is the central figure in *Luminous Mysteries.* The story focuses on the narrator's love for his wife, and on his, and her, uncertainty about whether the kidnapping she thinks she remembers really happened.

Rita's Mystery

Mayes rose to speak at the A.A. meeting, his first time giving testimony. He said, My name is Mayes Mello and I'm an alcoholic. People applauded. Mayes thought, Well, *maybe* I'm an alcoholic, but it was too late to take it back. He didn't want to disappoint. He had become very impressed with the people who attended the meetings. They were all wondrous. He had something he wanted to tell them, about the power they knew and relied on, and how it was manifested to him.

My wife is Jesus, he said. He chuckled. Just kidding. What I mean is that Rita is like Jesus. She has a quality. She's extraordinary. Yet, my Rita says that no matter what, you cannot plan your life. Did Jesus ever say a thing like that? I don't think so. Jesus understood something other. I don't know that Rita means it; she might be only trying to fit in with all of us unenlightened ones. I mean, even I know that to at least some extent you can plan your life. For instance, if you eat a cake a week, you get fat, so you can plan to get fat that way or you can plan not to. I plan not to, for instance. Or, if I want to know how a metal alloy behaves at sixty below, I drop the temp on that sucker and watch it crack. I'm a cryophysicist, and I'm sitting okay, having gone from high-school science-teaching, through the higher academia—specimen that I was—to practical research of the behavior of mass in the too-cold climates of space. I planned the whole trip. Rita, I should think, ought to respect that.

Jesus said that what you do now determines how you will be later. That's what he meant: to know the future, study today, what goes around comes around, you reap what you sow. I believe that. Anybody just glancing ought to see that it's pure common sense. But Rita, my wife, is like Jesus in that she does everything right instinctively. She is like the Buddhas and bodhisattvas I've read about. She's got a really good heart, is what I mean, and she loves everybody. Even the guy that kidnapped her. That's what I'm trying to get the police to understand. Rita is originally sinless.

She asks what past event, what past present, led to her being abducted, assaulted, and then arrested for public drunkenness—for drunk driving—and caused her picture in the paper, her arrest on television? She was on her way to work, damn it.

She doesn't think anyone believes her. She doesn't blame anyone, really; she understands how it looks. She was drunk, and driving. But she expects people to be charitable, to believe the truth.

I can tell she even suspects me of doubting her because sometimes she cries and she won't let me comfort her. She quotes to me my belief in cause and effect—if she's in trouble, then she caused it—assumes my complete faith in that logic. I admit, I don't understand.

The police, of course, and the D.A. certainly think she's lying. Her lawyer, maybe he believes and maybe he doesn't. He keeps asking her to tell the story again. Did anybody see her in the car with the guy? Did she phone anyone at work before leaving home that morning? Is there anyone—a neighbor, me, the paperboy—who can say that she even intended to go to work, that she's telling the truth? I tell them, yes, she's telling the truth, she intended to go to work.

Still, she's a drinker. All our friends know that. But she's not a drunk. She doesn't get drunk in the morning and miss work. She couldn't keep a job that way, not a teaching job anyway. She's called in a few times and gotten substitutes, but for the flu, like anybody else.

Now the principal is hinting that her calls have had a pattern. Monday morning calls. He's said that maybe now that she's gotten this attention she can get the help she needs.

The head of our library branch, where Rita tells stories to the preschoolers on Saturday mornings, has suggested that she discontinue her visits until this is all straightened out. So she's putting up with this suspicion and betrayal, and she loves and forgives the principal, the librarian, and especially the guy that's done this to her.

If we could just find him, everything would be better.

But Rita only half wants to find him. Certainly, she doesn't like being thought a liar, and it's embarrassing—indeed stunning—being perceived as someone you absolutely are not. But she knows the man is in pain and she would not want to cause him any more. The police aren't even looking for him. When they question her, she tells the same story every time, a little different here and there as she remembers things, forgets things, finds something or other more or less important.

She was just two blocks from home, at the traffic light, and she saw the man approaching in the side mirror. But she didn't think to do anything. Her door was unlocked. Bums are always on the corners, and the only thing different was that he was in her mirror this time, coming up beside the car. That was strange, and when she thought to run the light or lock the door it was too late. He was pushing her over onto the passenger seat. His odor paralyzed her, shocked her, made her cringe. He smelled like excrement. Like excrement and b.o. and rotten teeth. And *he* must have run the light because she realized they were speeding, the world outside the car blurring by.

He wore an unbuttoned blue shirt with green stripes tucked into beltless pants, and the dark skin of his chest was ashy-gray. It was cold that morning and the heater had not yet fully melted the frost on the windows. She had on her coat and gloves, and a knit hat and scarf. His pants were filthy, the color of tobacco, with black stains like grease and white stains like snot. His shoes, badly scuffed wing tips, had no laces, and he didn't have socks on his gray, cracked ankles. He reached inside his shirt and pulled out a gun. It had a short barrel. That's when he looked at her sidelong with huge watery eyes.

"I'll kill you," he said.

"No," she said.

He cursed her viciously, vulgarly.

His stink was so strong it was in her ears. She vomited.

"Looks like you had breakfast," he said, and snorted a laugh.

"Let me out," she said.

"I'll kill you," he said. "Messing up my day with this mess." He shook the gun at her and then put it back in his shirt.

As always, she had flung her purse and briefcase on the backseat. She wanted to reach back for a tissue from her purse, but she also didn't want to call attention to herself. She thought about his stealing her money and credit cards, and the hassle of canceling everything.

But she was embarrassed by the vomiting, so she reached back. He grabbed her arm and snatched the bag. The car swerved, nearly hit a truck in the next lane, and he caught the wheel and straightened. She tried on the spot to remember that truck but couldn't. Immediately it was gone.

The man took from the purse her fat wallet filled with receipts, cards, photos. Then he turned the bag over and flung it around. Pens, makeup, gum, checkbook, and tissue littered the seat and her lap, landed in the pool at her feet.

She wiped her mouth with a tissue, cleaned the dashboard as best she could. She thought about me, she says, and our daughters. She felt sorry for us, who wouldn't know what had happened to her—who'd learn maybe months later that the skeleton found in the distant woods was his missing wife, their missing mother. Black female, mid-to-late fifties. And imagining that made it all seem unreal to her, as if she were predicting the end of a made-up mystery.

When Rita tells her library stories, you feel as though you are in them. This is because when she tells them, *she* is in them. You sense that in front of her eyes there is a transparent screen on which her tales live and through which she observes her audience. And the audience, through the service of the same transparent screen, observes the tale and the teller. She stands there wearing her caftan, waving her cow-tail switch, and the myth of the origin of sleep awakens, or the story of the clever spider and the palm gourd begins to creep and speak of itself.

Yet she is holding something back from the police and her attorney, and that is why they don't believe her. I do my best to persuade them, to speak without saying what she doesn't want me to say. We differ about what should be known, although even if I could tell everything, my power to persuade would be less than hers.

It has been a month since the mystery. She yelps in her sleep. Usually I wake her as soon as she starts, but once I was in the basement washing a late-night load of clothes when I heard her. She got so loud I was honestly surprised she didn't wake herself. I shake her, is what I do. She stops with a grunt and a whimper. Always, somebody is chasing her. That son of a bitch. Yet, she seems afraid only when sleeping. When awake, she's angry, disappointed, but laughing and forgiving.

I used to say, Rita never meets a stranger. She's become good friends over the phone with the wife of the man who delivered our living-room tables last year when we were redecorating. I don't know how it happened. She'd never seen this woman in person, just some photographs the deliveryman showed her. She served the guy ham sandwiches and tea for lunch and looked at his snapshots, and somehow she's talking to his wife about who knows what. Troubles, it turns out. Their teenage daughter was pregnant. Later, we sent the baby some toys. We gave them some money when the guy had to have a leg artery sewn to his heart, to replace one that was damaged.

She has invited people over at the least provocation. She meets someone from Ontario, for example, where we used to live, gives them our address and tells them to come by anytime, as if we all have so much in common. If she meets someone who is going to Ontario, she gives them our old neighbors' addresses. So far none of these strangers has actually shown up at our door, and I don't know who has visited our old neighbors at my wife's insistence. I tell her it's dangerous to be so open, so giving, so trusting. She thinks I'm saying you're not supposed to like people so much. Maybe I am. She could be inviting over a killer, a robber, a vampire. I should hope that during her kidnapping she did not invite the kidnapper to our home, this man she dreams about.

She told me that after she got sick, when they were out of the traffic, on the outskirts of town, she felt hot and realized that the heater was on full blast. She switched it off and yanked loose her scarf, pulled off her gloves, unbuttoned her coat. She tried to breathe deep but his smells stopped her. She wanted to lower a window, but she looked at the man and realized he would be cold. His knuckles were scabbed, his fingers long and creased. The stubble on his face seemed as stiff and black as brush bristles, some of them ingrown; white, pus-filled bumps dotted his cheek and chin. He was skinny but muscled, like a scavenger animal, a hyena. Hair grew thick down his neck.

He steered the car onto a ramp to the interstate, heading west. As the ramp rose and they sped along the bridge across the river, she gazed out over the top of the town—churches, schools, houses, office buildings. She thought, this is what it's like to die, leaving everything familiar, accelerating, unable to stop.

He didn't kill her, obviously. He drove way out of town, got on some narrow backroad that split fields of dried cornstalks. She tried to talk to him and he cursed her. Cursed her for hours. Around ten, he made her buy bourbon at a rural package store and forced her to drink it with him as they drove empty two-lanes. They drank in a parking lot of an abandoned gas station along some piney country road. The concrete lot was crumbling, tough old winter weeds grizzled in the cracks. She tried not to swallow the liquor, but he held the gun to her throat and ordered her. She swallowed what she dared and then he drank some. They took turns like that. It was a half-gallon bottle. He raised the tilt wheel out of the way, leaned their seats back some.

As I said, Rita knows how to drink. First of all, she made it look like she was swallowing a lot, but she wasn't, and second, alcohol doesn't go straight to her head. She can hold it pretty well. She had a lot by now, though, and it was creeping up on her. She could sense the man was feeling better. It was clear that he relied on alcohol to ease his pain. She was worried he'd get the idea to rape her.

She began to imagine that when he drank, he left some of his pain in the bottle; and that when she drank, she first swallowed his pain away and then breathed in her well-being. That was the exchange—his pain for her health. And he became jollier. He said they were going to drive to Las Vegas, spend her money, and when the money ran out they would use her shining credit. He said she could buy him a house on a lake, in Africa, on Lake Victoria, and what kind of name for an African lake was that?

"What's your name?" she asked.

He let out a breath, let his chin slump to his chest, the bottle between his legs. He told her to get out of the car, and as she did he got out too, came around to her. The wind was whipping—ballooning and flapping his open shirt and molding his pants to his pipe-thin legs.

Straight on, he had a wide face, winglike cheekbones, eyebrows that met in a

V in the middle, and beautifully shaped, cold-white lips. He hit her. She ducked and his fist grazed and split her eyebrow. She fell back against the car and he rushed her, groping for her breasts through her coat. She felt nothing much, random and unpleasant pressure, as if drugged and submitting to a foul-smelling search. Then, as if he could not be satisfied, could not make himself felt, he gave up, let his arms go limp as he leaned on her, and breathed into her knit hat.

He rolled off and pushed back, arms pinwheeling like a stumbling cow town drunk. He ran tiptoed away from her but stopped at the corner of the building. He turned and, in an afterthought, pulled his gun and pointed at her with the length of his arms. For seconds he steadied it. Then he backed away and disappeared.

But while he had stood there sighting her, she had seen a radiance about him, a gleaming silver-gold sheen issuing from him like the spiny fins of a phosphorescent fish.

After he was gone, the whole scene was radiant—the tall, dry, pale grass in the ditch across the road, the black, bending pine trees with their silver-needle quills, the disintegrating parking lot, the glowing rust of the gas pumps, the white concrete-block building. She took her glasses from her coat pocket and put them on, to verify what she was seeing. The car was the most beautiful she had seen it, the paint like a clear, green glaze over chrome.

Light was in everything during her drive away from there, during her woozy, disoriented search for a phone booth. She doesn't know how far she drove before she slammed into a tinseled, shimmering tree that seemed to swoon out of the middle of the road. The road itself had seemed as bright and straight as a sheet of glass.

The police believe her bleeding head resulted from the wreck. She wasn't wearing a seat belt.

There is little evidence of the man. There were fingerprints other than hers found on the half-empty bottle but Rita can't remember where they bought it, and the police say the prints could belong to the salesman. They don't match any known criminal's. No distinct suspicious prints anywhere else, not even on the purse, not that the police looked very hard. Nor can she remember where the old gas station is, despite our drives around to look for it.

So, right now, it doesn't look good for Rita legally. She failed big-time on the Breathalyzer test. She won't tell the police about the vision—refusing to be ridiculed for something as powerful as that and sad that it would be received with the knowledge that she was drunk. She was plastered, blitzed, looped. If she had planned it, she says, there would be no suspicion attached. If she had planned it, she would be in control. Nothing, she says, can account for what she's gone through.

But I tell them, for her faith in me and for my faith in her, that she was not injured in the car wreck. That bruise is no steering-wheel mark over her eye. In fact, she remembers something the police could verify. When the state trooper found her she was sitting upright behind the wheel, the front end accordioned, the motor running, and the heater on low. Her eyeglasses were on the floor between her feet, neatly folded, reflecting blue-white light back at her, as if placed there for her, for when she was ready for the whole truth to be revealed, again.

Charlotte Holmes

In her collection *Gifts and Other Stories,* published in 1994, Charlotte Holmes portrays a series of individuals who, for one reason or another, are dissatisfied with their lives. The title story, presented here, concerns an alcoholic unwilling to believe that she deserves the life and the partner that have come to her. It is written in a spare, minimalist style reminiscent of Raymond Carver. Holmes was born in Ft. Gordon, Georgia, in 1956. After undergraduate study at Louisiana State University, she earned an M.F.A. at Columbia in 1980. She has held a number of editorial positions, and her work has appeared in such places as the *New Yorker, Antioch Review, Carolina Quarterly,* and *Southern Review.* Holmes is currently an associate professor of English at the Pennsylvania State University.

Gifts

In the gray light I could make out the mattress striped in blue ticking, sheets roped against the footboard; in the night the quilt had fallen to the floor. Palmer's arm curved around his head, and as stronger light seeped in around the edges of the windowshade I saw the white mark of his absent wristwatch. His jeans and green corduroy shirt crumpled on the cushions of the chair. I stood in the doorway until he turned over and looked at me. He said my name, then I sat with him and began smoothing back his hair.

After he left I showered and dressed. I made coffee. While it brewed I smoothed the *Examiner* out on the counter. I read the news and marked the classifieds, clipped notices for immediate openings while I drank my coffee. I didn't need to call to know that each job I was qualified for would have a catch—no benefits, weird hours, bad pay. I put the clippings end-to-end along the counter and then I put them on top of each other in a neat stack. I drank another cup of coffee.

Bo-Bo jumped into the kitchen window and looked in, rubbed against the screen and tried to meow. No sound came out. He looked at me with his one good eye and waited. I raised the window, pushed open the screen, and with two delicate steps across the drainboard he was inside. I rubbed my hand down hard along his knobby spine and he flattened against the counter, purring. I felt gristle and bone under his gritty fur. He opened his mouth and rasped a meow, then closed his teeth around my fingers.

A long time ago Bo-Bo was a gray kitten with a red ribbon tied at his neck, a valentine from my husband. Missy named him, confusing the red bow he wore with the word we used for her countless small wounds. Missy's fifteen now, long-legged and jittery—nothing like she was when I left her, a skinny seven-year-old curling her hair around one finger and waving goodbye from the door of her father's house.

I'm thirty-eight but no one believes it; my face is round and unlined, the face of a woman of thirty, maybe thirty-one but it's not how I looked at thirty. At Christmas when Missy was small I used to tell her about Santa: a broad face and a little round belly, and I'd put my hands on my stomach, ho-ho-ho to make her laugh. I'm bloated now, round the way a dead animal is round. Anyone thinks I'm pretty, it's because of my hair, still tinted copper and cut at Emporium, my extravagance.

Along with the many credit cards in his wallet, Palmer carries a California license that says he's nineteen, but when he buys liquor the clerks don't ask for an I.D. Feature-by-feature, his face is young, but I know how he fools people: he moves slowly, he thinks before he speaks, he wears an old tweed sports coat with his jeans. When he talks, his eyes cut into you the way broken glass would if you'd let it.

When the coffee was gone I spent some time on the phone; I took a nap; I washed out the bathtub. I wrote letters to people who might hire me. I fell asleep in the chaise on the patio and when I woke up, the day was over, Palmer was out of school, off work and already on his way back to me. The *Trib* came at five and I clipped more classifieds to add to the stack.

After Palmer showed up with two bags of groceries I filled two tumblers with ice and he popped the seal on the Jim Beam.

"I bought some steaks, too," he said. "And Sara Lee cheesecake for dessert."

"Fancy."

"Any luck today?"

"Kelly Girl called after you left. I worked half a day at Packard. They said they might need somebody for permanent part-time in the spring."

"That's great," he said, and we lifted our glasses. He held the bourbon in his mouth for a few seconds before swallowing, put the glass on the counter and cupped my shoulders in his hands. "I missed you today," he said. "I missed talking to you. I spent all day potting poinsettias. A hundred-sixty-five potted poinsettias, can you believe it? They're the ugliest plants in the world. I can't figure out why people still buy them. Come January they'll be in garbage cans all over Palo Alto."

"They're not so bad," I said. "They look real Christmasy."

He shook his head. "My mother's always had poinsettias at Christmas and I thought she was the only one in the world who still bought the damned things. I figured they would've gone out of style by now."

I smiled. "That's funny," I said. "When my daughter was born I remember how surprised I was that she woke up so much in the night. People would tell me how tired I was going to be with a new baby and I thought they were crazy—talking like they lived in another century." I looked out the window, at my yard sprouting dandelions and chickweed. "Maybe I'll drop by sometime and buy a few plants for the patio." I meant this to be funny, but Palmer didn't laugh. Working at that fancy greenhouse on El Camino had convinced him I should take better care of my yard.

I rubbed my hand along Palmer's face. His cheek was rough with stubble, but across the temples the skin was smooth as a girl's. I could taste the bourbon in his mouth when I kissed him.

"I'm glad it's Friday," I said.

"T.G.I.F.," he murmured against my neck.

"The Grunts Is Free."

"Thought it was 'The Gin Is Free.'"

"That's even better. But no gin tonight. It's bourbon."

"I have to work tomorrow," he said.

I pulled away. "But I told you. Missy will be here tomorrow." I picked up my drink and leaned back against the counter.

He looked embarrassed. "I guess I forgot," he said. He folded his arms across his chest. When he did this, his shoulders hunched and he looked like a schoolboy, a kid in trouble. "Sorry," he said.

"You're afraid."

"I just don't think I ought to be here. I'll end up insulting her and she'll go back home thinking we're both a couple of jerks."

I put my drink down and took the steaks out of the grocery bag, peeled off the plastic wrap and sprinkled the meat with salt and pepper.

"Missy will like you," I said.

"She may like me, but she won't like it that I'm with you. She won't like it that we're together. She'll find a million reasons why I shouldn't be here. Whatever I am, she'll hate."

"You sound like you've had practice with this," I said without turning around.

"I know what I'm talking about."

"Well, you don't know Missy. She's a great kid."

"Carla, I used to date girls her age," Palmer said.

When I didn't say anything he left, went out the back door and into the yard. When I looked out, I saw him standing underneath the eucalyptus with the empty glass in his hand. It was December, the rainy season. The sunlight was pale on the silver leaves of the eucalyptus and on the waves of Palmer's brown hair.

When my husband filed for a divorce I wasn't thinking much about what my life would be like without Missy. There was no custody battle, none of the bitter stuff you read about in the papers. I moved out of the house and the domestic agency Scott called sent Mrs. Eakins, a woman in her fifties who moved quietly into the downstairs guest suite and eight years later, she's still there, making breakfasts, arranging dinners, taking Missy to ballet and gymnastics class. After the divorce, I went twice to the house on a whim and Mrs. Eakins answered the door. She was polite but she kept me standing on the porch.

I got a job working part-time in Public Information at a college and that was fine, I made enough money and met some nice people. The office was cheerful, with six big windows overlooking a courtyard almost silver with debris from the huge eucalyptus trees that surrounded it. But one afternoon about a year ago I got so tired I had to rest my head on my desk after lunch; when I woke it was dark outside and my supervisor was thumping me on the shoulder. As she talked, not unkindly, about rest, detoxification, treatments that had worked for people she knew, the paper curled from my typewriter like a wave about to break, and the words I'd typed looked in danger of slipping to the floor. I kept staring at them as her voice went on and on, wondering who could be held accountable for such an arrangement of the alphabet. She said ". . . of course we'll be happy to reconsider you for the position if you'll accept treatment, if you'll only help yourself," and I realized that on the page the words were toppled together in a nonsense rhyme, the one Missy and I used to sing, *Gimby, gumby, shimble-shanks, hush-a mush-a, thimble thanks.* I read them to the woman and her mouth closed in a hard red line. She sent me home in a taxi.

Now I spend all day at home, a bungalow in the shade of the few trees that still grow between the expressway and the creek. My husband bought me the house for his own peace of mind, he said—he wanted to be sure I had a decent place to live. A high redwood fence keeps out the neighbors, and I have the sound of traffic for company. Sometimes when I can't sleep I'll bring a pillow and quilt out to the chaise, and lie there listening to the freeway noise until I fall asleep. It's a peaceful sound like the ocean, cars rolling back and forth like so many million drops of water in a narrow gray sea. When I get lonely I drive to a club near the exit ramp, and it's easy to find somebody to talk to.

That's how I met Palmer. I sat beside him at the bar and already felt the warm dizziness easing through me. When I touched him he looked at me, familiar as a friend, and my face went hot in the dim light. We drank tequila that night and he wanted to talk—stories so broken and confused I took them for a drunk's ramble and stopped trying to follow. I kept watching his face as he talked—the coolness in his blue eyes, the brittle curve of his mouth, the high arch that made the nose seem a little too long. When he saw me looking at him instead of listening, he smiled as if he understood. He rolled down his sleeves and said, "Let's take a drive." We took my car. The traffic was stop-and-go and we were drunk by the time we hit the interstate. Palo Alto had been gloomy, November drizzle slicked the streets, but the interstate was a solid wall of fog. Only the spires of trees were visible here and there along the embankment.

On the beach Palmer took the kite I'd bought for Missy and the ball of twine from the back seat and began running. The fog seemed to weight the air and the kite rose only a little above his head, the red silk tail billowing with his effort. I put my hands in my jacket pockets and watched until Palmer became only a man running away and then even less, a shape being gathered wholly into the fog. I brought out what was left of the tequila and settled back against the cliff.

The waves filled my head with the sound of their coming nearer and diminishing, so insistent I felt they would reach me before Palmer came back.

Hours later, Palmer's cold hands woke me in the dark and his mouth moved hard against my mouth. He said he had dropped the kite when he found the body of a seal floating in the surf.

"Suddenly I wasn't drunk," he said. "At first I thought it was a person. Then I thought it was a tire. I didn't know what it was, Carla. I kept wading farther out, trying to see what it was so you'd know."

He was soaked to the skin. I made him take off his clothes at the car and he wrapped himself in a blanket. The ocean chill seemed to have gone bone-deep for both of us. On the way home I stopped at Eddie's and bought more tequila.

Bo-Bo leapt off the hood of the car and walked slowly, loosely, as though his bones were tied together with string. He stopped and sniffed up at the steaks on the grill. He licked himself, then brushed against Palmer's ankles.

"Bo-Bo," Palmer said, squatting to ruffle the cat's ears, "you are one wretched cat."

Bo-Bo dropped onto his back, grasped Palmer's hand with his front paws and began to chew the outstretched fingers.

"You've hurt his feelings," I said.

"Some people think it's all instinct, that cats don't have feelings," Palmer said.

"What do they know?" I said. "He's showing you how much he cares."

Palmer smiled. "Yeah, sure. I used to have a cat. She was never this neurotic."

"What happened to her?"

"Dead," he said. "She had a litter when she was about seven months old, and we couldn't get rid of the kittens. I put free cat signs up at the supermarket, everything, but nobody wanted those cats. My mom finally trashed them."

Bo-Bo lay quietly in front of Palmer with his yellow eyes narrowed. When Palmer picked him up and spread him across his lap, a small cloud of grit drifted out.

"I'll get you a cat," I said. "Tomorrow. After Missy gets here we'll all drive out to the shelter and pick out a kitten."

Palmer didn't look up, but shook his head slowly as he moved his fingers through Bo-Bo's thin fur. "I don't want it," he said. "It wouldn't do any good." His shoulders under the blue shirt looked rigid, and he held himself so completely apart that for a minute I felt that I was sitting alone in the yard. But when I leaned over and touched him, Palmer was real, solid. I tousled his hair.

"Oh well," I said. "Doesn't matter. I forgot your mother. I guess she hasn't changed her mind about cats."

"She hasn't." He looked at me steadily. "Make me feel better," he said. "Say something."

I rattled the bits of ice in my glass and held it out for a refill. "Dame Trot and her cat led a peaceable life, when they were not troubled with other folks' strife," I said, remembering a nursery rhyme I used to tell to Missy.

Palmer laughed. "Tell me how you got Bo-Bo," he said.

"A gift," I said. "He turned out to be a nice gift, too, but I didn't think so at first."

"Whose gift?" Palmer said.

"What?"

"I said, whose gift? Who gave him to you?"

I put down my drink and got up to turn the steaks. "Scott always thought I needed things to take care of. He gave me plants, an aquarium, the cat, you name it."

"Missy."

"Sure. Her too."

"Did you love him?" Palmer said.

I bent down over the grill. "That's a good question," I said. "I used to wonder about it sometimes myself."

"Doesn't it bother you?"

"That I've stopped wondering? No, of course not."

Palmer leaned back in his chair. "Does it bother you that I want to know about him?"

The coals were white and my face felt warm from the heat. "It's okay that you asked. I don't miss being married, if that's what you're after."

"It isn't. I mean, it is, but I'm asking something else, too. Look, there he is, some fancy doctor who lives in a fancy house with your daughter, and here you are with me."

"So?" I looked around. "There are worse places to live, believe it or not. You've lived a sheltered life if you think it can't get worse."

"That's not the point."

"No? Then what is?" I sat down and picked up my drink.

"Listen, don't get mad. I'm just—I don't know, curious or something. I mean, here we are together. We make love, we have some good times, a few drinks, what have you." Palmer rocked his chair down and rested his elbows on his knees. He looked a little drunk; he cupped his chin in his hand and stared at the rainwater puddled around the roots of the eucalyptus.

"And?" I picked up the bottle of bourbon and poured another shot into both our glasses.

He took the glass and held it. "It's like—well, you know when I'm with you, when I'm inside you, say, and I look into your face I feel like the woman I'm with isn't you at all."

"You *are* drunk."

"Don't make jokes. I'm trying to say something. Right now, talking to you, it's hard to believe you're anybody's mother, that you were ever anybody's wife. But other times that's all I can see about you."

I shrugged. "Maybe that's your problem."

He looked up, then ducked his head and smiled. "Probably."

I liked to look at him like that—his shoulders in the work shirt were broad, and he held his head down and a little to the side, sheepish. It was such a boy's face; I could imagine it in the stupor of its childhood sleep, eyes closed and lips parted, one hand open on the pillow. But then Palmer stretched his legs onto the chaise, nudging against me. The soft suede mocassins he wore were so old the stitching at the toe had broken, just at the point where his big toes pressed. And I remembered that under the washed-out corduroys his long legs were tan and muscular, warm when he wrapped them tight around me.

What could I tell him of all those years of fidelity and loneliness? I imagine there are days—maybe weeks—when Missy and Scott forget me. I'll be waiting at an intersection, or filling out a job application, or even making love, and I remember that I have a child somewhere, a daughter who was pulled from my body fifteen years ago, whose first words I listened for, whose hands I held between my own and taught to hold a spoon and wash themselves. And I wonder why that wasn't enough—what in me was so impatient that I couldn't bear her childhood out? But before I know an answer, the traffic light will change, my number will be called, the man holding me will cry out my name in the darkness.

"Marriage," I said. "It has good points and bad, like everything else. I just married the wrong person. When you do that, a part of you goes a little crazy after a while. You start wondering who you hate more—yourself for getting into such a fix, or the other person for not being what you want."

Palmer shook his head. "I can't feature being married," he said.

"Oh, come on," I said. I smiled at him over the rim of my glass. "You'd make a terrific husband."

"Yeah?"

"Sure," I said. "You'll see. Someday you'll find somebody nice and it'll be fine."

He looked at me for a few minutes. Then he shook his head. "You don't know what you're talking about," he said.

The wind rifled the leaves of the eucalyptus and kicked up dust in the yard. I sat in the chaise after dinner with a quilt tucked around me. We had run out of ice an hour or two before and the bourbon tasted warm and smoky on my tongue. Palmer sat in the chair beside me, drinking. He'd put on his tweed jacket but his hands trembled around his glass and I asked if he was cold.

"I like winter. I like cold weather," he said. "When I was a kid, we spent New Year's at Tahoe. Snow and ice. Chains on your tires. In Tahoe it gets really cold. Colder than this."

I pulled the quilt tighter. "Maybe. I'm not interested in winter. To me it's something finished, there's nothing to wait for anymore. I like fall—just when the air begins to look different, bluer, and the leaves start to change." I thought for a minute. "It's a lot like making love."

"How?" he said.

"What I like best is knowing it's going to happen. I like that feeling of inevitability more than the sex."

"You're a little crazy, you know that?" Palmer said, and sipped his bourbon.

"Well, the sex is okay, too," I said. "With you."

But then he didn't want to talk about it. He bent his head and wobbled his glass slowly on one knee.

I felt we'd been drinking for hours, but now Palmer didn't seem drunk at all, only difficult to focus on. Bo-Bo came slinking out of the bushes and jumped onto the chaise. He nuzzled at the quilt, and I turned back one edge to let him climb under.

"My old pal," I told him.

Palmer looked over at us. "You could do anything to that cat," he said. "He might bitch, but give him ten minutes and he'll be back rubbing himself on your leg, wanting to be friends again."

"He gets lonely," I said.

"Or hungry."

"Maybe to him they're not so different." I pushed the quilt down and reached for my glass.

Palmer didn't say anything, his face didn't change. He lifted his glass to his lips and set it down again without drinking.

I took another drink and said, "Listen. I want you to meet Missy. She looks just the way I looked when I was her age, but she's nothing like me. You can tell by the way she dresses—even her jeans are ironed." I pulled up the quilt to show my wrinkled pants. The zipper was unzipped and my underwear showed. "Nothing fits me anymore. I used to wear a size 8. Can you believe it, with this belly? My skin's bad now, too. The color, I mean. It looks sallow against my hair. My hair's the only thing about me that still looks decent, and that's only because I pay somebody to keep it that way."

"Carla," Palmer said.

"It's true," I said. "I used to be a lot better looking."

"You're still pretty," he said. "You'd be prettier if you took better care of yourself. You gave Bo-Bo half your steak."

"I eat when I'm hungry," I said. "I don't get hungry anymore. I don't know why I'm so goddamned fat. I can remember when I was nursing Missy. I had an appetite like a truck driver and I never gained an ounce. I'd wake up in the middle of the night to feed her and end up having eggs and toast or a sandwich before I went back to bed. I liked those nights. She'd look almost drunk lying in my arms. But if I moved her, even the slightest way, she'd wake up and begin to feed. And then she'd doze off again."

I watched Palmer lift his hand to his cheek and rub along his jaw. "How did you lose her?" he finally said.

I picked up my drink. "Like a glass slipper. Like a hen that lays golden eggs. You name it. It's just the same."

"No," he said quietly. "It's not. I mean, that night in the bar, you drifted in and you said the right things. I liked it. I needed you. But I could've been just anybody sitting there. And what if I didn't need you? Would that have been it? One night getting drunk together, a fuck on the beach, then nothing? I mean, how many times have you done that, Carla?"

I looked for his face coming out of the shadows. "Well, you weren't just anybody," I said. I tried to look at him more closely—wanted to see if the expression on his face was anything like what I heard in his voice—but either the bourbon or the darkness kept me from it. "Meeting you in a bar has nothing to do with Missy anyway," I said.

"Then why don't you have her?"

"Maybe I didn't want her. Or maybe Scott wanted her more."

"He must have loved you," Palmer said.

"Well, he was wrong."

Palmer poured more bourbon into his glass. I was beginning to feel the drinks, and the cold wind against my face made me sleepy and uncomfortable. I wanted to stop our talk, to go inside and make a place for myself in the bed and sleep until I didn't feel bad anymore.

"So I'm the terrible one," I said, to end it. "But living with him was terrible too. Even this is better. At least I don't have to apologize to anybody for the way I am. I can do what I damned well please. I call my own shots here."

Palmer seemed not to have heard me. "That night in the bar," he said. "That first night. It was like you were coming to me from some place we should have always been together. I was so strung out that night . . ." he rolled his glass between his palms and looked to me. "I don't know," he said. "When I came in from class that afternoon my mother was there with her boyfriend—she was in this little robe, and he had on a pair of swim trunks. And he kept telling me how wonderful it was that we have a pool. I started thinking about my old man, how he wasn't really so bad, you know. You'd look at my parents together and see nothing, just a regular couple. But what was between them must have been hell. My old man never got over it. Even when he was dating a chick with big boobs and driving a white Porsche, he couldn't understand why my mother had 'done that' to him. And he always saw it that way—when she started going out, it was something she was doing to him, it was a personal attack. He died four years ago. Had a heart attack on a sales call—keeled over in somebody's reception room."

I reached for him, touched his knee and almost fell out of the chaise. "Listen," I began.

He steadied me. "Doesn't matter," he said. "Another story, another night. I was talking about something else."

"The bar."

"Right. So finally, the guy left and my mother and I started talking. In about five minutes, she was raving. She told me if I didn't like her life to get the hell out, and started screaming that Dave—Dave with bikini trunks and the rank aftershave—was the only person who cared for her, that I've never loved her, that I blame her for the divorce, for my father's death, for my crummy grades in school, the whole works. When I walked out, she was throwing things into the pool—books, dishes, clothes, stuff out of the refrigerator. She said she'd drown herself."

"Would she?"

Palmer shrugged. "This happens about once a week. I keep thinking I'll get used to it. When I left the house I didn't want to see anybody. And then an hour later there you were. I mean, it's so damned random. I could have gone to another bar and met someone else, or I could have told you to get lost."

"Maybe you should have."

In the silence that followed, Palmer came to sit beside me on the chaise. His face looked brittle, and his pale eyes were hollow in their sockets.

"Why can't you just be what I need?" he finally said. When I didn't answer he put his hand under my chin and turned my face toward him. "You're not Missy's mother. Not anymore."

"You're right," I said carefully. "She's been without me half her life. We don't have much in common anymore. When she's not here I try not to think about her. I don't want her to exist for me unless she's standing in the same room."

Palmer's hand tightened on my chin. "What does exist for you?" he said. "This crummy little neighborhood? That godforsaken cat? Any loser who comes by wanting a fuck?"

I pulled free of his hand. I wanted another drink very badly. I wanted to lie down some place warm, not to talk anymore. I felt around on the ground beside the chaise for my glass. I found it, but when I went to pour in more bourbon the bottle was empty. Then suddenly Palmer was taking things from me—the bottle, the glass, the quilt finally—and as he weighed me down with his body he said so softly that he could almost have been talking to himself, "You love me. Say it. Say you love me."

When I woke it was still dark, and I lay on my side with my face pressed into Palmer's chest. The cold night air bit my shoulders and I pulled up the quilt but it wasn't large enough to cover both of us. I moved my hands underneath Palmer's shirt, along his ribs, and he stirred a little, his arms tightening around me. The smell we gave off was whiskey and the sweet, grassy smell of sex, and it lay so lightly around us that it seemed almost a part of the night.

For a long time I listened to the noises rolling in from the freeway. A car sped by out front and I heard a man yell "Hey Carla! Car-la-a-a-a!" over the fading noise of its radio. Palmer mumbled something and I stroked his face lightly, soothing him back to sleep. He huddled close. I don't remember waiting for the night to pass, but when I opened my eyes again the trees over our heads hung their leaves into fog and everything around us was the air getting colder.

Mary Hood

Few writers portray human character as well as Mary Hood. She has a naturally empathetic ability to see through to the hearts of her characters, to show their deepest feelings and sensitivities, in a way that is neither sentimental nor dispassionate. Her first two collections of stories, *How Far She Went* (winner of the Flannery O'Connor Award for Short Fiction in 1984 and the Southern Review/Louisiana State University Short Fiction Award) and *And Venus Is Blue* (1986, for which she won the Townsend Award), established her as an important American writer. Her novel *Familiar Heat,* set in south Florida, was published in 1996. Hood was born in Brunswick, Georgia, in 1946, and has lived most of her life in Woodstock, Georgia. She earned a B.A. from Georgia State University in 1967. Contemporary in many of her concerns, her early fiction was usually set in the small towns of the north Georgia hills just outside the suburbs of Atlanta. More recently, she has begun to explore characters in other settings. "Virga," set in the American Southwest, is a fine example of Hood's finely drawn evocation of character.

Virga

"Red River Valley" was the song the old woman was humming in Clark's back room when Ada Yazzie knelt before her to wash her feet. The man wouldn't wait on them till she finished. "Nothing personal," Clark said again. "Store policy. Old folks can get a little"—he searched for the word—"rusty, yeah. No offense."

The old woman knew enough English but didn't bother with his, never lifted her gaze past his suede and snakeskin boots, mainly kept her eyes shut, and went on humming. She was ancient. If the sun and dry winds had withered her, they had also preserved her. She had survived by turning her back, not by entreating.

Ada had seldom touched the old woman. They both jumped from the cold hard water, the latherless soap, the sulfurous brown paper towels. She worked lightly, no scrubbing. Ada ignored the man. She had to slip past him to the lavatory sink. Her hands and her heart hurried; she had liked the leathery way the store smelled when they first walked in, but now she was holding her breath against the man's cologne and that camphor smell from the toilet. The basin and the bowl had years of rust stains, the porcelain dulled by harsh and useless scouring. Ada wanted to turn the taps on full, and let the water rush out and swirl, to fill her hands, and drink from them, and sling them dry afterward, but she didn't. She was as careful as though she were home, and the water had come miles to her in a drum on Albert's truck, and she were accountable for each drop.

The old woman seemed asleep, except for the humming. They had walked for two hours after Albert Yazzie's half-ton blew a gasket near Sunrise. It got towed south to Winslow, but they walked and hitched there.

"She was clean when she set out," Ada said.

"Jesus! When was that? Kit Carson's last ride?"

There was no one around to enjoy it, no other customer to dilute Clark's attentions. He settled his shoulder against the doorframe, a shoebox under one crooked arm. He stared down.

As soon as Ada patted the soles of the old woman's feet dry, and stood, the man pulled up the bench and sat. When he measured the old woman's foot he had to use the children's Brannock device, her little hoof was that hard to fit. She wasn't hard to please.

"Like these?" He dangled a kid-size pair of deerskin oxfords from two fingers. Red. That was what she had said, the only word she had spoken. She watched him tie them on her feet and then she stood, turning her back, fishing a trucker's wallet up from under her velveteen shirt. Clark was watching her in the mirror, spying, a little smile for how easy it was. All he was stealing was a look, but he knew better; not looking away was Anglo, knowing he wouldn't answer for any insult. Ada caught him. Watched him in the mirror he was watching the old woman in, until he realized he'd been caught. Ada knew what those mirrors were for; Maxine had caught Ada just like that, three years ago in the camp store mirror, had caught Ada's reflection stealing Tampax when she was twelve years old and still talking to her doll and getting answers . . .

Then Ada's brothers had been in the video game room blasting away with the money they'd found in a pay phone coin return. Ada and the old woman were on the bench out front watching the day drain off behind the San Francisco Peaks, waiting for Albert's truck to come from the grocery store and pick them up. Henry and Bernard kept on playing, faking the games and sound effects when their money ran out, setting Douglas on watch at the side door to catch Eddie's signals—all he was good for so far, too short to even see the screen in the booth, and unable to concentrate on pleasure the way he could focus on dread. Plus, when he shrieked he could strip varnish. It was better than a whistle or a horn. And all he'd yell was "Albert!"

Albert Yazzie was a hard man, careful and practical. They didn't call him father. They called him sir. He took his responsibilities seriously, and he didn't want any help when he laid in supplies. Once a month he shelled out for generic cans by the caseload, lard by the bucket, flour and meal like a Mormon, and he didn't want any of what he called their bubblegum suggestions wrecking what little he had left for a beer budget.

He did most of his drinking at home or on the way; in town he bought it one can at a pop and took his time. He paid for it with scrabbled-up coins or single wadded bills, to fool anyone who might be hoping for a piece of his Park Service check cashed that morning and stashed in his left boot.

He took care of his family, but he was no Ranger Rick. He had a reputation: no one had to throw cactus at him to make him buck. His right boot was the one with the knife, not to get into trouble but to get him out of it. "While I'm breathing, I'm toting," he said.

When he stopped at any of the little lunch spots to bean up, always alone, he'd order the cheapest fare and spoon it down in a blur hurry, drain that one beer then head for the door. He never stayed long, never stood for a round. When owl heads at the bar asked, "What are you saving it for?" he'd hardly pause to think. "Generator and satellite dish" was no answer, it was a Santa Claus dream, so he'd glance out the door at wall-to-wall Arizona and say instead, going for the laugh, "Rainy day." It could have been his nickname, but he didn't have one, not even in the army, not even with his kids. No one called him anything but Albert.

He liked to drop the kids off before he shopped, and the old woman too—his grandmother's sister from Two Grey Hills. Since he had discovered the dinky campground store and playground west of Dry Lake, he dropped them there. It was miles off the main drag and away from the strip malls. If they stayed in town, what they did—the old woman too—was look at things and decide they needed them. One time it was refrigerator magnets. The youngest one, Eddie, had the kind of tantrum over them that no threat or distraction can cure; there was heartbreak in it, and grief, like being stripped of love and hope and left raw and exposed on a bleak rock brow for the vultures. He didn't cry like that—none of them had—when their mother died. This was craziness, all these tears for plastic butterflies. "We don't have a refrigerator," Albert kept trying to explain, louder and louder over Eddie's riot. The store manager came, and a deputy, so Albert bought the magnets.

All the way home Eddie had sat bunched on a lambskin in the corner of the cab snubbing and snuffling and chewing on the corner of the package. He lost interest before he lost the magnets later, but for a while he stuck them to the sides of this steel drum or that, or the fender of the truck, or the washtub, eye-high to a three-year-old, proving whatever it was that needed proving.

Albert made sure after that episode the kids didn't tag along with him. He'd charge the older ones to watch out for the younger, and all of them to stay out of the manager's hair. Maybe he'd give them money, enough for one arcade game each, or candy or popcorn to share. He expected them out front—their chip bags empty and the last salt licked from their lips—when he drove in, and no trash, literal or figurative, in their wake. He wanted to keep things smooth between him and the campground.

When he came to pick them up, he'd top off the truck's tank at the diesel pump and brim the jerrycan with unleaded for the lanterns. Before the store had changed hands, he and the night clerk—sometimes a geezer, other times a local kid just past the birthday which made it legal—would knock back a couple of cans of Albert's beer still sweating from the grocer's cooler. Meanwhile, in fair exchange, the kids would be around back at the hose tap, filling rinsed-out gallon milk jugs with city water. It made better coffee than the alkali stuff windmilled into the tank at the tribal reservoir.

Albert hadn't pushed his luck about the tap water lately. He didn't know the new owner, Maxine. She wasn't the clerk type; she was the boss type, and her own steady hand had painted the warning over the old Bardahl sign: New Management.

Maxine came out of the store, leaving the door wide open, propped with a chunk of lava. "*Ya ta hey!*" she said to Ada and the old woman on the bench. Ada didn't answer. The old woman nodded, inviting her to sit beside her. From a pocket in her red flannel underskirt, she drew a weaver's comb, offering to sell it for tobacco. When Ada saw it, she stood up. She walked around. Albert didn't want them trading, but Ada didn't have a say about the old woman. The old woman had not been a weaver for many years, and she kept her wallet from dying of starvation with these plundered little handfuls. There was always someone who'd pay.

Maxine examined the comb; she was interested in the old ways and means. Didn't her cash register stand on an antique wood and glass showcase filled with local rocks and fossils and bits of bowls and tools? Everything labeled, even the old thumb-buster pistol and part of a fire-scarred trapdoor Springfield she had sifted out of the debris in the canyon where trash had been cairning up for years over the bones of a Navajo vengeance against bride stealers. Maxine stressed that she did not collect bones, even if she could have told sheep from horse, man from maiden, Apache from Diné. She had other rules too.

"I can't take this," Maxine said, handling the comb. The old woman looked at her, signaled Ada to come translate. "Museum quality," Maxine said. It was handcarved and smooth with decades of lanolin from the wool. "I can't afford it. No way."

"No way," Ada said.

The old woman stood abruptly. She was spry. "*Ya ta hey,*" she said with an angered shrug. She moved off across the graveled lot, beyond the fenced-off LP tank, to sulk by the road with her back turned.

Maxine hustled after her.

Ada didn't follow. Maxine's English, even with her Sonoran accent, was good enough if the old woman weren't so stubborn. "Too good, too much. No trade," Maxine was saying. "Worth too much." She glanced Ada's way, appealing for help. She tried her native back-country Spanish when Ada held out.

The old woman let her rave, then bottom-lined, in English. "No trade. Cash dolla."

They were silhouettes: Maxine taller and sturdy in her Levi's, her broad hands heavy with their seven turquoise rings gesturing across the gap between her and the desiccated little weaver bundled in skirts and velveteen. Maxine lit a cigarette for each of them.

Silence while the old one smoked and Maxine considered. Ada sat on the bench alone, and waited. She could hear her brothers in the game room. None of them had ever so much as touched a ten-dollar bill that was his very own. They had nothing yet that was their very own except their blood, nothing worth pawning or selling or trading away. Ada touched her silver barrette, her mother's, a bride gift. That was out of the question, of course. She watched the two women smoking. They might have been landforms, dark against the last light in the world. They were a mile high. There was nothing between them and the first clear stars but those sheer mouthfuls of smoke.

They were laughing! They had forgotten all about Ada. Maxine was pointing with her whole arm across the desert, northwest toward the Vermilion Cliffs where heat lightning shimmered. Underfoot, through the marrowless cooling bones of the earth, Ada could feel the tremor of the westbound Santa Fe, mile long, miles off. The old woman was shaking her head. The wind had dropped, but sounds of traffic on the highway were still blown away like the smoke around their words.

The campground was empty. Under repair. Only the store was open. The sole customers were Ada's brothers still horsing around in the game room, out of coins now, but rapt and rowdy at doubles table tennis, their sneakers squealing on Maxine's fresh wax job, their shouts ping-ponging with each swaggering score or missed shot—nothing to Ada but background noise. She was used to them; she knew them by heart. The boys were making their points and the old woman and Maxine were out in the dark dealing for dollars and Albert was Billy Hell-knew-where. Not there, that was the main thing. Ada slipped from the bench then and went into the store. The door was still wide open. She really thought that all she was going to do was look at the shackled bird.

Maxine had a sage-green parrot with a tiny silver anklecuff and chain tethering it to its beak-stripped perch. It could move back and forth and even fly over to the counter and step along on its crippled-looking feet. From time to time it croaked caustic Spanish in a shrill, tired way, as though it had learned from someone old and bitter. Something in Ada hoped the chain would break, but she was afraid too of what the bird might do with freedom. She picked a grape from the bunch in the feed bowl and rolled it along the counter. The bird nabbed it and slowly palpated it with its dark and leathery tongue that was like a tiny gloved finger. When it had swallowed, the parrot ruffled itself all over, flew to its perch, spread its wings, and flogged the air. The noise was like the sound in Ada's dream that past winter, the final dream she had had as a White Shell Girl, before she changed into a woman.

In her dream a tree fell, a tree larger than any she had ever seen alive. As large as the trunks in the petrified forest. There were no leaves on the tree, for it was winter, and there was snow. The land was white. When the tree had begun to fall, Ada saw that she could not stop it, and she did not try. She simply watched. The tree slowly tipped toward the earth, and when it finally struck, the snow hushed the sound. The tree split like a pod along its lightning-hollowed length. From the opening flew birds, east, south, west, and north, dozens of birds like bats from a cave, or swifts spiraling upward in skeins, all kinds of birds, all sizes, all colors—jays, larks, thrashers, wrens, doves, hawks, sparrows, desert birds, mountain birds, waterhole birds, cave birds, fetish birds and real birds, birds brown as owls and birds bright as coral and turquoise. They flapped free and flew with a card-shuffle sound, higher and higher in the clear sky, and were lost in the sun, leaving no trace, no track, not even a feather. Ada's heart beat like a pot drum as she stepped up to the hollow trunk, bent, and looked in.

Among the dry splinters and limed walls of the tree's heart there was one brown knot. It looked like wood, but a slight wind turned the soft feathers and called Ada to put out her hands to it: a bird! She deeply pitied its sudden ruinous exposure, its deathly stillness.

When she lifted the bird to her, it was warm. She knew then this sleep wasn't death, but life waiting for its season. Since there was nowhere else to shelter it, she put it inside her shirt. She felt its tiny cold feet uncurl and grip to her as it resettled in its sleep, in hers.

Ada had slept all the rest of the night on her back, her hands lightly doming over her heart to protect the little bird dreaming in her dream. When she woke, the sun was already well up and Albert was outside shaking the frost off the blanket on his truck hood, hoping for one more crank from that old battery. It was a school day. Ada stood quickly, and in her sleepy confusion as she felt the first lunar trickle down her thigh she thought she had—despite her care—crushed the little bird, and this was its warm blood leaking, not her own. Then she understood the movie at school that gave all the science but not the magic. Ada decided she would tell no one about this Changing Woman business. The old woman was her only female kin close enough for confidences and yet not open to these, holding it against Ada that she had been born to a Zuni mother, not Navajo.

"Let *them* teach you," the old woman had answered when Ada asked her if there would be a singing ceremony and a blessing cake.

But how could they teach her, when she had never seen any of them again after her mother died and they cast the death sand and cloth into the river? Albert had vanished for four days while his wife's spirit traveled to the underworld, and when he came back, purified and safe from haunting, they had moved away from Zuni, where the roads were paved and the broken bottles sparkled under streetlights, and family and neighbors lived nearby.

Ada's mother's mother had had a washing machine and water in the kitchen from a tap and a flush toilet and bathtub. They had used bar soap that smelled like clover. For almost a year Ada had been taught by the nuns. Her school uniform had been starched, with a smell of wintergreen and lemon, and ironed smooth, and the meals cooked with electricity. Only the ceremonial bread had been baked outdoors.

Albert had moved them back to his own people, a winter house on dry land, and another place near stream water for summer grazing for the horse and sheep. The stream was ankle deep, never even wading depth, and nowhere along its length a hole where a person could float or bathe. Ada learned other ways. She watched the old woman and learned how to be private in the bushes at the summer place. At the winter lodge there was an outhouse. And a wooden crate up in the piñon tree for an icebox. She got used to drinking powdered milk and washing in cold water and wasting nothing. Chores toughened her hands, but her skin was too thin to do what the boys and Albert did, taking up a live coal in their fingertips to use as a match.

No matter how nice the clothes smelled when she folded them into the black bags to bring home from the laundry, everything—winter and summer—stank of fire smoke and frybread, even, despite Ada's best efforts, her own long hair. A year earlier Ada had gotten a free sample of shampoo at school from a girl who sold Avon. The shampoo had the scent of berries and vanilla, and when Albert smelled it, he reacted as though it were contraband, perhaps shoplifted (how else?) candy, or more impossible, perfume. He ducked inside and lit the lantern. His shadow reached to the wall. It dodged and trailed as he searched. He sniffed his way through the hogan till he located it. He pulled Ada out of his own shadow. "On you? That's you? Where is it?"

She thought he meant the shampoo. She said, "It was a sample, it's all gone."

"No, it's not," he said. "I could smell you out by the corral." He leaned closer. "Did you roll in it? Bring it here."

Ada found the empty packet, no bigger than one of those single portion sugar servings. He read it, read the list of ingredients, pronouncing them all, proving something. " 'No animal testing'?" he read, and threw it in the stove. His hands were tough enough he didn't even hurry touching the handle.

"Your hair," he said.

"It was free."

"Plenty to do in the barn," Albert warned his sons.

The boys got out then, even Eddie, who ran after them up the slope in boots not quite all the way on, lurching as he tried to zip his jacket, crying, as always, over the gap between himself and his heart's desire.

Now Ada was alone. The old woman was already gone, somewhere in the hills since noon, looking for a dark lamb she had dreamed about losing.

"Nothing's ever free," Albert told her. Just what he said about the government "commodities" and school lunch. He was like the coyote who sniffs the bait and trots on. Ada thought of the way the boys checked every pay phone for coins, and how she never left a penny on a sidewalk, even face down. Things worse than bad luck.

"You hear?"

"Yes, sir."

He flipped the hair on her shoulder with the back of his hand. "You get that stink off of you by dark or I'm cutting it off." He picked up the horse's bucket where he'd thrown it on the way in, and dipped it full of water from the blue barrel. She thought at first he was going to wash her hair himself, or maybe dunk her head in something he used on the stock, but he went on past her as though she weren't even there. He whistled; the mare trotted up to the fence, and he put his hand on her neck, talking low. The boys gathered to him also, like doves around a puddle. Eddie said something and they all laughed. That was when Ada's face burned like fever.

They didn't use shampoo. The boys and Albert used bar soap, or soapweed when they were camping, and all Ada was was trouble. She'd learned early if she wanted to soothe her chapped hands, she'd better use lard, nothing Albert had to buy special. That's what it was, this time, about the shampoo. He hadn't begun that other crazy stuff yet, about her being fast, about her "looking for trouble." She had gone past the White Shell stage by two years or so when he started that. He had never noticed her changing, and then one day he did. He seemed to be angry all the time, full of blame for crimes she hadn't even thought of.

Albert knew how to make soap and tea and medicines from the desert plants, and if she had asked him, he could have helped her find and brew snakebroom to ease her stomachaches, but she was ashamed to ask. Ada made do; she wore clumsy rags to school and got monthly supplies from the nurse, but when school was out for the summer she had to think of something else.

She did not intend to steal from Maxine. It all happened gradually. First the open door and the way the parrot flapped its wings and reminded her of her dream. Then the coin-sized little fossil like a crushed bug, labeled "400,000,000 years old," in Maxine's showcase. Eight zeroes. Ada counted them twice. "If that was dollars, I could own the world," Ada told the parrot. The bird made her uneasy, watching. She was glad when it turned its back and went to sleep, hunched, indifferent; it reminded Ada of the old woman, the way she could pull the blanket on its wire and shut out the whole world. Even though Ada was inside it with her, in the same sleeping space, she knew she had been left alone.

Suppose I could buy anything in this store, Ada asked herself. She walked up and down the aisles looking but not touching. She stood in front of the sunglasses kiosk. She lingered at the magazine rack. She leaned against the freezer unit and studied the ice cream novelties. She glanced at the candy counter, the kitchen utensils on their hooks, the detergents and mousetraps and insect repellents for hikers and rockhounds. She stepped over the metal detector. In the end, she touched only what she took, and she stole only what she needed. She did not pretend it was someone else's hand; she did not pretend it wasn't happening. She did not think at all. She had the single box concealed in back between her skin and waistband; plenty of room in her brother's hand-me-down jeans. They were boy-cut; she wasn't. She had her oversize T-shirt pulled loosely down in back and was about to go outside again and sit on the bench when Maxine came in to get the dollars for the old woman's deal on the weaving comb.

Maxine put the comb in the locked showcase. She made a label too. She was writing it as Ada was halfway out the door. "What's her name, anyway?" Maxine asked. "She says she won't tell me."

Ada turned around. "She won't."

The mirror was behind Ada, a circle mirror like a hubcap, high up on the wall. Maxine swiveled on her desk stool, adjusted her glasses, and gave another look. "X-A-P-M . . ." she spelled, then said, "Well, well now, how do you spell *Tampax* backwards?" She could read it plain as that, through Ada's old T-shirt. Could see the blue package where Ada had stuck it. Ada didn't cry. They just looked at each other.

"My father was *un hombre de campo*," Maxine said. She made a fist and shook it. "Like rock." She gestured toward Old Mexico. "Country on four sides. My mother—" She studied Ada, made a shot in the dark. "How long has your mother been dead?"

Ada didn't say anything. She took the box from its hiding place and laid it on the counter.

Maxine did not act as though this were in any way extraordinary. "Glad to," she said. She rang No Sale on the cash register and bagged the supplies and handed them back. Transaction complete. Maxine asked, "Is that all you need?" Ada just stood there. Finally Maxine put the package in Ada's hand. When the girl turned to leave, Maxine said, "Welcome to the club."

That was how their friendship began.

Albert ended it three years later, the Saturday his engine blew and the old woman bought the red shoes. The truck had been towed to Simpson's All-Nite All-Rite Garage. When Ada and the old woman left Clark's shoestore, they headed that way, walking till the sidewalk ran out. Traffic was heavy for a Monday because of Memorial Day weekend, and tourists cruised slowly along the street, rubbernecking the jewelry and "native" crafts spread on camp tables and blankets and pickup tailgates. On the outskirts, a winter's worth of hammered silver and sky-blue stone strewn in the sunshine. Business was brisk. The old woman knew many of the sellers, and she zigzagged across four lanes to visit. The crepe soles on her new shoes had thawed ten hard years from her stiff gait. Ada dodged after her.

The late spring sun had charmed Ada's denim jacket off; she tied its sleeves around her waist. A fuzzy-armed fellow with a freckled hand reached to Ada's ear and touched the ring. "Is that—"

"No, sir," Ada said, and moved past him. The crowd blocked her way. She lost sight of the old woman, but she could hear her talking to someone at Jenny Tsotsee's booth. The man who had touched her earring caught up. "How do you know what I—"

Ada sideslipped into the throng and left him behind. She threaded past the tables and trucks and up the graveled grade to the Santa Fe rails. She made a visor of her hands and stared hard through the shimmer. She could see Albert's crew cab on the pocked asphalt apron where the tow had dropped it off its hook. It wasn't even in the workbay yet. When they pushed it in, it would still be hours, maybe all night. A long night, dozing on plastic chairs somewhere public with fluorescent lights buzzing, or maybe Albert would herd them all to the truck stop, and they'd prop each other up in a booth, nursing cold milky coffee and making their ketchup on crackers last, trying to look like customers rather than vagrants, the way they got through it when Eddie had pneumonia and the clinic kept him three days.

Albert had told them to gather at Simpson's for lunch. By the sun they were near noon, but they had missed Albert by twenty minutes. He and the parts man were already on their way to Holbrook, the nearest place open, for a head gasket. Albert left them a message, to be there at four o'clock, or—"And I quote," the mechanic said—"'ya ass is grass.'" Albert had left them two bucks each and makings for a do-it-yourself lunch—bologna and loaf bread, a bag of corn chips. If they wanted Pepsi, they could throw their money away on it. He wouldn't.

They set to, even the old woman. Ada and the younger boys ate in the truck, doors wide open. The old woman sat in there too, but Henry, the oldest, had hopes, maybe even plans, and kept pacing back and forth on the shady side watching the road for Frank Luo, who had already circled by twice, inviting him—"You seventeen, *what* permission?"—and Ada too, if she wanted, "Just to ride around."

He backed so hard the little car hunkered down, squealing. Then he goosed it, kicking up sand. They had to turn away to keep the grit out of their food and eyes.

"I'll be back," Frank warned.

Ada started not to go. But it was hot and Eddie was a dead weight in her lap where he had fallen over, and the old woman and Douglas and Bernard were already conked out, catching up on sleep lost in their early start. Ada wasn't tired, but if she had been, where would she stretch out? On the three bags of dirty laundry in the back?

Ada checked the time. Almost two o'clock. She didn't really want to go, but Henry meant to. He was bouncing up and down, stiff-legged, on the balls of his feet, raring. Frank looked excited too, but in that glazed and jittery way he always looked, like the boys at school kiting on white-out and Magic Markers.

"Going as far as Dry Lake?" Henry wouldn't ask flat out, just hint, and hope.

"What's out there?" Frank glanced at his fuel gauge, then his watch. Before Ada could say "laundry," Henry made arcade noises and mumbled, "Mortal Kombat, Whirlwind, ThunderJaws," in a robot voice.

He tapped himself on the chest. "Looking at Whirlwind all-time high."

Frank said, instantly, "Ya not."

"One-oh-eight-one-two, two twenty," he said.

Ada knew Frank didn't have a clue. "Ten million, eight hundred and twelve thousand—"

"ArchRivals," Henry said, like she wasn't even speaking.

Frank's face lit up. "BasketBrawl?"

"Hell yeah," Henry agreed.

And just like that they slapped palms. They got in the front seats, and Ada risked their temper by how long it took to stuff the three bags of dirty clothes in the back seat and then wedge herself into the Civic on top. It was a quarter a load cheaper at the campground to wash, and only a penny a minute to dry. Ada figured if the garage didn't get the truck repaired by dark, they'd be spending the night in town anyway. At least this way, it wouldn't be in a laundromat, lugging clothes up and down the road at all hours like a string of ants hauling off whole raisins. She squirmed herself upright and balanced the bleach bottle on her sneakers. The detergent was her armrest. As they bounced along, she counted time. If she planned everything just right, she'd more than make it, have the clothes clean in the bags, her own self clean in her clean clothes, and her hair dried under the hand dryer on the wall in the restroom with plenty of time to spare for Frank to get them back to the garage by four.

Even so, she hurried. Frank went on through the store to the game room. At least Henry carried one of the bags in. He dropped it at the door of the laundry, and vanished. Maxine helped Ada get the other two in. Ada overfilled the machines because she had only the two dollars. Albert hadn't given her the money for the wash yet. She had some change in her pocket, and she had enough. As soon as the machines were churning, Maxine stopped back by. She had Ada's shampoo kit, which the girl left there each time. Shampoo and a comb, towel, one of Albert's shirts big enough for a coverup. Ada ran to the ladies room and stripped, put on Albert's shirt, and ran back to the laundry with her clothes, stuffed them in the wash, and fled to the showers. She wore the towel around her shoulders like a shawl, as though she were just coming from the pool. Maxine had no pool. Ada liked to look that way, even though she was dry.

Soon enough she was wet. She always went to the farthest stall, pulled the canvas curtain, and spun the handles all the way to hot, so the water would be warming up as she laid out her things on the bench: shampoo, creme rinse, shower gel, luffa mitt, and pumice stone for her heels, knees, and elbows. She even had a tiny jar of cream for them, after. "Skin polish," it was called, as though she were furniture, or shoes. All of these things she had afforded over time, and at great sacrifice. She had learned how to look for *sensitive* on the labels; that meant there was no fragrance, or very little, any of which she could attribute to the laundry detergent, if Albert mentioned it on the way home. She had first kept her things in a grocery bag, but Maxine had presented her with a large plastic food saver with a snap-on lid. Ada kept it and the towel in a nylon backpack which Maxine hung on a hook in her storeroom. Sometimes Ada woke at night and thought about it hanging there, safe, secret. For a long time Ada did not have her name on it, and then she did. The first night she had left it there labeled, she felt as though she had given herself away. She felt she had done something wrong. Like the old woman said she felt when the tourists wanted to take her picture and then just drive off with her in their camera, forever.

Even though she loved the toiletries and the ritual, what Ada loved most was the water. She gathered her hair up in a coil and pinned it with the barrette, to keep it off her shoulders while she bathed. She stood adjusting it to its fullest hottest blast, till her skin smoked in the cool air, then she turned off the hot and let the cold humble her. She dialed up moderate steam, she reached to the shower head and aimed it low, she stood on one leg and sanded her heels smooth as river stones. She had a razor and she used it. Albert would never know—how would he know? She wore jeans and tees and jackets, she wore socks and ugly shoes. She scrubbed her skin with the luffa mitt and foaming gel, and rinsed and rinsed till suds swirled around her ankles. She always did all this before she unclipped the smooth silver barrette and let her hair fall.

She had lathered twice and conditioned and was letting the water comb her long hair into obsidian sheets, had turned her back on the spray and then swung around—water streaming over her crown and shoulders, and then her upturned face as she reached for the handles to turn them off—when Albert kicked the door open, splashed through the water draining into the center of the dressing room floor, and found her. He didn't call her name, but Maxine did. Maxine ran behind him saying, "Ada!" and then "Mr. Yazzie, no!" and then "You can't," and "Ada!" again. But by that point he had ripped the canvas curtain to one side of the stall and reached right in, catching Ada by the hair.

He dragged her naked from privacy into the dressing room by the lavatories and mirrors. "Look at yourself," he said. "Look at what you are."

Maxine said, "*You.*" Maxine said, "You look at what *you* are. I'm calling the law and I'm bringing my gun back when I come"—here she had the shirt the girl had been using for a robe and was trying to get it onto her wet arms, Ada trembling, Maxine shaking, and Albert so steady—"and I won't be late." Maxine got the shirt onto Ada's other arm, and began to button it. "Let go!" she said, fiercely. And he did, only to take hold of the girl's hair.

Ada had her eyes shut. Ada was inside, behind her eyes. Ada was somewhere between times, like that backpack hanging on its hook.

Maxine ran. But what difference did it make by then? Albert had already kicked the bench out of his way, and all her little kit, comb, razor, barrette, and polishes had gone flying. Some of the bottles broke. The shower was still running. Ada listened to that. That was what Ada heard. When Albert opened his knife, she didn't know what it was. She didn't brace or flinch till he cut; he cut just once. Right above his fist wrapped in her hair, he freed himself with one fierce swift downward slice. His hand was trapped but nothing would stop him. He was in control; he cut the hair, only the hair. Not himself, not Ada. He cut the middle of her hair off right at the back of her skull, one rich fistful. He left a gap on the right and a hank over her other ear. That was all he left, and that was all he cut. No fixing it, no hiding it, she'd have to lop the rest with her own hands and the sheep shears. It would be shorter than Eddie's after they shamed him home from school with lice.

Albert let her go then, and walked out. At the door he threw the hair down, so when Maxine came back, with a pair of clean jeans, she stepped on it and screamed. Albert and the boys were in the laundry, even Frank Luo was helping stuff the dryer—hot clothes into the same old bags, not folding. Nobody said a thing. Ada dressed and got her feet into her shoes, no socks. She wasn't crying. She went to the hot-air hand-dryer and ducked under its jet to groom her hair. When the air went over the blank place, she reached up and felt it, slowly, and still she didn't cry. She didn't look in the mirror, or at the floor. She just waited.

"Honey?" Maxine said.

"He'll be back," Ada explained. Waiting.

"Let's go," Albert said at the door; this time he didn't barge in. One of the campers had come, and was watching. Several were gathered in the parking lot, looking and then looking away. The boys had the laundry out to Frank's car by then, but Albert had come in a wangled Park Service pickup, and after a moment, Frank and Henry slam-dunked it into the back. One of the bags split. The sky looked bad, really bad, and they could hear thunder. "Nah," Henry said. Like he knew.

Maxine, with her little pistol, followed Albert out. "Listen to me," she said. But he didn't even slow down.

"You be glad this thing's not loaded," she said. That made the boys laugh.

"Aw-right," she said, "listen to me."

Ada pushed past her and got into the truck.

"Not up here," Albert said, like he could smell something. Ada got out and stepped up on the bumper and over into the bed. Henry rode in front.

"Don't go," Maxine told Ada.

But Ada was only fifteen.

"Citizen's arrest," Maxine told Albert. Frank Luo had his Honda cranked and revved, and was out of there. Nobody even waved. "What do I tell the police when they get here?" Maxine said to Albert. At least he had rolled down his window.

"Tell them they missed me," Albert said, and drove off.

He picked up the others at the garage. The truck wouldn't be ready for three days. The old woman rode up front, with Henry and Eddie. The rest—"Shake and bake time," Bernard said—jostled along in back. The wind dried Ada to the bone in only a few miles. Her hair—the barrette was gone—flew and whipped. The sky was dark and promising, clouds heavy with water already beginning to fringe at the bottom so that she drew her breath, to catch rain scent on the land. She rode with her back braced against the side of the truck, facing north; she could see all the sky from east to west. The clouds ran ahead of them, and behind them. Plummy rich clouds with the rain falling in long gray and silver streaks. Virga rain, rain that falls but never hits the ground. A desert kind of rain. Maybe a bird besides the thunderbird could fly through it, go up where the rain was, like the nuns' kingfisher flying through the rainbow. But there was lightning, sometimes hail, and other dangers. The thunderbird could catch the lightning in its claws; his hurled bolts hit the ground, but the rain did not. In a land so dry, it was enough to hope that the sky itself would somehow have the good of the storm, though it never refreshed the earth. She could imagine that, how that could be, but she could not imagine why.

Ha Jin

Xuefei Jin (Ha Jin is a pen name) was born in 1956 in Liaoning, China. At the age of fourteen, during the Cultural Revolution, he joined the Chinese army and served for six years. This experience has proved a major influence in his work. In 1985 he immigrated to the United States, and by 1990 he had published his first collection of poetry, *Between Silences.* He began teaching in the creative writing program at Emory University the next year, and a succession of poetry and story collections quickly followed. He won the Flannery O'Connor Award for Short Fiction for *Under the Red Flag* in 1998, the PEN/Hemingway Award for first fiction for *Ocean of Words,* also in 1998, and the National Book Award for Fiction and the PEN/Faulkner Award for Fiction in 2000 for his novel *Waiting.* In all, since 1992 he has published two collections of poetry, five story collections, and three novels. Place is an important force in Jin's work, but it is not the place of Georgia or America. He writes in English exclusively about the land of his birth. Jin has said, "If I am inspired, it is from within. Very often I feel that the stories have been inside me for a long time, and that I am no more than an instrument for their manifestation. As for the subject matter, I guess we are compelled to write about what has hurt us most."

Too Late

It began as a bet at the Spring Festival. After the feast, the soldiers of my company were playing chess and poker, chatting and cracking roasted peanuts and sunflower seeds. In the Second Platoon some men were talking about women and bragging of their own ability to resist female charms. Gradually their topic shifted to the Shanghai girls at the Youth Home in Garlic Village. How were the girls doing on the holiday eve? What a pity there was no man in their house. Who would dare to go have a look and ask if they miss their parents and siblings?

Someone said he would pay a Spring Festival call on the girls after eleven. Another boasted that he would take a bottle of wine to that house and have a cup with them. Emboldened by alcohol and the festive atmosphere, they indulged themselves in the big talk.

Then Kong Kai declared he dared to go and sleep on the same brick bed with the girls. This was too much. Everybody thought he just wagged his tongue, and they told him to draw a line somewhere if he wanted to talk sense. But a few men challenged him and even proposed a five-yuan bet. To their amazement, Kong swung his quilt roll on his back and set off for the Youth Home.

There was only one young man living at that house, but he had left to spend the holiday with his family in Shanghai. Unlike the country women, those city girls had tender limbs and looked rather elegant. They knew how to use makeup and wore colorful clothes.

Kong entered the Youth Home and dropped his quilt at the end of the brick bed. The five girls were too shocked to stop him. He climbed on the bed, spread his quilt, lay down, and closed his eyes. For half an hour, they didn't know what to do about this man, who wouldn't respond to their questioning and tittering and instead was sleeping or pretending to be asleep. They brought out candies, chocolates, and frozen pears in the hope of inducing him to open his mouth, which like his eyes was shut all the time. They even cooked him a large bowl of dragon-whiskers noodles with garlic, ginger, and two poached eggs, hoping the fragrance might arouse his appetite. Nothing worked. One of them put a few lamp-soot stains on his face, saying, "This makes him look more handsome." They giggled; still he remained motionless. Finally, the five girls decided to keep watch on him by turns throughout the night, for fear he might do something unusual once they went to sleep, though they knew Kong by sight and didn't feel he was a bad man. Each of them sat beside him for one and a half hours while the rest were sleeping at the other end of the large bed. The oil lamp was burning until dawn.

On hearing of the incident at daybreak, Commander Deng and I set out for Garlic Village right away. It was crisply cold, and a large flock of crows were gliding over the snow-covered fields, clamoring hungrily. A few firecrackers exploded in the village that sprawled ahead like a deserted battlefield. Among some wisps of cooking smoke, two roosters were crowing on and on, as if calling each other names. In the north, the Wusuli River almost disappeared in the snow, and beyond it a long range of cedar woods stretched on the hillside like a gigantic spearhead pointing to the Russians' watchtower, which was wavering in the clouds. Though day was unfolding, the Russians' searchlight kept flickering.

When we arrived Kong was still in bed. The girls were all up, some washing clothes while others were combing and braiding their hair. They looked jubilant, humming light tunes and giggling as if something auspicious had descended on their household. At the sight of us they stopped.

"Lock up the door and don't let anyone out," Commander Deng cried. With a mitten he wiped the frost off his mustache, his deep-sunk eyes glinting. He spat a cigarette end to the floor and stamped it out. Orderly Zhu executed the orders.

Kong Kai heard the noise and got out of bed to meet us. He didn't look worried and gave us a toothy grin. His broad face was smeared with soot, but he still had on his fur hat, whose earflaps were tied together under his chin. I felt relieved; it seemed he hadn't taken off his clothes during the night. We brought him into the inner room and began our questioning.

It took us only a few minutes to finish with him. He tried to convince us that he had slept well. That must have been a lie. How could a young man sleep peacefully while a girl was sitting nearby with her eyes on him all the time? And another four sleeping on the same bed? Didn't he know his face still had stains of lamp soot on it? But we didn't ask him those questions, for it wasn't important for us to know how he had felt and what he knew. We cared only what he had done.

Convinced that nothing serious had taken place, we put him aside and brought in the girls one by one. Each questioning was shorter than two minutes. "Did he touch you?" Deng asked a tall, pale-faced girl, whom we had got hold of first.

"No." She shook her head.

"Did he say anything to you?"

"Un-un."

"Yes or no?"

"No."

"Did he ever take off his clothes?"

"No."

In the same manner we went through the other four girls, who gave us identical answers. Then we brought our man home, believing the case was closed. On the way back I criticized Kong briefly for intruding into a civilian house without any solid reason, especially on the Spring Festival's Eve, when the Russians were most likely to cross the border and nobody was allowed to leave the barracks.

At once Kong became a hero of a sort. Those foolish boys called him "an iron man." Together with his fame, numerous versions of his night adventure were circulating in the company. One even said that the girls had welcomed Kong's arrival and lain beside him by turns throughout the night, patting his face, murmuring seductive words, and even drawing a thick mustache on his lip with charcoal, but the iron man hadn't budged a bit, as though he were unconscious. We tried to stop them from creating these kinds of silly stories and assured them that the girls were fine, not as bad as they thought. They'd better cleanse their own minds of dirty fantasies.

A month later Kong's squad leader, Gu Chong, was transferred to the battalion headquarters, to command the antiaircraft machine gun platoon there. Gu suggested we let Kong take over the Fifth Squad. Indeed Kong seemed to be an ideal choice; the men in our company respected him a lot, and he was an excellent soldier in most ways. So we promoted him to squad leader.

Who could tell "the iron man" would be our headache? In a few weeks it was reported that Kong often sneaked out in the evenings and on weekends to meet a girl at the Youth Home. There were larch woods at the eastern end of Garlic Village; it was said that Kong and the girl often wandered in the woods. I talked to him about this. He said they had gone in there only to pick mushrooms and daylilies. What a lie. I told him to stop pretending. Who would believe the iron man had become a mushroom picker accompanied by a girl? I wanted him to quit the whole thing before it was too late, and I reminded him of the discipline that allowed no soldier to have an affair.

One Sunday morning in April, Orderly Zhu reported that Kong had disappeared from the barracks again. Immediately I set out with Scribe Yang for the larch woods. When we got there we came upon two lines of fresh footprints on the muddy slope. We followed them. Without much difficulty we found the lovers, who were sitting together by a large rock. They saw us approaching, and they got up and slipped away into the woods. We walked over and found five golden candy wrappers at the spot. I told the scribe to pick up the wrappers, and together we returned.

Scribe Yang said he recognized the girl, whose name was An Mali. The tall, pale-faced one, he reminded me. I recalled questioning her and didn't feel she was a bad girl at all, but a rule was a rule, which no one should break. Kong was creating trouble not only for himself but also for our company. We had to stop him.

Soon the leader of the Second Platoon reported that there had been confrontations between Kong and some men in the Fifth Squad. One soldier openly called him "womanizer."

In May we held the preliminary election of exemplary soldiers. As usual, we had all the guns and grenades and bazookas locked away at the company's headquarters for five days, for fear somebody might be so upset about not being elected that he would resort to violence. There had been bloodshed during the election in other units, and we had to take precautions.

All the squad leaders were voted in except Kong Kai, though three of his men got elected. The soldiers complained that Kong had a problematic life-style. Commander Deng and I worried about the results of the election, particularly about Kong, so we decided to talk to him.

After taps, we had him summoned to our office. The kerosene lamp on the desk was shining brighter with the new wick Orderly Zhu had put in. I walked to the window to look out at the moonlit night while Deng read a newspaper at the desk. Beside his elbow lay a blue notebook and a pen; whenever he came across a new word, he would write it down. He had only three years' education.

In the distance a Russian helicopter was flickering and hammering away among the stars. The hills beyond the border loomed like huge graves. I was wondering how Kong had started the affair. When we had questioned him and the girls three months before, we had been quite certain nothing had happened to him. How did the seed of love enter his brain? Was it because she had smeared lamp soot on his face?

Kong's stocky body emerged on the drill ground coming to the headquarters. I returned to the desk and sat down by Deng. "Take a seat, Little Kong," I said the moment he stepped in.

Straight to the point, we asked him what he thought of the election, and he admitted he felt bad about being voted out. His almond eyes kept flashing at us. I handed him a cigarette, which he declined.

"Three months ago," Deng said, "you were 'an iron man' in your comrades' eyes, but all of a sudden you become a womanizer to them. How can you explain the change?"

"I'm not a womanizer."

"Let's get this straight," I said. "When we picked you up at the Youth Home, you said you hadn't done anything with the girls. Did you lie to us?"

"No, I didn't."

"Then how did you hit it off with An Mali?" Deng asked. Kong remained silent, biting his bottom lip.

"Little Kong," I resumed, "there must have been something between you two which you've hidden from us."

"No, I didn't hide anything. I didn't know it when we came back together."

"Know what?" Deng said.

"The note. She left a note in my breast pocket. I didn't know it till three days later."

"Let's have a look at it." Deng stretched out his hand, and Kong slowly took out his wallet and produced the note. Deng read it and then passed it to me and cursed, "Bitch."

On the scrap of yellow paper there were these few words:

I know you. Your name is Kong Kai. — An Mali.

No one could say that was a secret message or a love note, so I said to Kong, "There's nothing unusual in this. It doesn't explain the affair."

"I was curious to see how she knew my name."

"So you went back to her?" Deng said.

"Yes."

"Shame on you two!"

I didn't feel the girl was in the wrong. Kong was the one who had broken into the Youth Home and then gone back to look for her, so he should be held responsible. However, it would be impracticable to order him to cut the affair at one stroke. He was a man and should break it off on his own initiative, so I switched the topic a little by asking him how he was going to make sure he would be elected an exemplary soldier at the end of the year. He said he would try every way to gain enough votes. We knew that was an empty promise, for as long as he was carrying on the affair, he had no chance of being voted in. Commander Deng got impatient and said, "Comrade Kong Kai, you know, you're already a dishonored man. You want to know how your men feel about you? They told me they felt fooled by you. Your task now is to regain your honor and make them respect you again. Otherwise how can you command the squad?"

Kong lowered his eyes without a word. I was impressed by Deng's pointed speech, to which I couldn't add anything. By nature, Deng was a reticent man. Obviously this matter had been preying on his mind for a while, though we had talked of it only twice. I felt bad, because I was the company's political instructor and Party secretary and I should have done something about the affair before the election.

After Kong left, I admitted my negligence to Deng and promised that I would try every means to stop the affair. Deng was always forthright and said we should have taken action when I showed him those candy wrappers three weeks before.

The next morning I sent Scribe Yang to Garlic Village to investigate the girl. I told him to go to the production brigade's Party branch first, look through her file, and find out all the information about her and her family background. "Trust me, Instructor Pan," Yang said with a smile. "I'm a professional sleuth." He swung a thin leg over a Forever bicycle and rode away with the handle bell tinkling.

Then I set about writing a report on our preliminary election to the Regimental Political Department. I had graduated from middle school, so the writing wasn't difficult, and I finished it in an hour. Having nothing else to do before lunch, I considered Kong's case again, particularly the girl involved. I remembered she had a pleasant voice. On National Day the year before, we had heard her singing an aria from the revolutionary model play *Seaport* at the marketplace. She worked in the village's tofu plant, where our cooks would go to buy dried bean curd and soy sprouts. Though tall and delicate, she wasn't pretty, and there were freckles on her cheeks. She often reminded me of a giant fox in human clothes. Among all the girls at the Youth Home, I would say she was the least attractive.

The scribe returned at noon. I was shocked by the results of his investigation:

> An Mali, 23, female
> Family Background: Capitalist
> Personal Class Status: Student
> Political Aspect: Mass
>
> An Long (An Mali's father), male, died in 2
> Class Status: Capitalist; owned two textile mills before Liberation
> Political Aspect: Counterrevolutionary

The true nature of the affair was clear now. If he knew her family background, Kong must have lost his senses and ignored the class distinction. As a high school graduate, he must have read too many Russian novels, in particular Turgenev, whom I had once heard him praise beyond measure, as though the story-maker were as great as Lenin and Stalin. Kong acted like a petty intellectual, who believed in romances and universal love.

After exchanging views on the new discovery, Deng and I decided to talk to

Kong again. The next afternoon, when the other soldiers were wearing straw hats and hoeing potatoes on the mountain, Kong sat in the headquarters answering our questions.

"Did you talk to An Mali?" I said.

"Not yet."

"When do you plan to do it?" Deng put in.

"Probably this weekend."

"Comrade Kong Kai," I said, "do you know what her family background is?" He nodded.

"Then why do you fool around with that capitalist's daughter?" Deng asked.

"She's not a capitalist, is she?"

"What? You don't mind having a counterrevolutionary capitalist as your father-in-law?" Deng thumped the desk.

"Commander Deng, Mali's father died years ago. She's an orphan now and I'll have no in-laws. Besides, she was born and raised under the Red Flag like me."

"You, you—"

"Kong Kai," I broke in, since Deng was not his match in this sort of verbal skirmish, "your offense is twofold. First, you violated the rule that allows no soldier to have an affair; second, you crossed the class line. Chairman Mao has instructed us: There is no love without a reason, and there is no hatred without a reason; the proletariat has the proletarian love, whereas the bourgeoisie has the bourgeois love. As a Communist Party member, to which class do you belong?"

Kong hung his head in silence. Deng launched an attack again. "What can you say now?"

No answer.

"You're ill, Little Kong," Deng went on in a voice full of comradely affection. "Everybody gets ill sometimes, but you shouldn't hide your illness for fear of being cured."

"Today we called you in," I added, "because we care about you and your future. We want to remind you of the dangerous nature of the affair."

Seeing that he seemed too ashamed to talk, I thought it better to dismiss him, so I said, "We don't need to talk more about this. You understand it well and must decide how to quit it yourself, the sooner the better. If you don't have anything to say, you're free to go."

Slowly he stood up and dragged himself out, with his cap in his hand.

"You should've ordered him to quit it," Deng said to me. I was surprised and didn't say anything. He went on, "He's so stubborn. How can we let him lead the squad? It's all right to fall into a pit, but he simply refuses to get out. How—"

"Old Deng, let's give him some time. He promised to quit it."

As I expected, Kong entered the larch woods with the girl on Sunday. This was necessary, because he needed to meet her once more to break it off; I didn't ask him to report progress. I wouldn't give him the wrong impression that I enjoyed seeing young people suffer. As long as he quit in time, it would be fine with me.

I met Kong several times the next week. Judging from his calm appearance, it seemed he had disentangled himself. But the following Sunday, Scribe Yang, who had been assigned to keep an eye on him, reported that Kong had sneaked out. I told him to go look for Kong in the larch woods and bring him to my office immediately, together with the girl. An hour later, Yang returned empty-handed and said they were not in the woods. Then I sent him, with the orderly, to search the village. They spotted the lovers, who were lying in each other's arms on the sandy bank of a stream, under a wooden bridge, but the couple slunk away at the sight of the searchers. Yang and Zhu returned with a used condom as evidence.

I was worried and dispatched the orderly to the Fifth Squad to wait for Kong and bring him over the moment he returned.

Kong arrived at my office two hours later. He said he had talked to her, but it didn't help.

"How come?" I asked.

"She cried her heart out. I can't bear to hurt her. Besides . . ."

"Besides what?"

"I've promised to marry her."

"What? That's out of the question. You must stop it."

"Instructor Pan, Mali isn't a bad girl. She loves the Party and Chairman Mao. You can go ask the commune members."

"I don't want to judge whether she is good or bad. You're a Party member and must not marry a capitalist's daughter. Do you understand?"

"Please help me, my instructor!"

"I am helping you, to get out of this mess." I lost my temper, though I was well known for being patient.

"No, I can't hurt her. It's too much for me."

"All right, let me lay bare everything here. You must make your choice between that girl and your future. If you choose her, you'll be expelled from the army."

"Damn," he cried. "I can't decide."

"Then let me help. Tell me, can you give up your party membership for her?"

He stared at me in silence and seemed overwhelmed by the dark picture. I continued, "What would your parents say if they were here? Would they allow you to take a capitalist's daughter as your bride?"

"No, they wouldn't."

"Right, because it would bring shame to your family. Tell me again, don't you want to be an exemplary soldier and send home a red certificate?"

He didn't answer. I asked again. "Don't you want to be an officer someday and command troops?"

I took his silence as acquiescence. "See, you've been lightheaded these days and never thought of the price you'll have to pay. No man in his right mind should ruin his future this way. I don't mean you shouldn't have love. We are all human beings and have emotions, but there are things more important, beyond love. A lot of revolutionary martyrs sacrificed their lives for the Party and the New China. Didn't they have love? Of course they did. They loved our nation and the revolutionary cause more than themselves. Now you are merely asked to quit an abnormal affair, but you say you can't. How can the Party trust you?"

He remained silent. I felt my talk had struck him hard and was boosting his determination, so I ordered, "Write her a letter and say it's over." To comfort him some, I added, "Little Kong, it's not worth it to make such a sacrifice for a girl. A real man must never put a woman before his career. I tell you this not as a Party secretary but as an experienced elder brother. Believe me, someday you'll marry a girl better than An Mali in every way. For the time being, it may hurt, but you'll get over it soon."

"All right," he muttered, "I'll write her a letter."

"Good. After you finish it, bring it over. I'll have it delivered to her. This may make you feel better."

At dinner I told Commander Deng about the talk and assured him that this was final. He also thought it was wise to resort to writing and having the letter delivered for Kong, because that would prevent him from seeing the girl again. In the evening the letter arrived, and we were surprised by its ludicrous brevity. Deng complained, saying we had to make Kong write another one, but I felt this would do, short as it was. The letter read:

June 12

Mali,

    Please forget me. I love you, but we belong to different classes. There is no way for us to be together. I will not see you anymore. Take care.

Kai

With my fountain pen I deleted the words "I love you, but," so that the writing became pithier. Meanwhile, I couldn't help wondering why Kong hadn't written a full page. He was one of our best writers. Very often he read out his long articles at lunch to the entire company, showing off his verbal command. A typical petty intellectual.

Immediately we dispatched Orderly Zhu to the Youth Home with the letter. An hour later he returned and reported that the girl had burst out wailing when she read it. Good, it struck home, we all agreed.

I was awakened by Commander Deng around three the next morning. He said Kong Kai was gone. I jumped out of bed, and together we went to the Fifth Squad. At first we were afraid he might have defected to Russia, but after seeing his uniforms and submachine gun, we felt that was unlikely. No one would defect empty-handed; besides, the Wusuli River was high now and Kong was a poor swimmer. Yet we sent out the Second Platoon to the river searching for him. Then Commander Deng, Scribe Yang, and I hurried along to Garlic Village, believing Kong was more likely to be at the Youth Home. But on the way we ran into a band of militia, who said they were looking for An Mali, who had disappeared after reading the letter. This information scared us, because we thought the lovers might have committed suicide. We returned immediately, woke up the other three platoons, and began combing the nearby fields, woods, ponds, and cliffs. The soldiers never stopped cursing Kong while searching.

Many villagers joined us in the search, which continued for a whole day, but there was no trace of the couple. The Regimental Headquarters was somehow convinced that they were alive and had eloped, so it sent out a message to all the police stations in the nearby counties and cities, demanding to have them detained. That had never occurred to us. Who would imagine two bedbugs could jump to the clouds! Now the nature of the affair changed entirely, and they became criminals at large. If they were caught, Kong would be court-martialed and An Mali would become a current counterrevolutionary. "I'll blow that bastard to pieces if I get hold of him," Deng kept saying. For two days we were at a loss about how to deal with the situation; there had been no precedent in our battalion.

We believed they would be caught within a month or two, because there seemed to be no place for them to hide. Wherever they went, they would be illegal residents and easily identified by the police and the revolutionary masses. However, China was such a large country that you couldn't deny there might be a village or a small town where they could settle down. Our regiment sent people to Shanghai and Kong's hometown in Jiangsu Province, but the couple had never shown up at either place. Three months passed; still there was no news of their whereabouts. To punish me and Deng for our negligence, the Regimental Political Department gave us each a disciplinary warning. Deng was mad at me, because he believed I hadn't taken strong measures in time to stop Kong and should have borne the responsibility alone. There was bad feeling between us for at least a year.

The next summer I received a letter two days before Army Day. It had no return address, though the postmark revealed it was from Gansu Province. It contained only a photo, black and white and three by four inches in size, in which Kong Kai and An Mali sat together with a fat baby on their knees. Kong looked silly, but obviously healthy and happy; his hair stuck out like a magpie's nest. His bride smirked a little to someone beyond the camera. They looked like peasants now, and both had put on some weight. The background was blurred, perhaps deliberately, and there seemed a hillock behind them. In the upper left corner hung these words: "A Joyful Family." After spitting on their faces, I turned the picture over and found a big word in pencil: "Sorry." I couldn't stop cursing them to myself. My first impulse was to send the photo to the Regimental Political Department, but on second thought I changed my mind, not because I didn't want to have them caught but because I couldn't afford to stir up more bad feeling between Deng and me. In addition, our superiors might reconsider my involvement in the case, suspecting Kong had maintained a correspondence with me. No, to send the photo on would be to set fire to my own house. So I struck a match and burned it, together with the envelope.

Greg Johnson

A native of San Francisco, Greg Johnson completed his under-graduate studies at Southern Methodist University in 1973 and earned his M.A. there in 1975. He received his Ph.D. at Emory University in 1980. Johnson has written in many different genres: poetry (*Aid and Comfort*, 1993), novel (*Pagan Babies*, 1993; *Sticky Kisses*, 2001), and short story (*Distant Friends*, 1990; *A Friendly Deceit*, 1992; and *I Am Dangerous*, 1996). He has also written books on Emily Dickinson and Joyce Carol Oates, including a biography, *Invisible Writer: A Biography of Joyce Carol Oates* (1998). Johnson received the O. Henry Award for short fiction in 1996 and was named Georgia Author of the Year in 1991. Since 1989 he has taught in the English Department at Kennesaw State University.

Crazy Ladies

Every Southern town had one, and ours was no exception. One year, my sister and I had an after-school routine that included watching the Mouseketeers on TV, holding court in the neighborhood treehouse we'd built, along with several other kids, in a vacant lot down the street, and finally, as dusk began and we knew our mother would soon be calling us to supper, visiting the big ramshackle house where the crazy lady lived. Often she'd be eating her own supper of tuna fish and bean salad, sitting silently across from her bachelor son, John Ray, who was about the same age as our parents. Becky would slither along through the hydrangea bushes, then scrunch down so I could stand on her shoulders and get my eyes and forehead—just barely—over the sill of the Longworths' dining-room window. After a few minutes I'd get down and serve as a footstool for Becky. More often than not we dissolved into a laughter so uncontrollable that we had to race back through the bushes, snapping branches as we went, and then dart around the corner of the house to avoid being caught by John Ray, who sometimes heard us and would jump up from the table, then come fuming out the back door. He never did catch us, and to my knowledge was never quick enough even to discover who we were. Naturally his mother didn't know, and didn't care. But there came a time—that summer afternoon, the year Becky was thirteen and I was eleven—when the crazy lady took her obscene revenge.

For me, that entire summer was puzzling. Our father, the town druggist, had begun keeping unusual hours. We could no longer count on his kindly, slump-shouldered presence at the dinner table, and when he did join us there was a crackling energy in him, a playfulness toward Becky and me that he'd never shown when we were younger. And while our father, a balding and slightly over-weight man in his forties, had taken on this sudden, nervous gaiety, our mother underwent an alarming change of her own. Her normally delicate features, framed by fine, wavy auburn hair, had paled to the point of haggardness. There was a new brusqueness in her manner—she scrubbed the house with a grim ferocity, she made loud clattering noises when she worked in the kitchen—and also a certain inattention toward her children, a tendency to focus elsewhere when she talked to us, or to fall into sudden reveries. This bothered me more than it did Becky, for it seemed that even she was changing. In the fall she'd be starting junior high, and she'd begun calling me "Little Brother" (with a slight wrinkling of her nose) and spending long hours alone in her bedroom. All through childhood we'd been inseparable, and Becky had always been called a tomboy by the neighborhood kids, even by our parents; but now she'd started curling her hair and painting her stubby nails, gingerly paging through movie magazines while they dried. What was wrong with everyone? I wanted to ask— but when you're eleven, of course, you can't translate your puzzlement into words. For a long while I stayed bewildered, feeling that the others had received a new set of instructions on how to live, but had forgotten to pass them along to me.

One humid afternoon in August, the telephone rang; from the living room, we could hear our mother snatch up the kitchen extension.

"What?" she said loudly, irritated. "Slow down, Mother, I can't make out—"

At that point she called to us to turn down the TV; from my place on the floor I reached quickly and switched the volume completely off, earning a little groan from Becky. She sat crosslegged on the couch with a towel wrapped tightly around her head, like a turban. We'd been watching *American Bandstand.*

"*You* turn it up," I said, with the same defiant smirk she'd begun using on me.

"Hush," Becky whispered, leaning forward. "I think something's wrong with Grandma."

We sat quietly, listening. Our mother's voice had become shrill, incredulous.

"Why did you let her in?" she cried. "You know she's not supposed to—"

A long silence. Whenever our mother was interrupted, Becky and I exchanged a puzzled look.

"Listen, just call John Ray down at the bank. The operator, Mother—she'll give you the number. Oh, I know you're nervous, but—Yes, you can if you try. Call John Ray, then go back in the living room and be nice to her. Give her something to eat. Or some coffee."

Silently, Becky mouthed the words to me: the crazy lady.

I nodded, straining to hear our mother's voice. She sounded weary.

"All right, I'll call Bert," she said, sighing. "We'll get there as soon as we can."

When she stopped talking, Becky and I raced into the kitchen.

"What is it, Mama?" Becky asked, excited. "Is it—"

"It's Mrs. Longworth," Mother said. Absent-mindedly, she fiddled with my shirt collar, then looked over at Becky. "She's gotten out of the house again, and somehow ended up in your grandmother's living room." Briefly, she laughed. She shook her head. "Anyway, I've got to call your father. We'll meet him over there."

But what had the crazy lady done? we asked. *Why was Grandma so frightened?*

Why were we all going over there? Mother ignored our questions. Calmly she dialed the pharmacy, setting her jaw as though preparing to do something distasteful.

Within five minutes we were in the car, making the two-mile drive to Grandma Howell's. Dad was already there when we arrived, but he hadn't gone inside.

"Well, what's going on?" Mother asked him. She sounded angry, as if Dad were to blame for all this.

He looked sheepish, apprehensive. He always perspired heavily, and I noticed the film covering his balding forehead, the large damp circles at his armpits. He wore the pale blue, regulation shirt, with *Denson Pharmacy—Bert Denson, Mgr.* stitched above the pocket, but he'd removed his little black bow tie and opened his collar.

"I just got here," Dad said, helplessly. "I was waiting for you." Mother made a little *tsk*ing noise, then turned in her precise, determined way and climbed the small grassy hill up to Grandma's porch. Dad followed, looking depressed, and Becky and I scampered alongside, performing our typical duet of questions. *Do you know what's wrong?* Becky asked him. *Why did you wait for us?* I asked. *Is Mother mad at you?* Becky asked. *Are you scared of the crazy lady?* I asked. *Scared to go inside?*

I asked this, of course, because *I* was scared.

Dad only had time to say, uneasily, that Grandma's St. Augustine was getting high again, and I'd have to mow it next Saturday. It was just his way of stalling; he'd begun evading a lot of our questions lately.

The front door was already open, and as we mounted the porch steps I could see Grandma Howell's dim outline from just inside the screen. Then the screen opened and I heard her say, vaguely, "Why, it's Kathy and Bert, and the kids . . ." From inside the room I heard a high, twittering sound, like the cries of a bird.

In the summertime Grandma Howell kept all the shades drawn in her living room; she had an attic fan, and the room was always wonderfully cool. It was furnished modestly, decorated with colorful doilies Grandma knitted for the backs of chairs and the sofa, and with dozens of little knickknacks—gifts from her grandchildren, mostly—set along the mantel of the small fireplace and cluttering the little, spindly-leg tables, and with several uninspired, studiously executed paintings (still lifes, mostly) done by my grandfather, who had died several years before I was born. A typical grandmother's house, I suppose, and through the years it had represented to us kids a sanctuary, a place of quiet wonder and privilege, where we were fed ginger cookies and Kool-Aid, and where Grandma regaled us with stories of her childhood down in Mobile, where her family had been among the most prominent citizens, or of her courtship by that rapscallion, Jacob Howell, who'd brought her northward (that is, to our town—which skirted the northern edge of Alabama) and kept her there. Grandma liked to roll her china-blue eyes, picturing herself as a victim of kidnapping or worse; through the years she refined and elaborated her act to rouse both herself and us to helpless laughter, ending the story by insisting tongue-in-cheek that she'd met, and adjusted to, a fate worse than death. (Grandfather Howell was a postal clerk, later the postmaster, and by all accounts a gentle, kind, rather whimsical figure in the town; it was always clear that Grandma had adored him.) Now, at sixty-one, she looked twenty years younger, the blue eyes still clear as dawn, her figure neat, trim, and erect, her only grandmotherly affectation being the silvery blue hair she wore in a tidy bun. On that day I decided she'd always seemed brave, too, even valorous in her quiet, bustling self-sufficiency, for that afternoon I saw in her eyes for the first time a look of unmitigated fear.

"Yes, come in, come in," she said, still in that vague, airy way, trying to pretend that our visit was a surprise. Then she turned back to the room's dim interior—her head moving stiffly, I thought, as if her neck ached—and said in a polite, tense, hostessy voice: "Why look, Mrs. Longworth, it's my daughter and her family. We were just talking about them."

Grandma Howell nodded, as though agreeing with herself, or encouraging Mrs. Longworth's agreement. The twittering birdlike sound came again.

By now we were all inside, standing awkwardly near the screen. Slowly, our eyes adjusted. On the opposite side of the room, and in the far corner of Grandma's dainty, pale-blue sofa, sat Mrs. Longworth: a tiny, white-haired woman in a pink dress, a brilliant green shawl, and soiled white sneakers, one of whose laces had come untied. The five of us stared, not feeling our rudeness, I suppose, because for the moment Mrs. Longworth seemed unaware of our presence. She kept brushing wispy strands of the bone-white hair from her forehead, though it immediately fell back again; and she would pat her knees briskly with open palms, as if coaxing some invisible child to her lap. It was the first time I had encountered the crazy lady up close, and my wide-eyed scrutiny confirmed certain rumors that had circulated in the town for years—that she wore boys' sneakers, for instance, along with white athletic socks; that her tongue often protruded from her mouth, like a communicant's (as it did now, quivering with a sort of nervous expectancy); and that, most distasteful of all, the woman was unbelievably dirty. Even from across the dimmed room I detected a rank, animal odor, and there was a dark smear—it looked like grease—along one of her fragile cheekbones. The palms and even the backs of her hands were filthy, the tiny nails crusted with grime. Like me, the rest of my family had been stunned into silence at the very sight of her; it was only when her tongue popped back inside her mouth, and she cocked her head to begin that eerie, high-pitched trilling once again, that my mother jerked awake and abruptly stepped forward.

"Mrs. Longworth?" she said loudly, trying to compete with the woman's shrill birdsong. "We haven't met before, but I'm—"

She gave it up. Mrs. Longworth's head moved delicately as she trilled, cocking from side to side as if adjudging the intricate nuances of her melody— which was no melody at all, of course, but only a high, sweet, patternless frenzy of singing. (For it was clear that Mrs. Longworth thought she was singing; her face and eyes, which she still had not turned to us, had the vapid, self-satisfied look of the amateur performer.) She would stop when she was ready to stop. My mother stepped back, then drew Grandma closer. They began a whispered conference.

"How did she get in?" my mother said hoarsely. "Why did you—"

"It happened so fast," Grandma interrupted. Her face had puckered, in an uncharacteristic look of chagrin. "I was outside, watering the shrubs, and suddenly there she was, standing in the grass. Right away I knew who she was, but she looked so—so frail and helpless, just standing there. Then she asked for a glass of iced tea. She asked in a real sweet way, and it was so hot out, and she didn't *act* crazy. But once we got inside . . ."

Grandma's voice trailed away. I saw that her hands were shaking.

"You *know* what happened the last time she got loose," Mother said. She was almost hissing. "Wandered down to the courthouse and started screeching all kinds of things, crazy things, and then started taking off her clothes! In broad daylight! It took four men to restrain her before John Ray finally got there."

Becky whispered, excitedly, "But doesn't he keep her locked up? At school the girls all say—"

"Yes, yes," Mother said impatiently, with a little shushing motion of her hand. "But she manages to get out, somehow. I've never understood why John Ray can't hire someone to stay with her in the daytime, or else have her committed. My Lord," she said, whirling back upon Grandma, "just imagine what could have happened. People like her can get violent, you know."

"Ssh. Kathy, please," Grandma said anxiously. She glanced back at the crazy lady, who had continued trilling to herself, though more softly now. "She isn't like that, really. I don't think she'd hurt anyone. In fact, if you'd heard what she told me—"

"Mother, the woman's crazy!" my mother whispered, hard put to keep her voice down. "You can't pay any attention to what she says."

"What was it?" Becky asked, and though I was afraid to say anything, I seconded her question by vigorously nodding my head.

"Hush up," Mother said, giving a light, warning slap to Becky's shoulder blade, "or I'll send you both outside."

Now my father spoke up. "Listen, Kathy," he said, "we ought to just call John Ray down at the bank. He'll come get her, and that'll be that."

"I've a mind to call the police," Mother said, and I looked at her curiously. She had sounded hurt.

"She hasn't done anything," Dad said gently. "And anyway, it's none of our business."

Grandma pressed her hands together, as if to stop their shaking. "Oh, if you'd heard what she told me, once I brought her inside. I gave her the iced tea, and a little saucer of butter cookies, and for a while she sat there on the sofa, with me right beside her, and she just talked in the sweetest way. Said she was just out for a walk this afternoon, but hadn't realized how hot it was. She said the tea was delicious, and asked what kind I bought. Hers always turned cloudy, she said. And I'd started thinking to myself, This woman isn't crazy at all. She dresses peculiar, yes, and she should bathe more often, but people have just been spreading ugly gossip all these years, exaggerating everything. Anyway, I gave her more tea, and tried to be nice to her. She kept looking around the room, saying how pretty it was. She noticed Jacob's pictures, and couldn't believe he'd done such beautiful work. She asked if I still missed him, like she missed Mr. Longworth, and if I ever got lonesome, or frightened. . . . And it was then that she changed, so suddenly that I couldn't believe my ears. She started talking about John Ray, and saying the most horrible things, but all in that same sweet voice, as if she was just talking about the weather. Oh, Kathy, she said John Ray wanted—wanted to kill her, that he was going to take her into the attic and chop her into little pieces. She said he beats her, and sometimes won't let her eat for days on end, but by then she'd started using her husband's name— you know, mixing up the names. One minute she'd be saying Carl, the next she was back to John Ray. And pretty soon she was just spouting gibberish, and she'd started that crazy singing of hers. She said did I want to hear a song, and that's when I came to phone you. I didn't know what to do—I didn't—"

Tears had filled her eyes. Mother reached out, taking both her hands. "Never mind, you were just being kind to her," she said. "Bert's right, of course—we'll just call John Ray, and that'll be that."

Grandma couldn't speak, but her blue eyes had fixed on my mother's with a frightened, guilty look. It was then that Mrs. Longworth's eerie trilling stopped, and we heard, from the sofa: "Bert's right, of course, we'll just call John Ray. And that'll be that." The voice was sly, insinuating—it had the mocking, faintly malicious tone of a mynah bird.

I looked at Dad. His face had reddened, his mouth had fallen partway open.

"Would you like some more tea?" Grandma asked, in a sweet overdone voice. She inclined her head, graciously, though it was clear that she couldn't bring herself to take another step toward Mrs. Longworth. But the crazy lady didn't seem to mind.

She cocked her head, and at the very moment I feared she would resume her weird singing, she said in a casual, matter-of-fact way, "No thanks, Paulina. I like the tea, but it isn't sweet enough." And she smiled, rather balefully; her teeth looked small and greenish.

Grandma began, "I could add more sugar—"

"Do you have Kool-Aid?" Mrs. Longworth asked. "That's my favorite drink, but my son won't let me have it."

"Yes, I think so," Grandma said, uncertainly. "I'll go and look."

"Red, please," Mrs. Longworth said. "Red's the best."

Grandma hurried back to the kitchen, leaving the rest of us to stare awkwardly at the old woman, while she looked frankly back at us. She had a child-like directness, but her eyes glittered, too, with the wry omniscience of the aged. Particularly when she looked down at Becky and me, her glance seemed full of mischief, as though she were exercising her right to a second childhood. And there was something in her glance that I could only feel as love, born of some intuitive sympathy. Young as I was, I remember sharing Grandma's thought: This woman isn't crazy at all.

For the moment, her attention had fixed on Becky. She held out a dirty, clawlike hand, as though to draw my sister closer by some invisible string.

"You're a pretty girl," she said, in the tone one uses for very young children. "Such pretty hair, and those cute freckles. . . . I used to have freckles, when I was young. I was a pretty girl."

She shook her head, as though hard put to say how pretty. "And I had nice dresses, cotton and gingham, all trimmed in lace. I'll bet you like pretty dresses. Your little nose is turned up, just like mine was."

Becky looked spellbound; her face had paled. "Thank you—thank you very much—" she stammered.

"Would you like to have some of the dresses I wore?" the old woman asked. "They're up in the attic, in a special trunk. We'll steal the key from John Ray. The dresses are safe, no bloodstains and none of them ripped. You could wear them to church, or when the young men come calling." She raised one finger of the still-outstretched hand. "But you'd have to bring them back. You couldn't steal them. We'll sneak them back late one night, when John Ray's asleep."

Becky tried to smile. I could see how scared she was, and I stood there hoping Mrs. Longworth wouldn't turn to me. Somehow I felt safer, being a boy.

"I—I don't know—It's real nice of you—" Becky couldn't put her words together.

"And you still have pretty clothes," my mother said suddenly, stepping forward. "That's a lovely shawl, Mrs. Longworth."

The crazy lady glanced down; she pulled the shawl tighter around her shoulders, as though she'd suddenly felt a chill.

"I had a cashmere shawl, pale gray," she said, "that my husband gave me. It was before John Ray was even born. Mr. Longworth went up to Memphis, and afterward he showered me with presents. An opal ring, too. And a set of hair combs. I was a pretty woman, you know. I still wear shawls, but it's not the same. This one's green."

She spoke in a circular, monotonous rhythm, as though reminiscing to herself; as though she'd spoken these words a thousand times. It was a kind of sing-song. I thought again of her birdlike trilling.

"Well, it's very pretty," Mother said.

"It's *too* green," the crazy lady said, "but I think it hurts John Ray's eyes. He has weak eyes, you know. When he goes blind, I won't have to wear it."

Grandma came in from the kitchen, carrying a tray with six glasses and a large pitcher of Kool-Aid.

"It's raspberry, Mrs. Longworth," she said as she put the tray on the coffee table. Her hands still shook, and the glasses clattered together. "I hope you like it."

She poured a glass and held it out; Mrs. Longworth grasped it quickly, then took several long gulps. She closed her eyes in bliss. "Oooh!" she cried. "Isn't that good!"

Grandma maintained her brave smile. "Kathy, would you and Bert like—"

"No, Mother. We can't stay long, and Bert has a phone call to make. Don't you, Bert?"

"Yes—right," Dad said awkwardly.

"How about you kids?" Grandma said. She was trying gamely to make all of this appear normal; then, perhaps, it would somehow *be* normal. That was always Grandma's way. But, much as I loved her, I was afraid to join in anything the crazy lady was doing. Like Becky, I stiffly shook my head.

Mrs. Longworth emptied her glass, then held it out to Grandma. "More, please," she said. While Grandma poured, she said (again in that matter-of-fact way): "You might not believe it, but I don't get good Kool-Aid like this. John Ray says it rots my teeth and my brain. I can drink water, or coffee without sugar." She made a face. "And if I don't drink it, John Ray gets mad. Now Carl, he never got mad. But my son is going to cut me with a long knife one of these days, and hide the pieces in the attic, all in separate trunks. When it starts to smell, he'll throw the trunks in the river."

She took the second glass of Kool-Aid that Grandma shakily handed her. Then she sighed, loudly, as if the details of her gruesome demise had become rather tiresome. "My son works in a bank," she said, "and his teeth are big and strong. So he can have sugar. If I try to sneak some, he pinches my arms, or hits me with a newspaper. That hurts, because he rolls it up first and makes me watch. The pinches hurt, too, but not always. He works in a bank, and so he knows all about locks and trunks and vaults. He has a map, so he can find the river when he needs it. I should be able to have red Kool-Aid, and to sing. I used to sing for Carl, and sometimes I sang to John Ray when he was a baby. Now, he's tired of taking care of me. He says, 'Don't I have a life to live? Don't I?'" Again she spoke like a mynah bird, pitching her voice very low. "That's what he says, and that's why he wants to cut me into pieces, and why I have all these bruises on my arms. You want to see them? It's not fair, because my singing is pretty. Carl said I had a prettier voice than Jenny Lind, and he heard her in person when he was a boy. He's dead, though. You want to hear me sing?"

She stopped abruptly, her eyes widened. She waited.

"Would you like some more Kool-Aid?" Grandma asked, helplessly.

"Bert, you and Jamie go back into the kitchen. We'll wait out here with Mrs. Longworth." My mother gestured to her ear, as if holding an invisible telephone.

Dad said, "Come on, sport," and I joined him gladly. I glimpsed Becky's look of envy and longing as we escaped into the dining room, and finally back into Grandma's tiny kitchen.

"What's wrong with her? Why does she say those things?" I asked breathlessly, while Dad fiddled with the slender phone directory. I tugged at his arm, like a much smaller child; my heart was racing. I wore only a T-shirt and short pants, and I remember shifting my weight back and forth, my bare feet unpleasantly chilled by the kitchen linoleum.

"Just simmer down, son," he said, tousling my hair in an absent-minded way. Frowning, he moved his eyes down a column of small print. "Ah, here it is. First National." And he began to dial.

I didn't understand it, but I was on the verge of tears—angry tears. When Dad finished talking with John Ray, his eyes stopped to read the little chalkboard hanging by the phone. "I can't believe it," he said, shaking his head. "It's still there."

Grudgingly, I followed his gaze to the chalkboard, and for the hundredth time read its message, in that antique, elaborate hand: *Paulie, Don't forget Gouda cheese for dinner tonight. I'll be hungry at six o'clock sharp. (Ha ha) Jacob.*

If Grandma was out when my grandfather came home for lunch, he would leave her a note on the chalkboard. But he hadn't lived to eat that Gouda cheese—he was stricken at four that afternoon, and died a short while later—and Grandma had insisted that his last message would never be erased. Mother disapproved, saying it was morbid, and more than once I'd seen Grandma's eyes fill with tears as they skimmed across the words yet another time. But she could be stubborn, and the message stayed.

"You'd know it was still there," I said, sniffling, "if you ever came with us to visit Grandma. But you're always gone."

The resentment in my voice surprised us both. My father's clear brown eyes flashed in an instant from anger, to guilt, to sorrow. He shook his head; the gesture had become familiar lately, almost a tic.

"Well, Jamie," he said slowly, licking his lips. "I guess it's time we had a little talk."

And for five or ten minutes he did talk, not quite looking at me, his voice filled with a melancholy dreaminess. He told me how complicated the grown-up world was, and how men and women sometimes hurt each other without wanting to; how they sometimes fell "out of love," without being able to control what was happening. He knew it must sound crazy, but he hoped that someday I would understand. Things were always changing, he said softly, and that was the hardest thing in the world for people to accept. Even my mother hadn't accepted it, not yet; but he hoped that she would, eventually. He hoped she wouldn't make it even harder for all of us.

The speech was commonplace enough, though startling to my young ears. As he spoke I kept thinking of Mrs. Longworth, and how she'd talked of her husband who had died, and how everything changed after that. I felt the cold, sickish beating of my heart inside my slender ribcage.

"But will Mother turn crazy, like Mrs. Longworth?" I asked, imagining myself, in a moment of terrified wonder, turning mean like John Ray. "Is it always the ladies who go crazy?"

Dad looked stymied; nor did I know myself what the question meant. I wouldn't even recall it until decades later, visiting my sister Becky in the hospital, where she was recuperating from a barbiturate overdose after the disappearance of her third husband. It would come back to me, in a boy's timid, faraway voice, like the echo of some terrible prophecy, a family curse. After a moment, though, my father reacted as though I'd said something amusing. Again, he tousled my hair; he smiled wearily.

"No, son," he said gently. "It's not always the ladies. You shouldn't let Mrs. Longworth get to you."

"But she said—"

"She's a crazy old lady, Jamie. She has nothing to do with us—don't pay any attention to what she says."

Hands stuffed in my pockets, one foot rubbing the toe of the other, I stood looking up at him. There were questions I wanted to ask, but I couldn't put them into words; and I somehow knew that he didn't have the answers.

"Now," Dad said, with a false heartiness, "why don't we—"

It was then that the kitchen door swung open, and there was my mother; she looked back and forth between Dad and me, as though she didn't recognize us.

"Honey? What is it?" Dad said, panicked.

"We—we couldn't stop her," Mother began, wildly. "She took off the shawl, then started unbuttoning her dress, that filthy dress—"

Dad crossed to her; he gripped her firmly by the upper arms.

"Calm down, Kathy. Now tell me what happened."

My mother was trembling. She said, haltingly, "Mrs. Longworth, she—she said she would show us, prove to us how cruel John Ray was. Before we could say anything, she started undressing. She undid the dress, then slipped it down to her waist. We—we just stared at her. We couldn't believe it. There were bruises, Bert, all over her arms and chest. Big purplish bruises, and welts. . . . And she said, *John Ray did this*, in that little singing voice of hers—"

Dad had already released her arms. He went to the phone and dialed again. For a moment my mother's eyes locked onto mine. I'd never seen her lose her composure before, yet for some reason I was filled with a remarkable calm. From that moment forward, everything was changed between us.

"Oh God," she whispered, grief-stricken. "How I wish Becky hadn't seen."

Dad hung up the phone, then led us back into the living room; he kept one arm draped lightly around Mother's shoulder. John Ray had arrived, and sat on the sofa beside Mrs. Longworth. Her dress and shawl were in place, so it was hard for me to envision the scene my mother had described. Mrs. Longworth sat staring blankly forward, as if her mind had wandered to some distant place. John Ray held one of her hands, and sat talking amiably to Grandma. He was a big-chested man, almost entirely bald, and had teeth that were enormous, white, and perfectly straight. He smiled constantly. He was telling Grandma about all the times his mother had been "naughty," wandering into a department store, or a funeral parlor, or a private home. He hoped she hadn't been too much trouble. He hoped we understood that she meant no harm; that for years she hadn't had the slightest idea what she was doing or saying.

A small, terrible smile had frozen onto Grandma's face. She stood near the front door, her arm around Becky, who looked pale and dazed.

"She—she wasn't any trouble," my mother gasped.

"Oh no, none at all," said Grandma.

There were a few moments of silence, during which the five of us stared at the Longworths, John Ray giving back his imperturbable smile and Mrs. Longworth seeming lost in the corridors of her madness, her mouth slightly ajar, her hand resting limply inside her son's. I tried to picture John Ray beating her, or shouting his threats of a gruesome death. I decided it could not be true.

When the police arrived, neither John Ray nor his mother protested. The officer spoke to Mrs. Longworth by name, and returned a few pleasantries to the smiling John Ray. As he followed them out the door, the officer gave a knowing, barely perceptible look to my father, who nodded in acknowledgment, then turned his attention back to us.

"Well," he said, jovially, "why don't we all go out for an ice-cream sundae?"

Beyond that, I can't remember clearly. I don't believe that anyone, including myself, ever talked about the incident again; there was a tacit assumption between Becky and me that we would not resume our spying on the Longworths, but they continued to be tormented by other kids we knew. I remember feeling, for years afterward, that life had become disappointingly routine. Evidently the police hadn't charged John Ray: he was still working at First National by the time I left home for college. Nor had anything untoward happened to Mrs. Longworth: one night, about three years after wandering into our lives, she died peacefully in her sleep. It was whispered around town that John Ray was wild with grief.

By then, the tensions between my parents had all but vanished; my father's unexplained absences had stopped, my mother no longer seemed angry or depressed. Grandma stayed absorbed in her garden, her knitting, her memories. Becky had plunged headlong into her adolescent social career, and with great effort had attained her obsessive goal: popularity. It seemed that I alone had changed. Violence had failed to erupt, and I became uneasy, tense, and vaguely suspicious. If I could have foreseen what would happen to my sister, I would not have been surprised. Like her, I left the South as soon as I was old enough, relocating in a big, overpopulated city where violence is commonplace. Although I often worry about Becky, and Mother, and even Grandma, I know there is no reason to feel guilty, just as there is no logic to the dream I've had, recurrently, for more than twenty years: a dream in which I open a door to find the three of them perched on a sofa, cocking their heads from side to side, trilling their songs of madness and despair.

Sheri Joseph

Sheri Joseph grew up in Memphis, Tennessee, and attended the University of the South. She then moved to Athens, Georgia, and studied under James Kilgo in the creative writing program at the University of Georgia. She thinks of herself as a writer of short stories and was encouraged as a writer by Stan Lindberg, the late editor of the *Georgia Review,* which published "The Waiting Room." Joseph describes her novel, *Bear Me Safely Over* (2002), as a cycle of stories focused on two individuals, a gay young man in a small Georgia town and his friend, a young woman, both trying to find their place in the world. Both the novel and her shorter fiction demonstrate Joseph's sensitive understanding of the dynamic forces governing relationships between people and within families. Joseph says, "I tend to see people in patterns of connectedness," and this is clearly evident in the sad burden of the family members in "The Waiting Room."

The Waiting Room

He had a way of insinuating himself into her life, even miles away, and his so-called living will was a perfect example. Who but her brother, she wondered, would think to draw up such a paper at the tender age of thirty? Among its morbid clauses, it speculated in detail on his potential vegetative state, an imaginary Warren beneath white sheets and hooked to machines. It galled her to know how such an image would seem to him romantic. And this from a man who was not even sick—at least, not physically. His crowning touch was to make her the executor. Their mother was still alive; she should have been the one. But he would have Libby alone pull the plug, insist on it, and hold her in thrall that way among his private papers as if it were some great joke on her.

Warren had always had a disagreeable sense of humor. When she was sixteen, seventeen, he had used it on the boys who came to take her out. There had never been many, and no doubt there were fewer once Warren had met them at the door. "She'll be a few minutes," he informed one. "She's doing another one of those treatments for lice." When Libby found a boy who would not be chased away, Warren spied on them as they said goodnight before the door, tape-recorded their conversations, and played them back—machine under the napkin in his lap—in the midst of a family dinner. But then, as her mother had reasoned, he was just a boy, and boys have so much energy.

Libby's response had been to hold her tongue and wish to be grown. *To be grown and away from here*—every night she had closed her eyes on that desire. It wasn't just Warren she wanted to escape, but her old-fashioned, well-meaning parents and her own long, awkward body. She wished for grace and poise and independence, for a life free of entanglements. In time, she made her small escape: to college in Boston, then back south to a job as an office manager for a Macon law firm. She was near her family, but far enough away to satisfy. Her mother remained in Valdosta, a few hours' drive, and Warren—no telling where Warren could be at a given moment, but he seemed to orbit the state, never lighting too far away, never pausing in one spot for long. In his grown life, he was as restless and homebound as a housefly. He had never learned to value his independence.

The odd thing was that when she finally found the house near Macon she knew she would buy—a little country house on two acres—and felt herself poised on the edge of a permanent life, her first thought was, "Where is Warren, now, in relation to this place?" She saw herself as a figure firmly planted on the neat white porch of a home all her own, and her brother always at some measurable distance, in one direction or another, as if radar could trace his movements.

He would need her. Whatever he tried, he would ultimately fail, and she would hear from him. It wasn't his fault, the doctors said now, but that he was ill. Manic-depressive. Bipolar. Lately, even suicidal. She couldn't imagine how such extreme-sounding terms had come to be attached to her brother. Not that she hadn't watched him progress from the earliest stages—through mood swings that had lost him first one job, then another, all the while slowly destroying a two-year marriage. The highs could be as bad as the lows, those manic fits that sent him rocketing in pursuit of new ideas, new careers, new investments. But it was the lows, finally, that made Libby and her mother stop saying, "Oh, that's just Warren. You know how he is."

"I don't understand it," her mother would moan now over long distance. "Why must he behave so? Could we have done something, back then? Did we do something? Wrong, I mean?"

Sometimes, for an answer, Libby recited the doctors' explanations that she had learned by heart. But her mother refused to hear Warren reduced to physiology, the helpless vessel of chemical flux, and truthfully Libby couldn't even convince herself. This was Warren—their Warren. Whether in the grip of inspiration or of the sadness that could crush him to tears and immobility, he was childlike. He was never so very different, in fact, from the boy he had been— except that now the impish glint in his eye was often accompanied by lucid self-analysis. In such moments, Libby couldn't help suspecting him of feigning the illness, at least some of the time, to amuse himself.

She didn't tell her mother her suspicions, though she imagined they were shared ones. Always she calmed her mother's obsessive questioning in the same definite way: "It just doesn't matter. It makes no difference at all."

In her two-bedroom home with its sunny rooms and pecan-shaded yard, she was still waiting for her life to begin. She was thirty-five now, uninvolved. She would have liked to find a man to marry and share the house with her—there was always that. She would have liked to think of children. But with Warren looming at every horizon, she felt already involved. Any phone call could signal disaster, the imminent dismantling of her rudimentary life.

In the dusk of late spring she sat on her front porch, unable to enjoy her peace. She had not heard news from his quarter in months, and yet his very absence was a demand, a little roothold on her thoughts. She was alone but for the fireflies glimmering out in the yard, and each one reminded her of the tip of his cigarette. Wherever he was at this moment, there was no doubt in her mind that he was alone in another dark and smoking a cigarette, just like these glowings of himself that found their way with seeming innocence onto her lawn. She struck up a conversation with his ghost.

Warren, why is it that you can never leave me be?

Simple, he responded. *You are my blood.*

I won't be responsible.

Ah, but you are.

It always happened—even when Warren was no more than a shadow of her own invention—that their talking turned quickly to argument, and from there to the teeth-gritted stalemate that sustained them.

When the call came, she answered with an edge to her voice, as if they were still in the midst of a fight only set aside the night before.

Warren said, "Libby, don't start with me, not now. I need you to come to Atlanta *right* away." Already his voice was an octave higher than in his relaxed state.

"Oh, Warren, really." She twisted the phone cord tight around one finger until it hurt, the tip filled with trapped blood. "You know that boy who cried wolf—"

"This is no joke. I've never—" He gasped, tried to continue.

"Okay, okay. What is it?"

"I'm in jail."

"Jail! Christ . . ." He had never yet fallen so low. The family, she thought, had never fallen so low. "What in the world have you done?"

"Nothing! It's a mistake, some stupid bureaucratic—they say it's for traffic tickets. *Parking* tickets, mostly. They won't let me out until I pay."

Libby stood half-crouched toward the phone, locked in that wrestler's posture until her joints began to ache. Though white sunlight filled the kitchen, where only minutes before she had been buttering toast, she could see his smoking ghost-face floating again before her. The face had the gall to crack an I-told-you-so smile. Yes, she thought, aiming the butter knife at the apparition, with you there's always something to be paid, isn't there?

She straightened, smoothed her skirt, looked at her watch. Seven-thirty. She had a few minutes to spare before she had to leave for work.

"I can pay it," he went on fretfully. "If I can get out of here, I can put my hands on the money. But I need you to come post bail. Can you come right away?"

"Dear, I have to work." Libby heard her own voice at the edge of becoming her mother's, the older woman's diction and crisp enunciation. "You know how it is with those of us who live in the real world."

She made some quick calculations. It was Friday. She could leave right after work, be in Atlanta before dark if she had to. She wished it were any other day of the week—Thursday at the least—so she could claim her greater obligations in Macon. Her job was, he well knew, the only obligation she could claim. And surely it wouldn't hurt him to sit in a cell for a few days.

"You don't understand," he went on. "I need some things from my apartment. They won't let me have my medication."

"What do you mean, they won't let you have it?"

"They won't send anyone to get it. They say it's a controlled substance so it's not allowed in." His breathing shook like a frail rope bridge across the gaps that fell between his words. "I need you to come. I don't know what I'll do."

"Oh, Warren." If it was the truth at all, she knew it wasn't the whole story. He twisted everything to exaggeration. She wanted to ask him to put someone in authority on the line.

But the mood was real. He wasn't always this way: the crying, the veiled threats, all his fault lines shuddering at the surface. So often his calls were elaborately, luxuriantly casual. He would tell her how well he was "functioning" and make bright references to his latent tendencies. One day soon—he might say— I'll make such a pretty corpse of myself. Oh. Sorry, Lib. Just a joke.

"I'll come," she said. "As soon as I can."

She had meant to go sooner. There were a few essentials at the office that needed to be taken care of, and then they could spare her for the afternoon. She even announced that she would be leaving at the noon hour on emergency family business; her job was classified as "highly responsible" so she needed no one's permission. But as such, it prevented her from delegating, so the day dragged on with phone calls no one else could handle, payroll "emergencies," the thousand details of office management that added up to no great import, though each in itself was a crisis.

At five-thirty she was still at her desk, after the last of her co-workers had departed for happy hour. The phone rang. It rang eight times, each one seeming louder and louder as she sat listening, and then her voice mail picked up. A man's voice, out of the deserted air, informed her that the prisoner Warren Suter had attempted to hang himself in his cell. He had been taken to Grady Hospital in downtown Atlanta.

Attempted. The word was with her like a passenger on the drive. Meaning, he didn't succeed, as he had never yet managed to succeed at anything he tried.

Not three different colleges, his various jobs, his brief marriage, nor the two or three or four (difficult to count) past attempts on his own life. Once he claimed to have taken pills—not the ones prescribed—and an hour later was having his stomach pumped. Once he had called and talked in such detail of hanging himself that she ran for her car and drove straight to Savannah, where he was hiding at the time from his wife. When Libby arrived, she found him calm and alive, making pancakes. Only later did she learn that he had called their mother in the interim, that he had regaled even her with his self-indulgent bullshit—no concern for an old woman's dignity or her heart. And now, there was no telling by what margin the latest attempt had failed. "For once, Warren," she grumbled aloud, "do something right."

One time, at lowest ebb, in a pay-by-the-week motel outside Atlanta, he had succeeded in cutting his wrists and made no call, left no note. That once, he had been near death. In the hospital she had found him unfamiliar, so wasted and pale against the sheets, his breathing a painful effort in her ears. She had wept without control. She had held his hand and said goodbye, had let go, and when he rallied and recovered she had almost hated him for it.

At twilight, just past eight o'clock, she pulled into the Grady Hospital parking lot. At first she didn't want to believe she had the right place—that bland brown crate of a building that looked like low-income housing left over from earlier in the century. But that was it—Grady Memorial Hospital.

Despite appearances, her arrival here felt like a return, a homecoming to a despised place. I will not go through this again, she told herself, not knowing what she could have meant. For how could she stop any of it? She had no control, as always. Their mother would have to be called. And it would be Libby, from a hospital pay phone, who would have to disturb her mother's peace and Uncle Frank's as well—Frank would need to fetch Libby's mother and drive her to Atlanta. He would probably also alert the rest of the south Georgia cousins, who might come along after him, might bring their children too. Libby could see them now, all gathered in the waiting room for yet another family reunion at Warren's behest. He had no consideration.

She gave his name at the nurses' station and was directed to a seat in the hallway. Around the corner she could see the regular waiting room, half full of dejected people—poorly clothed families with small children, an elderly man with an oozing bandage on his arm. She tried not to look at them. She knew she was in a bad part of town, and no telling what a Friday night would be like in such a place. Later there might be drug-induced frenzies, boys with knife wounds, gunshot wounds. She shuddered to imagine her mother in their midst. But it was early yet, and the halls were calm. She hoped a doctor would arrive and remove her vigil to somewhere private before all bedlam erupted.

Within a few minutes, a young woman in a white coat stopped beside her. "I'm Dr. Feldman," she said, unsmiling, though her voice conveyed an aggressive good cheer. "I'm a resident."

Libby stood and shook the offered hand. Dark, straight hair fell halfway down the doctor's back. The crown of her head was on level with Libby's collarbone.

"You're Warren Suter's sister?"

She nodded, stooping. "Libby." Her throat felt dry, and she cleared it loudly.

Dr. Feldman looked down at the chart on her arm, seemed about to speak, but Libby couldn't stop herself from going on. "I know," she said, haltingly, "what he did. They told me. Those people from the jail. He's done this before, you know. It's hardly a surprise to me, since I've lived through all this already. I know all about hospitals and treatment and psychiatric evaluations and prognoses—" She stopped, horrified at herself.

Dr. Feldman looked up at her steadily with dark-browed eyes. Her mouth tipped into an odd, froggish frown.

Libby laughed. "He's alive, of course."

"In a manner of speaking," said Dr. Feldman. "I'm sorry, but he appears to be brain dead."

Libby felt herself exhale. That meant alive, of course, breathing. She took care not to speak aloud this time, though she couldn't stop her lips from moving, her mind from racing and tumbling. He was in some sort of coma, unreachable, maybe brain-damaged, but it wasn't as if Warren had such a perfect mind to begin with. Perhaps it was only the sort of shutdown required for healing. Yes, that was it. She had known all along that he would be alive. By the time they let her in to see him, he was sure to have some sort of grin sneaking onto his sleeping face.

"Excuse me," Libby said, with careful decorum. "I need to call our mother."

Warren slept beneath yet another sheet that made her think of the endless laundry of these places, the terrible turnaround of bedclothes and the innumerable bodies that had touched this very one. There was death caught in its fibers. And yet Warren seemed to draw from it nothing but life. She remembered from the last time the face of death on him, bleached as gray-white as the laundry he slept in. His face had seemed no more than a skull then, with papery skin. Now all his flesh was flushed pink; his cheeks pulsed with blood. She studied his face and found minute twitches among the muscles there; his clean-shaven jaw actually seemed to sprout, as she watched, a ground cover of coarse brown hairs. There were more machines this time, pumping and hissing and beeping all around him, but they seemed only to suffuse his limbs with an energy that threatened to lift him off the bed at any moment.

And for all that, she knew, he was dead. Only the body remained breathing and beating, and only by the effort of machines. She knew that now. It was just so difficult to believe. His skin was warm, the flesh of his hand resilient, the nails pink. She tried not to look at the awful scars left on the wrists—a sort of embarrassment now on a body that could no longer tuck them under sleeves. She stroked his hand and pressed each nail, watching it turn white and then flood pink on release, instantly. If he could see his own body now, so ready to rise and walk, he might have had second thoughts. Already, she believed— fickle, impulsive boy—he was having second thoughts.

The last time, after cutting his wrists, he had opened his eyes in three days. He had opened them on Libby, opened his mouth on silence, too weak to crack a joke. "You're coming to live with me," she had said, softly, fiercely. "I have the room. I'll make the room." He had nodded without a fight, tears pooling as she kissed his forehead and felt that skull on her lips. But he never came. He checked himself out one day, went to gather his few things from the blood-stained room he had been renting, and moved to another town, another job, alone. Who knew what drove him from one place, one decision, to another?

He had been a normal, happy child, if a trifle oversensitive. The smallest of losses affected him, at times, like a mortal wound, a sudden shock of awareness of all earthly loss. But the next day, he would be himself again—oblivious wise-cracker with the dazzling grin. As an adult he was always happy in a new place, a new college, a new job. He spoke with such delirious excitement in the early days of each life he chose—*this time* he had the answer to it all—that Libby rarely had the heart to remind him of all those other false roads to salvation.

He could be, had been at times, happy in Libby's presence. So often when he returned to her after a long absence, he grabbed her and lifted her bodily, effort-lessly, from the ground so that she felt as airy as a dancer. He would fold and crush her, not release her for minutes, spin her about so that she understood that she, too, was life, and he never wanted to let go.

He had always had that gift for marshaling the body's awkwardness, its em-barrassing encumbrances, into order under his will. How had he grown so ag-ile, to be able to dance her about in a way that she could never move herself? She was nearly jealous of him for that power, as he well knew. Though he was no longer cruel, as he had been in childhood, he was not above reminding her that she had never managed to outgrow her teenaged body. He still made jokes of her long limbs.

It wasn't that he meant to embarrass her, but that bodies were so simple to him. Long before this final assault, he had dealt with the problem of his own sound body, and the result was stunning, cold, efficient. Unplug the machines, donate the organs, burn what remained. Though of course he had placed that body, the task of its redistribution, in her hands.

Their mother arrived in the morning, escorted by Uncle Frank and his daughter, Libby's cousin Gail. Libby booked them all into the same downtown hotel where she had spent the mostly sleepless previous night.

Mrs. Suter greeted her daughter with a silent kiss in the hospital corridor, then stood tall and austere for the better part of an hour beneath a perfect helmet of silver hair. The lines that furrowed into her lipsticked mouth were like seams to seal it closed. Both family and strangers sensed that she must be buffered in her silence, not touched, referred to but not addressed.

The first thing she managed to say was, "It won't do to have him here." They were in the waiting room, Mrs. Suter regal enough to transform her molded plastic chair into a seat of state.

"What do you mean, Mother?"

"I'll need to make some calls, of course, and we'll have him transferred to somewhere more appropriate."

"By all means," Frank said, who had been nodding since she began to speak. Frank had the sort of face that tended to disappear from notice, though a recent gray beard offered him more definition. For ten years now, in addition to providing most of Mrs. Suter's transportation, Frank had managed the family furniture store in his brother's place, since Mrs. Suter considered it unseemly for women of her generation to work. Yet in all matters, to the smallest detail, her wishes were consulted. Their alliance had become such that Frank reflexively anticipated the direction of her thoughts, hoping to beat her to an agreeable position.

"There's that place up north," Frank suggested, "outside the perimeter—"

"Don't be ridiculous," Libby said. "He's not going anywhere. There is nothing that can be done for him elsewhere."

Mrs. Suter turned a reproving look on her daughter. "Libby, my dear, you have always been the fatalist of the family."

"No, *Warren* was the fatalist," she replied evenly.

Mrs. Suter sucked her chin back toward her throat and blinked several times. "I don't think we need that sort of talk right now."

"I'm sorry, Mother. I know."

Dr. Feldman appeared and introduced herself to Mrs. Suter and the others. Libby hoped her mother had been educated enough during Mr. Suter's long illness not to react immediately against a "woman doctor." In the doctor's upturned face, close at her mother's shoulder, there was great concern, careful deference, as she led her queenly charge toward Warren's room, Frank and Gail following while Libby remained in the hall. Feldman was after the organs, Libby suspected. But it didn't matter, so long as her mother was kept happy.

Twenty minutes passed before they emerged, and Libby could see immediately that her mother had withdrawn again behind her silence. "We'll go and get settled in the hotel," Uncle Frank whispered to her. "Why don't you come along and get some rest?"

"I'm fine. I'll stay here." She thought of kissing her mother, then thought better of it and stood wavering like a stalk.

"I'll stay with Libby," Gail said, rescuing her by the hand. "We'll go find the cafeteria."

For a moment Libby met the dark eyes of Dr. Feldman, who stood down the hall just outside Warren's door. Libby felt the need to speak to her, as if she had something urgent to say but couldn't think of what it was. The doctor seemed to understand.

"This should never have happened," Gail was saying, over a bowl of chili in the crowded cafeteria. Libby had a hard time concentrating on her cousin's creek-burble speech, which so far had struck on sympathy, on Mrs. Suter's demeanor during the drive, and on Gail's own husband and twin boys left at home. It was often hard for Libby to believe she was related to this round-faced blond with her preponderance of curving flesh, carried with the same emphatic assurance she used in speaking.

"Somebody is responsible for this," Gail insisted. "Somebody should pay."

"Yes," Libby said uncertainly. Her own food sat cooling on the tray before her.

"I mean, it's outrageous. It's gross incompetence. You don't allow someone in Warren's condition to be left alone in a cell like that. And to not let him have access to his prescribed medication—it's a crime. It's just like murder." She flailed the air with the back of a hand. "Rights have been *violated* here, and I mean severely. What did he hang himself with anyway?"

"Hmm? Uh, bedsheet, I think. I don't know."

Gail frowned. "Oh, Libby. Maybe this isn't the time. But you really do need to look into this. We must *sue* whoever is responsible. And I would say *that* is certainly the county. Or would it be the state?" Her eyes flashed over a poised spoonful of chili. "But *you* work for a law firm."

"Let's not talk about this. There's no use. My mother would never stoop to such measures. And besides, what good would it do?"

"Well, they must be made to see their error, of course! Nothing will ever change if you don't sue."

"It's not their fault. It was his decision."

"Made without the benefit of *prescribed* medication, under extreme circumstances. What kind of trumped-up charges—who gets put in jail for a few traffic tickets in the first place? It's wrongful imprisonment!"

Libby dropped her head into her hands. "Oh, God, I'm sorry," Gail said, reaching for her arm. "Really, Libby, I'm just angry and you're not ready to listen to all this."

"No, I'm glad you're saying it. You're right. All those things are true, I'm sure, but I just . . . can't think about it that way. He's put us through this waiting for so long, this waiting to see what he'll do to himself—and when. It's horrible, but I can't help thinking, at least it's over now. There's no more to wait for."

Gail was silent for a minute, her fingertips resting on Libby's arm. Then she said quietly, "Your mother thought he was doing better. You don't know. Maybe it never would have come to this."

Libby spent the early afternoon alone with Warren. He seemed more settled in his sleep now, as if he had merely cycled deeper than dreams but might again return to the surface. His jaw was darker, she was certain—he was growing a full beard. She brushed a thumb over the new growth, lifted a piece of tape that held a cotton ball over one closed eye, and the lid did not scroll open like a shade, as she half expected. She touched his still eyelid, returned the cotton and the tape.

"I hope . . ." she said, then stopped herself. So often she spoke to him aloud when he was nowhere near, but now, in this room, she couldn't tolerate the sound of her own voice. *I hope,* she thought, *that you killed yourself, Warren. I hope you did this to yourself and it wasn't me who did this to you. I hope, at least, that I didn't want this.* Distantly she recognized her own emotional numbness, some inability to feel what she needed to. It would come, she suspected. *Unless I'm dead. Unless I simply can't feel anymore.* She imagined herself drifting this way endlessly, between life and death, the horror of feeling nothing ever again.

Dr. Feldman came up behind her and put a hand on her shoulder. "I hate to think of him alone, in here," Libby said. "I mean, I know he's not here. But still."

"I realize this is a difficult time—"

"Yes. I know why you've come. He must be unplugged. I should tell you, he wants to donate his organs, whatever can be used. There is a living will."

Here you are, Warren, center stage, last dance of the hopeless romantic. In the gold light of late afternoon, the family had gathered around his bed, and Libby couldn't help thinking, with an internal clenching, how pleased he would be to witness the scene. He had waited years to bring it off, and it was beautifully lit, just the right acoustic undertone from the life-support machines. In spite of him, she was determined to be practical.

"I can't say that I see any reason to rush this," Mrs. Suter said. She stood very still, posed in a shaft of that gold light, several feet from the bed.

"We should get a second opinion." Frank paced between the bed and the window, rubbing his hands together. Gail sat in a corner chair with her cheek cradled in one hand, her eyes half closed.

"That's been taken care of," Mrs. Suter said dryly. "I'm not suggesting we behave as if we had any ultimate choice in the matter. Poor Warren."

Libby stood at Warren's head, across the bed from the others, prepared for a battle over what little remained. Dr. Feldman had left her pager number and gone home for the day, leaving Libby to resolve the family's decision. Another doctor, the one in charge of organ harvesting, waited to be notified as well.

"I think we ought to proceed," she said. "Take care of matters now, while we're all here. There will be papers to sign for the organ donation."

"Pardon, dear?" Libby's mother was not hard of hearing, though the machines did whir and click between them.

"He made it quite clear, Mother, that he wishes to donate his organs."

"Out of the question. I will not have such morbid things discussed in this room."

"Mother, stop it. You know it's the right thing to do. Someone else can benefit. And *he* wanted it."

"Well, I have never heard—! Some silly paper, some notion of your brother's . . . I don't recall organ donation being so important when your father passed."

Libby sighed. "That's because Daddy had nothing left to donate."

Suddenly she had a premonition of her *next* trip to the hospital—Warren long dead with her father—when she would be presiding over the reclining body of this woman, her mother. Mother would be next, if not poor Uncle Frank. No, these places were not through with Libby yet. They would not be put behind, forgotten, but instead always loomed in the future, waiting with sure patience.

"I certainly don't like this." Mrs. Suter sniffed, fished a handkerchief from her purse. "Not one bit. I would prefer not to be asked to think in such terms. It's so demeaning—that my son's body is so many spare parts to these people! You realize we have no control over where they would go. *Anyone* could get them."

"That's the general idea." Libby felt a burning deep in her stomach, an old complaint. Her hand trailed of its own volition over the pillow beside her and into Warren's lank hair, fingers twisting into the roots.

"They would have to cut him open. No. It's out of the question. How would we present him for the funeral?"

"In an urn, Mother. He wants cremation."

Mrs. Suter gasped, looked to Frank and Gail for assistance. "Perhaps Jeannie should be consulted," Frank offered weakly. Jeannie was Warren's ex-wife.

"That's not necessary," Libby said softly. "We can call her for the funeral, but she's no longer a part of his life."

"What funeral would you be speaking of, my dear?" her mother interjected, pressing the handkerchief to the corner of each eye. "What shall I do with an urn? He has a *plot* beside his father, beside *my* mother and father and—"

"You can bury the ashes, for all I care. And put a stone above them." She raised her hand, a fist, felt with a shock the strands of her brother's hair pulled loose and caught among her fingers.

"I don't believe I care for that tone, Elizabeth."

Frank stepped in. "Really, how can you talk about what he wants? We agree that . . . well, he's gone, right? He has no wants. What matters now are his mother's wishes, his family's wishes."

"We *are* the ones left alive, after all," Gail added petulantly. "We're the ones who have to leave our homes and our children whenever he—I mean . . . he's made his share of decisions for the week, that's all I'm saying."

"I'm sorry." Libby drew the caught hairs distractedly from her fingers. "Mother, I don't mean to be insensitive. But Warren is no longer here to defend himself. He left his wishes with me, and I'm not especially happy about that myself. But I intend to see them carried out."

"Please. Just . . . give me a minute." Her mother sounded more composed, more resigned. "I'd like to be alone with my son."

Libby was startled to find that she had gathered enough of Warren's hair from her fingers to form a full lock, shiny brown, glazed faintly with the oils of his scalp. *Oh, Warren—I'm sorry.* She kissed her fingertips and laid them at the corner of his mouth, where his lips closed on a tube crossed with tape. Tied like a great umbilicus to one of the machines, the tube from his mouth held visible beads of moisture—the heat of his breath condensed there, clinging not with ferocity but with a kind of patience. On his skin she felt the burning of life still in him, intense as the fire they would feed him to, reducing the corpus to ash so that nothing unused was left behind—no second chance, no do-overs. The one thing he had ever done right, it seemed now, was the living will.

"I'll be waiting outside," Libby said, and she walked away.

By the next day, Sunday, she had tendered the document Warren had left with her, and the family signed the necessary papers for organ and tissue donation. It was all as the doctors advised. There was no need to wait past the weekend to pull the plug. They needed to take only long enough to make the arrangements for cremation, for the memorial service to be held in Valdosta. Later there would have to be an investigation. Gail insisted, Frank insisted, and finally Mrs. Suter agreed, that someone would have to answer for their loss—but all that would wait.

Libby was exhausted. She was ready to return to Macon and sleep in her own bed, but it would be days before she would be free of the remaining obligations. In a stupor, she sat through the last gathering around Warren's bed, now attended by more of the family, who had trickled in with gradual but automatic reflux from around the state. Libby nodded to each cousin and aunt and uncle on arrival, and they allowed her to remain cocooned, silent and protected, as though she had become her mother.

In the end, Libby was alone with Warren and Dr. Feldman. Not even her mother wanted to witness the last breath. Dr. Feldman, though, had come in on her day off to see Libby through the procedure they had agreed on. "He's not exactly my responsibility anymore," she confided to Libby. "But I'll feel better about it this way."

As it turned out, there literally was a plug that would stop every machine at once, and Libby would be allowed to make the disconnection with her own hands, as if to do so were a great privilege. Yet it was a right she demanded. Dr. Feldman had explained that it would be better to leave him plugged in, for the sake of the organs, but Libby refused to say good-bye to his living body. They moved him to the operating room; she would pull the plug there.

There was nothing more to it. A simple cord that supported his life, held in her hands where he had placed it. When she touched it, round and ridged and heavy, a physical thing, she knew that it was also the very cord that bound her to her brother. His last wish was that she should lay hands on it, break it—and then he would be beyond the power to make any further demands of her. So she removed it from the wall, and the machines sighed into silence. She felt dizzily unattached to the action, as if she were floating above herself, as if she were in danger of being lost from the earth altogether. Warren must feel that way now, she thought, released like some child's balloon into the stratosphere, trailing tubes like string beyond the grasp of human hands. She would catch him back again if she could.

She watched as Dr. Feldman unhooked the IV lines, removed the hose that attached to the tube in Warren's mouth. She expected the doctor to remove the tube as well, but she left it alone, a straw reaching into the empty air of the room. Libby touched the end of the straw, hoping to feel something—a warmth, at least, some final hint of him. But there was nothing. She couldn't bring herself to kiss him again. Beyond the curtained glass, she knew, the organ harvest teams were poised and waiting for her to withdraw.

In the waiting room, there was a quiet family reunion in progress. Libby found a chair at the edge, drew her knees up to her chin, and instantly her composure collapsed in tears. Her hair fell over her knees like a privacy curtain, and she hoped no one would notice her there at all. Above her, Warren drifted on a black, glittering current of air, dimly visible, so high, and Libby felt herself stretching as if on tiptoe to reach him. He stretched downward through stars, past planets, one hand reaching to brush the tips of his fingers against hers. Nothing more. But he smiled, she thought. Smiled.

Some time later—she couldn't have said how long, except that few of her family members had altered their positions in the room—she rose and went past them, and then down the hall. She thought perhaps she was looking for a restroom. But the tips of all her fingers vibrated oddly, and she had the growing sense, clarifying to conviction, that Warren was not dead in the least, that he had only played out his greatest joke yet. Dr. Feldman was nowhere in evidence; instead Libby found a startled nurse, to whom she tried to explain her need to see Warren. "That room isn't ready," the nurse told her, but Libby answered that it didn't matter. Whatever the conditions, she had to see him, immediately.

At Libby's persistence, the nurse relented and led her back through the locked double doors. And then she was alone in the room again, beside his sheet-draped body, amid the silence of the machines. The operating team must have made its exit in a rush, leaving behind medical refuse and trays that crooked at odd angles as if shoved hastily aside. On a tray close to the bed, she noticed a sponge damp with a rusty orange surgical scrub, still pinched into a finger hold. Beside it, a curved set of pincers gaped open, the blood caked and drying in the gaps of its delicate teeth.

His blood. She would have to burn it: all the instruments and sponges, as well as this stained sheet that now covered the empty container of his body. Is that what he had meant for her to do? To clean this room once the doctors had left? His eyes, still shut beneath their X's of tape, stubbornly refused to answer. He had always been this way, she told herself, so willful and perverse—always. What more did she expect of him now? The straw still reached from his mouth, and she studied it from a distance until the clear tubing seemed to go milky opaque, the way a cold pane of window glass might fog under his breath.

She thought of how her own windows, back home in Macon, fogged that way in winter and cleared again, lit with the sun. As the pecan trees let go of their leaves with each colder, shorter day, so the house would seem to open out, brighter than before. In winter she liked to take her reading into the back bedroom, the one that had no other use; by winter light, it was the best room in the house. Now she felt herself standing at the threshold of that room, and Warren seemed to lie safe in the spare bed, under her grandmother's double-wedding-ring quilt and a gauze of the palest light. She went to him and stood quietly beside his bed as if he were sleeping—no tubes here, no tape. After a while she found his upturned wrist beneath the sheet, lifted it carefully so as not to wake him. As if stitching she slowly trailed a finger back and forth over the ridge of the shocking scar that persisted—even in this room and her best dream of him, her most careful effort.

James Kilgo

James Kilgo was born and grew up in Darlington, South Carolina, but after study at Wofford College and Tulane University, he moved in 1967 to Athens, Georgia, where he lived until his death in 2002. In the early 1980s, in the midst of a career as a teacher of southern and American literature at the University of Georgia, Kilgo began writing newspaper sketches about hunting. These led to a more formal series of personal essays on nature, friendship, and family, which were collected in 1988 as *Deep Enough for Ivorybills*. A second essay collection, *Inheritance of Horses* (1994), and a novel, *Daughter of My People* (1998), followed. His final book was *The Colors of Africa* (2003). In "The Resurrection of George T. Sutton," set in South Carolina, Kilgo explores themes that lie at the center of all his work: family, memory, storytelling, and the past.

The Resurrection of George T. Sutton

Growing up in a graveyard convinced me from an early age of the persistent presence of the past. Our house did not actually stand among tombstones, but it was next door, close neighbor to the Methodist dead. The church that buried them had long since moved to a better part of town, leaving the graveyard to weeds and briars. By the time I was born, it had become a gloomy wood, home for possums and haven for wandering drunks. In summer thunderstorms, large limbs sometimes crashed down upon the tombstones, and when autumn came, drifting leaves covered the broken slabs. Yet some stones remained upright in the deep shade, often wearing hanks of Spanish moss, their stained faces carved with the angels and bleeding lambs of nineteenth-century piety.

With the other boys on my street I played cowboys and Indians among the monuments, and one summer we even built a tree house in a huge laurel oak that stood just within the graveyard. But we were always out of there by dark, when ghosts began to stir. At bedtime, from the window of my room, I could watch the restless dead gathering at the edge of our yard. You can imagine what my dreams were like.

On the other side of the graveyard, where the trees thinned out and sunlight prevailed, stood a structure that looked like a green, leafy cabin. Its walls were high fences of wrought-iron spears, its roof a blanket of kudzu, peaked twice like a circus tent. At each end, heavy iron gates barred entrance. By the time I was ten, I suspected that the darkness within concealed a story—some shameful secret of murder or suicide carved in granite.

One afternoon two of my friends bet me a dime that I didn't have the guts to enter the kudzu castle, read the monument, and return with "the secret of the crypt." Spurred on more by the dare than by the dime, I raced home for a flashlight, then back to collect. One of the iron gates was ground ajar, just wide enough for a skinny boy to squeeze through. Down two stone steps—a trembling descent into the underworld—my bare feet recoiled at the squishy carpet of leaf fall, but I probed bravely with the beam of light and kept moving. Directly before me stood a granite spire. I could see nothing on the first side, but on the opposite face I discovered a woman—a Victorian lady in bas-relief, head bowed in sorrow. Something was written beneath that scene, but paying no attention to the words, I rushed back to the sunlight outside and told my friends that the secret was a grieving lady. Pictures didn't count, they said, and kept their dime.

When I was twelve my family moved to the other side of town, but unlike the Methodist church I was unable to leave the dead behind. Ever since, I have been a hunter of lost tales, an old-story archaeologist, brushing dirt from brown bones and seeking articulations.

Having grown up on that same street, my father had played in the graveyard too, but whenever I asked about somebody buried there, he'd say, "That was before my time, Son. You'd have to ask Doctor Whit about that." He meant Doctor Whitfield Mackenzie: an authority on the lore of our town and reported to be the best storyteller in that part of the state. "Whit needs to write those stories down," you'd often hear somebody say, " 'cause they'll sho die with him if he don't."

Most of Doctor Whit's material was apparently either too bawdy or too grotesque for children, however, and by the time I was old enough to listen to his stories, he had lost his voice to cancer. I was sixteen or seventeen then, one of a small group of boys who had begun to realize that the whole town was a graveyard and Doctor Whit its chief custodian. We took to dropping by his house in the afternoons, where we'd find him in his bathrobe, sitting at the kitchen table, drinking rum and grapefruit juice. He seemed to enjoy our company, and despite the tracheotomy, he tried to entertain us with old Darlington anecdotes. At first the sounds he uttered shocked me—electronic and uninflected, more like those of a robot than a man. And with each costly word the little flap of gauze fluttered at his throat.

Some of us talked about writing his stories down at that point, but no one got around to it. Then, before I finished high school, Doctor Whit died. What I remembered of his tales after he was gone was little more than headstone information—such as the hanging of a black girl by Union officers in 1866 for stealing a silver mirror from her mistress. (The mistress happened to be sleeping with one of those Union officers—Doctor Whit liked that story because of what he thought it said about Yankees.) Or the talk about a mulatto woman named Ella David, said to have been beautiful, and her hit-and-run death as she—in the company of a prominent white man—was walking away from his broken-down automobile at three o'clock one morning. Or the bizarre case of a man named Sutton—an important name in Darlington—who set his brother's corpse in a buggy, put a hat on its head, and drove it all over town.

From what I could gather, the brother had died under mysterious circumstances in his law office on the public square, and Sutton had placed the body—sitting up as though alive—in the buggy and drove it around town. The next day, for some reason, he drove the corpse across town to the dead man's house and there called a barber to come shave it. After the body was buried quietly, the rumor spread that the dead man had supposedly gone to New York where he had caught a boat for France.

By the time I began to realize that such old tales were worth saving, it was almost too late. I no longer lived in Darlington, and most of the others who might have remembered Doctor Whit's stories were also dead. Once, during a visit with my parents, I asked my father about the Sutton brothers. "That was a little before my time," he said. "I bet Whit Mackenzie could have told you."

Finally, I called one of the guys who used to sit with us at the doctor's kitchen table and asked if he remembered the Sutton story.

"One of them committed suicide by drinking poison, didn't he?"

"Suicide? I didn't remember that. Do you know why?"

"Something to do with fraud? I'm not sure. I think he was supposed to have escaped to France or somewhere."

But that's all my friend remembered.

With each generation, I suppose, such stories pass from a town's collective memory into an oblivion of lost tales. With the Sutton story, however, I felt that I could actually see—as on a movie screen—the familiar courthouse square and, circling it, the brothers in their buggy. It seemed all in living color at first, yet it stiffened before my eyes into a black-and-white cartoon which, in turn, disintegrated into scraps that blew away in a roaring wind.

Only after I had conceded that the Sutton story was irretrievable (and had all but forgotten it myself) did one of the scraps, caught in crazy metaphysical vortex, blow back into the present and land, literally in my lap. The scrap was a copy of an old document, forwarded to me by my father. "Dear Son," his note began, "Cousin Paul found the enclosed buried among some papers in his basement. He has no idea whether it's fact or speculation—and no idea how this curious account passed into his hands. See if it's not the same story as you heard from Whit Mackenzie."

The document was a photocopy of a manuscript written on blank paper in a crabbed hand, undated and unsigned:

> Mr. George Tilghman Sutton is the subject I am writing about. I'm not sure that I have his middle name right. It dos't sound just right. He used to go by his given name initials but G. T. dos't sound right either altho it may be.
>
> He was president of a small independent cotton oil before it was taken over by Carolina Cotton Oil Co, the present corporation in Darlington. He was supposed to make big profits and paid large dividends, thereby was able to sell much stock. By selling stock he was able to buy or build other mills. In time by paying such large dividends he found he needed more money so he opened a

bank where Mason Daniels had his insurance business. He would use the bank money to keep his business going. I don't think he had any idea of stealing but he had a big ego to be known as a big business man. He kept two fine horses and William, who drove later for Dr. Paul Bent, drove for him. Taking him to the mill, driving him to Florence to take a train for New York where he was supposed to attend directors meeting of some big corporation every month. He lived diagonal across the street from our house before he bought the big house with a fountain in front of it on Cashua Street. Mr. Sutton was in big style riding behind the two high stepping horses with William driving. He never mingled with the people. I don't recall hearing anything about his wife or ever seeing her or about them going to church.

At his directors meeting he would pass around Oxford cigars costing 10 cents each—now they cost probably 25 cents. Have them all smoking and in a good humor then he'd read his phony report. One thing he failed to count on, however—all the directors were not dumb. Mr. Benton Charles got suspicious and made a trip to Charleston to check on a quantity of oil Mr. Sutton claimed was stored there among his assets. No oil was found. Mr. Charles went immediately to the Judge and got an injunction—seizing the books of the oil company and closing the bank.

Mr. Sutton wired his brother Hugh in New York to come down and tell him what he should do. It is a disgrace among the Sutton clan to go to prison and the only alternative is suicide. So Mr. Sutton came in the drugstore that late afternoon. He bought a hair brush and other articles then casually asked me for two oz. carbolic acid. I found that we had none melted and told him it would take ten or fifteen minutes. He said not to bother and went to the corner drugstore where the bank is now and bought four ounces carbolic acid which he took to his uncle's law office where Tommy Gardner's law office is now located. Hugh was waiting for him. Mr. Sutton sat down and Hugh poured the acid in a glass and mixed it with some whiskey and handed it to his brother who drank it. It was late afternoon—light enough outside but with no light in the office one couldn't see clearly. Hugh phoned for Dr. Tilghman Bent. He came and found the dead man sitting in a chair and Hugh standing by. The doctor pronounced Mr. Sutton dead and permitted, at the request of Hugh, the removal of the body to his former residence. The doctor was too frightened at this crazy man's commands that all he could say was OK. So one on one side and another on the other they walked the dead man down the stairs and across the sidewalk to his carriage so any passerby wouldn't know what was going on. They had John Doyle to come up next day and shave him. The report got out that Mr. Sutton got away and caught a boat in New York and was in Paris. This swiftly went from mouth to mouth and built up to such an extent that the people actually made Dr. Bent half way believe that it was a dummy that he pronounced dead and the coroner likewise—also the barber. The report was so persistent that Judge Madden actually ordered that the body be dug up to make sure that it was not a dummy which they buried. He is buried in the cemetery on Orange Street. Nothing was ever done about Hugh's part in the affair.

Clearly, the anonymous author was the druggist first approached by George Sutton. Neither my father nor Cousin Paul had any idea what his name might have been, but that was merely incidental. The story had been hovering out there all this time—*wanting to be told,* waiting for someone whose sympathy was strong enough to bring it forth. Now that this much of it had come to me, I had to do something about it. The document contained enough news to get me started.

That big house with the fountain in front of it on Cashua Street, for example, had to be the old Terrell place—during my childhood a flaking facade screened from the sidewalk by a wrought-iron fence and a tall stand of weeds in the yard. The fountain, large and ornate, stood in the center of a wide walk leading from the gate to the front steps. I had been told that a Jewish merchant had built the house some time around the turn of the century to please his bride, who on their wedding trip to Venice had been delighted by the Doge's Palace and wanted one just like it but on a smaller scale. They had named the extravaganza "Villa Valentina," but within a year of its completion the young wife died. Eventually the house was owned by the Terrell family, but before that apparently it had been George T. Sutton who bought it from the heartbroken husband—probably at a good price.

That house must have been the showplace of Darlington during the years of the Sutton residency. Remembering it in ruins, I could imagine the fine carriage, with William perched above those high-stepping horses, swinging through the pillared gate onto cobbled Cashua Street, the well-dressed Mr. Sutton looking neither to the left nor the right.

Using the manuscript account, I could follow Mr. Sutton to his bank on the corner of the square, to the board room filled with expensive cigar smoke, to the train station in Florence ten miles away. I could even walk with him up the stairs to his uncle's law office, for I had climbed those dark old stairs myself as a child going to the dentist. But I had real trouble following him into the office on that last day of October when he sat down with his brother, just in from New York, and explained what he aimed to do. *With no light in the office one could not have seen clearly,* according to the druggist, who hadn't been there. If he or Doctor Whit had quoted even one statement by either of the Suttons, enough might have been revealed for me to understand how a man could help his brother commit suicide. As it was, the two figures merely flickered, silhouettes on a silent screen.

A week after receiving the manuscript I drove to Darlington. The "cemetery on Orange Street" was the old Methodist graveyard that I had grown up in. I had no recollection of any Sutton buried there, but if I could find his headstone I would at least know for sure that George Sutton had died. And that, in turn, would prove that he had lived.

A drive-through branch of the Carolina National Bank now stands on the site of what was once the Villa Valentina, and the Sutton brothers certainly would not recognize the square now. The building where George Sutton had died was gutted by fire long ago. And during the sixties our progressive city fathers demolished the domed and columned courthouse that had stood in the center, erecting in its place a six-story concrete shoebox. At the corner where an elegant opera house once stood—one of only three of its kind in South Carolina—people now park their cars for easy shopping. Progressive thinking had reached all the way to the shady little street of my childhood and bulldozed the house where I was born and the house next to it, making room for a row of condominiums. It did stop short of moving the dead—the Methodist church saw to that—although in cleaning up the old graveyard, they failed to restore to their proper places the broken and vandalized tombstones.

Still, even without the landmark trees, I go straight to the crypt of the grieving lady. Unfenced and stripped of kudzu, the plot lies exposed to the sun, smaller than I remembered. I had thought it was sunken, two steps down. Had I imagined that? I am almost afraid to look for the grieving lady, but there she is, too good to be true, though younger than she had seemed when I was a child. The inscription I once suspected of containing a dreadful secret suggests that the man for whom she grieves was her husband:

> This last act of devoted affection is
> Performed for him who sleeps below,
> But memory embalms him in the
> Shrine of a sorrowing faithful heart.

No scandal after all, though George Sutton's wife must have wept like that. In fact, the carved figure is almost close enough to George's grave to play the role of his widow. Without having to take another step, I spot it—just beyond the further obelisk, alongside the Orange Street sidewalk—a small granite stone inscribed

GEORGE TILGHMAN SUTTON
Jan. 8 1872–Nov. 3 1910.

No wonder I never saw the marker. In those days it was hidden beneath a carpet of kudzu.

Why, I wonder, did the widow choose this graveyard, already out of use by 1910, especially when the Suttons had always buried their dead in Grove Hill, the large public cemetery on the other side of town? Maybe the rest of the family begrudged George a site, forcing someone like Tilghman Bent, on behalf of the desperate Mrs. Sutton, to importune the Methodist Board of Trustees to find room for one more in this crowded old field. Lying solitary between the sidewalk and the grieving lady, his grave looks like an afterthought.

Even so, the town apparently found this innocuous little headstone an unacceptably prosaic conclusion to such a scandalous story. Some of them, according to the druggist, actually believed that old George was living it up on their money with a beautiful foreign woman in some French Villa Valentina, while a dummy occupied his grave. I find it hard to understand how Tilghman Bent, who examined the body and then assisted Hugh Sutton in hauling it out to the carriage, was ever persuaded that George was anything but dead. It's even harder to believe that a man as earnestly sober as Judge Wilbur Madden was prevailed upon to order the opening of the grave.

The judge was still alive when I was a child, living in a columned brick mansion only a block away from our house. I remember him as a small man, fussing among his camellias or seriously gathering eggs from his henhouse, and I was a little afraid of him. Even when his grandson Billy came from out of town for summer vacation and I was invited over to play, we lowered our voices when the judge came through the room. Judge Madden was strictly business.

I can see them gathered here on a cold night—let's say in February of 1912—the judge and Tilghman Bent, John Charlton the coroner (also the undertaker), the sheriff, and two gravediggers. The gravediggers work by lantern light, which throws long shadows on the curtains of Spanish moss. If a man, walking home late from work, pauses to see what's going on, the sheriff sends him on his way. Doctor Bent takes a drink of whiskey from the bottle that he's been hiding in his coat, and the judge stands as silent as a graveyard statue. They all hear the hollow grating sound as the spade strikes wood.

What they find is a corpse all right—they can tell that without having to look—but Tilghman Bent leans forward with the lantern long enough to make sure that it is in fact poor George. Then they bury him again and go home to their warm houses.

But I, having returned after thirty years to the backyard of my childhood, sit musing once again upon the bones of the past, George Sutton's old bones, trying to understand.

When faced with the odd behavior of Southern gentlemen, especially of that day, one does well to remember that they tried to live by a code of chivalry. Since chivalry makes no sense apart from ladies and dragons, I must consider the shadowy Mrs. Sutton, of whom the druggist surprisingly knew nothing besides the fact that neither she nor her husband ever went to church. George Sutton's reason for drinking acid instead of using the quicker bullet may have been to conceal the guilt implicit in suicide, but I prefer to believe that he chose that terrible alternative as a way of sparing his wife the shame of being widowed by his own disgraced hand. That would have been a noble gesture for a man who had stolen the life savings of poor people, but in Southern gentlemen the chivalric ideal often persisted after all else was gone.

Hugh Sutton is another matter. What kind of man would mix a carbolic-acid cocktail for his brother, sit and watch him drink it, then prop up the corpse in a buggy and take it for a ride?

I walk over to the grieving lady. The slant of the afternoon sun casts her in bold relief. Leaning against an urn that stands on a pedestal, she weeps into a handkerchief. A naked foot that I did not remember peeps out from beneath the hem of her gown, suggesting a bedroom intimacy, and suddenly it occurs to me that perhaps another woman grieved for George Sutton too.

Let's call her Edith, make her a New York widow in her early thirties, and suppose Hugh had the misfortune of falling in love with her. She would have found his Carolina accent delightful and adored his courtly manners, but as Hugh grew more fervent she would have made it clear that, dear boy though Hugh was, she was still in mourning for her husband. Then George came to town. Hugh would have introduced Edith to his older brother at a small gathering of mutual friends, and I can see her deciding on the spot that one could not go on forever living in the past.

When George began making monthly visits to the city, he was no longer welcome at Hugh's place. He had to stay at a small hotel in Washington Square—a little finer than he could really afford, but Edith was a lady of discrimination. Except for Hugh's priggish disapproval, the arrangement suited George beautifully. And Hugh would get over it in time, George said. The boy had never had a chance with Edith anyway—hadn't she told him that—so how could he think that George had stolen his girl? Clearly Hugh did think so, however, and he nursed his resentment. Yet when George's telegram arrived, Hugh boarded the next train south.

Let's rewind the film now and add the sound: The train pulls into Florence at about four o'clock on a Friday afternoon. Hugh steps down from the platform, recognizes George's driver William, and hands him his valise. During the forty-five minutes it takes to drive to Darlington, Hugh tries to doze, but the questions that kept him awake half the night in his rocking Pullman berth won't let him nap in the carriage. George's wire said only, "Trouble. Stop. Please come now. Stop." Hugh knows little of George's business affairs, but he figures the trouble has to do with money. George has been spending a world of it lately on his trips to New York, and, since George said please, the trouble must be bad. He can't imagine what George thinks he can do. Probably help him devise a legal ploy to nullify his debts. George has never been troubled much by scruples.

October has been a dry month in South Carolina. The carriage toils through deep sand, and the leather seats are powdered gray with dust. Hugh did not try to shave in the swaying coach that morning, and all day he's been looking forward to a barbershop. He rubs his sandpaper jaw and decides to have William drop him off on the square.

As they approach town they drive past small weathered shacks on both sides of the road, past black children playing in the yards. Then the carriage clatters across the Atlantic Coastline tracks, and Hugh notices they've finished a new tobacco warehouse on the left, an encouraging sign of local prosperity. A shiny yellow automobile turns into the street up ahead, putt-putting toward the square. Darlington may enter the twentieth century yet, Hugh thinks. Soon he can see the dome and columned portico of the new courthouse, standing on the ashes of its predecessor, and beyond that the clock tower of the new opera house, completed just before Hugh moved to New York. Five of five, the clock says.

When they reach the corner where Main and Pearl enter the square, William turns left—not the way to Cashua Street or to the barbershop. "William, where are you going?"

"Mr. George say bring you to Mr. Ned's office."

The horses swing wide through the turn, and William pulls them to a halt at the curb. Hugh steps down, gives the man a quarter. As the carriage pulls away, he enters the doorless dark vestibule and climbs the groaning stairs toward the office where he first read law. At the top and to the right he faces the familiar gilt letters on the window of the door: EDWIN A. SUTTON ATTORNEY AT LAW. Beyond the door the rooms are dim with late afternoon light. Hugh anticipates the mixed odor of leather and tarnished brass. He wonders if he should knock, decides against it and turns the knob. "George?" he calls.

"In here."

Hugh crosses the outer chamber to his uncle's office. George is sitting slumped in one of the upholstered chairs, his fingers braided before his face. He looks to Hugh as though he's been sitting there for a week, but he manages to get to his feet and extend a listless hand before dropping back into the chair. Hugh is shocked by his brother's appearance. Usually well groomed, George has not shaved in several days; he wears neither collar nor cravat, and his famous waxed handlebar hangs ragged upon his lip. In the close air, Hugh can tell that he hasn't bathed.

Hugh opens a cabinet, finds a quart of State Dispensary whiskey and two glasses. Assuming the role of host, he asks, "May I fix you a drink?"

"No," says George.

Hugh sits down in the chair behind the desk, studies his glass in the light that comes through the window at his back. People have always said that he and George resemble one another. The features of their faces do share the strong Sutton stamp, but George of late has grown considerably thicker than Hugh, and his face is darker. Has George been drinking too much? He seems sober enough at the moment. As Hugh waits for his brother to begin, he notes with wry pleasure that George has chosen the chair in which for forty years a succession of wretched men and troubled women have sat, rehearsing their tales of self-justification, while he, fortified behind Uncle Ned's massive desk, occupies the seat of the counselor.

"They locked me out of my bank, Hugh. Out of my own goddamn bank, if you can believe it." George speaks in a low voice, uninflected, almost catatonic. His black eyes reflect no light.

"Why did they do that, George?" Hugh knows that he sounds more like a lawyer than a brother, but he can't help it, or won't. George seems not to notice.

"I don't know."

"What do they say?"

"It was Benton Charles—a back-stabbing son of a bitch if there ever was one. Didn't have the decency to come to me first. Came back from Charleston, went straight to Wilbur Madden. The bastards locked me out of my own bank."

George has been close-mouthed about his business affairs for so long, Hugh thinks, that now when he needs to be forthcoming he can't break the habit. "Why did he go to Charleston?"

"I don't know. To verify some oil, he says."

"Oil you reported as an asset?"

George nods.

"Did he not find it?"

"He says not."

"Why didn't you show them the invoice? You do have the receipts, don't you?"

"They've all turned against me. Even Benton. They seized my books."

Same old George, Hugh thinks. No matter the trouble, it's never his fault. "I'm going to have to know more than that before I can help you, George."

George is silent for what seems a long time, merely staring, expressionless. Finally he says, "There's nothing you can do."

"You got me all the way down here from New York to tell me that?"

George mumbles an answer.

"I didn't hear you."

"I need you to say it was a heart attack."

"To say it was . . . what in the name of God are you talking about?"

"That's all you have to do. Just say it was a heart attack."

"George, for God's sake—"

"I'm not going to jail, Hugh."

"Is it that bad?"

"That's what they say."

"Okay, George, but listen. We can work this out. If it's money we're talking about, I can help. Not a great deal, but some. We can find the rest some other way. We'll hire the best lawyer in the state, should it really come to that."

"I'll not stand trial, Hugh. Not in this county."

"I know, George, but there are ways to avoid that. If you'll stop talking nonsense and tell me what I need to know, we'll figure something out."

"In just a few minutes now I'm going to get up and go down to Townsend's. When I get back we'll have that drink."

For the first time that afternoon George manages a flicker of a smile, but the room darkens as he speaks. It seems to Hugh that the temperature drops ten degrees, twenty degrees. He begins to shiver. "George. For God's sake. Think of Nell."

"That's exactly who I am thinking of. Otherwise I'd just use this." He draws from his coat pocket a well-oiled revolver. It gleams in the soft light.

Something in Hugh Sutton caves in. "There must be another way," he says again, but his voice lacks conviction.

As though invigorated by the hard, weighty object in his hand, George's voice grows stronger. "Well, there's not. So you listen to me. When it's over I want you to telephone Till Bent. He shouldn't be drunk yet—not this early. Tell him I'm having a heart attack or a stroke or something. I'm sure Till knows about this other business"—George waves his hand vaguely toward the square, the courthouse, the padlocked bank on the opposite corner—"I'm hoping he'll think that caused it. But if he don't, Hugh—if he sees the truth, I mean—you're going to have to make him understand. That I did it for Nell's sake. You tell him that, you hear. Think what the bastards would say, Hugh, what it would do to her, and make Till understand."

Hugh rises and turns to the window. The light, as weak as it is, blinds him for a moment. The clock strikes the half hour. A wagon creeps along the street below, an old black man driving an ancient mule. Hugh has never known his brother to plead for help.

"Will you do that?"

"George."

"Will you?"

"I don't know, George."

"God knows I'm sorry to have to ask it of you."

Hugh's knees buckle. It has never occurred to him that people who commit suicide might be in control enough to ask their brothers to help. Addled, Hugh hears the sighing of the springs in the chair, hears George say, "I'll be right back."

Townsend's Pharmacy is directly beneath the law office. George emerges· sooner than Hugh expected. Without his hat he looks half-dressed. Instead of turning the corner toward the door to the stairway he crosses the intersection, walking purposefully toward the Darlington Apothecary on the south side of the square. Two men meet at the corner below, greet each other with a handshake, and stop to talk. Hugh can see only the tops of their hats—a couple of good citizens on their way home from another day of keeping store. They'd be talking about George, he reckons, secure in the confidence of their own decency, shaking their heads. Sh, here he comes now, they're probably saying, as George crosses toward the corner where they stand. He passes without speaking and disappears from Hugh's view. The two men watch him as he goes.

Hugh hears George's feet on the stairs. The door opens and closes, and George enters the room. He takes a bottle of clear liquid from its sack and places it on the desk beside the whiskey. Then he returns to his chair. Hugh stares at the bottles, mesmerized by the amber glow of the bourbon in the chilly light, the only spot of color in the room.

"I'll take that drink now."

Jesus, Hugh thinks, he really wants me to do it. Isn't it enough that I've come eight hundred miles, to shiver in this unheated room? Not to mention whatever I've agreed to do afterward.

"I just don't know that I can pour it, Hugh. If you could do that for me . . . with a little whiskey."

Hugh reaches for the dispensary bottle, trying to hold steady. He has just begun to realize that, for the first time in their lives, George is allowing them to be brothers. Hugh manages to pour two fingers of whiskey, then—his hand shaking noticeably—he adds the acid, all four ounces. The darker liquid swirls, diluted by the lighter. The concoction looks as harmless as bourbon and water. Hugh picks it up, walks around the desk, and hands it to George. Then he turns away and pours another whiskey for himself.

"I don't reckon you've talked to Edith lately?" George asks.

The question stuns Hugh. "No. I never see her."

"I guess not."

Edith, he thinks. For God's sake.

"She's a firecracker," George says. Hugh turns as his brother raises his glass. Before he can stop himself, Hugh lifts his in response. As though needing that gesture as a sign of permission, George drinks. Before he has finished, Hugh walks over to the window.

Lights have come on in the stores around the square. The men are still talking on the corner. George makes a terrible gagging noise, but Hugh remains at the window. George's breathing grows labored, interrupted by sounds that Hugh has never before heard. On the sidewalk across the street, a man comes out of the barbershop next door to the apothecary. It's Harvey Thompson, a man he hasn't seen in years. Hugh rubs his chin. George makes a sound that sounds like *Hugh,* and his brother almost turns. George says it again—if in fact he's saying anything—but Hugh remains at the window, his hands gripping the sill. He doesn't see how either one of them can stand it much longer.

Later Hugh will not remember calling Tilghman Bent nor waiting for him to arrive. Perhaps he remained at the window, except for the time it took to ring the operator, insensible of passing time, of the sprawled corpse, of his own name. He will have no recollection of what he said when Till answered the telephone, but he will never forget the heavy creak of Till's feet coming up the stairs, nor the look on his face when he spotted George, nor the way he said, "Oh Jesus."

Till Bent lowers himself heavily to one knee, says, "Light that lamp, son." As Hugh strikes a match, the doctor applies his stethoscope, listens for a moment, then shakes his head. The room grows warm with light. The doctor discovers a glass on the carpet and raises it to his nose. Through the rich aroma of bourbon he detects the odor of phenol and says *Jesus* again. Gripping the arm of the chair in which George lies, he hauls himself to his feet.

"It was the damnedest thing I ever saw, Till. We were just sitting here talking, and all of a sudden George broke out in a sweat and started clawing at his throat. I ran in there to call you on the telephone, and when I got back he was gone. It was just that quick."

"What did he use, son? Carbolic acid?"

As if poleaxed, Hugh Sutton drops to his knees. Clutching the edge of the desk, he lowers his face and begins to sob. Till Bent lifts the younger man by the elbow and guides him into the chair; then, finding Hugh's glass, he pours him a shot of whiskey. "Drink this," he orders, and he takes a swallow himself straight from the bottle. "Now, son, I want you to get aholt of yourself. I'm going to ring John Charlton. I'll be right back."

Hugh jumps to his feet. "No!" he says, placing himself between the doctor and the door. "You stay right there, Till. This was a heart attack, you hear. I don't care what you smelled in the goddamned glass: George died of a heart attack, and that's what we're going to say. George said to make you understand."

Hugh gulps some whiskey before going on. "He was thinking of Nell. He said it would be up to us, Till, up to you and me, to protect her. He was counting on us."

Tilghman Bent needs to sit down and think about that. And he needs another shot to help him think more clearly. Gripping the bottle by its neck, he drops into the unoccupied chair beside the corpse. After a while he says, "Okay, Hugh, but we still need to call John Charlton. But listen now: John'll do what I tell him. He'll go along."

"No, Till, I can't let you do that."

"I have to, son. Otherwise, what are we going to do with George here? You don't plan to take him to the undertaker yourself, do you?"

"I plan to take him home, Till. But I'm going to need your help."

"You're upset, son. Sit back down now and have another drink. You know you can't do that."

"Yes I can, Till. I'm going to. And don't you try to stop me."

Till Bent opens his mouth to speak, but a wild look in Hugh's eye helps him decide that for the moment it's better to play along. So he rises heavily from the chair. "How are we going to do this fool thing?"

Hugh takes hold of his brother from behind and the doctor lifts the feet. George is heavier than Hugh expected, and Till Bent has trouble backing down the steps. At the bottom Hugh gently lays the body down, removes his hat, and places it on the head, taking care to push it down tight so that it will stay put. "Let's lift him up now and walk him out to the buggy. Come on, Till. As though he were drunk. If we see anybody, just say he's sick."

Together they heave the corpse to its feet, arrange its arms around their necks, and walk it, feet dragging, out onto the sidewalk. There is no one in sight.

The Sutton mare and the doctor's horse, hitched side by side, shy at the approach of the strange trio. The mare pitches her head against the fastened reins, snorts, and backs away. Till Bent has to leave Hugh to manage George on his own while he tries to catch the mare's rearing head. But Hugh cannot get his brother's body into the lurching buggy without hugging it to his chest like a sack of fertilizer. When at last he has humped it up onto the floor board, he climbs into the buggy from the other side and pulls George up onto the seat beside him.

In all that tug and struggle George has lost his hat, and Hugh notices that one of his shoes is also missing. "Forget the goddamn shoe," the doctor says. "Let's get this madness over with."

But Hugh insists on retrieving it. Back at the buggy, he slips the shoe onto the dead man's foot, as deftly as a shoe salesman, and laces it tight. On the seat again, he spreads a lap robe across the legs, taking care to arrange it just so, all the while mumbling to himself—or to George. At last he raises the folded roof, grabs the back of George's coat collar to hold him in place, and tells Till he's ready.

A hazy autumn twilight lies upon the town. Gas lights flicker in the gloom.

The mare is eager to get to the barn, and with only one hand Hugh has trouble keeping her reined in, but he can't let go of his brother. As they rattle past the Confederate soldier on the courthouse lawn, Hugh begins to talk to George. "Just take it easy, Bubba," he tells him. "It's going to be all right. We're almost there."

Hardly a soul would have been on the street at that still hour, though a month later half the people in Darlington claimed to have seen the buggy enter the square. Some insisted that Hugh drove all the way around the courthouse, a full lap and a half, before he turned down Cashua Street. Others swore for a fact that they saw him go around several times, as though he were caught on a merry-go-round—might be circling still, they said, if the doctor had not intervened. But the truth is that Hugh could not have kept the mare from home if he had wanted to.

Tilghman Bent was outdone by Hugh's insistence on taking the body to the house, but having participated that far, he just took another drink and played it out, telling people the next day that George Sutton had suffered a heart attack in Edwin Sutton's law office. No, he wasn't seeing visitors, not even Mrs. Sutton; his condition was perilous. Hugh shut himself up in the bedroom with the corpse and stayed there until Saturday night when it became evident even to him that George could not last much longer. By the time the doctor was allowed to pronounce the dead man dead, the barber John Doyle refused to shave the corpse.

Anyone driving past on Orange Street can see me sitting on this tombstone, for the woods that grew on this acre when I was a child have been cut down. No doubt they wonder what business I have in such a place. George Tilghman Sutton rests in peace, I hope, buried twice and mourned forever by the barefooted lady a few feet away. But I wonder about Hugh. Did he spend the rest of his life in New York City, hiding his dreadful secret from the people he knew? Or did he confess to every man he met how he learned to be a brother? I'd like to read his epitaph, but not knowing where he's buried, I'll have to settle for what the druggist said: *Nothing was ever done about Hugh's part in the affair.*

Carol Lee Lorenzo

Carol Lee Lorenzo was born in 1939 in Atlanta, Georgia. She devoted most of her adult life to acting and to writing fiction for young adults and has published three novels in that genre. In 1995 she published a collection of stories entitled *Nervous Dancer*. Written for adult readers, this collection earned her the Flannery O'Connor Award for Short Fiction. Lorenzo has taught fiction writing at Callanwolde Fine Arts Center in Atlanta, Emory University, and Oglethorpe University. Her stories have been published in *Primavera, Pennsylvania Review,* and *Epoch.* Her story "Nervous Dancer" is a skillful and unrelenting examination, by indirect and allusive means, of the forces that weigh on personal relationships, especially those involving parents.

Nervous Dancer

We do not leave the ocean's side, but follow the thin, worn-out highway on the hard ridge of shells and sand cliffs. We see over the swells of the ocean, night trying hard to come down. Still a crack of white light stays between the ocean and night. It is as if someone keeps reaching up and tearing night off at the bottom.

For a minute, I feel lonely in the car with Julien, my husband. We should not have come here—to my mother's house—for vacation. I am not feeling so good away from time schedules, crowds of strangers, and tight deadlines of the city that keep pushing us forward from one event into another. In the city I do not have time to ponder that I love my mother but do not like being around her.

Julien does not know my mother well. He does not know that she hates men. He knows her in the casual way of her coming to the city to visit, bringing her own washcloth, soap, and a homemade dessert, to sleep fitfully on our living room couch. Julien has never met my father, but he has spoken to him by phone. Ten years ago, when I felt desperate to marry Julien, it was then that my father chose to leave my mother's house.

The car headlights are on; it looks like Julien is following the two beams instead of the road, carefully following the color yellow.

The dog, which I hold on my lap, pants heavily, a wild taint to her breath. I crack the window as if for a heavy smoker. I feel I am inside her lungs.

We get to my mother's turnoff, a white wooden sign scarred by wind. On the turn, the empty shells slide under the tires.

I talk to Julien, his face warm and appealing in the intimate dash light, our voices brushing together feathery wings of sound. "Why have we come?" I ask him. "As a child, the two times I never liked to spend at home were holidays and Sundays."

"You have a responsibility to your parents," he says. "You have a relationship with them." But then he, too, says, "I do miss our friends. We shouldn't have come on vacation alone."

We find the cottage atilt on one of the stationary dunes, hardpacked ground shaped like swells of water.

Outside the car, I feel I have Julien's scent all over me. But it's just that we've been in the car so long together. (Perhaps we both smell like my dog.) It makes me uneasy walking toward my mother's cottage in the falling dark with Julien. I do not know the ground well. I cannot hold his hand, he is carrying our two cases. Somehow our intimacy seems flagrant now that I am bringing my marriage—actually for the first time—into my mother's house, her home base instead of ours.

My dog squats in the yard and I lift the black knocker to the front door. When my mother opens it, my dog is dancing, tethered on the end of the leash.

"You finally got here," she says for welcome.

"We never told you what time we'd come," I say. I see she is dressed like me—in odd colors—a combination not quite expected. She's in blue and copper.

"You've brought that dog," my mother says. "You're too old to always have a dog with you. Do you still sleep with them? I've tried to keep you from putting your face in theirs and to never breathe in their breaths." She pushes the door back till it catches and it's safe for us to pass through. She precedes us into her house.

Julien has been looked at but not spoken to. It is he who unsticks the door and crosses the rug to shake my mother's hand. They nod at each other.

Thinking maybe my father's in town, I look around to see if there are still signs of him in here. There are only signs of me ten years ago—which unsettles and unwelcomes me. Photographs here and there, framed on walls and tables, all from when I was a kid and pleased her by not being any different from her, not yet grown up. My dog tries to go to her; I hold on.

"Put your bags away," she says. For a second I wonder if she will let me sleep with a man in her house. "The guest room—take the hall on the left." Julien takes my case and his. I hear him clicking a couple of lights on as he goes.

"It still surprises me that you ever married," says my mother as soon as Julien leaves. She enjoys telling secrets just loud enough for the other person to overhear. "After your living through my marriage, I was disappointed that you married someone who looks just like your father."

"You used to say in front of everyone that you wished I would grow up to be an old maid or a nun, then you'd be happy. Didn't you want me to ever learn to share?"

"Do I really look like her father?" asks Julien, back quickly. He doesn't like the dark and there are no streetlights out here.

I tell my mother, "Julien is trying to figure out just what he really looks like. It's one of his hobbies."

In the tiny kitchen, my mother gives the dog water out of a pie pan. She doesn't like to touch animals, but she takes care of them.

On the counter is a huge bouquet of garden flowers, such bright colors.

"Why, Mother, you never bring flowers into the house," I say. "You treat them like yard animals."

"For you, Eulene," she says. "I know you love them by your bed."

"Do I?"

"You know," says Julien, "I'm interested in what I look like alive—other than in a mirror."

"You look like Avery, when I first fell," says my mother. "He's old now. I saw him just the other day driving in the car ahead of me."

"But since he left us," I say, "I often see him driving in the car ahead of me, no matter where I am."

"No, he's really here. He's following the Blues; the Blues are running. I got in touch for you." Her voice is bitter. "You know how important fish are to him. He loves to go fishing," she tells Julien, "but he never eats them. He can hardly get one to stay down."

She has made us a very delicate and moist cake. She offers Julien two pieces because he's a man. I'm glad when he refuses. I know my mother believes being overly generous is polite, but she will make fun of you if you accept.

"You still drink milk?" she asks, when I've poured myself some.

I never took her teasing as good humor. When you show hurt, she doesn't stop. I'm a bad sport. She tries to teach me humor by teasing me, but I'm only embarrassed.

We walk the dog together. Julien stays behind reading the same newspaper he read this morning. The dog runs, her hind legs hopping with excitement. The sea air leaves a film that draws my skin. The air catches in the young trees in my mother's garden. The trees are noisy with air, like watery waves which the ocean breaks on the beach below us and then seems to break again in the trees above us in my mother's garden.

The wind changes. My mother notices and says, "Eulene? What's the matter?"

There is a moistness between me and my clothes. "Nothing." Ocean air makes me uneasy. I feel as if everything is too loose. The curl is coming out of my long, heavy hair, which I still wear to my shoulder blades. My hair and my skirt blow forward; my hair gets in my mouth. It tends to get into everybody's mouth, Julien always says.

"How do you like having gray hair, old girl?" my mother asks.

Just this year a little white has come in at the center of my hairline. "Sometimes Julien thinks it's fascinating; sometimes I think it's nauseating," I say. "Like the beginning of the pattern in a snakeskin, I tell him."

I see her decide not to tease me about my hair. When I was little, I used to go behind the house and play pretend in the walled-in patio. It was safe and engrossing to talk to myself. This oddity of mine kept my parents from getting what I felt was too close to me. When I do it now, whisper to myself, and Julien interrupts with "Did you say something?" I tell him, "I'm talking to my dog."

We walk down long, gritty steps to the black beach, leaving the lights behind our shoulders. We are standing in just the hollow, swelling sound of the ocean. My mother has taken me some place that I am not safe. She's with me, yet I cannot reach out for her. My dog sees for me. I follow her breath beside my leg. Wet sand crusts my shoes. Back up the steps in the electric light, the sand sparkles and I knock my shoes together and the sand falls. My dog's claws hook at the wood.

I take a deep breath of salty, cold air and look up. The stars are out and look like they are riding away from us. We go inside with the dog, where it seems quieter without the surge of the sea, and my mother hugs me. My arm under her hand is warm.

I think I hear a tape playing somewhere far off along the ridge. I hope it will play over and over again until I am deeply asleep tonight.

Julien has made accordion folds out of the front page. We say good night to my mother and the dog doesn't want to go to bed yet, so I leave her in the hall and take the flowers with me, thinking my mother has done for me something she doesn't like but she knew I would like.

In the guest room, the door is locked and I knock once. Julien is already undressed. "I'm so white," he says, looking surprised at himself naked. "I'm so white that I'll tan red." His naked whiteness makes him loom large. I feel his feet are as big as my head.

Sheets have been left to be spread out. Julien holds them up. "She gave us the wrong sheets." Two king-size sheets, and the beds are single, narrow, and stuck to the floor. "Who's going to tell her?" he asks.

"Well, you don't have anything on." Irritated, I put the flowers close to my bed near the edge of the table. I take the sheets, and when I get to the other end of the cottage to my mother's room, I find the tape is playing in there. Only my dog is in the room, stretched out, listening to Chopin. Just when the Chopin tape ends, she relaxes the one huge curl at the end of her tail. I take off her pearly collar, undressing her for bed. That funny little protective covering chases across her eyes, and though she looks at me she is falling asleep.

My mother is not in the other rooms that I check. It is dark inside and out, and I can't tell where the walls are. I want my mother but I will not call out for her. I want my dog to follow and I do not make her.

I pull a light cord that skins the top of my hair. My old bedroom is this unrecognizable storage room now; thank heavens she didn't keep it. I find the linen closet and in the top of it are a few boxes. Then I realize they were once presents—opened, looked at, and never used. I am repelled by my mother counting, saving, but depriving herself of presents.

My face is raw with anger at my need to avoid my mother and to have seen what she values—abstinence—and to know that I find what she values valueless.

Back in the guest room with the same sheets, Julien and I share the kinship of my stupid moment. We support each other this way. He takes one king-size and I take the other. I listen for my dog, then remember removing her thin aluminum I.D.'s. I wait till I have the bathroom to take off my dark, opaque stockings and put on my long-legged pajamas. I think the only private thing about me is my pretend and my legs. I have bad legs. I think my mother has passed them on to me, these legs in a net of fine broken veins, though I know I did it to myself. I have broken my veins from ten years of giving myself birth control pills. It strikes me suddenly that I do not even have sex so often. Yet, religiously, I continue to give myself the cycle of pills.

I don't want a child. My breasts are too small. I don't understand what size my mother's are. I have checked her bras and they are two sizes—36B and 36C. To me, her breasts seem to hang from her shoulders. I got the idea of no children from my mother. My mother doesn't like children. I am an only child.

I am addicted to wearing dark stockings and it is the way my friends remember me, I know—that I hide my legs. For my breasts, I do nothing. For my legs, I have continued my dancing lessons. I am tall and thin and taut with a consciousness of my body that I don't like. My father started me dancing when I was three. He said I was a nervous child and he believed that dancing would cure me. We both have continued to believe it even after time has proved it untrue. Instead of going to lunch at work, I take ballet; I practice though I never perform.

I take my king-size sheet to bed and roll up in it, bound and bandaged in my mother's wrong sheets. "Linens are so personal," complains Julien. He reaches out to the table lamp between us and puts the three-way down on the lowest.

The small window looks bright now. The pull and slip of the ocean is loud. The rhythm of it sets me off, rollicking and whispering through my prayers. I ride my childhood path of prayers as erratically and as slumped as I had sat astride my bicycle, always slightly to the side, ready to give up, get off, bail out. I lose my way and start my prayers over. Finally, I ask that my vacation be over soon, and that God protect my mother from herself, and from me. My father almost gets left out because he's so complicated. I gain heart and continue and ask God to give him peace, but not in the form of death. For the last, I ask slowly that I always have the strength to save myself when I need it.

My eyes keep opening during my prayers. Julien is watching. "I've been reading your lips," he says. "You are haunted by things that no one cares about but you."

The novel we've brought to read together is in Julien's hand. We read to each other the well-ordered words, running them down the delicacy of our closeness, relaxing us both.

We lean and touch lips, his sticking to mine for a second. I feel that thick peak to his lips—a thickness people generally get from sulking or playing the trumpet or nursing. Then he is lost in himself, sitting back on his bed, rubbing his eye. For all his pleasing good looks, he has a lazy muscle in one eye. It causes his eye to look stranded in his face. His fingers automatically find it and his eye slides to the side away from us, the focus floating from me in uncertainty.

"Don't mess with your eye," I say. He reaches down and touches his penis.

We turn off the light and stay quiet. Trying to get comfortable in my mother's house, my body jumps twice on the edge of sleep.

Sometime during the night, we both wake. The old moon has moved while we were sleeping and now at the window it looks like a white hole for escape. Julien makes a noise in the dark, secretly fooling with his eye, and I think I see a shadow slip out of his nose.

On the table nearest me are the flowers from my mother's garden. The flowers have opened wider. They are bigger—black, huge, primeval blooms.

"Maybe flowers do belong outside," I say.

Julien sits up in bed.

"What's the matter, love?" I ask.

"I don't know. I can't stay asleep."

I prop myself up, pillow raised against the headboard, my silky pajamas so close my breasts feel heavy, dream-filled.

"Is it your stomach?" I ask.

"I feel so different from the way I feel at home," he says. "The noise and light is different." He comes to me, bringing his own sheet. "At home we have all our stuff, all our friends. I feel so empty. I think my soul upsets my stomach." He is rubbing his chest.

"That's not your stomach. That's where your heart is," I say.

He rolls on top of me and I think that it is his weight that keeps me pinned to life. Without him, I would be right back where I came from, back home, not safe.

So many emotions, loose as live breath in the room, thrust, push, vibrations of feeling and thought. Our wedding floats through my head, sticks and stays. The reception. The raindrops, huge, pendulant, falling slowly through the trees into the groom's yard. The strong rain. Stop, start. Afterward we are all barefoot in fancy dress. Everyone on the thick, matted wet yard. Too excited. The grass felt like cold glass. And the dog barking, too excited. And the groom's father went over and hurt the dog to stop it.

One young man, younger than we, playing the sounds of ten instruments by pulling stops from an electronic keyboard. The music was vibrating, and sweet, and scary because the electronic system had gotten wet and dangerous to play.

Breathing in Julien's breath like it's his emotions, I almost hold my nose. During the thrusts from him and me, by mistake I call my mother's name. I scream it. It had rolled around in my head; he made it roll out of my mouth. I screamed for my mother who could make things happen, make this prickly adulthood disappear. Sex; what I wanted when I got it became something that terrified me, as it did her. In wanting to be so unlike, I proved to myself that I was like. My mother was powerful; she could make me like her. My mother could work magic. After all, she had made my father disappear.

Julien chased me along in sex play, I ran ahead, and he finished last. He came with his lip up and squinting like he'd gotten the seat in the sun.

I felt as if I were the winner, but was losing blood. Actually it was just transparent juice. But Julien beat me to the bathroom.

My mother has the clear voice of morning. She calls, "The sun's coming up. If you two want to see anything today, you'd better get out of that room."

My mother is looking at day coming from the other side of the island. She is in her flowered robe and the light has struck the top of her head.

I ease in, barefoot down the hall carpet. I walk in dew left from my dog's paws.

"Your dog stayed with me last night," she tells me, as if to prove what I love is easy for her to win over. "She's out now. In and out."

Over at the one windowpane in the kitchen, I look for my dog. But I can see only down the cliff, the window glass seems to be holding back the ocean. I shift to opening some cabinet doors, looking for a cup. On plates in the cabinets, fruit and tomatoes ripen. Mother always puts them away for the night—ripening fruit. She is afraid of night—and mice. I once saw a small jumping mouse, sitting, licking something on its feet, nesting in a broken conch shell on the stairs. I never told on it. I remember my mother saying she was afraid of my father only at night. It was then that he was the strongest. It seemed the dark made his nose look longer and his hairline recede, and it scared her.

"You'd better eat if you're coming with me."

My dog comes in from the yard. She is covered with pollen and doesn't want to be petted.

I decide to have a banana and a cup of coffee.

Julien calls from the hall and I go to get him. "Why didn't you wait for me?" he asks. "I've been sick this morning. I threw up a little piece of your mother's cake."

"I ate the cake. You didn't have any."

My mother has fixed Julien a huge breakfast, without asking. Julien is trying hard to be pleased. He has eaten too much on his washy stomach and is embarrassed. My dog lets out wind, and no one mentions it. I close my eyes and try not to laugh, my head aswim with glee.

Julien and I shower and talk through the warm steam and dress in our bright vacation clothes.

In the car, carrying a thermos of water for the dog, I ask, "What are we off to see?"

My mother says, "Your father."

Julien wants to go back and take another look in the mirror; we won't let him. "I never saw you so worried about your appearance," I tell him. A Polaroid camera stretches his pocket.

We sit in the back; my mother drives with the dog up front. "See how your dog takes to me when I don't even like dogs?"

We come around the elbow of land from the ocean to the mild river side. Julien practices his smile on me, and against the glass of a restaurant window we pass walking now. I haven't seen my father in so long that I'm scared.

We find him in the boathouse. He seems to be blushing, but I know it is his circulation. My mother believes that he can shut down his valves and go unconscious as you talk to him.

"Well, how-de-do," he says. He is not a conversationalist. He looks like a worn-out, hurt man who tells funny stories on himself.

My mother introduces Julien and then she asks Avery questions and he tries to guess the right answers. The water rocks in the slow slap of the tide leaving. My mother is not interested in the answers. She needs only to keep asking questions to feel in control.

Avery takes it all under the hood of a joke, but it does take its toll on him. He snaps his head around directly to me, for the first time. "How about you—are you still shaking your hands?"

"Oh," I say, extending my right hand to him to shake before I realize the intent is to hurt.

"I'm wrong," he says. "The word wasn't *shake*. It was *sling* your hands. We'd say, 'Where's she gone, off to sling her hands?'" He has caught my mother's attention and he and she are enjoying the joke.

I say to Julien, "I used to play pretend. I used to sling my hands in the walled-in patio in a little rhythm to talk to myself by. I used to play pretend till I was exhausted. Like I can dance now till I'm anemic." Now Julien laughs with me, not knowing but not wanting me to be alone.

My father makes a small face at Julien. Julien must have taken it to be friendly because he makes a small, friendly face back.

Above our heads, light reflected from the water spins and revolves on the steep arch of wood, a cradle upside down over us. My parents' voices carry up and away. The terrible smell of sea broth is running like thick rich cloth through my nostrils.

Avery leads us outside to the restaurant, politely nudging us ahead of him. "Do you still have my dog?" he asks me.

"No," I say. "I have my dog now. Our dog died. Remember?" But he has lied so much about everything, trying to guess the right answers to the right questions, that he has ruined his memory. He couldn't remember his dog was dead. I, who wanted to stop the conversation, continued it. "You remember, Daddy, you used to shout commands right after our dog did anything. If he rolled over, you'd yell, 'Roll over,' quickly. Same thing if he barked or ran. It made everyone laugh, the trick dog who did everything before he was told. That dog died years ago. You told me you took him on the front seat of the car with you to the vet's. He was so weak and cold and sick. You said, 'The vet gave him a shot, but the shot didn't make him get better.' The shot was to kill him, Daddy. You knew that." My pulse beat in my throat.

"Please, just stop your carrying on, now."

My truth made him slip farther from me.

Then he and Julien discussed all the things Julien didn't know about—boats, fish, cars, tools. Julien was a professional.

In the restaurant, at the round white table, everyone had the same Sea Platter except Avery, who had an egg-salad sandwich, though he was anxious about the mayonnaise because it goes bad so easily. My father took the rings of crust from his egg-salad sandwich; he saved the crusts.

"You still have your small appetite, Avery," said my mother. "One of the things I continue to admire about you." I felt that my vacation was going faster. My mother reminisced. I held my saliva. My father remembered what he did like; she remembered what she didn't like. He stayed safely a few sentences behind her.

My mother says, "You used to be attracted to businesses that had shut down. One night you left the car with me in it and went across the parking lot of a closed drive-in and reached for a broken metal sign and it fell on you. I was trying to protect you and as it hit you I screamed, 'Goddamn you.' And you pretended the sign hadn't hurt."

"What an odd thing for a woman to scream who is trying to protect him," I say.

"He always liked to read what was written on signs that had fallen over," says my mother.

"Why don't we get together more often?" I ask my father.

"I never think I feel good enough to see you," my father says.

"He hides," says my mother. "He doesn't want Eulene to see him lying down.

He thinks he's sick when he's only drunk. He drinks as seriously as if he were taking medicine."

Julien works at a mayonnaise spot on his shirt with his napkin and drinking water.

"Physically, things are looking up," my father says. "I have a heck of a lot of possibilities." His sea-colored eyes rise to meet mine. He is ready to leave.

Outside, he stops a minute under the running clouds. "You were always pretty," he says to me. "But too picky. There were too many things you wouldn't try or do. You couldn't sing. You never learned to swim. You liked to be alone."

"That's not true," I say. "I was alone. I loved things. I loved candy. I loved you best, Daddy."

"That's not nice," he says. "I think you should love your mother best."

He detours to one of the open boat slips where huge gulls are riding the water. He scatters his crusts and says the big gray gulls are so beautiful. Then he throws the last of the crusts and hits a gull on the head.

"Why did you do that?" I ask.

"I don't know. I was just trying to figure the gulls out." He draws his shoulders together, chilly. "It's so hard for me to pee anymore," he says. "If I don't pee today, I think I'll kill myself. I wake up in the night listening for noises that would make me want to pee and trying to remember when I pee-peed last."

Julien is now taking a Polaroid shot. My mother stays at the edge of the picture. She and Avery hang around each other for a minute. Avery sucks in his cheeks and says, "Two people married and in love, but we never believed in each other."

My mother says, "You don't fool me. You're so lonely that you'd say anything—even 'I still love you.'"

Julien covers the mayonnaise spot with his left hand and gives my father his right for shaking good-bye. The Polaroid sways on a strap from his neck.

My father squints at me, I can't see in his eyes, and says, "I think you're the only one who's never hurt me. But you live in such inaccessible places."

"I live in the city. They have maps, Daddy." I feel I should have taken the luncheon napkin with me and wiped my heart.

Julien stands at my shoulder. "Come see her dog in the car," he says quietly.

"Don't want to," my father says. "My dog is dead."

Inside the car, the dog's head is hidden under the seat where it is cool. I think I hear Avery call back. I turn. He is far away. I see him bend and look intently at the ground. It is my mother's voice that says, "I hope he hasn't found anything. He keeps finding things and sending them to me in a box by mail. It's embarrassing to open the box. Sometimes it's an old watch. Sometimes a barrette. Once a broken chain."

We get in the car and the dog gets on the seat. The air is sticky. The clouds in the sky are made of wet, gray clay. My mother gives the dog water in the cap of the thermos.

Disappointment is around Julien's mouth. He shows the Polaroid. "His hair is still dark but his face has turned gray," he says as we ride away.

Then my mother is crying, her tongue clicking.

Julien sits forward, fascinated by my mother's crying. His hand is open, but there is no way to help her.

"Why would he eat mayonnaise?" says my mother, rounding a curb tear-blind, skinning the tires against concrete. "He eats mayonnaise when it could kill him. He picks up things off the ground. He never gets over a dead dog." Her throat and nose roar with tears.

"Why are you angry about that now?" I ask. "I thought you hated Daddy."

"Because," she says, "I used to care."

By the time she gets us back to the cottage she's stone-calm and talking about swimming when the weather lifts.

In the kitchen, the dog drinks from its pan. While Julien blows up a rubber float for my mother, I put beach trousers on over my bathing suit. When the float is taut, we carry it down to the water.

The approach to the beach is abrupt. We walk down ribs of sand left by wind and erosion. Now we are on planks that shift and make a kind of stairs that I had been down last night. At the bottom, I think I see my own footprints coming to meet me.

The beach is full of stones. I bend in my trousers and pick up smooth pebbles, eggs, nut-shapes, sharp tips, swirls, and curdles—shapes water has ridden into rock.

They call me, impatiently. I stand straight too fast, eyes closed against them. Light flickers red through my eyelids.

"The ocean looks dirty," my mother says. She is gazing around slit-eyed in the glare. A few kids, looking very little because they are far away, are running in circles.

"Dirty. Because of the kids," I say. "When I was little I couldn't control it either." Thinking I could have helped my chilly father. A simple little cure. It's the sudden feel of lukewarm ocean water he needs. "Feeling all that water in my bathing suit, I always peed."

"Who cares about kids?" my mother says. "I mean fish, crabs, clams, turtles—they all do their stuff in the water."

Julien must have tried to swallow a laugh. I think I see spray fly out of his mouth when my mother winks at him. Julien is getting too juicy with my mother's good nature. Mother's awakening to like Julien now simply ruins him for me.

I walk sideways to the humped water. I don't want to be with them, but I'm afraid I would get lost without them.

"Where are you going?" asks my mother.

"To look for shells."

"They're all broken."

There is little walking space between the step-off of the ocean shelf and the slipping cliffs of hot sand. I glance at the few people at the beach. Everyone seems to be at the water's edge waiting to go in.

The full trousers I wear pop with the wind. My hair rises with sea wind and makes me a sun umbrella. I find a stone with a deep crease in it. It feels so good in my hand. I keep it and will hide how much I care for it. Incoming ocean is choking the narrow beach. I walk back with one foot in the water, a sloppy, slurping sound. I am laughing until I see Julien and my mother laughing at me.

"I knew you wouldn't find any good shells," Julien says.

"I collected a stone," I say.

"You don't have to worry about finding shells. I know that you brought a seashell from the city back to the beach with you in your case. You can take it out. You don't have to hide it. You hide such simple things, Eulene, that it turns them into the grotesque."

"I remember," says my mother, "Eulene as a child trying to learn to hide emotions and endure hurts. Well, you got poison ivy and hid it. You let poison ivy go and it got all the way up into your boopsey."

"I did not," I say. "I wouldn't do it. Oh, all right, I did."

We are all smiling and laughing with each other. I give the stone in my hand a squeeze.

"You just hide things and lie to try to keep your privacy," says Julien, understanding me.

"We haven't been in the water yet," I say. "Such a large body of water."

He has our book out, using his finger for a page marker. He peeks back into it and says, "I'm at a good part," and sets it on the float. He takes my hand and a small nerve in my body runs loose.

Julien leans against me and we watch my mother slit the slick top of the water and plunge in. "I wouldn't dare get in with her," he says. She splashes so much a cluster of wet bubbles grows around her. Then she's caught the bottom with her feet and is walking back up the underwater shelf. In and out, quick as a drowning. Back on the beach, the sun turns liquid on her. Her hair looks glass.

I wait at the wet hem of the ocean.

When Julien is in the water, I shed my cotton trousers without looking down and hurry into the water. My mother calls, "Eulene? What have you done to your legs? They're worse than mine."

Salt water fills my bathing suit. The underwater rocks are so slick I almost fall. I have to swim. I sink to my neck, up to my mouth. My hair spreads out, floats around me. I look for the line of sky to hang on to. "There's no horizon," I try to say. I spit out sea water. The ocean moves in and out in respiration. I relax and float, tethered onto the very edge of relaxation.

Julien pops up floating near me. We bob together. Since neither of us can harmonize, we quote a few lines together from Woolf about colors and old glass. The vacation begins working out. I tip my face to the side. White sun lines in the water run toward my mouth.

Julien reaches for me from underneath with his legs; liquid electricity vibrates in me, a pleasing shock in water.

My mother sits up abruptly on the dry float. She shouts at us, "It's time to go do something different."

"My endless vacation," I say.

She says, "When you still think you're young, you're never satisfied. I've saved all the pictures from the time I wasn't satisfied—pictures of my boyfriends. They're dying off now, of course, but I have their pictures. I could have married a dentist when your father came chasing after me."

"Mother," I say, "I wouldn't have been born if you had married a dentist."

"Half of you would have been. My half."

I go for my mother's ride, in my bathing suit and trousers, stone in my pocket, to see the wooden churches of the island. The churches drop afternoon shadows more intricate than their architecture.

I apply brown eye shadow to tone down the burn on my lids and walk carefully in the old, boggy cemeteries. Julien reads headstones aloud as we read novels at night. Then he gets something on his shoe and has to rub it off.

We nap in the car while my mother drives. I wake with wrinkles on my face from the car velvet. The soft tissue under Julien's eyes has swollen.

At the cottage, we have a cold dinner. The dog eats from my hand. My mother comes out into the walled patio with a jug of tea, ice chiming against the glass sides. Light falls through the holes in my straw hat; it falls down into my lap and onto the pot of flowers beside my chair. Everywhere I go, the designs fly along with me on the flat flagstones, over my shoes. The ocean way below calms for sunset. Then twilight comes, a bluish airspace between each of us, as if we are close to stepping inside each other's fragments of dreams.

"I'm trying to write a letter," my mother says. She has eaten with ink stains on her fingers. "I do keep friends to write to, but I have such trouble deciding what not to tell them." The tea pitcher is between us. "I don't use sugar because it's not good for you," she says. "But I put some in for you. I don't like sweet. Is it all right?"

"You're making me feel so comfortable," says Julien.

The tea is too sweet, it drives the taste down to the root of my tongue.

I touch my dog. She kicks her hind leg convulsively and stretches her mouth into a black fur dog grin.

That night, in the bathroom, I put on a white batiste ankle-length nightgown. Nothing moves tonight, only me in my batiste gown.

"Something's happening," I say. "I don't know what."

Julien honks, "Huh?" at me as he slides down into the right-size sheets. Mother has made our beds this time. "It must be happening just to you. I don't feel it," says Julien, already searching through a book for something interesting.

I find my stone in my beach trousers pocket and slip it under my pillow. I sit beside it and say, "I need to feel better."

He turns his head from me into the sea silence of the room. A roll of deep water. Another sea silence. "I'm afraid, Eulene. If we say it out loud, we won't recover. It may be a mistake to put everything into words. Words are cruel."

Something sharp and deep is riding on my breath. "My mother never says anything out loud. She just thinks it. I believe in saying it out loud." My voice! A child's skinny, scabby, sulky one.

"If your mother told you all that she thinks," he says, "how would you be able to stand to hear it all? Would you want to know it—how could you receive it? What if you knew what makes her hate? If she gave it to you, could you carry it?"

I curl my knees toward my mouth and bow to sleep, my pillow over my smooth stone. Later, in the dark, I wake to see Julien edging around the carpet, holding his penis as if it were a banister.

"Where are you trying to go? Don't wake up my mother."

"I'm lost in this room," he says.

"Don't wake her! She's so sensitive."

"I know," he says. "All those wrinkles in her face."

"No," I say. "It was my father who wrinkled her." I am up, too. Trying to catch him. Stop him. This is all too unreal. I touch myself to make sure my breasts are still there.

The shadows in the room are elastic. The room changes. The wind is up—it blows a small tree's shadow into the bedroom with us. I think it's laid a slippery spot on the carpet. Trying to get to Julien.

Near the door I slip and go down on the end of my white gown.

"Oh!" he cries out for me. He sees I am really down and he cries out, "Are you hurt? Are you hurt?" Then he comes down beside me and begins to hit me. He strikes me, yelling, "Get up! Get up!" On the third stroke I stand and the striking knocks the loose waist of my batiste gown up over my breasts.

My voice breaks. There are funny coatings over my vocal cords. I have two voices; another voice screams with me, "I want to go home."

Yet I cry it to him who is striking me, whose home it is, too. Because he is the closest I've ever been able to get to anybody, this man for whom I now feel hate. I am so slow. I feel tears dropping from my eyes. I try to catch them in my hand, but I can't and they fall anyway.

Three times hard he's struck me. "We should have been just good friends," he says. Now he flops down on the bed, his back bent, as domed and ancient a shape as a carapace. "I've tried hard to keep loving you," he says.

My chest aches and stretches with the blood of shock. "But it's I who don't love you! I've hidden it all this time." I raise my breasts like plumes on a bird.

In the doorway, my mother surprises us. She stands half absorbed by sleep, wearing a fancy nightgown, old white yellowed as rich as cream, saved, ripened, so old it splits as we watch—tears without a sound. My mother, in her anger at what she sees in us, has torn the front of her nightgown.

"Go to bed, Mother," I say. "Just because I'm in your house doesn't mean I've lost the right to fight with my husband." It's as if fights are too intimate for her. My vision has one black dot jumping in each eye.

She says, "I wouldn't let either one of you be treated the way you are treating each other." She leaves with her nightgown open.

I thought I would scream or tear into the flesh of Julien's face. Instead, I sit down and put my feet up.

"Why did you marry me?" he asks.

"I am the promiscuous daughter of a promiscuous man," I say, "which is funny because I don't find sex satisfying. I don't even like it. I guess I married you to get rid of sex. When we do it great I love it, but then I always panic. Neither of us can take it all the time."

Julien looks tired. "I wonder if maybe I'm a homosexual."

"No," I say. "Homosexuals love somebody. You don't love anybody."

I listen to my dog in the other room scratching at the long nap of my mother's carpet.

"You and your dog," he says. "It sure is hard to be married to an only child."

"What are you thinking of now?" I ask.

He says, "I was thinking of aspirins."

We take bitter white aspirins together. Then we wait for the white, powdery morning to begin.

At some point, I slide into sleep. When I wake, my muscles are stiff and my eyelids tight with sun and windburn and I think I am alone. Then I find my dog is curled into the bend of my legs. I get up, dress, and find Julien in the kitchen just sitting. "I'm waiting to work up an appetite," he says.

My mother sets the table with dishes from my childhood. "I was known for never breaking things," she says. "Other people break my things, but I never break things." Today, she will not look at me.

I let my dog out for a minute. When she comes back, I leave her collar and tags on. "Want to go for a ride soon?" I say. She jumps all over me, her claws leaving white scratches down my arms.

We do not use any of the plates. I use a teacup and a spoon for honey. I do not want sugar. Because we all feel badly, and Julien has spoiled my face, I wait till no one is looking to eat directly from the honey jar—a mouthful of thick pleasure.

Minutes later, Julien puts his hand—the back of it—so softly against my marked cheek. He strains for me from his chair. He has never done anything so open and so tender before.

"I am the continuation of what's wrong," I say.

"So. You are going to sacrifice me?" He laughs.

I lean and get a spider of sun in my eye.

My mother has gone to her garden wearing ugly old clothes. She does not like sweat. She will not wear her good clothes for it.

Julien and I are alone, but for the dog biting and combing and scratching her coat with her claws. "I've put pressure on you," I tell Julien. "I've thought too much and put pressure on myself. So in the end I have to be the one to leave." Julien's eye is to the side. I rub it slowly to move it back in place.

In the room, I put my dirty things on top in the case, the city seashell still at the bottom. I do not need a souvenir of my vacation. I do not need the stone— it ends under my pillow.

Now with my case, my dog, and my pocketbook I find my mother in the yard planting leftover seeds from packets with lost labels. She will let them sprout and then see if she wants them. On her knees, she hacks away with a hand hoe at the black silk soil of her yard. "Goddamn, hell, shit, Goddamn them to hell," she says as she plants. My dog sits in a draft under the tree. My mother gets up in stiff jerks. "No reason for this," she says to me, seeing me, my case and pocket-book. "You do this to yourself. You always set yourself apart. Alone. What is so courageous about leaving?"

"I'm leaving Julien here," I say.

"Well, you always did love to play by yourself," she says.

He has come as far as the door, licking what looks like my honey spoon. "You told them at the office that you'd come back from vacation a different man," I say. "You have one more week." He lifts his head to me. This morning's shadow hangs to his side.

I thrust my case into the closed-up car; my dog sticks with the draft. The car inside is stuffy. I sneeze hot air and lower the windows to cool the car so I can get in it. I walk with Julien once around my mother's house. Near her hawthorn, we stop. "I was desperate to marry you, Julien." The starlings are overrunning the hawthorn. Julien and I make loud clapping sounds together to startle them and then we smell what they're after—crushed soft fruit fermenting on the ground under the tree. We flatten the grass with our shoes and I lead and tell him that I was wrong. "My mother doesn't hate men. She has only withdrawn from them to coddle her passion. Be careful."

"You're just angry and scared," Julien says to me, quite kindly.

I mask my glance at him, checking, thinking that I am actually leaving another Daddy with Mother again.

Next time we look at her, my mother's skin is slick. She is sweating the sweat she hates. Neither sun nor clouds move. "Julien's staying for a while to finish his vacation," I say. I move backward one step toward the car, an uneven stone shocking the bottom of my foot.

To help Julien, maybe, I ask, "Is Daddy really your failure—or your success, Mother?"

The dog climbs into the open car slowly. I start the car, it quivers with the air-conditioning. Still the dog pants. Her breath is the sharp smell of canned dog food.

I have something to say, but I cannot bear anything more. I put on my large sunglasses and think they will break the small bones of my nose. The dog beats her tail against me because she loves to ride. I catch myself in the mirror and think I must look like one dark lens to them; or maybe I'm just too small to see.

I look ahead, up the narrow road from my mother's house, and see a little boy fully clothed on a powerful motorcycle, and then a blond man bare-chested, painfully pedaling a bicycle. I am laughing and my muscles are hurting. I say, leaving Julien in my mother's garden, "I had no idea till today, Mother, that I had come here to punish you."

I swing the car into my side of the road, the wheel spinning in my hands. The dog barks and runs along the seat with pleasure. I am looking beyond us to the broken, scattered colors of the fields. It is me that's laughing and heaving in the air conditioner's air. But way below my heart, I can feel a kitten shaking in my womb. I am at the end of my vacation.

Frank Manley

Frank Manley enrolled as a student at Emory University in 1948 and earned his B.A. in 1952 and M.A. in 1953. After two years of service in the military and an instructorship at Yale, he received his Ph.D. from Johns Hopkins in 1959. He left Yale in 1964 and returned to Emory as a faculty member, retiring as a professor of Renaissance literature in 2002. A dramatist, poet (*Resultances,* 1980), writer of short fiction (*Within the Ribbons,* 1989, and *Among Prisoners,* 2000), novelist (*The Cockfighter,* 1998), and scholar (he has published editions of Sir Thomas More), Manley has had a distinguished career. In "Chickamauga," he describes in a darkly humorous yet emotionally affecting way the encounter of two individuals at the famous battlefield in Tennessee. One is mentally challenged, unable to read or understand much around him; the other is still grappling with memories of his service in Vietnam. For both, the Chickamauga battlefield, its maps and commemorative markers, becomes a metaphor for the inscrutable nature of war, the past, and history's meaning.

Chickamauga

When I am losing hold of myself, absolutely passive in the hands of the
great unknown forces that have shaped me, in those dark moments, grant,
O God, that I may understand that it is you who are painfully parting the
fibers of my being in order to penetrate the very marrow of my substance
and bear me away with you.
—Teilhard De Chardin

It was not a voice. It did not speak or call him by name or touch him on the arm
or shoulder to get his attention. It was more like breath. Like suddenly feeling
his own breath and waking at two o'clock in the morning to find his mouth
pressed in the crook of his arm, breathing the smell of his own skin, or pressed
against Forest's bare back, breathing the same smell. He turned suddenly, and
there it was, standing beside him—a man his own age or older.

"The blue ones say 'Go,' and the red ones say 'Stop,'" the man was saying.

"What blue ones?"

"The blue ones and the red ones," the man said, pointing to the Plexiglas
map of the Battle of Chickamauga on the wall beside him. The map was so big
it looked like a billboard. The Union forces were depicted by blue arrows moving south. The Confederates met them in red. The arrows swept and swirled
like sickles—broken edges and fragments of circles moving toward a vortex.
Except for the implicit motion, the suggestion of something out of control, the
map was almost pleasant to look at, it was so neat and orderly. It had nothing to
do with what actually happened there.

"Fucking arrows," the man said, smiling. The smile was disturbing. It didn't
fit. Something was wrong. He seemed to be sending two different, contradictory messages at once. Ventris Tidwell checked him out. Nondescript. Middle
height, middle weight, middle aged. Madras shirt, blue trousers. Thinning hair.
The only odd thing about him was the smell. It was too strong for after-shave. It
was more like a woman's perfume. The man was rank with it.

French, Ventris Tidwell decided. Or Welsh. He himself was a little of both—
French on his mother's side, Welsh on his father's. The man beside him looked
vaguely familiar, like one of his uncles. He not only smelled like a whore, he
talked like one too. And besides that, he lisped. Ventris Tidwell did not say "shit"

and "fuck" in ordinary conversation and was never comfortable with those who did, not even in the army. It was like child pornography, hearing someone lisp like that and say things like "fuck" and "shit." He expected "shit" any minute.

"I can see, but I can't read," the man said.

Ventris Tidwell hardly heard him over the lisp. It roared in his ears, and he kept straining for another "fuck," the same way a pianist reaches ahead for a difficult passage and misses the next note.

"You can't read."

"I can't read," the man agreed. "I told them that in the army. And they said, 'We'll test him. See if that fucker can read or not.'"

There it was. The "fucker" fell on Ventris Tidwell's ear like grace. It was all he wished for, all he ever expected. He hardly heard the man continue.

"They set me down in this room they got," the man said. "Squeezed me in, and they started buzzing."

"Buzzing?"

"Buzzing like fuckers," the man said gaily. The smile came on again like a great light. His entire appearance changed. Before he had seemed abstracted as though he was plugged in, listening to distant music on a Sony Walkman. Now he was focused the way a magnifying glass is focused. The smile felt like heat on his face, and Ventris Tidwell suddenly realized he was angry. He felt the blood pound in his head. The language upset him.

"This is a National Battlefield," he heard himself say. He noticed he was speaking in a stage whisper. It seemed to go with the polished floors and the clean windows and the shine on the freshly painted woodwork of the museum.

"It's like church. You don't say things like that in church."

The man ignored him. "I stood that shit as long as I could. Then I got up and walked around, and one of them fuckers said, 'Sit down,' and I stepped out the window."

"You stepped out the window?" He couldn't believe it. "What's your name?"

"U. S."

"U. S. what?"

"U. S. Hightower. My momma said, 'Call him Sonny.'"

"Listen," Ventris Tidwell said. "You stepped out the window?" He felt his heart lift again as soon as he said it.

It was the first grade, the first week of school. A nun had locked him up in the cloakroom, and he leaned against the wall among the hats and coats feeling like something hung up in there until he couldn't stand it anymore, and he climbed out the window and went home. They came looking for him a few hours later, and his mother hid him under the table. He heard them shouting in the other room—his mother asking what sort of women they thought they were, if they *were* women. She would never think of locking a baby up in a cloakroom, because she had one of her own. Speaking of him like he wasn't even hers, like he was some foreign baby in some far-off land where things like that were supposed to happen: dead bodies stacked up like cordwood beside the twisted tracks of the railroad.

Sonny Hightower smiled like a picture of a drunken Dutchman, radiant in his own confusion. Suddenly it all seemed all right—as normal as the National Park Service.

"I saw the window," Sonny Hightower said, "and stepped out, and they yelled, 'Go get him,' and one of them got me and took me in this other place and said, 'Here, read this, you say you can't read.' And I said, 'I can't read.' And they said, 'Read it. This is a test.' So I buzzed at it, and they said, 'Out loud. Read it out loud.' And I said, 'What the hell you call this, fucker?' and they said, 'Read it where I can hear it and tell if you can read or not.' So I buzzed at it louder, and they said, 'Hell, that ain't reading,' and I said, 'Hell no, I told you that, fucker.' And they said, 'He can't read. This guy's a moron.' And I said, 'That's what I been trying to tell you.' If I could read, I'd be in the army." He gestured at the glass cases full of the burnished relics of war.

"What you mean, you retarded or something?"

"Damn right."

"Is that your real name?"

"What?"

"U. S. You named for Ulysses S. Grant, or what?" It seemed appropriate at Chickamauga, a moron named Ulysses S. Grant.

Sonny Hightower ignored him. "Looks like a red light. You know how to drive?"

"What looks like a red light?"

Sonny Hightower pointed at the map of the battle. The red and blue arrows. It looked like a complicated traffic pattern, a cloverleaf on the interstate. Red for stop. Green for go. Then it came to him. Green for go? The arrows on the map were blue.

He was about to say something about it when Sonny Hightower asked if he had a sword.

"What? A sword?"

Sonny Hightower nodded his head. "You got a sword?"

"No."

"Me neither."

They fell silent, contemplating the map again. Ventris Tidwell thought of the time when he drove the interstate all the way to Dalton before he realized where he was going. It was like a river. He was carried by the current far past his destination. The cloverleaf shuttled the traffic, and the traffic moved on it wherever it went, going to its destination. Without the pattern, it would all gridlock. Same thing with wars.

"You ever kill anybody?" Sonny Hightower asked.

He did not know if he had killed anybody or not. It was a question he was careful never to ask.

"What you mean, 'kill anybody'?"

"When you were in the army."

"How did you know I was in the army?"

"The way you look," Sonny Hightower said. "What's your name?"

"Ventris."

"Ventris what?"

"Ventris Tidwell."

"Ventris Tidwell." He spoke as though he was testing it. "Don't sound like a name to me."

"My mother's maiden name." As soon as he said it, he knew that was no explanation. Names were not supposed to mean anything, but Ventris always seemed to contain some sort of suggestion of meaning. He never knew what.

"Sounds like it means something to me," Sonny Hightower said.

"That right?"

"Sounds like it's somebody knocked on the door waiting to get in, to me."

Ventris Tidwell nodded his head. He knew what he meant.

"Sounds like U. S. to me."

"What?" Ventris Tidwell was quick as a rat in the wall. "What you mean, U. S.?" And then he knew. "Well, shit. Who was Ulysses S. Grant?" he asked.

"What you mean, who was Ulysses S. Grant?"

"I mean, who was Ulysses S. Grant, you named for him like you say you are?"

"Who gives a shit?"

"That's what I figured."

"Look here." He went over to one of the display cases and tapped on the glass.

"U. S. Look at those canteens. U. S. This is a National Monument." The initials were everywhere in the room—on the belt buckles and rifles, the wallpaper, the maps and displays. They were carved on the lintels and woven in obscure red-and-blue patterns on the drapery shrouding the windows. "That ain't your real name. You just made it up."

Sonny Hightower began moving his hand in front of his face, slowly at first, then faster and faster, staring at the map of the battle. Ventris Tidwell did not know what he was doing. He looked at the face moving through the arc of the hand and fell into the same rhythm himself. It was like looking through the blades of a chopper and seeing the landscape split into fragments, mismatched circles spinning out of the sound of the engine, the gunships awkward as great beasts—buffalo or rhinos—lifting off like his own name in a thrusting of wind, the trees bending to the vortex, circling where they said was a village, burning the trees like flesh off a body, the face lifting, turning toward him, features burned beyond recognition.

"I don't know if I killed anybody or not," Ventris Tidwell said. "I was in Nam."

"Nam what?" Sonny Hightower asked. He had quit doing whatever it was he was doing.

"Nam what?" Ventris Tidwell asked. "Goddamn." He took two vicious steps and returned. "Vietnam," he said, pronouncing it to rhyme with *jam*. He looked at Sonny Hightower. It was like looking in a mirror and seeing himself not as he was but as he used to be, and he thought of an advertisement on TV. A politician walking down the corridor of a prison. Bars on either side painted green. The whole place painted green. All of a sudden he stops in front of a cell and turns to the camera. "When I'm president," he says, grinning like he got a mouth full of shit, "I'm going to put all the criminals in jail and keep them there." All of a sudden a guard rushes up and slams the door on him. It makes a loud noise, clanging and banging. Fucker's inside. They finally got the son of a bitch, Ventris Tidwell said to himself whenever he saw it. He was not innocent.

"Listen," he said to Sonny Hightower. "The army took me, but I wish they hadn't. They liked to've killed me."

"That's what they're supposed to do, ain't it?"

"I don't mean *them*," Ventris Tidwell said. "I mean *me*. They liked to've killed *me*."

"What's the difference?"

"What's the difference?" Ventris Tidwell couldn't believe it. "Listen," he said. "They killed my brother."

"Who killed him?"

"His own men." He spoke in confidence, lowering his voice and leaning forward. Sonny Hightower leaned back in the opposite direction. "The Americans," Ventris Tidwell said almost in a whisper. Sonny Hightower was too far away to hear.

"Who?"

"His own men," Ventris Tidwell said. "Our own army. Americans. They thought he was somebody else."

"Who they think he was?"

"How the hell do I know?" Ventris Tidwell shouted. He was angry. "What does that matter?"

"He's dead, ain't he?"

"What you mean? Of course he's dead. I just told you he was dead. His own fucking men killed him."

"That's why it matters."

"Yes."

"If they knew who he was they might not have killed him. They know he was your brother?"

"Listen," Ventris Tidwell said. "What the shit does it matter whose fucking brother they thought he was?" He stopped suddenly. "They thought he was the Viet Cong."

"The Viet Cong," Sonny Hightower said. He sounded amazed, as though he had just learned that Forest Tidwell was believed to be a Coca-Cola bottle.

"You know what I mean?"

"What?"

"The Viet Cong. You know what I mean?"

Sonny Hightower looked about the room as though searching for something.

"Shit," Ventris Tidwell said. "They thought he was the enemy."

Sonny Hightower looked like someone had put him in neutral.

"I mean the Americans," Ventris Tidwell said. "They thought he was the fucking enemy. His own men. They killed him." The words rose up like apparitions. "There wasn't even a body inside the coffin. They sealed it up and covered it with an American flag, and we didn't even know what was in there, it was so light."

"You mean there wasn't nothing there?"

"They said, 'Don't open it. These are remains. He was burned beyond recognition.'"

"You mean you didn't even get to see him? How'd you know who it was?"

Ventris Tidwell did not reply.

"I said, how'd you know who it was, you didn't even get to see him. It might have been the wrong one."

"Yes."

"What?"

"It was the wrong one."

"They killed my brother with a car," Sonny Hightower said. "They buried him, I knew who it was. I kissed his face, and they closed the lid, and I knew he was in there. That's how we're different."

"That's one way," Ventris Tidwell said.

"What are the others?"

"What others?"

"The other ways we're so different."

"We ain't so different."

"Yours didn't die right. That's one way. You got an empty box. Mine was full. I know what I got."

Ventris Tidwell nodded and started to leave.

"What about reading?" Sonny Hightower said. He looked suspicious. "Can you read?"

"Yes."

"Read that." He pointed to a large display on the wall.

"It was a haunted land," Ventris Tidwell began, and then stopped. "How's that?" It was a test.

"Don't stop now!" Sonny Hightower said. "Keep on going. Read it out loud where I can hear it."

"It was a haunted land," Ventris Tidwell began again. It did not occur to him to pick up where he had left off. He read all the *A*'s as *A*'s and all the *The*'s as *The*'s.

Chickamauga Creek was larger than most rivers in Europe. It flowed out of the mountains of North Georgia toward the lowlands of Tennessee through a rough and broken country, a sparsely settled region of gloomy woods and lonely cabins. It had been given its name by the Indians—Chickamauga, the River of Death. For the early settlers who lived on its banks it still retained that meaning, flowing in the heart of nature, eroding the edges of their fields, and then suddenly rising up wild and uncontrollable, sweeping away their loved ones and all their possessions. But the soldiers who arrived on its banks and began their blind, bitter struggle gave it new meaning, baptizing it afresh with their blood. Marching, the armies sang the words of the old hymn, "There Is a Fountain Filled with Blood." Chickamauga was that place.

"Don't stop!" Sonny Hightower said. He seemed to be charmed by the words as snakes are said to be charmed by music. "You ain't come to the end of it yet." He walked up to the display and peered at it. The type rose up over his head like a sign warning of a disaster.

"That's it," Ventris Tidwell said. "That's all it says."

"Well, shit," Sonny Hightower said. He walked along the base of the wall as though looking for a way out.

"What about that one?" He pointed to another display. It looked like the tombstone of a wealthy banker. "What's that say?"

"The Battle of Chickamauga went to nobody's plan."

"Go on," Sonny Hightower said. "Read the fucker. Don't just stand there."

A Brigadier General in the Union army summed it up perfectly when he wrote that Chickamauga was a "mad, irregular battle, very much resembling guerrilla warfare on a vast scale in which one army was bushwhacking the other and wherein all the science and art of war went for nothing." The country was full of trees and underbrush with little clearings here and there; nobody could see much of his enemy's position, it was almost impossible to move artillery along the narrow country lanes, both armies were sodden with weariness, drinking water was hard to find, casualties were extremely heavy, and by nightfall all anyone could be sure of was that there had been a terrible fight and that it would be worse tomorrow. They were the two bloodiest days of American Military History. More than a quarter of the 124,000 men engaged were killed, wounded, or missing; in some units casualties exceeded 80 percent.

Bruce Catton

"What?"

"Bruce Catton."

"What's that mean?"

"I don't know. Man's name that wrote it. Some kind of general."

"That's what I figured. Why didn't you tell me before you started?"

"What? His name? How the hell am I supposed to know that? I don't read backwards."

"Well, shit," Sonny Hightower said, leaning forward to inspect it more closely. The light on the surface was dazzling. "Don't ever do it again, you hear me?" He walked on past a cluster of flags and came to the next major display. He stood in front of it as though praying or expecting to absorb the message without reading it but simply by remaining there in its presence. Ventris Tidwell joined him. It looked like an enormous telegram so outsized it would have taken two men to carry it.

"Son of a bitch," Sonny Hightower said. He leaned forward and inspected the grain of the print as one might inspect the brush strokes of a painting.

"What's it say?"

William S. Rosecrans, Major General, U.S.A., Commanding, The Army of Tennessee, Chattanooga, Tennessee, to Henry W. Halleck, Major General, U.S.A., General in Chief of the Armies, War Office, Washington, D.C., 21 September 1863.

"Washington, D.C.," Sonny Hightower repeated.

WE HAVE MET WITH A SERIOUS DISASTER.

"We have met with a serious disaster," Sonny Hightower said. He sounded delighted.

EXTENT NOT YET ASCERTAINED. ENEMY OVERWHELMED US. DROVE OUR RIGHT, PIERCED OUR CENTER, AND SCATTERED

TROOPS THERE. EVERY AVAILABLE RESERVE WAS USED WHEN
THE MEN STAMPEDED. CHICKAMAUGA IS AS FATAL A NAME
IN OUR HISTORY AS BULL RUN.

"Goddamn," Sonny Hightower said. The whole thing conformed to what it
was saying. "Look how it looks. See that?"

"Yes."

"Looks like a train whistle. You know how to drive?"

"Yes."

"Me too. I ain't forgot it. My brother taught me. They don't give you a license
for driving unless you can read."

"I heard about that."

"I reckon so. Most folks have." He waddled on down the wall like a rat moving along its base.

Ventris Tidwell was reminded of a wall he had seen in the *National Geo-
graphic* with all these pictures of men leaning their heads on it and sticking
flowers in it or pieces of paper with messages on them. The wall was black. It
was covered with names. On the other side of the wall was nothing. It was just a
wall, and the men cried to it for help in their lives and pity and mercy on their
souls.

Sonny Hightower kept on going and stopped at the end. There in the corner
was the last message.

"What about that one?" Sonny Hightower asked. "What's that fucker looking
like that for?"

He was pointing at a grainy blowup of a young man with a round face and
slick hair that looked as though he had just combed it with water. He was wearing a bow tie and an open coat with large brass buttons running obliquely
down his chest like bullet holes. His clothes looked rumpled as though he had
been sleeping in them. His face was plump and well fed. In the crook of his left
arm was a felt campaign hat with a large brass H on the front above the brim.
The fingers holding the hat were tense.

Ventris Tidwell read the caption. "Sam R. Watkins, High Private, Company
H, First Tennessee Regiment, Confederate States of America." Underneath that
was a quotation.

"What's it say?" Sonny Hightower asked.

I got a piece of cold corn dodger, laid my piece of the rat on it, eat a little piece
of bread, and raised the piece of rat to my mouth. *Sam R. Watkins*

"Piece of rat. Well, shit. Looks like you, don't it?" He pointed at Sam Watkins.

"Like me?" There was no resemblance.

"Read what it says."

We remained on the battlefield of Chickamauga all night. Everything had fallen into our hands. We had captured a great many prisoners and small arms, and many pieces of artillery and wagons and provisions. The Confederate and Federal dead, wounded and dying, were everywhere scattered over the battlefield. Men were lying where they fell, shot in every conceivable part of the body. Some with their entrails torn out and still hanging to them and piled up on the ground beside them, and they still alive.

"That's all," Sonny Hightower said. "I know all about that"—waving his hand in front of his face like the blades of a chopper.

Some with their underjaw torn off and hanging by a fragment of skin to their cheeks, with their tongues lolling from their mouth.

Sonny Hightower touched his arm. Ventris Tidwell looked at him.

Some with both eyes shot out, with one eye hanging down on their cheek. In fact, you might walk over the battlefield and find men shot from the crown of the head to the tip end of the toe. . . . Dying on the field of battle and glory is about the easiest duty a soldier has to undergo. It is the living, marching, fighting, shooting soldier that has the hardships of war to carry.

Sonny Hightower was still holding his arm when he finished. They looked at each other for a moment. Then Sonny Hightower detached himself and wandered among the display cases.

"Look at this," Sonny Hightower said.

"What is it?"

"I don't know."

"What's it look like?"

"I don't know."

Ventris Tidwell went over and looked.

"Canteens."

They came in all shapes and sizes. Those still wrapped in cloth reminded him of dead bodies piled on one another in heaps until they no longer resembled individual human beings, not even dead ones. They were too piled. The piles were too neat. The piles looked like rows of canteens.

"Look at that," Sonny Hightower said.

Ventris Tidwell turned away in revulsion.

"Any more of them fuckers?" Sonny Hightower said, straightening up.

Ventris Tidwell looked around. The only other displays in the room were some photographs of Chattanooga and Lookout Mountain and the Moccasin

Bend of the Tennessee River. On the opposite wall between two windows looking out over a sweep of lawn was a large blowup of a trench full of dead soldiers. He walked over to it. Northern or Southern—he couldn't tell. They were all jumbled up together. It looked like the remains of some great disaster, some great wind that swept down and lifted them up and then flung them down to lie there like that, sprawled obscenely on their backs. They looked sexually assaulted. The trench was muddy. It was full of pieces of paper, books, scraps of wood, logs, shoes, pots and pans, dead bodies.

Underneath the photograph was the word: "CHICKAMAUGA."

That's it, Ventris Tidwell thought. The place was healed over, the debris cleaned up, the bodies buried. Rotten and eaten now. Even the bones leached out in the wet soil. But it was still there.

Sonny Hightower was standing directly in front of the photograph. "What's it say?" he asked Ventris Tidwell.

"Chickamauga."

"What?"

"Chickamauga. The Battle of Chickamauga. This's where it's at."

"That ain't here," Sonny Hightower said.

"Yes it is. That's where we are."

"Not me," Sonny Hightower said. "That ain't where I am. Shit." He laughed. "You read them all?"

"Except for the windows."

"The windows?"

"A joke. I was making a joke."

"A joke?"

"Forget it."

"I mean that story," Sonny Hightower said. "Any more about that story?"

"What story?"

"The one you were reading."

"Just the maps."

"Read that," Sonny Hightower said. He walked over to one of the maps and pointed at a blue arrow. "What's that?"

"A map."

"What's it say?"

"Thomas's Corps."

"What?"

"Thomas's Corps."

"What's that mean?"

"It means where they went. The men in Thomas's command."

"Well, shit. Read it."

"I already have. 'Thomas's Corps.' That's what it says."

Sonny Hightower went closer and scrutinized it, tracing the arrow slicing south.

"That's all it says?"

"Listen," Ventris Tidwell said. "You don't read a map."

Sonny Hightower looked at him expectantly. He was like some sort of animal in a field—a mule or a horse or a cow.

"Maps show what happened," Ventris Tidwell started to say, and then stopped, knowing that was not it.

Sonny Hightower waited.

"They're like diagrams," Ventris Tidwell said. "They show the movement."

"The movement."

"Yes. This is Thomas's Corps"—tracing the blue arrow. "And this is Longstreet's."

"Longstreets."

"Yes."

"Where's that?"

"Here." He pointed at a red arrow.

"That's Longstreets."

"That's right."

"What's Longstreets?"

Ventris Tidwell did not answer.

"Read it," Sonny Hightower said.

"I can't," Ventris Tidwell shouted. It made him angry. He was so angry he wanted to kill somebody.

"Listen," he said. "You don't know why you came here, and I don't know why I came here." He broke off.

It was like blind, lumbering armies marching around in the woods all day on and off the roads. They met at a place called Chickamauga, and the men whose lives made up those armies died there or lived through the fighting to die somewhere else. Like his great-grandfather, who was born and raised in Chattanooga and fought in all the battles around there on the wrong side, in the Union army, and came home after the war and went into the hardware business and had a family and lost his business and retired and lived with his only daughter until she died and then with her daughter until he died himself of old age or a bad heart or indignation or despair sitting in a chair in the side yard under a Yeats apple tree. And there was a reason. He was not killed at Chickamauga, and there was a reason. There was a pattern that guided men's lives. He could not explain it or say what it was, but he felt its wings. He felt the cold air of its wings.

"Damn right," Sonny Hightower said. "That all you got?"

Ventris Tidwell nodded his head.

"Then I'm obligated to you," Sonny Hightower said. "You gave me the information I needed, and I'm much obliged."

Ventris Tidwell was touched by the speech. It reminded him of the elaborate courtesy of people he had known when he was a boy. They adopted it in all their relationships with one another, even with their loved ones at home. There were still a few of them left in Chattanooga, on the heights overlooking the city, and in some of the wood-frame houses in the flats along the river.

Whoever took care of Sonny Hightower took care of him well. They kept him clean and had taught him his manners. He was like an elderly pet or a well-loved child. He was trusting with strangers. He knew no fear.

"You're welcome," Ventris Tidwell said, assuming the same serious air.

Sonny Hightower stood there waiting. He seemed about to say something. Then he turned and walked across the room. There were two doors. One was marked EXIT. The other said MAINTENANCE. KEEP OUT. They were side by side, with only a small display case between them. Both were paneled, both painted the same Williamsburg blue. Sonny Hightower was just at the point of having to choose between them when he turned and looked at Ventris Tidwell.

"The one on the left," Ventris Tidwell said.

But Sonny Hightower did not open the door. He turned instead and waved goodbye the same way children wave goodbye with their whole arm. Ventris Tidwell waved back.

Sonny Hightower stood there a moment. Then he came back across the room.

Oh shit, Ventris Tidwell thought. Sonny Hightower was on him like a dog.

"Now it's my turn to tell *you* a tale," Sonny Hightower said. He marched toward the center of the room, arms stiff at his side like an automaton. When he reached the middle he stopped and turned.

"Attention!" Sonny Hightower shouted. The sound filled the room like an explosion. "Attention! This is the captain. We're going down." He made an elaborate sinking motion with his hand. "Who knows how to pray?" He paused, waiting dramatically, then turned to Ventris Tidwell. "None of them know how to pray."

"Keep your voice down," Ventris Tidwell said. "Don't shout so loud." What would he say if someone came in and asked what was happening? He did not know what was happening.

"No one could pray," Sonny Hightower said. He had stepped out of the joke or story or whatever it was and stopped as though it was over. Silence seeped into the room like water. Ventris Tidwell felt like praying. But not for himself. It was such a crazy, useless story. It was not even a joke. It was nothing.

"That's some story," Ventris Tidwell said.

Sonny Hightower just stood there, eyes shut, arms rigid at his side. He seemed to have fallen into a trance.

Then all of a sudden Sonny Hightower shouted, "All right. No one can pray. We'll take up an offering. You got a hat?"

Ventris Tidwell did not know what to say. He had fallen down the rabbit hole.

"We took up the offering," Sonny Hightower said and made as though someone gave him a hat full of money. He stuck his face into it as into a mirror.

"This is the captain," he said, straightening up. "We're going down. Then the ship sunk," he said. "They all died." He gestured with his hand. It fell through the air like a leaf. "Now I told you a tale." His eyes were still closed. He still stood at attention.

"Much obliged," Ventris Tidwell said. Then he realized he was angry. He was so angry he wanted to kill him.

"What kind of story is that?" he shouted. "What you mean telling me something like that for? What's it mean?"

Sonny Hightower did not reply.

"It wasn't money. That what you mean?" He stopped abruptly. What was he talking about? Sonny Hightower was a moron.

But what was he doing here? What did he want? For there are no accidents. Ventris Tidwell was certain of that. His breath flowed out of him and returned. It filled the world like a balloon. And that was no accident. Sonny Hightower had come here today. He felt his breath coming and going. And that was no accident. There are no mistakes. Invisible pathways lead through the earth, currents of the air and sea beyond our means of comprehension. It all made sense now, just for a moment, until he looked at Sonny Hightower and realized there was no message. He was a moron. That was the message.

Sonny Hightower was still standing at attention, arms stiff, jammed down beside his legs like stripes on a convict. His fists were clenched as though he was about to hit somebody. The cordons and tendons of his neck were twisted like rope. His face was flushed. Ventris Tidwell watched as his mouth pulled back into his neck, baring his teeth. The whole body was like a muscle undergoing a massive contraction. A low sound rose from it as though forced out by the tremendous pressure. It was not the sound of a voice. It was the sound of the tissues themselves contracting.

Ventris Tidwell became alarmed. He glanced at the door to see who was coming. What could he say? He rushed over to Sonny Hightower.

"Keep it down!" Ventris Tidwell said. He began to shake him. "Shut up, goddamn it! Somebody's coming. They're going to hear you. What are you doing?"

Sonny Hightower fell over backwards and hit a display case. Ventris Tidwell expected to see it overturn or slide across the room and smash into something, but it was too heavy to move, and Sonny Hightower slid off and scuttled around on the floor as though he was trying to creep under it. His arms and legs were moving in different directions. The heels of his shoes struck the floor in an irregular rhythm. His arms flailed, and his head started to beat on the floor. The moans were increasing. The volume was louder.

Ventris Tidwell began to run. He was halfway across the room before he turned to see what had happened. He remembered something about biting one's tongue and ran over to the registration desk, got a few brochures, folded them lengthwise, and tried to force them into Sonny Hightower's mouth. The teeth were clenched. The head flung itself about in his arms like an animal seeking release. Then it was done, and he allowed the teeth to close on it. They snapped shut, and he thought of a turtle he had caught once in the Tennessee River. He remembered teasing it with a stick as big around as his arm. The turtle had seized hold of it with its beak and was still holding on when he cut off its head. He looked at Sonny Hightower's eyes. They were still open, but the irises had rolled back in his head. He looked like a fish.

That was it. Ventris Tidwell got up from the floor and started to leave. Someone would find him. He would come to sooner or later. His tongue was fixed where he couldn't bite it and drown in his own blood. Ventris Tidwell owed him nothing.

The paint on the door had such a high gloss that it reflected his image like asphalt after a rain. He pulled it open, and instead of the steps and the parking lot, the sweep of lawn leading up the hill that overlooked the battlefield, there was only a wall and a darkened room. It might have been his own heart.

Inside the room were obscure shapes such as he had seen in Southeast Asia, the clothes they were buried in rotted half off them. Some were on shelves. Others were hung up by hooks at the back, shoulders hunched over their ears. Skulls gleamed like plastic jugs.

He slammed the door and stumbled back. The light was like grace. It fell on him so suddenly that he was not only disoriented, he was completely bewildered. He had already closed the door and read the sign before he realized what it meant. The sign said MAINTENANCE. KEEP OUT. Inside were buffers, electric cords, coveralls hanging on hooks.

"Oh God," Ventris Tidwell said. "Oh God." He started laughing.

He walked over to the other door. A red and white arrow above it said EXIT. He wondered how he could ever have missed it. The doorknob in his hand was brass, part of a massive rim-lock set. He noticed how cold it was to the touch. All he had to do was open it.

Then he turned and went back, the noise of his heels coming after him like a shadow. Sonny Hightower's feet were sticking out from under a case of bayonets. Every so often they would move as though he was trying to pull them in after him.

Ventris Tidwell dropped to his knees and looked in under the case. Sonny Hightower had worked himself all the way to the back and was sprawled with his head and shoulders propped against the wall.

"What are you doing?" Sonny Hightower asked.

It seemed like the perfect question. Ventris Tidwell did not know what he was doing.

"I don't know," Ventris Tidwell said.

"I do."

"What?"

"Looking at me."

Ventris Tidwell laughed. "That's right. I came back to see how you're doing."

"Back from where?"

"I don't know. Nowhere. How are you feeling?"

"Fine as wine. How are you?"

"Fine as wine."

"What happened?"

Ventris Tidwell did not know what had happened. "An accident," he said.

"Where am I?"

"Under the table. You want to get out?"

"Sure."

"Give me your leg." Ventris Tidwell started to pull him out by the leg at the same time that Sonny Hightower kicked him away and tried to stand up by himself. He kept hitting the case with his back.

"I can't stand up!" Sonny Hightower shouted. "It's all over me. I can't move!"

Ventris Tidwell dropped to his knees, crawled under the case, and wrestled Sonny Hightower to the floor.

"Kneel down," Ventris Tidwell said. "Look here, like this." He crawled out. A few moments later Sonny Hightower crawled out after him. He continued to crawl until Ventris Tidwell put his hand on his shoulder and stopped him.

"Can you stand up?" Ventris Tidwell asked.

"I don't know."

"You want to try? You want me to help you?"

"Sure. Who are you?"

Ventris Tidwell did not know what to say. "A friend," he said finally.

"A friend. Where am I?"

"Chickamauga."

"What?"

"Chickamauga. Where they had the Battle of Chickamauga."

"I already been," Sonny Hightower said.

Ventris Tidwell laughed. "You look like you been."

"Fucker already read it to me. You ready to go? Let's go."

Ventris Tidwell was not certain what he meant.

"Take my arm," Sonny Hightower said. "You going to help me, that's how you do it. You carry my arm."

Ventris Tidwell carried his arm.

"My pins ain't steady," Sonny Hightower said.

"Your pins?"

"The pins on my feet. They're coming loose. My feet feel like they're wobbling off."

"You want to sit down?"

"Not yet. I got a tale to tell you about that."

"About what?"

"The pins on my feet. You want to hear it?"

"Not yet."

"It's too early," Sonny Hightower agreed.

They came to the set of doors, and Sonny Hightower headed straight for the wrong one.

"Not that one," Ventris Tidwell said.

"How you know?"

"I already been there."

"What's in it?"

"Nothing."

Sonny Hightower saw the arrow. "It got an arrow," he said. "This what we're supposed to do."

Ventris Tidwell knew that this was what they were supposed to do. The only problem was that he did not know why they were supposed to do it. The message said pray, and he had prayed all his life, but they were still going down. What do you pray to? The wall is nothing. On the other side is a vacant lot and another man praying.

"How you feeling?" he asked Sonny Hightower. It was as though he had just been given a gift but did not know yet what it was.

"Gooder than snuff," Sonny Hightower said. "How about you?"

"Gooder than snuff. You want to open the door?"

"Sure," Sonny Hightower said. He moved forward and tried to push it open with his hands, then with his shoulder. The door wouldn't open.

"Pull," Ventris Tidwell said.

The sunlight was blinding. Then his eyes focused, and Ventris Tidwell saw the whole world. The sky was endless as an ocean. It filled the horizon. There were no clouds. The air was like marble. The cars in the parking lot caught the light and sent it spinning, dazzling his eyes. The lines on the asphalt heaved in the heat as they walked across it arm in arm onto the grass and up the hill to the clump of oaks overlooking the battlefield and then down the other side to the row of trees in the far distance marking the place where the river flowed, the muddy Chickamauga, eroding the edges of the field and opening a way in the forest. Even now, here and there, he caught an occasional glint of light like something moving through the trees, a flash of something barely seen out of the corner of his eye. He thought of it as some kind of glory.

Judson Mitcham

Judson Mitcham writes poetry and fiction so well that few would ever guess he is a professor of psychology at Fort Valley State University in Georgia. Mitcham was born in Monroe, Georgia, where much of his work is set. He earned his degrees at the University of Georgia. His poetry collection *Somewhere in Ecclesiastes* (1991) won the Devins Prize and recognition for Mitcham as Georgia Author of the Year; his second poetry collection, *This April Day,* was published in 2003. Mitcham's poems have a strongly oratorical quality, as if they are written to be read aloud. His first novel, *The Sweet Everlasting,* was published in 1996; its story of an old man trying to make amends for the wife he betrayed many years before is painfully and lyrically beautiful. A second novel, *Sabbath Creek,* will appear in 2004. Mitcham is a skillful narrative writer, a poet and elegist of the family and the past. "The Light" illuminates the power of a memory that cannot be named or forgotten.

The Light

By a strange twist, the thought of God's anger only arouses love in me.
It is the thought of the possible favor of God and of his mercy that makes
me tremble with a sort of fear.
—Simone Weil

I have found a way to reach the woods near their home, unnoticed. From there I have watched the house like a thief—but what is it I would steal?—or like a voyeur trying to witness some passion in secret. That is what I am.

I have seen him sweep the driveway and take out the trash. I have watched her water the flowers. But mostly I stare at the house. It is across town from the one they lived in when I knew their son, so if there is a shrine inside, it is only a reconstruction, not the actual room left exactly as it was—where the angle of the guitar pick on the desk would have come to seem immutable with the last touch.

Yesterday, I saw him cut the grass, then rest for a while. I saw her come out the door with two tall glasses of what looked like lemonade. They sat on the front steps smiling and talking while they drank.

Today is the day.

When the doctor stepped through the door of the emergency room and told me Paul had died, I traveled into the smooth green shine of the hospital wall, gave the tenderest part of myself away to the surface, as if fascination could protect me; as if I could really journey off and leave my body—so awkward and stupid, so capable of error.

Believe me, you can stare at a thing until it almost heals you. You can listen to a noise until the quality of lullaby arises. You can travel endlessly into the most ordinary event or thought, if only you give your entire life over to it for a moment. And when you have lived this way, foraging for a particular kind of sustenance, each element may begin to fit, as in a dream—when the telephone rings and you realize you have been waiting, all along, for someone to call.

I can see the dirt road—red clay packed so hard that it gleams; deep ruts, ridges baked in their long molds, rigid as bone; a winding road rolling through the low hills of the piedmont, rocks rapping up against the underside of the car; here and there, stretches of loose sand challenging the tires, so the steering wheel turns in my hands.

We are riding out into the late afternoon one Sunday after a movie, down a road none of us is familiar with, the red dust billowing out behind us.

We have chosen this road for its remoteness, for the likelihood that at night no one travels it, and so a boy and a girl might drive out here to be alone. Fatigued by the long war movie, slightly queasy from the popcorn, happy to be almost lost, we are looking for places a car might ease off the road and not get mired in the mud, trying to find driveways leading to abandoned or burned-down houses. But we are bound for a place where we will each be touched in a way we cannot yet imagine.

I watch old couples.

An old man stands in line alone, buys two chili dogs, two soft drinks, and a single order of french fries. He sets the tray down in front of her on the table. They both keep their coats on, though it is relatively warm. They are clearly not in a hurry. The woman leaves the chili dog in the wrapping. The man flattens the paper out, and he eats leaning over it, bits of chili escaping the bun and falling with each bite. He keeps checking the front of his coat.

He is finished before she is, and wipes his mouth, sucking his teeth. He balls up the napkin, drops it on the tray, then looks around slowly, no visible emotion in his eyes as he watches the young people lining up for pizza. She does not look up.

When I awoke today, having made my decision, a quietness came over me. I made coffee, then sat on the sofa, looking out across the deck.

The dawn came in—a slow haze, mist between the branches—then the sky like a low blue flame, and the trees, in their stillness, like watercolors of trees.

"No, he's still alive," I heard her say—that woman I had never seen before and never saw again, who took it on herself to telephone Paul's parents. But within five minutes—or perhaps it had already happened when she hung up the pay phone and we walked back down the hospital hallway—he was gone.

I can summon no good image of that woman. I don't know if she was thin or stout or what color her hair was. I cannot offer the first detail about her face, but I would know her voice—would know it absolutely—that soft drawl with all the world in it.

I prayed in short breathless bursts of words not formed into complete thoughts or sentences. I said "God," and "please," and "no," groaned these words aloud as

I ran down the dirt road, not knowing where I was, wild to find help. Somewhere behind me, Paul lay bleeding from his mouth—Raymond kneeling beside him, repeatedly making the sign of the cross.

In the days to come I would remember a story from Sunday school: how a man walked up to a bad wreck out of nowhere, and without a word to anyone, ripped off the car door, overpowered the crushed-in steel pinning the little girl and her mother—simply willed his muscles and bones to accomplish the impossible, lifted out the woman and the girl, then suddenly was gone. Days later he was identified as a man who had lost his own wife and children to an accident, and who finally, in his rage and sorrow, had given himself over to the Lord—whose instrument, Samson-like, he had become that day on the road.

And I was a lean sixteen-year-old, finely conditioned from year-round sports, able to run forever, I believed. But when I turned from the wreck, took my loafers and socks off and began to run, what could I do but start off fast, in a flat-out dash? I knew, my whole body knew, the wrongness, the obscenity, of setting a pace, of loping off over the hill with a measured, medium stride. I ran as hard as I could—sprinted, churned, knees high, arms pumping—as if trying to steal home or as though I could see a finish line.

So it came to me—my education in the heavy body. With a boy lying near death I felt the earth take hold, felt gravity drip its syrupy liquid into my limbs, so that no will, no force of thought, no panic, no prayer could stop them from slowing down. The June heat sucked the breath from my mouth, set the light melting and swarming near the edges of everything, turned the air busy with nothing, and I moved as if underwater. But I did not stop. I did not sit.

They are stranded on the median of I-75, trying to cross three lanes of holiday traffic and get back to their car, parked on the shoulder. They are inexplicably in the middle of the interstate. There is no clear reason why they should have crossed the highway—no service station or telephone on the other side, only another open field, no houses.

They are poised to make a dash when there is a gap in the traffic, their angelhair whirling and fanning back in the fumey wash of the trucks and cars, their faces looking the same—not worried, but studious, gauging distance and speed. They hold hands, but neither seems to be about to lead the other, both providing ballast, steadiness. They disappear swiftly behind me—a sudden mystery in the late afternoon, though I know with some certainty what it is that I have been to them.

Sometimes I stand in the door to my son's room and look around at the clutter—clothes thrown across a chair, books lying open, his guitar against the wall, tapes stacked precariously on a shelf—and I see it frozen like that, never to be shuffled into another chaos by his own hand again.

I stand there, and I stand there, and I stand there.

Sunday afternoons my family used to drive out through the countryside in our old blue Chevrolet. Over and over, my father proposed the same activity: we were to search for something worth noting, whether by virtue of its beauty or its ugliness, its size, disarray, or unexpectedness—the quality we focused on did not matter.

We soon learned not to take a scattershot approach, pointing at everything. In this there was no pleasure, no return. We learned to take our time. My father drove so slowly on those days, we used to joke that he was practicing to drive a float in the Christmas parade. I remember one afternoon when he wouldn't pass a tractor.

We all saw the flock of starlings rise like a black veil from a field milky and thick with unpicked cotton. We all saw the fence made out of bedsprings, the bird dog asleep underneath a pulpwood truck leaning sideways on a jack.

Once, soon after we had pulled back onto the main highway, traffic slowed almost to a stop, and as we approached the wreck, my father made it clear that we were not to look, that he would not have his children gawking and rubber-necking at someone else's misfortune. But late one night on a trip to Daytona Beach, when I saw the flashing lights, I pretended to be asleep. Then I raised my face to the window just long enough to catch another face staring back—a deep gash underneath the right eye, swollen shut, and the other focused hard on me.

My earliest memory is of anger and tears, upon awakening from a dream in which I had flown a small yellow airplane with short square wings and a boxy fuselage. Though I had piloted the plane, I see it above me, there in the bedroom, climbing—the left wing angled downward, its tail near the top of the door leading to the kitchen. I remember the disbelief I felt, that my toy—my only means of flight—had been taken away. It had evaporated after that brief moment when it seemed to stall near the ceiling, no one at the controls.

Last night I dreamed, again, of wandering through an old house as large as a hotel, though it is someone's home. In this dream I am always looking for the right room. What is in the room, whether it is mine or someone else's, I do not know. I have never found it. I have tried many doors. Usually they are locked, but sometimes they open onto the outside of the house, so that if I step through, I will fall and keep falling, since the house rests on the edge of a cliff.

Perhaps the strangest part of this remarkably consistent dream is the way the hallways are thick with weeds—the broomsage knee-high—and there is a breeze blowing down the halls, always—a rising breeze, as though there is a storm coming in the house.

The next day, my brother drove me home from the hospital, and when we passed the junkyard, as we had to, there they were, lined up at the fence, pointing at the car.

I suppose it was something worthy of note—a rolled Corvair, all its tires flat, no glass left in the windows.

Sitting in the row in front of me, she smiles at the old man next to her, who has dozed off halfway through the movie.

When he opens their front door, my name escapes softly from his throat—like a breath let go—and with a tentative sweep of his hand, he shows me in.

They have both been sitting on the couch, reading the newspaper. She does not move or speak or in any way acknowledge I am there. Her face is classical in its immobility—a weathered carving out of the ancient world.

He sits down again at her side, leaving me to negotiate the room on my own. I remain standing. He leans over and whispers to his wife, but she does not answer.

Thirty years of whirling in silent orbits around the same dense absence and now the stillness of this room . . .

"Mrs. Bennett, for a long time . . ."

At the sound of my voice, her face breaks, her lips starting to tremble, as if some deep fault which opened up inside her long ago had again begun to shift. "Why did you come here?" she asks, though her eyes evade mine, focus on something beyond and make me want to look behind me.

Suddenly he is on his feet, moving quickly. "There's something I want you to see," he says, pulling me by the arm toward the hallway leading to the rear of the house. As we pass, she lunges at me and I throw up a hand to protect my face, but she wrestles me into her arms, kisses me roughly on the cheek, then grabs me above the elbow, her fingernails digging into my skin, then relenting—though she does not let go—and they both guide me deeper into the house.

The light along the wall is so golden, there must be a window at the end of that hallway.

But there is nothing I want to tell them now, and nothing I want to see. I only want to run, but they are holding me.

Ferrol Sams

A medical doctor and a longtime resident of Fayette County, Ferrol Sams was born in 1922 in Fayetteville, Georgia. After graduating from Mercer University in 1942, he studied medicine at Emory Medical University. He began writing in 1978, after years of practicing medicine. His first novel, *Run with the Horsemen,* appeared in 1982, followed by a sequel, *The Whisper of the River,* in 1984. A third novel, *When All the World Was Young,* appeared in 1991. Chronicling the life of a fictional character named Porter Osbourne, the three novels are loosely autobiographical. A collection of short fiction, *The Widow's Mite and Other Stories,* appeared in 1987; a collection of three long stories, *Epiphany,* appeared in 1995. Sams's skill with southern speech and character is especially evident in his humorous story "The Widow's Mite."

The Widow's Mite

I would be the first to admit that I wasn't born a Branscombe or yet a Vollenweider, don't you know? But still and all, I feel down in my heart that I'm as much of a lady as any of them. And down in your heart is where Jesus looks, and I hope it's only Jesus what looks down in there, for I've personally got no desire to. My stars alive, what may be going on even in my very own heart is enough to scare me to death. Which is what that psychiatrist was trying to tell me about that time. That it's what's down inside that you don't ever let out that's important, and we need to bring it up and face it and even talk to somebody about it. What he meant was me bring it up and talk to him about it and me pay him to listen. I'll tell you right now, I never went to him but once. It makes me mad as all get-out to go to a doctor anytime what's too busy to talk to me or worse yet acts like he's not interested in what I've got to say. I don't feel like he's proper earning his money. But there's something plumb indecent about going to a doctor that's not going to do a blessed thing but listen to you and charge you by the hour for it, and not even throw in no iron and vitamins or even a eensy-weensy B12 shot and has the nerve to tell you ahead of time that's the way it's going to be.

Well, they can keep their listening and I'll keep my money. I guess I wasn't born yesterday. And I guess I know a good doctor when I see one. A really good doctor has got a knife in one hand and hormones in the other and I mean he's coming at you. He's not sitting there in no leather chair with his legs crossed and sucking on no pipe and acting like if you got the money, he'll take the time.

Which is where I differ from the Branscombes and the Vollenweiders, for they throw their money around on you wouldn't believe what all, and I'd bet you five hundred dollars—if I was a betting woman, which I am not—that I've had more operations my ownself than the whole kit and caboodle of them together, and that includes their in-laws, too. Course they was all raised in big white houses or pillowed mansions or whatever you want to call them, and my daddy sharecropped and sawmilled from here to yonder and pieced that out by making a little whiskey now and then, but he never got caught at it, and at least I can truthfully say that not a drop of it has ever crossed my lips. Not even back when I had the cramps so bad ever time I minnerstrated that I'd holler and moan for two days hand-running, and my aunt what stayed with us after Mama died would beg me to take a dram and hush. But even when I was a teenager I was a handmaiden of the Lord, so to speak. I knew in my heart that ladies don't ever let down and drink alcohol, and Jesus can look down in there all He wants and He won't find even the first little old temptation to sin against my body with liquor.

Which is something that Waldene Branscombe has for sure and certain not learned yet. She buys all her clothes in Atlanta and has not ever took the down elevator when she walks into Rich's. Prances into the Regency shop there, she does, in the size sixes at that, and buys fancy clothes to wear to cocktail parties in Atlanta. She drinks liquor when she's at them, too, and she goes regular to one of them psychiatrists but has never yet had the first operation. Which we all have a pretty good idea of what's down in her heart, but if she shows the psychiatrist or yet Jesus more than she does the rest of us when she's flouncing around town in those lowcut, high-faluting clothes from the Regency shop, then somebody ought to be embarrassed, but it's sure not Waldene. I personally think she'd do better for herself just to go ahead and have something cut plumb out of her and be done with it.

People who was born with money don't have peacock brains about the real value of it and how to get the best return on your dollar. They spend it like it was always just gonna keep rolling in. She could get her gall bladder out for three hundred and fifty dollars, and I know that's a lot to shell out in one piece, but the psychiatrist will nickel and dime the same amount out of her over the long haul. And at least with the gall bladder out she wouldn't be bothered with gas for awhile, which is a great comfort and money well spent, and psychiatrists won't even discuss gas with you as I discovered that one and only time I went to one. Not that I for one minute want to be understood as saying I think Waldene's gall bladder is what ought to be cut out. I never yet caught Waldene in the unladylike conduct that gas causes and if I was going to recommend an operation for her I don't for the life of me know whether it would be to cut something out or put something in, but rich folks don't like to lay money out on something what's not a sure thing.

Take tithing for instance. Waldene wouldn't even consider that. She might spend a sight more than a tenth at Rich's, but a dollar in the collection plate is plenty on Sunday. I am a good Christian and always have been. I was born one, I guess, because I read my horoscope every day in the *Atlanta Constitution* and my Bible every night. And of course I have always tithed and been regular in the Eastern Star. I have flat set aside that tenth for the Lord even when I worked at the button counter at Kress's. Nobody could call me a religious fanatic or nothing like that, unless you was a Methodist, and of course they think that anybody what runs their lives by rules is a fanatic, which is the same as saying all of we Baptists are. Well, everybody knows about sticks and stones may break my bones but words will never harm me. That's not Holy Writ, as they say; it's just a saying. But it's so old and so true that it ought to be in the Bible. It would fit in real good in Proverbs like it was right at home. In fact, I may just write it in the margin of mine. In red ink. Like Jesus did all his talking in. The which I have already underlined the last chapter of Ecclesiastes in red, in fact I painted the whole white page of it with a red color crayon. I know as well as the next one that Jesus never said it, but all that about a virtuous woman, if he'd a thought of it he would of. And if I'd ever had a little girl, I was always aiming to name her Ruby and raise her up so that's what her price would have been greater than. That is one more holy piece of Scripture, I am here to tell you.

But I set out to tell you about tithing and how I became to look on it in an adult way and all. It's easy enough to give that tenth when you're making ten or twenty dollars a month, and if some emergency comes up and you're too sick to go to church on Sunday, you can always skip the tithe with a clear conscience— that is, if you're really sick and have been under a doctor and not just laying out because you didn't get your hair set or something like that. Even Jesus don't expect you to pay for something you don't get.

When you have a heap of money though, it makes you sing a different tune and do some real serious soul searching. You can almost understand how come the Branscombes and Vollenweiders are Methodists, although that is an extreme step and risking your immortal soul to eternal hell-fire and I wasn't never really tempted to change over. I am certainly not one to trade my soul's salvation for a mess of pottage. I have never knowed exactly what that was anyhow, but it sure doesn't sound very good. Bout like turnip greens or some such, and that's certainly not worth the risk of hell-fire.

Well, there I sat. All of a sudden I had an unborn baby in my womb and $125,000, cash, tax-free, in my lap. I had just that month turned twenty-one, which kept Pa from running my business although I did have to holler Law at him a couple of times to impress him that I was legal of age and also a widow woman to boot. If Pa had ever got his hands on my money or his nose in my business, it would have been Katy bar the door and shirt sleeves to shirt sleeves in about thirty minutes. I had only been married a year, and John George had in fact just took out the insurance policy as my anniversary present. It was our paper anniversary, like they say, and he was being appropriate, but it sure turned out to be a heap of paper. We made it double indemnity because it didn't cost but ten dollars more, not ever dreaming we was going to cash in on it so good and so quick. And, of course, we wasn't dreaming about Leon Jr. Talbott, either, whose mother was a Vollenweider.

Leon Jr. wasn't but fourteen and didn't have no business atall driving his daddy's Buick automobile across the playground at recess which it was also the ball diamond, but he done it. He done it on a dare, his friend L. M. Bottoms claimed, to prove that he could drive, and he was aiming to cut a doughnut out in center field and scatter them children like chickens, he said. Everybody in town knows Leon Jr. has got problems. He just never has been what you could call right. The very idea of him setting there hutten, hutten, hutten in a black Buick while them children finished their sack lunches, except for Little Bobby Brookshire whose Mama still packed his in a lard bucket even though he was in the eighth grade and fat as a killing-size hog.

The Board of Education had decided to put in outside lights for the ball diamond and had hired John George to do the wiring. He come down off his ladder when Leon Jr. scratched off and he seen that he was aiming for them children. John George hollered for them all to run and was trying to wave Leon Jr. off at the same time. L. M. Bottoms claims that they was all out the way except Little Bobby Brookshire who had to waddle in place of running, and that Leon Jr. would have hit him as sure as gun's iron if John George hadn't dived in front of that black Buick and give him a shove.

Even then everything would have been all right if Leon Talbott Sr. hadn't left that metal fence post sticking out the back window, but then he wasn't to fault for how could he have known that Leon Jr. was going to snitch his car to show out? Anyhow, when John George straightened out from pushing Little Bobby Brookshire to safety, that post caught him across the back of the neck going about forty miles an hour and cut his head clean off. They say it rolled almost to the pitcher's mound from out in center field, and even if somebody had of been at shortstop it wouldn't of made no difference, because everybody was just too stunned to even move until it quit rolling. It scraped a good deal of the skin off one side of his face and messed up his ear real bad. Luther and Son embalmed the head and body separate and then stuck them together, and although you could tell the shirt collar was riding a little high, we was able to open the casket at the service, which was a comfort to me. And I will say the insurance company never even raised a murmur about it and was real nice about paying off prompt. They never even done no whining about double indemnity. Course there was no way they could have said all that wasn't to be classified accidental death, and John George had even died like a hero and that was a comfort also. So was the insurance company in their own way.

Leon Talbott Sr. come to see me before the funeral with some papers to sign, saying I didn't lay no blame nor hold no claim on Leon Jr. Talbott. Everybody knows that every dollar in that family was Vollenweider, and they give me twenty-five thousand of them to sign the paper and said they hoped I'd build a nice house and be comfortable. I never let on to them about the insurance policy. What folks don't know won't hurt them and sometimes what they don't know helps you out a heap.

The only thing that really worried me about the funeral was that John George wasn't saved. I don't mean he didn't believe. I am sure that he did, but he hadn't never professed Jesus Christ as his personal Saviour out in public at the front of the church and all that and been baptized with the water and the Spirit. And every time that we was by ourself, so's we'd have a chance to talk about such, it seemed like John George always had something else on his mind and when he did he could sure distract you. I was aiming to work on him real hard for the second anniversary, which they say is tin and I'd rather of had John George saved than anything I ever seen that was made out of tin. But all things considered, I guess things turned out for the best. If we hadn't got the insurance, all our child and I would of had when it was over and done with would of been the twenty-five thousand dollars from Leon Talbott Sr.'s in-laws, and we could of made do real nice with that but we wouldn't have been so prominent in the church and the community.

I am still coming to tithing. It was about a month after the funeral. I know it was a month cause I had slacked up from going to the cemetery every day and had cut it down to three times a week, and after two months I was going to cut the trips back to once a month and then, of course, later I could just go on Christmas and Easter and John George's birthday. I know that only God sees our insides, but it don't hurt a thing to remember how hard folks look at the outside, and Faceville is strict about grieving widow women and the cemetery. The news leaked out about the insurance money and here come Brother Whatever.

That was my private name for him, of course, and I never let him hear me use it. His real name was Leland L. Laurens and he was the pastor of the First Baptist Church of Faceville, Georgia, and why we called it First Baptist I have never understood, unless it just had a grander sound to it, because it was the only Baptist church in Faceville. And still is, for that matter, unless you count the colored one and nobody ever does. I had found a home in the First Baptist and the congregation was, I wouldn't say more Christian than any I'd ever belonged to before, but certainly more what you would call genteel.

And I'd always liked the preacher well enough, too, although nothing like Mildred Mitchell, which her husband always said that when Mildred died she wanted to go to Leland, and she very nearly did when he got the call to Alabama and left Faceville for good. Die, I mean, not go to him. First place, he wouldn't of had her and second place, it would have flat tore Faceville up. She didn't have no use atall for the next two preachers we had at First Baptist and it wasn't for no reason in the world except she was still moaning for Leland L. Laurens, and them preachers was both just as involved and consecrated as they could be, and to this day Mildred don't do all she should in the WMU. I will say, though, that Leland L. Laurens was the cause of Mildred finally joining the Eastern Star, because when he left and Mildred dropped out of prayer meeting, WMU, and the Eve-to-Judith Bible Study Group, she had to have somewhere to get out of the house that was respectable and Eastern Star was it.

She went right on up, too. Within a year she was in the East and it wasn't but three years before she became Worthy Grand Matron. She would of done better to put it off awhile because Rotell Robinson was Grand Master that year and he can't keep from belching, even when he's in the East, which is not a suitable place at all for gas what with the ladies of the Court dressed up in evening gowns and all. Mildred had blue chiffon, the which it didn't do much for her, her skin being what I've always called sallow, but doctors nowdays don't know what you're talking about when you say "sallow." In fact, they don't even recognize "bilious" anymore.

And I know sure as I'm standing here that Rotell has got a hiatal hernia. I call mine "my hyena" and Dr. Mason always knows right off what I'm talking about. I told Rotell oncet that he ought to get hisself x-rayed and lose fifty pounds and he'd feel better, but he won't go to no doctor. All the Robinsons are tight with their money where doctors are concerned. Of course, the way I handle my hyena is when I know ahead of time I'm going out like to church or the Eastern Star, I get up early and take two enemas and you don't ever catch me belching in public. Or nothing else. A proper enema, if you give it right, is not only a tool of good health but makes you mindful of good manners. Rotell acted so disinterested I didn't bother to tell him about the enemas, and for that matter I've never told Dr. Mason. You can't ever be sure what them doctors have decided from one visit to the next that folks ought to give up. They can sure hem you in.

The reason I always called Leland L. Laurens "Brother Whatever" was that it looked like every time I got around him he'd wind up saying that. "Whatever," he'd say. The preachers in the little country churches I growed up in didn't have all that much education. They'd felt the call and got theyselves ordained and they preached on Sunday and worked at the Ford plant or some such during the week. But they was all full of the fire of the Lord and would talk to you and argue with you about the Scriptures all night long. Any church that is called First Baptist is bound and determined to have a preacher what's been off to college and to the Seminary, and of course they don't work. They just preach and visit.

Every time I would stop Leland L. Laurens on the street or even go by his office, which he called it his study (that comes from going to the Seminary, too, in my opinion), to discuss the way I personally was interpreting something I'd read in the Bible, he'd wind up rolling his eyes extra patient like and saying, "Whatever," and just keep walking on. Take, for instance, the first miracle, the one at Cana, where the Philistines or some such run out of wine when they was carousing at that wedding. I run into him on the curb one day just as the mail run and told Leland L. Laurens that my faith wouldn't let me believe that the Lord Jesus Christ condoned alcohol in any shape, form, or fashion or had anything at all to do with it. I told him that I had become to interpret that Bible passage as Jesus turned that water into plain grape juice, just like we have at Communion in First Baptist with the Nabisco saltines all crumbled up. It hadn't never sowvered or fermented, and that bunch of Vollenweiders and Branscombes whooping it up at Cana hadn't drunk anything like that in so many years they'd plumb forgot how good fresh grape juice tastes and that's how come they said it was the best of the evening. And that didn't take nothing away at all from the Lord Jesus Christ, for it's as plain as the nose on your face that it takes every bit as big a miracle to turn a barrel of water into grape juice as it does into wine. Leland L. Laurens shut his eyes for a extra long moment and then he says, "Whatever," and then he tipped his hat to Miss Lorraine Graham and walked on in the post office. And ever since that day I've been calling him Brother Whatever behind his back and down in my heart, where only Jesus can see and that psychiatrist wanted to go prying and plundering around except I wasn't about to let him.

If I'd told Brother Robert K. Price that interpretation, he'd of preached a whole sermon on it at the Holly Grove Tabernacle and have received at least two or three new souls into fellowship when he opened the doors of the church. Not that I'd trade back. Brother Price does murder the King's English—comes from not finishing nothing but the seventh grade and working all his life at Dundee No. 2 in Griffin. You can tell he is happy in the Lord, though, and he will always take time to talk to you. He told me oncet that when he was young he thought he'd be an evangelist. He was called to a little church in Dawson County way up in north Georgia for a whole week's revival. They guaranteed him twenty dollars plus all the love offerings he could get, which wasn't bad atall for that day and time. But Brother Robert K. Price had done bit off more'n he could chew as he very quickly come to find out. He come on back home on Tuesday and has been happy as a dead pig in the sunshine ever since, just preaching at Holly Grove and working at Dundee No. 2. He told me about Dawson County. Said he didn't mind the drums and cymbals but he wasn't going to do snakes for nobody.

Brother Whatever reads the Scripture as smooth and grand as Billy Graham and never stumbles over big words or hard names, and I do respect him for it as a man and as a servant of God and all that. I do wish, though, that every now and then he'd holler just a little bit. I never saw him raise a sweat over a sermon, and I never saw Brother Price wind one up lessen he was sopping wet. Now that's what I call the Fire of the Lord.

The day Brother Whatever come to call on me about my insurance money, I knew I had to have my wits about me, and I breathed a little personal prayer when I seen him coming up the walk.

I knew the news was out because Cousin Sara had went by Montine's to pick up a loaf of bread. The Bamby truck runs on Wednesday and Kate Greer always shows up to get a loaf while it's fresh and before everybody in town has had a chance to squeeze it or paw over it, she says. I do believe she is more conscientious than I am about germs. On top of which her doctor has told her that she has capillaries, so she is extra careful about a lot of things. Kate gets Rachel to set her aside a loaf under the counter in case the bread truck runs while Kate is taking her nap. Rachel is Montine's sister-in-law, and everybody in Faceville does love a family business. Cousin Sara heard Rachel and Kate talking about me, and Kate was saying that Leon Talbott Sr. had bought off Leon Talbott Jr. by paying me twenty-five thousand dollars.

Rachel said that wasn't the end of it by a long sight, that John Addison had come by and told Montine that a fellow had told him the insurance policy was for fifty thousand dollars, double indemnity. Course John Addison hadn't told who a fellow was, but anybody who's lived in Faceville long knows that it's a fellow always tells John Addison everything and they're usually dead center on the truth and John Addison has never yet the first time let down and told anybody who a fellow is.

When Rachel told Kate that, she said, "Well, now, hasn't she popped her butt in a tub of butter! I've got to run by Catherine's and tell her. Thanks for saving out the bread." Kate didn't mean no harm nor yet even no disrespect when she said that about my butt and the tub of butter. All it meant was that I'd done a heap better than anybody ever expected me to and they was surprised. It's just another one of those old sayings, although not one that I have ever even thought about writing down in red anywhere and most certainly not in Proverbs. I learned a long time ago that some old sayings are better than others, and to tell the truth, some of them don't hardly bear repeating. Kate, of course, will repeat anything. Almost anywhere. But, come to think of it, not to just anybody.

It was the day after that when Brother Whatever come a-calling, and I knew when I saw him what he had on his mind. He's always about a day and a half picking something up, but then Brother Whatever don't have a fellow and has to rely on the WMU. After five or ten minutes and a really sweet prayer, which Brother Whatever could do better'n anybody else—I mean he could flat bring the Heavenly Father right in the room with you when you were grief-stricken and all—he set down in John George's rocker and says, "Well, I hear you've come into a little money."

I was setting there thinking the whole time he had been praying. I knowed that he knew but he didn't know that I knowed that he knew, and that always gives a lady a little edge. So I come out with it straight. I said, "Yessir. John George had took out an insurance policy for fifty thousand on hisself for our anniversary present. It was our paper anniversary and I give him a Bible, one of them with Jesus talking to Hisself in red, that he could mark up whenever he got around to studying on it, and he give me the insurance policy. Next year I was going to get him baptized for our second anniversary, but I'm sure you understand, Preacher, that you have to go one step at the time and you have to walk before you can run, and that insurance policy was sure the first step to salvation on account of my intentions and all being so good, and I am not really scared about John George's soul. I figure if he's not with Jesus yet that sooner or later they'll find each other. After all, they got all eternity to do it in. The Bible says, 'Seek and ye shall find,' and I figure that applies to Jesus same as John George, and John George was sure a patient man, the which if anybody ought to know I do."

I explained about the policy being double indemnity and then I told it all. Like I said, I knowed he already knew it anyhow, so I told him about Leon Jr. Talbott and I asked Brother Whatever to pray for him because we all know that, regardless of how the law gets tangled up and confused about involuntary manslaughter and such, Leon Jr. Talbott had took another human's life and was in danger of hell-fire on account of it, double indemnity notwithstanding. Although it's a sweet thought I'd never had before that maybe the good Lord gives all of us double indemnity if our sins are accidental and we can prove it. Then so help me, he come out with it. "Whatever," he said.

That was a good sign I was winning. I lined it right on out: twenty-five from Leon Talbott Sr. and the Vollenweiders, fifty from the policy and fifty from the double indemnity.

"That makes $125,000, Preacher," I said. "And there's no sense atall in either one of us wasting our breath on the widow's mite. The which I'm a widow my own self now and I realize if that one in the Bible had amounted to anything or had anything besides just a mite, she wouldn't have had to throw it all in the collection plate at one time, she could have just give a tenth. You can't divide a mite, Preacher, there's not ten parts to it, I suspect, but I am certainly going to tithe my fortune which I have come up with so unexpectedly. I am grateful to God for His bountiful goodness and this fallen sparrow is going to repay Him and keep the hairs in my head numbered."

When I stopped for breath, Brother Whatever said, "Amen," and had a sharp gleam in his eye and I could tell he felt like I was losing ground. I never let on. I just kept talking. I could tell he had done his arithmetic in his head and he was dead certain that ten percent of $125,000 was $12,500. Well, I had news for him, and Brother Robert K. Price would of thought on the Lord giving double indemnity for a whole week at Dundee No. 2 and then come up on Sunday morning with a sermon that shook the rafters and brought new men in from the field of sin, as they say. But then some folks is so educated you couldn't inspire 'em for nothing, short of a lightning bolt and a thunderstorm.

Then I told Brother Whatever that I had been praying on my knees about this matter. I learned a long time ago that if you are going to have a argument that the first one what says he has been praying about it, just up front and open and all, has got a considerable advantage, like a school teacher or your grandparents or even a judge. It takes more than a average person to ignore you praying about something and go on with the sense behind what you was talking about in the first place. And if you say it was on your knees, then if somebody disagrees it sounds like they coming between you and the good Lord and they feel like they are more than likely to displease the Lord a little. The which I had been praying, and if it wasn't really on my knees, at least I'd thought about being on them, and Jesus Hisself says that thinking about something is the same as doing it, so I wasn't really lying.

I could tell that Brother Whatever believed it anyhow, for he looked down at them real quick-like. My knees. But they was crossed. Mama had learned us that soon as we was old enough to wear lipstick and silk stockings. You can't ever tell who's trying to get a peek, and it's better to be prepared and help your fellow man avoid even the appearance of evil. Some of them Branscombes and Vollenweiders can flop down on a sofa or yet a glider and take your picture from clear across the room, but I am a Baptist lady. That is no way to attract a man, besides the which you can't never tell what might come up that you've got no desire to handle. The only time I ever went to the Methodist church, Waldene Branscombe got to giggling with her cousin over the responsive reading, which it was about a rod that come forth out of the stem of Jesse. They kept it up plumb through Epworth League, and if you are going to get nasty-minded about the Holy Bible, no wonder you need a psychiatrist and all such. It is better to avoid the appearance of evil.

"Preacher," I said, "let me tell you about this tithe and ten percent business. You think we talking about $12,500 for the Faceville First Baptist, and I have no doubt in my heart that you are sincere in the light of what all you have learned at that Seminary in Louisville, but I myself know all about two plus two and ten percent and all, and I never had to leave Little Flock school house to learn it.

You think ten percent is $12,500 and that's what you looking at, but it ain't." I never say *ain't* because Mama preached at us about it and said it was common to say it, but didn't seem like nothing else would fit right then. Another thing Mama used to do was make us girls wear bonnets and gloves and long sleeves in the field so as folks couldn't tell we'd been out in no sun or ever touched a hoe handle, and I would pray that Waldene or none the other girls at school would come by and recognize me. Sister rubbed buttermilk on her face, too, up under the sun bonnet and all, because she was bad to freckle, but all I wanted was just not to be recognized.

"First off, Preacher," I went on, "you can drop the double indemnity. I feel like that's something the Lord granted because of good stewardship, like in the parable of the ten talents and all, and it didn't cost me and John George but ten dollars to start off with, so that's forty-nine thousand nine hundred and ninety dollars right there ought not to be tithed on again. That leaves fifty thousand, and from that we need to subtract at least ten percent because you know that the insurance company had done paid out that much on income tax and corporate tax and it is un-American to have double taxation or taxation without representation, which is what caused this country in the first place at the Boston Tea Party, the which Myrtle Crouch and me like to never of learned from Mrs. Cole in American History, but once we got ahold of it I bet you neither one of us will ever forget it. So that leaves forty-five thousand."

I could tell that he was weakening. The first sign is his eyes get sort of a glazed look they call it, and he quits looking at you plumb straight all the time.

"Now, Preacher, out of that forty-five thousand we ought to take the funeral expenses, to my way of thinking. After all, that was a very religious ceremony the way you preached it, and now we talking just a little about separation of church and state, but I won't do nothing more than just touch on that."

He took a deep breath and swallowed, but he didn't say nothing.

"Luther and Son's bill come to $2,445.50, which included the embalming, the solid copper coffin, the hearse, the funeral home, and twenty-four dollars for digging the grave. He's got the whole thing itemized, which is just good business and I do appreciate it, and he was real sweet and supportive and just wonderful through it all, but I disremember exactly where the fifty cents comes in at. So now we talking about $42,554.50.

"But from that we need to deduct the florist's bill. I don't want you to think I'm being cheap, Preacher, but all this was spent on John George, you know, and I have not been able to find the first thing in the Bible about tithing dead men. It stands to reason that if there's to be no giving or taking in marriage in heaven, then for sure and certain the tithe ought to be shut down, too. I paid out a flat one hundred dollars for that blanket of red roses and baby breath what was on the coffin with the one orchid right in the middle of it. Laverne wanted to make the orchid white to match the baby breath, but I liked the purple better, and it is still fresh in that little test tube what Laverne put it in and I've yet got it in the refrigerator. I have pressed six of the roses, and when the orchid starts to fade I aim to press it too, and then I can have them framed and hang them on the wall, under our marriage license.

"Also, while I was at Laverne's picking out the orchid, I come across this offering that I just couldn't resist, which you may have noticed at the head of the coffin. It was the carnations around the pink ceramic telephone that was laying off the hook and had golden letters under it that said, 'Jesus called.' Laverne charged me twenty dollars for the phone and five dollars for the carnations, but to me it was worth it. It's just so sweet and sentimental and tells it all, and I still choke up when I think about it. I have got the offering with the telephone on it in my closet, but I didn't press none of the carnations. They are so fat they'll stain the Bible or dictionary every time and they get flaky and crumbly when you finally do get them dried. Laverne wanted I should choose white carnations, but I stood firm on pink. That Laverne is really hung up on white, you have to watch her. And that's another $125 right there."

I took a quick look at Brother Whatever and knew I was doing all right. You could hear the air blowing way in the back of his nose when he breathed. But if he thought I was even close to being done, he had another think coming.

"Preacher, I hadn't told you yet about the house I'm getting built. John Milsapps is going to build it except for the brick, which James Callaway is going to put up. John George's baby and widow are going to have a brand-new house by the time the baby is born, and John George's baby is going to be raised in a solid brick house. James said everybody puts up brick veneer, but I argued him down and my house is going to be solid brick all the way to the roof. I told James that nothing else would do, since it was going to be built with John George's insurance money and I wanted solid brick for sentimental reasons if nothing else, because John George used to say that was what I was built like. James said solid brick tends to sweat, but I told him John George did, too, at least ever time he made that remark, and James said it was fine with him and we didn't need to talk about it no more.

"James is the best brick mason around, Preacher, even before he give up drinking, and John George told me one time that you wouldn't find no hogs in one of James Callaway's walls and I laughed fit to kill, but it turned out that's just brick mason talk, and a hog to them is a slanting line of bricks that is a monument to sloppy work when somebody stands off and looks at it. It's there forever and you can't hide it for nothing. I told James about what John George said and he come down on his price, too. He has got real respect for a widow woman.

"John Milsapps is a different cat. I had to talk cash at four o'clock every Friday to get his prices off any. He's the one what built K. W. McElwaney's house, and he'd make a dog laugh telling about how come they kept calling him back every year or so to put on a new addition. John's got a sharp tongue, but he's got a true eye and I've always heard that his corners are square. He give me a little trouble about me wanting two bathrooms, and I won't repeat his remarks about what a girl raised like me wanted with more'n one on the inside the house. It wasn't that I hadn't already heard the words he used at one place or another, it was just that his thoughts was what you would call coarse and a lady wouldn't repeat them. I know he'll make a funny story about it before he tells it down at John M. Jackson's store and it'll get all over town, but it helped me get another two hundred dollars off his bill. Course I had to let a tear come up and my chin tremble, but it takes that to make John feel guilty. I've knowed him since I was a little girl and Pa sold him whiskey now and then, which means ever Tuesday and Saturday, just between me and you, Preacher. John talks rough and blusters around like he's disrespectful, but he's got a heart like summer butter, if you know how to get to it. It's tedious, but it's all part of being a good steward, Preacher, of the earthly goods that the Lord has placed in our hands."

Brother Whatever had commenced to rocking, but he never said a word.

"I know you wonder why I'm telling you all this, Preacher, but it still has to do with tithing. John George use to say I ramble more'n anybody he ever saw to finally get to where I was headed for in the first place. The upshot of all that with James and John . . . and I hadn't even thought of it before but that sounds like I'd been dealing with the disciples, don't it? James and John. I declare. Course James Callaway's daddy wasn't Zebedee and John Milsapps has never been what you'd call all that close to Jesus, but still and all isn't that interesting? Anyway, for one afternoon and half a morning's dickering I got a solid brick, three-bedroom, two-bathroom house with a glassed-in sun porch for $8,400 instead of $10,000. The sun porch is nowhere near as big as Mrs. Vollenweider's, which is where I got the idea, but it'll hold a little sofa and also some ferns and African violets in the winter time. If you've been following along, that leaves $34,305.50. Right?"

He never said it then. He just said, "I guess so."

Then I told him, "The lot was four hundred dollars, which may sound a little high for no more'n one acre of land in this town, but it sets on a corner just one block from the court house and I hear tell that someday they're going to pave the street in front of it. Also it belonged to Mr. Hulon Gossett, and I didn't even try to dicker or talk cash with Mr. Hulon. He didn't particularly want to sell it in the first place, and Lord knows cash don't mean the first thing to a Gossett. Mr. Hulon's still got a nickel of the first dime he ever made. Now, there's somebody you need to work on, Preacher. I can promise you tithing has not ever crossed Hulon Gossett's mind.

"I got the deed drawed up real quick before he could back out, and that's another place I used my head. Did you know that lawyers charge you just for making a trip or two to the court house and filling out a little piece of paper? It comes from all that schooling. I tell you, education is driving prices up all over the country, and if somebody don't call a halt to it we may get bankruptured over education. The lawyer I got was Lester Creasey, who is good as any and better than most. On top of all that he was always one of Pa's best customers. About the third time I acted real cordial and told him I hadn't seen him since I left home and use to run into him and Pa in the corn crib all the time, he grunted and said by God, to hush, he wasn't going to charge me for drawing up that deed. Now, that's stewardship, too, Preacher, and I didn't cause him to stumble and use the Lord's name. Lester Creasey does that all the time anyhow. Did you know he's aiming to run for public office next fall? Everything helps, Preacher, if you're a good steward. Now, let's see. That leaves $33,905.50, don't it?"

Then I told him about the trust fund for the baby. I decided while Lester Creasey was in such an accommodating frame of mind I'd just have him tend to that too while I was at it instead of having to take time to work him up to it again, and besides it might be he wouldn't have his mind on it as good if it was any closer to election time. We put in initials, since we don't yet know whether the baby is a boy or a girl. R. J. Ruby Johnnie if it's a girl, which I hope it is on account of Ecclesiastes and all, and Reuben John if it's a boy. Either name gets in the daddy and the Bible, and you can't hardly beat that for anybody's name. Of course, what was of interest to Brother Whatever was that the trust fund was for twenty thousand dollars, which means that I can't ever again get at that money but it will be there for education when Ruby Johnnie or Reuben John needs it, whichever. And, of course, that sounds like an awful lot for education, but I believe on another one of them old sayings. It's, "If you can't lick 'em, join 'em," and I wouldn't write it in red or anything because it just don't ring right for that and I can't imagine Jesus saying it, but it is very true. By now me and the preacher was down to $13,905.50, and I declare he had broke just the lightest of sweats. His forehead was plumb shining.

"Ooh, Preacher," I said, "I was about to forget the headstone. It is not ready yet because they've got a three-month backlog, but that is going to cost me an even five hundred dollars. The reason it costs so much is account of the telephone. The letters and all worked out real good, for the Georgia Monument Company could carve 'Jesus Called' just as easy and a heap cheaper than 'Asleep in Jesus' or some such, but they're charging me plenty for that telephone with the receiver off the hook. I can't help it. I just had to have it. And if that's not good judgment I'll just have to answer for it later. Now, my figuring puts things at $13,405.50.

"That looks pretty good, but you know what, Preacher? There is such a thing as hidden costs, and a wise man and his money is not soon parted if he just keeps his head about him and thinks, and I am not talking about the Hulon Gossetts of this world who are rich because they never spent nothing. You know well's I do that the Gossetts don't even live in a brick veneer house, let alone solid. And they don't have a bathroom inside because Mr. Hulon says if somebody's too lazy to go outdoors to you-know-what, he's too lazy to live. That's stingy, that's not smart, because Jesus said, 'I have come that you should have life more abundantly,' and I am convicted that He certainly includes a commode and lavatory and tub and running water and all that. That is, if you can afford it. There is certainly nothing sinful about an outhouse, but Mr. Hulon Gossett is welcome to his. I can't imagine for the life of me Jesus Christ making a remark like that.

"Now, those hidden costs I was telling you about? I bet you hadn't for a minute thought about the premium John George paid out to the Prudential Company in the first place, but don't feel bad about it because I hadn't either. Not till I started adding it all up to see where I was and all, and all of a sudden I hollered right out loud, 'Why, that's a hidden cost.' And it was, Preacher. It's $826.50, and that balances out that other fifty cents that was on Luther and Son's bill, and I am glad to get shed of it because from now on we can deal just in round numbers and that's ever so much simpler. It's not that fifty cents is so hard to handle by itself. It's just that all of a sudden you remember that it's a half a dollar and a half of anything is a fraction, and as soon as I hear fraction it throws me back in Mrs. Barron's classroom, which is where I first heard of fractions and I have never to this day got over it yet. It was add fractions, subtract fractions, divide fractions, multiply fractions, and that old woman would yell and holler at you if you didn't learn 'em right till you had a headache and wanted to bust out crying and never hear of a common denominator again the longest day you lived. Mrs. Barron was a Christian and all and prayed real sweet every morning, but when them fractions hit at one-thirty in the afternoon, look like it brought the devil out in her. She hollered so mean I broke out in the hives. I did, too. And worse and still she locked Jane Dennis's bowels. Jane always was stubborn and had a temper herself, but nobody could stand up to Mrs. Barron, and Jane got that olive skin from her daddy's side the family and wasn't subject to hives. I've always felt like I'd rather put up with the bumps and the itching. Jane was in a real bad fix off and on for over two months and stayed constipated till summer vacation."

Brother Whatever was pretty restless. You could tell because he had begun to cross and uncross and recross his legs, so I settled back to business.

"Now, don't forget that we had saved up that money together, Preacher, me and John George, for that premium and that it had already been tithed on, so we get back to that double taxation again if we are not careful. And don't forget the ten dollars for double indemnity which I first added on back yonder when we started out. That comes to $836.50 and that brings us down to $12,569. Now that's the figure, Preacher, that my figuring shows that I owe the tithe on. And one-tenth of that comes out $1,256.90, and there comes them fractions at us again so I'm just going to round that off at $1,257 and forget about Mrs. Barron.

"Now, if you think I had forgot about the twenty-five thousand from Leon Talbott Sr. you are wrong. I have prayed over that too, Preacher. You know what that twenty-five thousand is? It's blood money, that's what it is. It's paying me for Leon Jr. Talbott cutting off my husband's head with a forty mile an hour fencepost and it rolling almost to the pitcher's mound before anybody could stop it. And Jesus Christ don't want any part of that money, I am here to tell you. Even if Leon Jr. is not quite right. What told me that was going back and reading about that poor, pitiful Judas Iscariot. You know he had sold out Jesus Hisself for thirty pieces of silver and got paid in cash, too, and then it turned out to be blood money. And what did Judas do? He hung hisself, that's what. They say it was on a dogwood tree but I can't find that anywhere in my Bible, and he laid the thirty pieces of silver there on a stump along side of him. It don't say that in the Bible either, but a stump would of been the logical place to lay it if you was going to do such outside instead of in a closet somewhere, which would of been more private and tasteful but Judas Iscariot probably didn't come from much to start with. Sometimes it don't hurt a Christian to use his imagination same as his head.

"Even the church back then wouldn't touch that thirty pieces of silver. And when you get to looking at my blood money it's really only twenty-five pieces of silver, but that's all right, for John George was certainly no Jesus Christ. I have got it in the bank at four and a half percent interest, and it looks like I'll never get away from fractions the rest of my life. I have not yet decided what to do with it, except I'm probably going to buy up some of this land around here for fifteen, twenty dollars an acre, but I know for sure and certain the Lord don't want no tenth of it. I know it down in my heart and that's where Jesus looks. So we'll say no more about it."

I could tell I was losing Brother Whatever. He was getting to his feet, and he opened his mouth and he said it. He came right on out with it. "Whatever," he said. It kind of croaked.

"Set back down, Preacher," I told him. "I am not done yet."

I reached down inside my shirtwaist and pulled out a check. That was where my grandma always kept her egg money, tied up in the corner of her handkerchief and stuffed down in there where it was safe because for sure and certain nobody ever messed with Grandma. She called it her titty bank, but of course I wouldn't even think of such a word in front of a man. He might read it in your eyes even if he was a preacher and get the wrong idea. I still had a little Evening in Paris bath powder left over from the last valentine that John George had give me, and that check sure smelled good. I sort of waved it at the preacher, and if he got any ideas besides clean and dainty from smelling Evening in Paris, then he's got a problem and I can't help him with it. Like Lurline used to say in the back seat, "I can hear you clucking but I can't find your nest." That don't even deserve to be wrote down, certainly not in red, but Lurline use to say it. And it worked, too. It cooled 'em off. Course I never looked in the back seat; that is not good manners. But you can tell a heap without having to see it and you can tell when things have cooled off. The way she talked helped, too. Lurline had a fancy accent to start off with and she kept on cultivating it, and that's why she's got such a good job with WGST now, and you can't listen at her and even guess where she was born at.

"Now, Preacher, in case you think this check is for $1,257, you are dead wrong and you have been misjudging me, the which Jesus tells us not to do less we our own selves be misjudged. Also it is my opinion that Jesus would of told us not to jump to conclusions if He had of thought to of said it. Even Jesus couldn't think of everything, Preacher, bless His heart. Sometimes we just have to haul off and do what we think is right out of our own minds and our own hearts, the which if you have got Jesus in there to start with then it's going to turn out all right in the long run, even if the New Testament is not always the rule book some say it is.

"For instance, I have never yet understood grace, no matter how much you preachers try to explain it. But I do declare I feel today like I am filled with it. Waldene Branscombe passed me yesterday when I was walking home with a sack of groceries. Montine would have delivered but the doctor says I need to walk. Waldene was in her brand-new bright red Packard coupe that her daddy just got her, and I hear it's the first one made since the War and old man Branscombe wasn't even on the waiting list. He's just got that much money and that much pull, don't you know? He had a little brass plaque mounted on the dashboard before he give it to Waldene what says, 'Seek ye first the kingdom of God and His righteousness and all this shall be added unto you.' The which I had heard about already because John Addison had told Montine that a fellow had told him about it, and that was even before the car was delivered. You can't get ahead of that John Addison. When Waldene offered me a ride, I climbed in because I wanted to see it with my own eyes. Not to say I had doubted John Addison and a fellow, because I have lived here long enough to know he's right more often than your horoscope and a heap sight more dead on it. And, Preacher, it's there all right.

"The which I think sometimes you can misuse them mottoes of Jesus. I mean that what you think may apply to you, the person over in the next field may think you're puffing yourself up and giving yourself airs. And there is very few people in this town who think that old man Branscombe was seeking first the kingdom of God let alone its righteousness when he was shortchanging sharecroppers and holding back wages on day laborers. Yes, sir, I had seen Waldene's car and I had heard about her plaque, and I had already acted on it. But I never said a word to Waldene about it nor told her what I've done. I'll just wait and give her a ride when my car comes. You see, Preacher, I've ordered a black four-door Buick touring car what's every bit as fine as Miss Lorraine's or Mrs. Vollenweider's. It's supposed to come next Friday, and it's got its own plaque on the front the glove compartment. My plaque says, 'In chariots some put their trust but my faith is in Thee.' I like never to found that verse but it's in Psalms, the which I am sure you already know chapter and verse, but the Bible is hard work for some of us. I can't wait for Waldene to see my plaque. But aren't you proud of me for not opening my mouth and saying a word about it, Preacher? When you know it's only human that I was busting to tell it? Now, if that is not grace, then I am not setting here."

That's when he said it again. "Whatever," he said. But he didn't move. To tell the truth, he acted like he couldn't.

"Now, Preacher, let's get down to business. And I do mean business, for that is what stewardship is all about, and just because you're a Christian don't in any fashion mean you're suppose to be a ninny about finances. Let us discuss this check which I had already wrote out and had ready before I seen you coming up the sidewalk, and I'm not telling how I knowed you'd be along this morning. You can wonder about that when you get around to it and have time to get over wondering about some other things. This check, Preacher, which you have already misjudged me about, since after all you're only human and jumped to the conclusion that it is for $1,257, is for $12,250. That is one-tenth of every nickel I got, including even the blood money what is in the bank and drawing interest at four and a half percent, the which you can be certain I aim to do better than that with it. If Little Hill Carstairs can buy them Hickory Freeman suits doing nothing but being president of the bank and paying me out four and a half percent, then I can do better than him, for he wasn't no better at fractions than I was and like to have drove Mrs. Barron crazy."

Brother Whatever was setting bolt upright like he had a wagon rod down his spine, and his eyes was bugging out so far they misted up his glasses. He didn't lick his lips, but he looked like he wanted to. He never said a word, and I believe "Silence is golden" is probably in the Bible somewheres, I'll have to look it up. If it is not there, then it soon will be.

"Preacher," I went on, and I had done put a firmer tone in my voice which you ought to do when you're really getting down to business, "this check is made out to the Faceville First Baptist Church and it is marked down in the corner 'the John George Higbee Higher Education Fund.' It is to be used to help poor children go off to college. Not a nickel of it is to be spent on sticks or stones or red velvet rope or pipe organs or stain glass windows or even yet on Lottie Moon. I have discussed it with Lester Creasey and he's already drawing up the papers."

Then I handed him the check and he stretched it out tight and looked at it real hard. If it smelled good to him, he never let on. The which I have never really and truly been able to make myself believe that when Elijah burnt all them dead bulls at Carmel it was a pleasing odor to the Lord. Land's sake, I can't even stand chicken feathers around the wash pot, let alone no burning bulls, and like it or not we are cast in God's image and that includes our noses.

The preacher said, "I don't know what to say."

I said, "Just say 'Whatever' and let it go at that."

He didn't ever take his eyes off that check, which makes me know the poor man don't even know he says that all the time.

"Now, Brother Laurens," I went on, "there is a catch in this love offering, the which that is what it is, since I have spent the last half an hour proving to you that I don't owe it. Not one penny of the $12,250 can be paid out, just the interest it earns. I mean, I been learning about principle and capital and all them words that sounded like Greek before. This is a present-day parable of the talents, Preacher. The good Master has give you $12,250. You gonna bury it? Or you gonna multiply it ten fold? Or better? I'm gonna increase mine, Preacher. So I can hear those blessed words, 'Well done, thou good and faithful servant.'

"Let's see what you and Jesus can do with yours. And I'm gonna be a watchful master over you. I'll ask a accounting of you every three months. Every quarter, don't you know, and there's them fractions again. Let's see what a educated man can do alongside a unschooled widow woman, Preacher. I'm gonna put mine in real estate."

Well, I thought for sure and certain I had give Brother Whatever more'n money. I thought at the very least I had planted the idea for a sermon in his head. And I did want to hear that one preached, too. Right out in the Faceville First Baptist Church with me setting on the front row right next to the Hammond organ. What I wanted was for him to preach a sermon on, "A good name is to be preferred above great riches," the which you'd think he would of tumbled to, but I be blessed if I was going to line it out for him.

Down in my heart that's all I wanted. A good name. That's all I've ever wanted, really. A good name.

Ever since Pa sold liquor.

Cynthia Shearer

Born in southeast Georgia in 1957, Cynthia Shearer grew up in a family much like the one in her novel *The Wonder Book of the Air* (1996). She has described the book as "a social history of Georgia told through members of my own family. It is autobiographical and based on stories that actually happened." She did not realize that she wanted to write until late in her work toward a doctorate at the University of Mississippi, where she studied under the writer Barry Hannah. Before joining the English Department faculty at Ole Miss, she worked for the Center for the Study of Southern Culture and, from 1992 to 1997, served as the curator at Rowan Oak, the home of William Faulkner. Her story "Flight Patterns" concerns the difficult relationship of a father with children he abandoned years before—he cannot bring himself to apologize, they cannot bring themselves to forgive, yet they cannot escape the links that bind them.

Flight Patterns

My earliest memory of my father? It's 1958. I'm three. He stands in the doorway. I'm next to my mother, with my cheek pressed against her grey wool skirt. – *Go . . . go . . . go . . .* is the word I keep hearing, and they are angry. My mother is crying, so I cry also, afraid of things I don't even have the words to name yet. My name is Phoebe.

When they fight at night, I run away across the street, open the unlocked screen door, and slip into my grandfather's big brass bed. In the mornings he sits with me in the front porch swing and we play the train game.

– *You want to take a ride on the Alapaha Star?*
– *Yes.*
– *You got your bag packed?*
– *Yes.*
– *What's in it?*
– *My red dress.*
– *What else?*
– *My red pocketbook.*
– *What else?*
– *My red flip-flops.*

He will never drive a train again. One of his legs has been amputated, he is an old man. But in the swing with my grandfather, I forget about those screamed words: *Go . . . go . . . go!*

My father goes. The boards of the walls seem to relax. Now we all sleep in one room, and my baby bed is beside the fireplace. We seem to eat crazily: cornflakes for lunch when there is no money and steak for supper when there is. I learn that it is terrible that I need new shoes. It makes my mother tired and tearful. Needing anything is bad, so I stop needing anything.

My red-haired sister, Allie, seems to be in charge of what I learn about the world. One day we steal eggs from a nest she has found across the tracks at an old black woman's house, and we learn how they will smash in our coat pockets if we ride the iron deer in a white woman's yard. Under Allie's tutelage I learn who in town has new puppies or old dirty magazines in their tool sheds. There is a strange roof on the ground at our father's mother's house; we break into it and play among the old radio parts there. Once on a summer morning she discovers our father's car parked at his mother's house, which is two blocks from ours. His mother will not speak to us, but she lets us in. He wakes up to find us staring down at him. We are wearing matching playsuits with giraffes on them.

– *Don't you like our new clothes?* we say, but we cannot get him to say they are pretty. Because our mother bought them. I am three, my sister is five. I sit in a chair by the door while she sings him piano lesson songs and makes him laugh. He has a nickname for her, "Red." I feel safer being an observer than a participant.

Another day my sister takes me to a little room in our house that has always been padlocked. She has picked the lock with my mother's nail file. – *Look,* she says, opening a tall North American Van Lines crate, strewing the floor with the bright confetti of shredded comics. She hoists out a brandy snifter as big as her head. It has a circle of roses etched around its rim. When she lets me hold it, I drop it. Its shards will remain there on the wood floor for several years.

This becomes our secret, that we burrow and tunnel through boxes stacked to the ceiling. There are golf clubs in a leather bag fuzzy with mildew, and a rotting brown-leather bomber jacket. Light, airy watercolors of the villages of Bermuda, fringed with oleander and hibiscus. Uncountable long-stemmed cocktail glasses, which we break having imaginary tea parties. We're more accustomed to the cheap, thick crockery from the local grocery store.

We pass the summer ruthless in the wreckage of our mother's former life, piratical. We break the tortilla holder shaped like a floppy sombrero. Abundant booty: a box of evening dresses, tulle-festooned, satiny-slippery. We fight over a green paisley one studded with green brilliants. I settle for the strapless pink and blue one with the rustly skirts. Damask napkins down my front: instant bosoms. Black lace mantilla over my head: Bat Masterson's girlfriend. Sometimes we play office with the stacks of old Air Force photostats, black pages with white print.

We venture outside in our regalia, carrying champagne glasses for effect. The kids from the housing project in what used to be our grandfather's peach orchard are not amused.

– *That ain't yours,* one little boy says. – *And it's a sin to drank.*

– *Well, you don't even own the house you live in,* my brother Field says. – *We do. You live in the projects. My grandaddy sold that land to the government. It used to be my grandaddy's land.*

We know that we are poor, and that they are poor, but we live in a big white house with green shutters, and they live in cramped little dark ones. We know that we are smarter than they are.

Our secret seems to be out. Field investigates the room. By sundown he has used three sterling silver platters for BB gun targets, brittle 78-rpm records for flying saucers. Tommy Dorsey, Glenn Miller, and Benny Goodman: *fling, zing,* over into what used to be our grandfather's peach orchard.

– *This is mine,* my brother says, pulling out a heavy wooden propeller. – *It was on my wall in Bermuda.* He drives the propeller into the soft earth, like a conquistador staking claim. It seems to me that he has a bigger claim on the earth than I do, partly because he can remember more of the time that is pre-history, when our mother and father were capable of talking to each other. Our mother, when she finally notices, simply makes us throw everything back into the room and tells us to stay out of it. Of course, we don't. A teak and bamboo teacart makes a terrific entry in a soapbox derby, and a burgundy damask and lace tablecloth is just the thing for a mongrel to have her puppies on.

Some months later, Field calls me to come listen to a record he is playing on the record player my father left behind. I hear music playing, and what I re-member to be my father's voice talking.

– *Listen, Phoebe. Daddy's talking about being shot down in the war,* my brother explains, and I look into his face and wonder why he has bothered to notice me. – *He fought against the Japanese. This is when they gave him the Silver Star.*

There is a big red book in our living room, with black-and-white photos of soldiers in it. Once my brother thumbs through it and shows me our father, sitting in the front row of officers, his legs crossed easily, squinting into the sun. For a long time I am confused when I look in the book by myself. I can't find him. They all look alike to me in their uniforms. I think that World War II is still going on, that my father is there, and that they play a lot of saxophones in the background there.

My grandfather dies, and I understand I am alone somehow now.

By 1963, sometimes my father comes from Savannah to take us to a town nearby to eat at a restaurant called The Purple Duck. I love these times, because I can sit in the back seat of his Rambler station wagon, smelling his old fishing things in the back, hearing the conversation of my older siblings pass over my head. Their presence deflects his attention from me, and I feel safe, watching them. I like being in his warm car.

One early fall afternoon I come flying out of my third-grade classroom at 3:10, and I see the Rambler station wagon. I run up with my sister, and she ex-plains that she has a piano lesson for the next hour. His smile fades, but he says he will take me fishing. He takes me to his brother's pond, out in his little brown wooden boat with green trim.

When I speak, he hushes me. He doesn't give me a fishing pole to hold. I sit facing him, my hands in the lap of the green party dress bought a few years earlier to go with my sister's red hair. I am worried that he is angry at me for wearing the dress. I study the whorls in the varnished wood of the boat seat between us. *Alapaha Star,* it says, and I want to ask him about this. I would like to think that if he doesn't love my mother, maybe he loved my grandfather the way I did. It begins to get dark, and my back begins to hurt.

On the way home, he stops at an old well. – *Bet you've never had well water before,* he says, registering a mild rebuke of my mother. He draws up an old metal bucket, reaches behind the well, and takes a dinged-up metal dipper, which he hands to me full of cold water. While I am drinking it, he says in his clowning-around voice, – *You'll never drink water this good anywhere else. I'm tellin' you like a friend. I used to haul so many buckets of water for my mama when I was your age, I felt like Paul Bunyan's ox.* He studies my face for a reaction. – *I've had water from all over the world, but it was never as good as this.*

When I'm getting out of the car, at our house, he hands me the string of small fish he caught, slick-slimy and walleyed dead. – *Give these to your mother,* he says, and closes the door and drives away.

This excites me. A string of fish is a joyous thing in the houses behind us, and I have seen the men come home and hand the fish to the women, who float them in red-rimmed white dishpans, then cut off their heads, slit open their bellies, and throw the little orange hot-dog-looking things to the cats. Then they cook the fish in big deep black skillets. I have even seen a big deep black skillet in the secret room of my mother's house.

My mother scowls when I hand her the fish. – *MORE work for me to do,* she hisses, and throws the fish, still on the string, out into the back yard. She curses our house, our clothes, our life. – *He could have been a general.*

My mother decides to dose us with more truth as we get older: my father is not with us because he doesn't love us. He loves to drink and dance with lots of different women. He once told her that he had better things to do with his life than to raise children. He has sudden unexplained absences, and he hangs around Navajo Indian reservations when he disappears. He was given the choice of retiring from the Air Force, at the age of forty-one, or being court-martialed; and that was the year we all crash-landed in my grandfather's house in Georgia, in the little town where he and my mother both grew up. In a drawer in her bedroom are manila envelopes of old Defense Department photos: my parents greeting Eisenhower, Churchill, and Anthony Eden as they step onto the tarmac at Kindley Field in Bermuda, my father accepting golf clubs upon retirement. My father is saluting and serious in these; my mother's face is seraphic as she beholds Eisenhower.

My brother and I press my mother for information. She tells us that she used to read the Bible when he was in the air. We ask her about my father's separation and retirement papers—and all the details, such as the women he was seen with outside bars and hotels, in addition to the empty tanks in the planes when he flubbed an alert as deputy base commander at MacDill Air Force Base in 1957.

– *Sounds like he was set up to me,* my brother comments. He is a draft counselor at the University of Georgia. It's 1968, and I'm thirteen. My brother has a deep, instinctive mistrust of military men. This is a time when Vietnam was writhing in all our minds like a sly oriental dragon.

– *The alert came through, and they couldn't get the planes off the ground.* My mother shrugs, as if that is the only explanation one needs.

My brother and I look at each other: the imaginary enemy was coming, and there was imaginary fuel in the planes: off with his head.

Field is 4-F. He lost an an eye with a cherry bomb, while my mother and father were attending the Army-Navy game. Now it is summer and he is home from college. He and the one other long-haired boy in town spend evenings on our front porch facing Main Street, discussing the act of war. My sister is in Savannah with my father for the summer. She is the only one who sees him. I am happy to be sharing the front-porch swing with rebellious long-haired young men, and I wish I had my own draft card to burn.

One night our discussion is interrupted when a young man with short hair runs shirtless, shoeless, and shrieking down Main Street and into the woods. We begin to hear screen doors slamming up and down the street—the men coming out from their suppers and TVs to go see who is screaming in the woods. So my brother goes, too. We can hear voices in the woods for a while, calls and shouts. Then my brother comes back.

– *It was Pierce,* he says. – *He got drunk and thought he was back in Vietnam.*

– *These people,* my mother snarls, and takes a long drag off her cigarette. – *They don't know what a REAL war is. World War II. Now there was a real war. This war is a moral atrocity.* She retires to her bedroom, with stacks of the Atlanta *Journal* and paperback Faulkner novels heaped in the place where most women would have installed a new man.

By the end of the summer my sister has returned, wearing long sleeves and pants, even in the swampy south Georgia heat. Her first night back, she and my mother sit in the kitchen crying and talking long after I have gone to bed. The next morning my mother explains to me privately that my sister's legs and back and arms are covered with old brown bruises. She had been out in an elegant Savannah restaurant with my father, who became drunk and combative with the waiters. She became afraid of him. She called a policeman to drive her to his house. He found her there, and beat her. When he sobered up, he bought her a new wardrobe and took her and his girlfriend to Hilton Head, to let the bruises heal.

– *Don't talk about it,* my mother tells me. – *We are not going to talk about it again.*

By the time school begins, the incident is buried beneath others. The schools are integrating. The first day of school finds my mother, an English teacher, standing in the elementary school yard, taunting some farmers armed with shotguns, like she must have taunted them as children.

– *So do you feel like a BIG MAN now? Showing your gun to a six-year-old child?* This man is on the local school board, and is a big deal in the Klan, if you can judge by the fear of the blacks. But the little black kids are more wide-eyed at my mother's wrath. One night there is a knock at the door, and my mother answers it, telling us to stay back. There is one of the farmers there. His gun is in the gun rack in his pickup truck.

– *I just wanted to see the pitchers of the niggers.*

– *What?*

– *They sayin' at the cafe you got pitchers of niggers on your walls. Just wanted to see what you teachin' your kids.*

– *The picture is in my classroom,* my mother said. – *Winslow Homer, The Gulf Stream. Come by and see it sometime.*

The townspeople stop speaking to us. My mother has causes instead of friends.

Books are what I have instead of friends. I read *Soul on Ice,* by Eldridge Cleaver, about his ambition to rape a white woman, to avenge all his oppressed ancestors. For one week in the summer, my brother makes me read the "Rime of the Ancient Mariner" to him in the afternoons, before he will agree to take me swimming.

My sister goes to a Methodist revival that fall, the kind where for one week out of the year everyone is fixated on the idea of being saved from something terrible. She goes down the rabbit hole of religion, never to surface again in quite the same incarnation that we knew her.

One day as I am leaving school, I see my father's new silver Chrysler parked in front of the school. He is waiting outside for us. What will it be this time, I wonder. A forced haircut just to show our mother he has the power to leave his mark on us? Expensive clothes that she can't afford to pay the dry-cleaning bills on? A two-hour wait in the car while he goes into a bar to drink? My sister runs to meet him. I hang back by the holly bush that grows outside the book room.

I can see my sister chatting with him, animated. I step between two girls I hardly know, and I walk right past his car, pretending to be so interested in what the girls are saying that I have no time to notice that he's there. And so he is out of my life for a few more years.

Now I'm twenty-one, and I neither smoke, nor drink, nor take drugs, though I hang out with a crowd that does, daily. I still hang back like the junkyard dog, because that is what I am good at. I live alone in a little rented house on the edge of a cotton mill district, with the scrawls of previous tenants' children still on the bare pine walls, and the apparently stolen tombstone of one James T. Hughes, killed in the Spanish-American war, as the front stoop. I support myself by waiting tables. I managed to get the job when my predecessor, an Air Force wife, cut her feet to ribbons running across broken glass to get away from her husband.

I come home from my waitress job and stay up all night sometimes, listening to music and reading, the poetry of Yeats, visions of Byzantium wheeling in my mind like some sugarplum mandala. I rarely see my mother.

My father has cruised into my college town in his new Winnebago, towing his old silver Chrysler for me. It is his one rite of fatherhood to give each of us a used car when we become seniors in college. It's my turn now. My mother has coached me to identify him with Nixonian politics, the military-industrial complex, male chauvinism, and all the other bugaboos of the decade. I have seen him perhaps three times in the previous ten years, and always within the safety of my brother's or a boyfriend's presence. But now my brother is a newspaperman in Atlanta and I am a college senior. And our father has remarried, a woman I don't like.

He and his wife have invited me out to dinner. It's as nice a restaurant as can be had in the town, with a lengthy wine list. His wife waits for him to tell the waiter what we will all have for dinner. I order a cheeseburger, so I can offend him twice over by ordering something inelegant, and ordering it myself. I am waiting for him to give me the line that he always gave my sister, that real ladies always wait to have men order for them. If he does, I will walk out.

My father makes a big issue out of ordering the most expensive wine on the list. I make a big issue out of not drinking any. I keep a closer eye on his highball glass than the waiter does. I know the precise number of blocks to the little mill house. I know the precise number of blocks to my boyfriend's apartment. I know the drill that seems to have been dormant in me for a long time. I just don't know precisely where the line is that my father has to cross before I will walk free of him forever. I even know the precise objects in my house I would crack his head open with if he ever so much as lifted a hand to hurt me. It is a fantasy I have had ever since my sister's bad summer with him. But for the moment, in the restaurant, I'm navigating under a different plan: always know my precise position: where the available exits are in relation to how drunk he is getting. Keep money and keys in pocket, not purse. Like any good guerrilla, I know how to watch and wait.

He drinks prodigious amounts, but he doesn't seem to get drunk. They drive me home and we say good-bye. I assume that it will be for quite some more years, and that the next I hear from him will be through his elegantly scripted postcards from places like Tempe or Gallup.

He shows up at my door the next morning, toolbox in hand. – *I have work to do here,* he says, and proceeds to nail weird shelves around. Bizarre places: thereafter I will think of him when I crash my head after brushing my teeth. He makes a pretty lamp out of a dimestore basket, hangs it over my garage-sale table, and puts a dimmer switch on it. My mother's anger is also in me: that he would think a dimmer switch to dine by is a necessity of life, when most nights I come home alone to wash the waitress smell of grease and nicotine off me.

He bumbles around my house, recognizes my refrigerator as one that used to belong to my mother's mother and hails it like a long-lost friend. I notice that he is not drinking. He quotes poetry to impress me, now that I am an English major. He used to be an English major, at West Point, he says, and this shocks me.

Nobody ever told me that. I tell him about finding some old textbooks of his in my mother's house, with fold-out maps of Civil War battle plans. He quotes poetry that I don't know. He has to identify it for me. – *Ever read Wilfred Owen?* he asks. – *Siegfried Sassoon?* I shake my head. He continues to tinker with the catch on the refrigerator door while I hold the handle he's removed. – *That's okay,* he says. – *"They also serve who only stand and wait."* He glances back at me to see if I know what I'm hearing and I don't. It's final exam week at the university and I am cutting class as we stand there.

– *Uh, Dryden?* I say. – *No. Alexander Pope.*

– *Nope,* he says. – *Don't you do your homework?*

That night I pick up a box of greasy fried chicken and we shove my books and papers aside to eat together, dirt-smudged and tired. I feel good, I feel easy with him. I feel like I am meeting myself coming and going. He grew up in the same schoolyard that I did, played basketball in the same circle of daffodils I did. – *I used to raid your mother's acorn piles and shoot them in my slingshots.*

We both learned to swim in the Alapaha River, by diving off the same cypress stump. We bicycled over the same sidewalks, bought penny candy in the same grocery store. We both breathed the same air as my mother as long as we could, and then we left.

By the second nightfall I have cut another day of exams, to accompany my father to the hardware store while he indulges in an orgy of shopping for me.

Jumper cables, gas can, pliers, hammer, fire extinguisher, deadbolts, window locks, fly swatter, hibachi. All the things he seems to be appalled that I don't possess. His wife joins us, bearing a Porterhouse steak. He goes down the block to buy scotch. She produces linen napkins, silver, and crystal that travel battened down in the Winnebago with them from Nova Scotia to Vancouver. – *He won't eat with paper napkins,* she says in her martyr's whisper. – *He gets very angry with me if—*

– *He ate greasy chicken last night off paper towels,* I answer, slapping my cheap forks onto the table.– *And he seemed to like it okay.* She looks puzzled and betrayed.

– *He just drinks too much and I don't think I can go on—*

– *That's why my mother threw in the towel,* I say. *He broke her nose twice.*

– *The sun is now retreating over the yardarm,* he grins from the doorway. He begins to grill the steak, making great effort to show me the correct way to do it, out of some need to impart something useful to me. There is something in him that is wooing me. Now that I am no longer the little girl in the hand-me-down dress helpless in the boat, he wants to be friends. He wants to show me that he is a connoisseur of fine steaks, wine, and women. – *Look at this woman,* he says to me, pointing to her. – *Doesn't she look just like one of those fine carvings on the prow of a Swedish ship? This is no ordinary woman you're looking at. This is my mate.* He pulls her up to dance around the room to a Mills Brothers record he has fished out of his Winnebago. He sings along. – *Be my life's companion and we'll never grow old; I'll love you so much that we'll never grow old.* I understand that he delights me in some way, though his music enrages me. Those silly little love songs, *Picture you upon my knee, just tea for two and two for tea . . . Oh can't you see how happy we would be?*

I watch him drink his way into the late hours, though I have another final exam the next day. His speech becomes grandiloquent. He tells me fantastic stories: how he delivered a baby in a taxicab on the New Jersey turnpike, how he lifted a tree off his Uncle Artie after a tornado ripped through Alapaha before I was born. I no longer keep my eyes on his glass and the door simultaneously.

But you vanished when I was being born, I think.

But I have become a connoisseur of fine lies and a sucker for fantastic stories and grandiloquence, so I listen amiably, sifting out who he is by seeing what it is important for him to lie about. – *Tell me about when you were shot down over New Guinea,* I say, companionably. Tell me how things fall apart.

– *Ancient history,* he says, waving his hand, deflecting the thought.

Soon they depart, the Winnebago like some grounded zeppelin with a bass boat in tow, out of my life again. My whole house seems to sigh and relax. I am tired. I have had little sleep in three days. I go to see my professors whose classes

I have been AWOL from. I explain that my father, an alcoholic, had shown up unexpectedly, and that I chose to spend the time with him. They let me make up my exams.

I get a postcard from my father some months later, in handwriting so stark, lean, and elegant that it makes me ache to know the person who produced it: *The sight of 13 Winnebagoes belly up in an arroyo can give one a healthy appreciation of the value of the left turn signal. How you doin' down there in radioland? — Dad.* On the front: the Hotel del Coronado, resplendent in sunshine, clouds, and airbrushed stucco.

In 1985 I get home from work and my answering machine tells me: *Beep:* my not-quite-ex-husband loves me and will never consent to divorce. *Beep:* my boss wants me to work harder to persuade the Pentagon that it is in the interest of national security to buy us a new podium. *Beep:* my not-quite-ex-husband tells me that he wishes he'd never met me and if he sees me again he will kill me.

How can he say this to me? He couldn't hurt a fly. He is someone almost old enough to be my father.

I made the decision to leave the marriage in a moment when I seemed to understand my father. I was in a motel bar in Eufala, Alabama, wishing my husband would ask me to dance.

He shook his head, annoyed. I seemed to have consigned myself to a life of no dance.

After a moment there was nothing but this weird padded silence in the air. His long, thin fingers looked like foreign objects to me. Then a song cut through like an announcement in an airport:

> Stay on the streets of this town
> And they'll be carvin' you up, all right.
> They say you gotta stay hungry.
> Hey, baby, I'm just about starvin' tonight.

From some old memory, two images roared up across the synapses at the same time: me in my married kitchen with the window cracked and the radio on low; the Jews in the gas chambers looking for the cracks at the last minute: *Air, air.*

I looked out the window of the bar, across the river to the blinking bridge lights, and the steadier lights of the little fishbait stores across in Georgetown, and I saw it: *radioland:* right out there in the black air: the messages that crisscross and occasionally connect, hovering over the softness of the rivers and the unyielding cities. Amazingly simple statements, hanging out there to be intercepted and confirmed:

– SOS . . .
– Are you a believer?
– Prepare for liftoff . . .

I kept creasing my napkin and sipping my drink, until, toward the bottom of the glass, I swallowed one molten swallow that seemed to slide like shooting silk, *down down down,* until I could feel it glowing somewhere deep, like a heavy golden pear, and hanging by a thread. It was all quite simple. There are certain unalienable rights in this world. One is to dance to the music of one's rightful radio tribe, and another is to form a more perfect union.

I had not yet found the man I belonged to: someone who could accept it with equanimity if I ever confessed that I sometimes lie awake in the dark feeling like a cyclops, wondering if radioland is not some holy huge place where it all ends up, melded into one soft sussuration: the protests of the sheep as Noah led them into the ark, the cry that Shakespeare's mother made, and the patter of Navajo code talkers blending with stray drumbeats from the first time Benny Goodman did "Sing, Sing, Sing." And I wanted someone who could face with courage the prospect of stepping barefooted in the dark on a Tinkertoy or a cold mashed banana. And so I knew that I must never, ever touch the man across the table from me again, that it would be wrong to do so.

Which brought me to this stage of divorce: I need an air-traffic controller in my life telling me that it's time to eat or sleep, and that I am going to survive. My lawyer's secretary has watched me delete possession after possession on my divorce papers, the way someone might watch a fox gnaw off its leg to get out of a trap.

– Do you drink? she asks.
– Not really, I joke. *– Is it too late to learn?*
– Well, come with me tonight. I know a guy you'd like a lot. He's divorced, too.

But I'm avoiding men. They might sense how I am like an ex-con recently sprung from the slammer: suspiciously gaping and blinking in the sudden light of their presence: *Gee, when did they take the tailfins off the Cadillacs?*

I prefer to go to a little cafe around the corner where the men have learned that I will drink my two margaritas in solitude. I sit there wearing my first bikini tan in six years, still the junkyard dog who needs to be quieted by the proximity of the human species. But no real contact, please.

Then I go home.

I sit there in my first divorced dusk.

I remember that it was dusk that did me in in the first place, made me marry so I would have a man to cook for at dusk.

I sit like I'm washed up on an empty island somewhere, waiting for the Lilliputians to arrive.

I call my mother. She can't understand why I would leave a man who is neither a drunk nor violent, so she tells me about her new dahlias. – *I don't give advice,* she says, – *especially about THAT,* avoiding the word *marriage* as if it were an epithet.

I call up my brother, working late at his newspaper. – *Shit, shit,* he repeats like a mantra. – *Oh, little Phoebe.*

I call my sister and ask her to tell me about Jonah and the whale, like, what exactly did Jonah *do* with himself once he got out of that belly.

– *He praised God,* she says, without missing a beat.

My own personal guess was that he found a small tight cave and stayed there curled into the fetal position for a while.

After several calls around the country, I find my father. He is at something called the Trophy Bass Lodge in Georgetown, Florida, where he goes when he and his wife have had enough of each other's company for a while. I can hear a jukebox in the background, a heavy honky-tonk beat, and the rich human complaint of the saxophones.

– *So, how you doin' down there in radioland?* I ask. *Radioland* has come to mean the little backwater towns I have always ended up living in, or the places he goes to hide.

– *Doin' fine,* he says. – *They got bass big as Spanish mackerel here.*

I want to *be there,* with all the old men and their fishbait. My father's voice is all scotch-warm and wise through the eight hundred or so miles of telephone cable.

– *In a divorce,* he says, – *the potential for holocaust is real. You can't spend too much time lollygagging around in the wrecked fuselage. You got to explore the new terrain. But who you are has taken you this far, and who you are will take you any place you want to go. Just cultivate a sense of ironic detachment.*

He squires his sentences around like Gene Kelly dances with women: a masterful turn here, a droll pause there, an incremental repetition of the fun parts. – *Bitterness is a form of mental laziness,* he says, and I know that he is referring to my mother, who has nursed her wrath along with her dahlias for years. – *It means you can't grasp the big picture.* He lets that sink in. – *There is a young woman here that I watch,* he continues. – *She gets out in the middle of Lake George in the biggest goddam boat around. And she is the mistress of her own vessel. The rest of us old geezers just get out of the way. You got to be like that babe in the Bayliner boat. You can't pay too much attention to that skinny cat playing that sad violin offstage—it'll mess up your sense of comic timing. You got to be like that babe in the Bayliner boat. Ironic detachment.*

He offers to meet me for a visit at Warner Robbins Air Force Base, in Georgia, on his way to a West Point class reunion. He blows into that place in a slightly smaller Winnebago, his old one having been declared too large to be legal. He and his wife meet me outside the gates, to get me in. The sentry does not salute him; my father chews him out, indicating the colonel's star on his windshield. The kid knows the drill and apologizes profusely.

My father is ready to hit the bar at the officer's club as soon as he has checked us into the VIP Suite. – *He's not well,* his wife whispers to me as we both stand at the same bathroom mirror applying makeup, dressing for dinner. – *We should never have left Savannah. We talked about divorce all the way up from Winter Park. He just drinks entirely too much, and I don't think that I can go on*—

Shit, shit, I tune her out with my brother's mantra. I am nervous. It has been many, many years since I have slept under the same roof as my father. I notice where all the exits are. I remember that my brother always parks his car head out when he visits my father, ever since the time he offered my father a joint rolled in flag paper and had to make a fast retreat—not because of the grass, because of the desecration of the flag. I put my car keys and my money in my skirt pocket and we head for the bar.

I explain to my father the problems of my job, of milking the federal government for strategic-studies money when you are located a thousand miles from the Washington Beltway think tanks.

– *All you need are the ideas,* he points to his temple. – *Nobody has a monopoly on the truth.* He has had three scotches to my one margarita, and his words are attaining that drunken cadence that can mesmerize me on the phone. I drink faster, to catch up to where he is.

– *Ideas,* he says tapping his temple. – *Go do your homework. Wars don't start in Washington. Wars begin out in radioland. Do you know that? Do you know what I'm talking about? You know why I went to West Point in 1935? Because I was tired of giving my mama my shoeshine money to feed me with.* Olivia's face softens, and I wish in that moment to know all the things about him that she knows.

– *You don't need Janes, just get a map. Look for the places where the people are fed up with being unfed. Look for where the malcontents mass along the borders. Look at that dude out in that jungle, homo sapiens human being, and he suddenly starts digging Dallas on his neighbor's satellite dish, and his baby needs a brand-new pair of shoes. War. Two, five, ten years down the road.*

– *But I work for people who just want to make speeches about rivet patterns on Japanese Zeroes, planes they flew forty years ago.*

– *A Zero is a worthy topic of study,* he says. I sense that he is tired of the discussion. He waylays a group of pilots coming into the bar. – *Lissen,* he says to them, at that stage of drink where you are open to whatever might flower around you. – *I have a female member of the species homo sapiens human being here who is bugging the goddam hell out of me with questions about aircraft. Would you care to field the questions for a while?*

It turns out that they know a tad about aircraft. They are the Thunderbirds. My father has to find out all their names, ranks, and hometowns. Only one of them is drinking, the one from Red Cloud, Nebraska, who almost bought it this afternoon when a bird flew in front of his intake vent right before he chandelled.

– *Lissen,* my father coaches him, leaning forward, – *Lissenamee, Lieutenant Thackeray Phillips of Red Cloud, Nebraska.* My father points to the band. – *You hear those funny noises in the air? Those little ruffles and flourishes and beating of tom-toms? That stuff is called music. Take a lissen to that stuff, man. That is the sound of a human soul that knows the difference between drag and lift.*

The lieutenant leans backwards, enduring his second indignity of the day, being told how to act by an old geezer. His politeness is standard Air Force issue.

My father is in his element, eloquent in the altitudes of alcohol. – *And it is imperative that when you hear that stuff in the air that you get up and dance, shake a leg, trip the light fantastic. What are they teaching you in flight school? Get up and fly, man. There are females in the world languishing.* He gets up to demonstrate, pretending to pat the fanny of a stout woman dancing with her back to us, escorted by a dignified old general-looking fellow.

Olivia shoots me a look—*Help*—and I go dance with him. I am at that stage of drink where I can't tell which is the soft-petaled thing opening, the universe around me or me. My father is portly, but graceful. We dance, pausing only to have new drinks. The band does a cover of Springsteen's "Pink Cadillac," and we find that it is a magic thing, to dance to a saxophone joke about Adam and Eve. If nobody can touch us, it's because we've become the same person. I am him, young; he is me, old. We circle each other, smiling: *Hello, me. Long time no see.*

He can boogie like a college boy, or samba like a sailor, or float around as graceful as the *Hindenburg,* no feet, nothing to tie him down to earth. His wife sits patiently, looking exactly like something carved on the prow of a Swedish ship. The club is closing down; the waiters have all the chairs upside down on the tables. Not only have we skipped dinner, we have closed the place.

My father and I sit down a minute, oblivious, admiring each other's funny freckly hands. – *I have your hands,* I say, and there is a very thin membrane of something tough inside me, holding back a lifetime of tears waiting to spill on his calluses. We vow that if all else fails in my life, we will simply go into the fishbait business together in Key West.

– *Can you do this?* he calls when we are walking back to our rooms. He jumps up on a three-foot-high retaining wall that scallops the sidewalk we're on. He walks it all the way back, agile as an alley cat. He is seventy and has had more scotch-and-sodas than I could count. I am thirty, have had three margaritas, and I want to curl up on the sidewalk and lay me down to sleep. When he kisses me goodbye the next morning, I smell the fresh scotch. He's still cruising along, holding altitude, coasting over the tops of the heads around him.

Later I describe it all to my mother over the phone, omitting all my margaritas.

– *He used to do that every weekend,* my mother says. – *He broke my nose one time because I asked him for money to buy groceries.*

I cut her off before she can get to the part where I am conceived in what essentially amounts to an act of rape, and where he disappears for three weeks when I am due to be born, and how she almost dies having me, and how he beats her up when I am two weeks old. I know it all already, and keep it filed in the same place in my mind where he, in perpetuity, beats my sister Allie in an elegant pastel Savannah apartment, or burns my brother's hand with an alabaster cigarette lighter, to teach him not to disturb the symmetry of the coffee-table items. It's what we have in our family instead of a photo album.

– *I really feel for Olivia,* my mother surprises me. She's been doing a lot of that lately, now that I have joined the sacred sisterhood of the divorcees. – *I always felt like marriage was just legalized prostitution,* she said, as if she suddenly needed to confess a past felony. – *I used to pray that he would die,* she says. – *I used to pray that his plane would crash.*

I want a drink, I think. *The potential for holocaust is real.*

My father mails me a photocopy of a letter, dated June 1942, that he wrote to a woman in Santa Fe, as printed in an Albuquerque newspaper. It described to her the last moments of her husband, his navigator, one Winston Fite, after they were shot down by a Japanese Zero off the coast of New Guinea in the Battle of the Coral Sea. He told her how much the man had loved her, and named the precise latitude and longitude where the plane went under.

I want a drink when I have finished reading it. I have several. I sit in the wisteria and drink my margaritas and listen to Benny Goodman. Pretty soon I feel like I've got squatter's rights to the stars, and I can handle the massive dose of history that I have been given. He knew the drill. Know your latitude and longitude the moment you begin descent.

Soon after, on a bright summer morning, I read a tiny box in the Memphis newspaper. Lt. Thackery Phillips of Red Cloud, Nebraska, crashed into the desert outside Las Vegas, to the horror, amazement, and edification of a cheering crowd that had paid to see the Thunderbirds perform, applauding even as the flames erased him from the earth.

When I walk into my mother's hospital room in 1986, my brother, Field, takes one look at my face and thinks up a phony excuse to walk with me down the corridor. We wander without really knowing where we are, and I tell him that the doctor used the word *terminal,* and in that moment I understand what it must be like to bayonet someone who's been trained not to flinch. I tell my brother everything the doctor has told me, everything from the futility of surgery to the availability of little old polyester ladies who have no better thing to do than come keep the deathwatch and plump the pillows. He takes a long, even breath. – *We better get in there,* he says, – *or she'll start getting paranoid.*

We weave back through the sterile honeycomb of labs, gurneys parked in hallways, waiting rooms. – *Look,* he whispers, eyeing a shrunken old white lady asleep in a wheelchair, twisted into the fetal position. She is clutching a pink plastic baby doll. They have matching lipstick, fire-engine red, and matching wildly thatched hair. – *Dada art,* he whispers to me. I love him fiercely, proud to be breathing the same air that he breathes.

Back in my mother's room, he turns in a passably good performance of the man he was a few moments before. – *Jesus, Mother,* he teases, rummaging through a Whitman Sampler someone has brought to her, – *you've hogged all the goddamn Brazil nuts.*

A few days after Christmas, when I am trying to answer my mother's mail, I find a lush expensive Christmas card from my father. To her. The first time in my life I can remember his writing to her.

– *Wishing you a joyous and peaceful Nativity,* the card reads. No note, just a signature. I study the illustration on the card, a blue and silver and green sketch of a Bayliner hauling a fresh-cut fir tree across a frothy glittering lake. Maybe ten seconds elapse before the scream makes its way up out of me.

She can't hear me, though. She's already floating on Demerol. The phone rings. She is oblivious, enchanted by the antiquity of her own hands.

It is my father. *Ah,* I think, *nice little bit of closure here.* He will talk to her. He will tell her he is sorry. She will tell him she is sorry. They will not die hating each other. He will be a father to me, and say the grandiloquent words that will help me live through this.

– *There are certain documents I must have,* he says, breathless at some automatic-pilot alcohol altitude where the air is thin. – *Photostats. You need to know the truth. Ask and it shall be opened unto you. Ye shall know the truth and the truth will set you free.*

Nothing will ever set me free from the knowledge of the world he is giving me in that moment. *Ironic detachment.* It means getting *yourself* out of the wrecked fuselage, forgetting the rest of the injured.

– *You have not always been told the truth by your mother,* he says and I look over at her. She is smiling beatifically at "Wheel of Fortune," the only show she recognizes anymore. "Sentimental Journey," she guesses correctly, without benefit of most of the consonants.

– *I have to go help Mother,* I say. This is no lie. She is picking at the buttons of her gown, convinced they are pills she needs to take. I am afraid she will fall off her high bed. – *Nobody has seen those papers in years.*

But he hasn't heard anything I've said, because he hasn't stopped talking. He is still talking about the truth setting me free as I put the phone back in its cradle.

I try to persuade my mother to lie back down, and the phone rings again.

– *This. Is. Your. Father. Speaking. You. Do not. Hang up on. Your. Father,* he is saying, full of what registers in my mind as rage and hatred.

I slam the phone down. *Come on, come on, old man. Your moment with me has come.*

The phone rings again. It is his wife, ever sweet-voiced. – *He asked me to see if I could get you on the line. There seems to be some problem with the line,* she says.

– *It's not the line,* I snarl.

I write my father a letter that night, my kamikaze rage burning me up before I finish: *Last time I heard, phone conversations were intended to be dialogues, not monologues. If you want conversation with me now it will be sober, and you will do me the courtesy of listening when I tell you something. You never stuck around long enough to notice it, but I am the toughest and meanest of your offspring. I am the most like you. If you give my mother one moment more of grief during what is left of her life, one of us will live to tell about it, and it won't be you.*

Soon I go next door to my aunt's, and ask her to come show me how to give a bath to someone who can no longer move a muscle. – *I'm not asking you to do it for me,* I say. – *I'm asking you to show me how.* She is a nurse. She says, – *I remember the first time I saw you. You were nineteen days old. You all were a sorry-looking sight when you stepped off that plane. Your mother had a black eye from where he'd gone after her—*

– *Why?* I ask.

– *Some trouble they had in Bermuda. He didn't think that you were his baby.*

I want a drink. I want altitude, solitude. Solid alcoholtude.

My brother and I take shifts, spooning liquid Demerol into her, sleeping in turns. In the final days, my mother goes back in her mind. She welcomes Winston Churchill, she has tea with Queen Elizabeth. The pain intensifies and she goes back to 1921 or so, calling for the old local doctor who took her tonsils out.

– *Go tell Dr. Moore,* she beseeches me, her face full of bewilderment at the war that is being fought inside her. – *He will fix me.* She goes further back: *A, B, C. One, two three.* She goes back to an infant's rosebud-mouthed whisper, and then she's gone.

The funeral home man shows up within an hour. He has a pink carnation in his lapel. He is none other than Most Popular Boy in my brother's high school class. He is carrying his little music stand with the little satin-covered quilted book, all white and lovely like an albino Valentine. He used to sit in my mother's office and negotiate for graduation. She sat in his a month ago and selected her coffin from a brochure. She chose the cheapest one. She never did like Mr. Most Popular.

The farmers and their wives come with dishes of food, sign the albino Valentine book. We have to get the pallbearers together. My mother has managed to yoke together, nonviolently, and in public, the white racist mayor and her black yardman. Over her dead body. My brother and I break the seal on the bourbon bottle before we ride out to the cemetery to show Mr. Most Popular where to dig.

The sheriff, one of her students, comes to lead the entourage to the little Alapaha cemetery. The physician stands amazed, maybe at the knowledge that he lost thousands of dollars in her decision to ride out the cancer at home, or maybe at the knowledge of how she ran forward in her mind to greet death like a long-lost lover.

My earliest memory of my child?

I come to, in my hospital room, to the sound of my new husband's voice. He is cradling our newborn daughter in his hands, crooning to her, – *What are we going to do? Your mother can't stay awake, and she walks like an old Chinaman.* I know that I am smiling at him, but I don't know much else, except that I have recently acquired some horrific memories, and there is a thin, thin membrane of drug between me and immense pain and those memories.

I swim up out of the Demerol long enough to hear him singing to our daughter, easing her troubled passage to earth because Mommy is momentarily blotto. The nurse is holding her out to me. My first sight of her: tiny hands clasped together, like a mezzo-soprano in a mouse opera might. It's like they are giving me my very own papoose to have, and from it are issuing whimpers of bewilderment at being born into the species *homo sapiens* human being, the bright lights, the big loudspeaker. But she seems to know who I am, and where to go for lunch.

My husband stands by to catch her if I am too woozy to hold her, and I push the blanket aside to inspect her fully.

She has my father's face.

It's like a slow fist of love slamming up through me. It's like the heel of God upon my neck, to give me back the same configuration of face I've always feared, to give it to an infant I love with ferocity. It's like being inducted into some secret chapter of species *homo sapiens* human being.

I uncurl the little fists. The thumbs are my husband's, a familiar arc in miniature. – *Look,* I say. – *She has your hands.* I am quite relieved by this, as if this gives her some greater purchase on happiness than to have hands like mine.

My husband calls my brother and sister to tell them of the birth. He does not call my father, because I don't want him to. In the first year of my daughter's life I don't want to see or talk to my father, for reasons that don't have anything to do with me. I have this child, and she is too helpless to know where the exits are. Every time I look into her face, I also see my father as an infant, and I feel as if I am learning to love him from his own infancy. But I feel an obligation to my daughter to filter my father out of her life, the same way I stopped drinking coffee and alcohol.

I do not question why I must do these things, and my husband doesn't question it. I seem to be flying on instruments anyway. I can hear some other woman's baby cry in the supermarket and the milk will rush into my breasts, staining my blouse. I can no longer read newspapers; they will pipe wars and rumors of wars into my house. One night after several weeks of awakening every hour or so at night to nurse the baby, I dream I have become the ragged mother coyote, mother superior I saw once, milk-swollen, trotting oblivious alongside buzzing traffic in Wyoming, in transit either to her babies or to her next meal, or lost.

My last memory of my father? Olivia calls a few days before he dies. – *Don't let him know that I called you,* she says. – *But can you please call him? He has talked and worried about you all day. But don't tell him I suggested it. He get's so angry if* . . . she trails off.

My father has ripped out his IV tubes a week before, and thrown his TV through his window. I dial the hospital number that she gives me, at the appointed time when she will be there to act surprised and hand the phone to him.

Who is this weak old man I'm talking to? He acts like we just saw each other days before. The truth is, we've each been locked into our respective aeries of outrage for so long, we hardly remember what the original fracas was. There is something in him that is still wooing me to be his daughter.

He tells me he understands why I haven't brought the baby to see him. – *You've got a good thing going,* he says, already sambaing with the angels at 30 milligrams of morphine a pop. – *I didn't want to spoil it for you,* he says. – *Man. Woman. Baby. Winter. Fire. There is probably nothing else, sweetheart. Nothing else but love.*

He mentions the time I walked past him in the schoolyard. The tears are like acid in my eyes.

I keep waiting for something that feels like apology from him, for what he did to my sister. He seems to be fishing for what feels like apology from me. He tells me through gritted teeth how he used to park his car a few blocks down from the house to watch me ride my tricycle up and down the sidewalk.

I do not believe this. I am no longer a sucker for a good story.

– *You used to stop and make imaginary phone calls in the crepe myrtle bush,* he says. – *Up and down the sidewalk you went. Up and down.*

The crepe myrtle bush.

There is no choice but to believe, the cold floes of old anger loosening, creaking. Almost like making it out of a wrecked fuselage, being frightened by the new terrain.

Within days I'm sitting with my brother and sister in a cemetery in Savannah, and even though I am expecting the salutatory gunshots, they give me the confusion of fight or flight. I want to rise up and gore the enlistees with their own bayonets. A military funeral is a cold, dead thing, even if you are basically a raging heathen. I come away from my father's funeral feeling like his life has not been celebrated in the manner he would have wished. It ain't over till the saxophones complain.

– *The sun is now over the yardarm,* Olivia says, back at the motel where we are staying. She produces a silver flask of scotch. I keep trying to get my brother and sister to listen to a tape of Clifton Chenier doing "In the Mood." As if that will evoke our father's presence. They don't want to hear it.

So I hang back like a junkyard dog in my expensive dress and my high heels, sorry that my father was not around to take it all in. He would have loved the spectacle: the opportunity to chew out the soldier in the honor guard whose left shoe was not spit-and-polish perfect. He would have marveled at the nicest piece of Dada my brother and I have ever seen: a funeral wreath of red, white, and blue carnations, shaped like a B-17. From the old geezers at the Trophy Bass Lodge, Georgetown, Florida. I am sorry that he is not here now to have a drink with us after we have taken off our shoes.

It wasn't a B-17, was it, I would tell him. *It was a Flying Fortress.*

Oh, really?

Well, your brother told me that your name is in this book called Heroes of World War II, and—

I made that up.

I figured. Never could locate it. So I looked up the Battle of the Coral Sea, matched your dates and coordinates with what I found, and figured out that you were one of the scouts sent out looking for the Zeroes. You were three miles out of Port Moresby at eighteen thousand feet when one came at you. He wrote in his bomb report later that he knocked out your tail and your left wing. All of the crew were alive when the plane pancaked, so he kept strafing you. You told a Melbourne newspaperman who interviewed you that every time he came back over, you would dive as deep as you could, and think of all the women you had to get back to. When the Zero left, you swam to shore, alone. The natives passed you from tribe to tribe until you made it to base. It took two weeks. You weighed ninety-eight pounds and had dengue fever.

On the morning that your father got the telegram saying you were missing in action, your brother, a C-240 transport flyer home on leave, just happened to read in the Atlanta Constitution that you had made it back. That was the first time he ever saw your father cry. The second time he saw your father cry was later when your baby brother, a tail-gunner on a B-25, was shot and killed by MP's outside a Negro nightclub in Montgomery, Alabama, for refusing arrest after going AWOL. He was sixteen. You all called him Red, and he had enlisted by lying about his age. When they found out his age, they had sent him home, but he just enlisted again in the next county.

You were given the Silver Star for gallantry in action. Red was given a quiet soldier's burial, with none of your other three brothers present. You all told your mother he'd been killed in combat, and she never knew the difference. You were all flying bombing missions or talking airplanes down out of the sky on radios, or trying to fly food into the Pacific theatre. You were a local luminary, the light of which blinded you and Mother both to the fact that the potential for holocaust is real. Did you know that she used to read the Bible and pray while you were in the air?—

How do you know all this?

I do my homework.

Then you ought to know that a B-17 and a Flying Fortress are the same animal. Not bad though, for a dame. It was more like ten thousand feet than eighteen. I musta lied.

Tell me about the time you threw the TV through the hospital window.

Ancient history. Lissen at that music. Mercy. I refuse to believe that a child of mine cannot learn to samba. Come here.

And I'd come there. And I'd look at him and say, – *Hello, me. Long time no see.*

And he would forgive me.

Charlie Smith

Charlie Smith's "Park Diary" may not seem a short story in the traditional sense. It has only three paragraphs, no characters, and no plot. What it offers instead is the all-consuming obsession captured in the opening sentence. Smith is both a poet and a novelist. A faculty member in Princeton University's creative-writing program, he was born in Moultrie, Georgia, the son of a state legislator. He earned his undergraduate degree at Duke University and his B.F.A. from the University of Iowa's Writer's Workshop. His first story, "Crystal River," was accepted by the *Paris Review* in 1977 and won the Aga Khan Prize for Fiction. His first novel, *Canaan*, appeared in 1984, followed by *Shine Hawk* in 1988, *The Lives of the Dead* in 1990, *Crystal River: Three Novellas* in 1991, and *Cheap Ticket to Heaven* in 1996. His poetry collections include *Red Roads* (1987), *The Palms* (1993), *Before and After* (1995), and *Heroin* (2000). His work is marked by lyricism, violence, eroticism, confessionalism, and deep probings into the human psyche.

Park Diary

There are four hundred fifty-seven names for heroin. I have learned eighty-two of them. The drug sellers tell me the names, the pushers, the smack heads, the needle-specked little boys pulling their pants down to display their swollen red puds tell me, the girls with the scratches on their arms tell me, sports at McDonald's tell me, former users tell me, a woman I met at Al-Anon, ex-junkie attending meetings because her boyfriend went back to drugs on her and beat her up, threw her down the stairs, pushed her naked into the street and left her there cowering until by chance a Universal Fellowship soup wagon came by and a (kind) soul gave her a blanket and a quarter for the phone: she tells me; and ex-hippies tell me, and a street preacher from Kansas tells me, and a cop, and a couple of social workers and a Chinese wallpaper salesman going down in flames at a party in Soma Dahlberg's penthouse tells me—*White Horse, Shiny, Doubloon, Red Day, Flash, Hot Jimmy, Alphabet Local, Crank, Pearl, China Day, Johnny, Elmo, Ajax, Yellow Blaze,* are the names of heroin—*Columbus in Heaven, Deliquescence, Rainbow Roustabout, The Jeweler's Daughter, Ambivalence,* are the names of heroin—*Six Years after the Hurricane, Dead Mothers in the Highway, What is Thinkable Is Also Possible, Sweetest Love I Do Not Go For Weariness of Thee, Jumbo on Wheels,* are the names of heroin—*From This Valley They Say You Are Going Do Hasten To Bid Me Adieu But Remember The Red River Valley And The Cowboy Who Loved You So True,* are the names of heroin— and Rae tells me, like a woman speaking Japanese to the mirror, Rae tells me the names she has invented for heroin, tells me the names of her love for it, the names of what she has given up for heroin, the names of her desire and its completion, she tells me that for an addict heroin is a country with its own seasons, its own accents and inflections, its intonations and emphasis, a country of rituals and perfections, country of lonely farm lanes, and of young girls washing their hair in buckets, of children suddenly lost in a piney wood looking around; she tells me that heroin is a division of purpose and a hotel on a beach in Normandy, she puts her hand on my arm and the dry skin of her fingertips is a form of speech I have heard before, the slight erasing, shifting, whispering sound of her fingertips on my skin is the sound of a policeman weeping into his hands, and of this she tells me, of this policeman and his name which is another name for heroin, and tells me the secret mysteries of rainy nights in Nebraska where she was born, where the rain fell on the fields breaking down the green wheat—which is another name—and she tells me of the names of heroin lodged in the mouths of women dead of cholera in Bangladore, tells me the names of heroin mentioned in the abridgements of certain recent court proceedings, tells me the combined law of averages that will sweep all names of everything else that lives into the sea; Rae tells me the names and I listen, I listen to her voice that is the voice of my wife become the voice of a mad woman, and she tells me this is another of the names of heroin and I write this in my book and later say the name over to myself in case some night when my life depends on it I am asked the name and I tell them and she's freed; each of us, she tells me, naming names, is the host; each of us, she tells me, heroin calling itself *Little Mary* in her veins, is standing in the doorway, she says, like Christ just after he gets the news that everyone else in the world, but him, got crucified.

. . . smell of fish in the entranceway of the store where I buy my typing paper . . .

. . . the plane trees on the terrace beside St. Patrick's Cathedral: thick, dark green leaves, blood-fed . . .

". . . Your ass is as black as mine . . ."

Benjamin Prang says, *Accept that the world will never be healed.*

I take my earphones off, step out of the chair and sit down on the floor. Rae speaks to me, but I don't hear her. So often these days I don't hear her, or don't listen, don't want to know the latest disaster unveiled. But then I do. A mystery leaks into my ears, a noise, a sound shaping and reshaping, blips and muted screeches, whisperings and soft pleading asides, the parts of speech—fat triphthongs, musty ablauts, bilabial fricatives take shape, I hear her, hear her speaking to me from the background, from the corner of the room she has taken over, from her chair, from the side of the bed where she dips her fingers into a pan of warm water, dips her hands and begins to wash her bruised arms as she sits looking out the window at summer bullying the trees in Washington Square Park; I hear her voice, the monotone, the unvariable persistent elegant phrasing, the complaints and observations probing the air, entering me impersonally, wheedling and begging, commanding, dividing me from myself, whittling new ornaments of feeling we might turn wonderingly in our hands, gauds and trickery, silky shaped phrases for a life, for the day and its merciless divisions, all apparent at once in each word, by now nothing left out between us, nothing without its hidden and its obvious meaning.

And all meanings the same, she might say, lifting her beautiful ruined face to the light, turning toward me, smiling blankly as if I am a picture of myself held up to remind her of what life once was in a place she has forgotten.

Melanie Sumner

Melanie Sumner was born in Rome, Georgia, in 1964. She left home at seventeen, studied in Boston, taught in Senegal, reported the weather in Alaska, and for eighteen years lived in New Mexico before returning to settle with her family in the town of her birth. Not coincidentally, perhaps, her first book, a story collection titled *Polite Society* (1995), focuses on a young woman trying to get as far away from home as she can. Sumner's next book, a novel titled *The School of Beauty and Charm* (2001), moves closer to home as it describes the situation of a nonconformist young girl growing up in a conventional small-town Georgia family that loves her just a little too much. "The Guide," set in North Africa, was first published in the *New Yorker* and is one of the stories in *Polite Society*. Ironically titled, it describes how a woman becomes increasingly lost, geographically and emotionally, as she is tricked and confused by a foreign culture that she comes to understand no better than she understands herself.

The Guide

At the gate of the Grand Hotel de Mali, a brothel that served as an inn for the rare tourist in Oulaba, Darren reached inside her shirt and paid off her first guide. The child had only carried her pack up the short path from the road, and his dark eyes grew round as he took the one-hundred-C.F.A. coin into his fist. Immediately, the other boys attacked him, snatching at the money. "White lady!" one of the children shouted in French. "We all led you here. We are all your guides, and you must pay all of us!"

Darren shook her head, banged the gate shut behind her, and went down a dark corridor. Behind one of the closed doors a whore wailed. Her voice rose and fell like a siren, now laughing, now crying, following Darren down and around the halls to the courtyard, where the sound of television drowned it out. A black-and-white set perched precariously on a stack of crates, balanced by two rabbit ears. Beneath the screen, Malians sat on mats, mesmerized by a fuzzy, French-dubbed episode of "Dallas." They barely turned their heads as the small, pale American wearing a man's felt hat crossed the courtyard to the bar.

"Bonsoir, Madame," she said to the stout woman leaning in the doorway. "Je m'appelle Darren." She asked for a room for the night.

The hotelkeeper looked her over. She uncrossed her arms to wipe her hands on the faded *pagne* cloth wrapped around her hips and reaching to her ankles. Then she folded her arms back over her chest and returned her gaze to the white woman in bed with a lover on the TV screen. The gold ring in the hotelkeeper's nose glinted in the dim light.

From a shadowy corner of the room, a boy stepped forward. "Bonsoir, Madame Darren," he said. He bowed low, like a magician on stage, and said in French, "Please excuse my mother, for she doesn't speak the languages of the first world. My name is Jaraffe, and I am at your disposal." He offered a brilliant smile. "American, I presume? Americans are my favorite people. How do you find Mali? If you care to see our cliffs tomorrow, I am pleased to be your guide. You are tired. Perhaps you would like a beer? I suggest the imported beer. Normally, of course, one can't find such luxuries in Oulaba, but this is your lucky day." He lifted his thin shoulders in an elegant shrug.

She wanted to laugh at him, but she was stunned by his beauty. He was slender, with skin the color of honey, and silky black curls that fell into damp ringlets at the nape of his neck. His nose was precise and delicate; his lips curved salaciously, blood-red against small, even, white teeth. A new T-shirt, several sizes too large, slid off one shoulder, baring the bones of his chest. As she studied him, he kept his head demurely bowed, hiding his eyes beneath their lashes, but suddenly he raised his head and stared back. He had the yellow eyes of a cat.

"How old are you, Jaraffe?"

"Me? Well, I am thirteen. No, not thirteen. Did I say thirteen?" He affected a bemused chuckle and stretched himself up taller. "I am fourteen, actually. Almost fifteen."

"I'll have the imported beer," she said, sure that he would return with a flat, warm Gazelle, or something worse, and a long explanation. She sat down at a low, rusty table and rested her head in her hands. In a few moments, he reappeared with an icy bottle of Heineken. She held her hand out for it before she caught herself.

Then she narrowed her eyes in the expression of jaded wariness that she adopted in her dealings with Africans. The expression was fake. She was alone and, more or less, lost. In a leather pouch hanging from her neck and tucked inside her khaki pants she had five hundred dollars, more money than the average African earned in a year. If she had to, she would pay an outrageous price for the cold beer, and the child knew this. "How much?" she asked.

"For you, my friend, seven hundred C.F.A."

"Six hundred."

He shrugged, handed her the bottle, and returned to a stool in the corner. After a weary sigh, he removed a crumpled cigarette from his shirt pocket and approached her again. "Do you have a light, Darren?" When she shook her head, he found some matches in his pocket, smiled apologetically, and, lighting his cigarette, sat down beside her.

The game began. Darren considered telling him that she had not invited him to sit with her, but she was too tired to get tangled in the absurd exchange that would inevitably follow such a statement, and, after all, Jaraffe was only a boy.

Three days ago she had set out from her Peace Corps station in Senegal on an odyssey to Timbuktu, and since then she had not had a moment's respite from African men who considered any young, white woman travelling alone to be public property. Her furious protests were as delightful to these men as if they came from the mouth of an unbranded cow wandering in their fields. On the first hour of the train ride from Dakar to Bamako, a note was pressed into her hand:

Hello my American frend. I find you is so very nice for me. So yes you pleese me. I love you. Now we will be together. Nice.

For the next twenty hours, no matter where she sat on the train, the man wedged himself beside her, smiling indulgently at her rejections. He did not consider himself rude.

Now, having gained a seat at her table, Jaraffe sailed into the relationship. "Are you married, if you don't mind my asking?" Smoke curled softly out of his lips and hung in the moist air between them. He wasn't inhaling.

"Yes," she lied.

"Your husband is an oil tycoon, perhaps? Or a doctor? It's none of my business. I myself will be a surgeon. When I have saved enough money, I am going to America to study medicine. Now, when I am not in school, I work as a guide. I give most of the pay to my mother, of course, but I save what I can for my journey to America. Perhaps you and your husband would like me to take you to the cliffs tomorrow? We can go and return in a single day, if you like."

"I wasn't . . . my husband and I weren't planning to go to the cliffs."

With a wave of his hand, he dismissed this detail. "I know the cliffs. The other boys will ask to be your guide, but, unfortunately, they are all liars and thieves."

"Thanks for the information, but we don't need a guide."

He smiled at her bad French and continued. "For you, my friend, I will only charge fifteen thousand C.F.A. a day, or fifty American dollars if you like. You see, I must go into the cliffs tomorrow anyway, because I have a secret mission there. My father is a marabout—a magician, if you will. He can turn rocks into coins, he can make your enemies run when they see you coming down the path, and he can make it rain." He paused, watching her with his yellow eyes. "He can make the dead rise again."

Darren nodded.

"I see that you don't believe me, but that is understandable. Even in a country as great as America, you have never seen anything like this. Tomorrow my father is coming here to show his magic in the courtyard, and then you will see that Africans may be poor, but we have special powers." When she glanced over his shoulder, he said, "All right. This is a special price for you only. Thirteen thousand C.F.A. It's all settled."

A gendarme stomped into the room, pushing a drunk ahead of him. "Jaraffe!" the drunk shouted. The boy jumped up to run from the room, but the drunk lunged and punched him in the face. Then Jaraffe's mother came forward, and with one smooth swing of her arm she struck the drunk on the temple. He slid down in the gendarme's arms, his head hanging to one side, his mouth open. Jaraffe was gone.

"*Voilà.*" cried the gendarme, who was also drunk. He shouted gaily in Bambara as he dragged his prisoner across the floor and propped him against the wall like a sack of millet. The woman crossed her arms back over her chest and said nothing. Again, the gendarme cried, "*Voilà!*" He was a handsome, barrelchested man in a khaki uniform, with skin as black and gleaming as the pistol that hung in the holster skewed around his hips. He turned his attention to Darren. "Excuse us, Madame!" he roared. "*Bonsoir. . . . Madame américaine? Ou Madame française?* I hope we are not disturbing you."

"*C'est Madame américaine,*" she said firmly.

"*Monsieur Gendarme. Enchanté.*" He thrust his hand forward. "*Bière!*" he shouted, and dropped down on the bench beside her. "Are you in Oulaba to visit our spectacular cliffs?"

"No," she said. "I was on my way to Timbuktu. I was going to fly out of Mopti, but—" She stopped, remembering that he was a gendarme. In Mopti, the police had discovered that she wasn't carrying the *license de photographie* they required of all foreigners with cameras. The fine for this crime was the camera itself, or jail. Using the alibi that she was going back to her hotel to get the permit, she had jumped into the first available jitney, ending up in Oulaba, a town that wasn't even on her map. Now she forced a thin smile. "The boy here, Jaraffe, offered to be my guide. Do you know him?"

"You want Jaraffe? I'll sell him cheap." He slammed his fist on the table, shaking Darren's bottle, and threw his head back to laugh.

"Is he a bandit?"

"No! I can't sell bandits cheap. The bandits are expensive!" He howled at his own joke and then composed himself.

"*C'est 'Madame' américaine, ou 'Mademoiselle'?*"

"*C'est Madame.*"

"I like your hat, Madame," he said. He peered under the brim at her face. "Give it to me."

"Tomorrow," she said.

"Ah, you know Africa too well!" He shouted for Jaraffe. The doorway to the bar remained empty. "The boy is ashamed," said the gendarme. He took a drink and turned the bottle around in his broad hand. For a moment his brow creased into deep lines. His voice became maudlin. "That's the boy's father," he said, inclining his head to the drunk on the floor. Darren turned to look at the man slumped against the wall. His robe was torn and soiled to the uniform gray of fools' rags, and the nails on his hands were twisted and yellow, like the nails of a madman. A thin line of blood dribbled from his slack mouth.

Three whores walked into the room, dressed in tight miniskirts and stiletto heels. They laughed at Darren in her hat. One of them sat beside her and said, "You are my sister." She reeked of beer and cheap perfume, and her painted mouth was frightening.

Darren motioned to Jaraffe's mother, who led her across the courtyard and down the corridor to a door she opened with a skeleton key. The room had a concrete floor and walls, and near the ceiling there was one tiny window with no pane, crossed with iron bars. The foam mattress on the floor was covered with a dirty *pagne*. "*Merci, ma mère*," said Darren. The woman almost smiled as she tucked Darren's two bills into her bra. Talking rapidly in Bambara, she locked and unlocked the door several times, and Darren nodded. "Yes, I'll lock it," she said in English. "Thanks."

In the morning, in the bloody light of the rising sun, Darren saw the cliffs for the first time. They rose up and shimmered all around the dusty village like huge gold nuggets piled by the hands of giants. No matter where she turned her head, she saw the low, golden mountains, scintillating in the sun like broken glass. They drew her toward them. Reason told her that mountains are generally farther away and higher than they seem, that she was an inexperienced climber and would not be safe out there alone; but although Darren always put on a great show of being practical in front of other people, when left to her own devices she was as hapless as a child alone on the moon.

Her only concern was that Jaraffe might find her and insist on being her guide, so she shouldered her pack and hurried down the road. At the market she stopped to fill her pack with whatever seemed edible: dried dates, canned sardines, a strange fruit that rattled when she shook it. "Cheese?" she asked. "Bread?" But the women just shook their heads and laughed, holding out their rough palms for money. She wondered how Jaraffe had been able to get his hands on a Heineken. He was not among the pack of children who followed her to the edge of town, calling "Hey, white lady, look at me. I am your guide!"

The children escorted her to the banks of a muddy river where young women waded with their *pagnes* pulled up over their thighs, balancing brightly colored plastic buckets on their heads. One of them knelt and drank. They all watched curiously as Darren pulled off her expensive new hiking boots and rolled her jeans up to her knees, and when she waded across with the pack on her back, they shouted to one another and laughed.

"*Au revoir!*" the children yelled from the bank. "*À bientôt!*" The bravest boys smacked their lips to make loud kissing noises as she went down the narrow, sandy path and curved out of their vision.

She had to keep herself from breaking into a run. The desert opened up all around her, and she gulped the fresh air until her throat was parched. Within half an hour she began to burn. The sun bored through the sunscreen on her face and arms, resting on her soft, freckled skin like a warm iron. Already, the stiff leather of her boots was cutting blisters on her feet. She didn't care. She shifted the light pack on her shoulders and marched on, imagining telling her brothers in Tennessee about this adventure. As a child, she used to stand crying in the doorway when they left the house in their oiled hiking boots, shouldering heavy packs of Bunsen burners, gorp, and powdered eggs. "We girls have to stay home," her mother said, and she tried to teach Darren how to knit. What was a lap of tangled yarn compared to entry into the horizon? When the boys came home, smelling of woodsmoke, sweat, and leaves, she ripped out every stitch she had painstakingly knitted in the sweater sleeve. "I'm a prisoner!" she yelled. "I'll run away! You'll see!" Her mother told her to keep her voice down, and the brothers smirked.

As the sun rose higher, the cliffs lost their golden sheen and became hot, dry rocks. Darren had no sense of measure; the mountain could have been a thousand or ten thousand feet high, but the top of it seemed rather close to the clouds. When she began her climb, some of the rocks tipped under her weight. There was no sound but the dry scrape of her breathing and the slide of her boots.

Then the silence broke. "Darren!" a thin voice called. She looked at the bare rock all around her and up at the wide, empty sky. "*Madame Darren!* I am here!" Two yards away, through a wide crack in the rock, Jaraffe poked out his curly head. Her heart sank.

"*Quelle bonne surprise!*" he exclaimed, slithering out of the rock and landing on his feet like a cat. A purple bruise shone around one eye. "Here I was, just going along on my secret mission, all alone, and I find Madame Darren, my American friend!" He grinned from ear to ear. "And you're all red and tired but still so beautiful. Were you frightened and lonely? Dismiss all your fears—your guide has found you."

She had been warned about this. If she refused his services out here, he would follow her back to town and tell everyone that he had guided her but she had refused to pay him. If she did accept him now as a guide, there would be no one to witness the bargain, and he might do the same thing.

"Where are your shoes, Jaraffe?"

He glanced down at his dusty feet as if he fully expected to find shoes there, then looked up and shrugged. His hands were as small as sparrows, and when he held them out by his sides, palms up, he appeared to be the most vulnerable little boy on earth. Suddenly she was furious.

"How much do you charge for this tour?"

At the nasty tone of her voice he raised his eyebrows in a perfect arc. He dragged one toe along the rock. "Two hundred American dollars."

She laughed, and he joined her in a child's falsetto. She raised her hand to him. "You are a child, and you will speak to me with respect!" When he ducked, she was ashamed of herself.

Out of reach, he smirked contemptuously and said, "Well, of course, I am actually here on a secret mission for my father, as I explained last night, and so if you choose to follow me, well, then I assure you that you will see what no tourist ever sees. I thought you were my friend, and so I had planned to show you a cave filled with Dogon burial treasure. But this obviously bores Madame, and so I beg her pardon."

"You lie, boy." He looked at her, and for a moment she was afraid, but she continued, raising her voice. "There is no sacred treasure, and your father is not a magician."

"You lie!" he yelled. "You don't have a husband. You lie, and also you speak French like a dog!" He stepped back from her and mocked her accent, laughing in a high whine.

"Your father isn't a magician, he's a drunk."

Blood rose to his cheeks, and his eyes turned almost black. "Whore! Dog-French white-lady whore!"

"Well, you've lost your fancy manners, haven't you?" she said softly in English. "You snot-nosed little brat."

For an instant he gazed at her mouth, wrinkling his smooth brow, as if the words still hung about her lips and might be grasped, but then he turned his head away. "I don't understand your language, and I hope the hyenas eat you."

"Five thousand C.F.A.," she said in French. "Or fifteen American dollars. That's the price, if I see the Dogon burial cave." He spit. Then he jumped, from one rock to the next, leaping the boulders like a goat until he was gone.

Soon she heard his spook sounds—strange whistles and long, sad wails echoing in the caves inside the cliff. Clinging to the rock, she inched her way toward the sky. At noon, when she stopped to eat, her body trembled. Sweat stung her dry lips, salting the food as she put it in her mouth. The warm, heavily chlorinated water was delicious, and she was sorry she hadn't brought more than one canteen. She removed her hat, stretched out on the rock beneath an overhang, and dozed.

First, she sensed his presence. When he was close enough, she smelled his sweet, child's sweat, already familiar.

"Six thousand C.F.A.," she said, without opening her eyes. He did not answer. Instead, he touched her sunglasses, and then her hair. He was leaning over her face now, so close that his breath stirred the tiny hairs in her nose. She felt the wet, exquisite curve of his lips on her ear, whispering in a strange tongue. Then she sneezed.

Abruptly, she sat up. "What is your problem?" she yelled in English. He stared at her mouth, his eyes large and dark, the purple bruise glistening. He smiled hopefully. "If this desert were hell, you'd be Satan," she said. She continued to speak in English as she busied her shaking hands with the water bottle. She gave him a drink. "Where are your shoes? Are you hungry? Here, eat." She set out the dates and sardines. Pressed close against her legs, he began to eat with feline fingers, sucking all the sugar from the fruit and all the oil from the fish, finishing everything she dropped before him.

When he had eaten his fill, he said, "Seven thousand C.F.A." Without waiting for a response, he tossed her pack across his narrow back and began zigzagping up the side of the cliff. She faced the first boulder he had mounted, fingering the smooth surface for a grip. Then she jumped, catching the top of the rock with her hands, scraping her knees and elbows as she lugged herself over the edge. From a perch far above her head he looked down and said in heavily accented English, "What is your problem?"

He told her to remove the hiking boots and hang them around her neck. As they climbed, the soft pink soles of her feet became familiar with the wrinkled face of the rock, and she moved more swiftly, but no matter how quickly she climbed, Jaraffe skimmed ahead of her. His bronze legs disappeared against the rock, and his blue shirt melted into the sky. Only his black curls stood out against the horizon, and, when he turned, the flash of his smile. She did not look down.

At last, when the sun was easing down over the mountain, Jaraffe stopped to rest. She handed him her canteen, and he drank half of it. She took two short drinks, hesitated, took a third.

"Where is this Dogon cave?"

"Here."

"Where?" There was nothing around them but rock and, far below, the tiny squiggle of a sand path cutting through a velvet desert. When she climbed around the rock where they were resting, she saw a field cut in furrows as thin as pencil marks, dotted with Dogon farmers.

He rolled over and grabbed her ankles, whispering, "Come back, you fool. The Dogons will see you. We are on sacred ground!"

She edged back against the wall. "Don't grab me," she said, whispering back despite herself. "I am older than you. Respect me."

"The dead are older than you. Respect them."

"Shut up."

"Shut up," he mimicked in English.

She lowered herself into a sitting position, keeping her back to the stone. For the first time it occurred to her that they wouldn't be able to get back down the cliff before nightfall. Her hand played with the cap of the canteen, twisting it back and forth.

"I'm going into the cave," he said. "You may follow me if you so desire. In the case of catastrophe, you are not my responsibility. I'm just informing you. Americans like to know these things beforehand."

"Jaraffe, we have to spend the night up here. You told me we could make the climb in one day."

"Maybe I will find you some beautiful earrings, or some money. But if you are complaining I won't give the present to you. Then I will give it to one of my other girlfriends, or perhaps I'll keep it for myself."

She ignored the girlfriend reference. "We need water," she said.

"I am going on my secret mission." He rolled his eyes in cool mystery. "Are you coming?"

The entrance to the cave was blocked by a boulder. "Otherwise," Jaraffe explained, "the hyenas would eat the corpses." They stood on either side of it and rolled it away. Jaraffe asked for Darren's flashlight, peering over her shoulder as she dug in her pack for it. He switched it on, dropped to his hands and knees, and crawled behind a scraggly bush, and, after a second, Darren knelt down. She followed the pink soles of his feet into the tunnel, slapping her hands over the thin edge of light that moved behind him. She could smell something rancid, like a rotting steak. Jaraffe began to hum. The hum reverberated in the narrow shaft, sounding in her bones as she and he wound down into the belly of the mountain. Then they turned the last corner, and Jaraffe stood up and moved the circle of light around the room.

It was filled with human skeletons. They were stacked from the floor to the ceiling. Some of them were seated along the walls, behind urns full of beads and trinkets. The flashlight threw quivering strips of light into the stark eyeholes, the gaping jaws, and the thick spaces between the yellow ribs. They stank.

Jaraffe sang. It was a low, mournful tune, full of strange notes and nonsensical words. They stood beside a pile of corpses. The bottom of the heap was nothing but dust, and the human bones seemed to rise out of this, a shoulder pushing up, a jaw jutting out, a broken hand digging back down into the powder. In the middle of the stack the skeletons were complete, and at the top, near the ceiling, scraps of faded pagnes hung off the bones. It was as though the corpses on top had grown out of the dead lying beneath them. It was as though Darren and Jaraffe, panting and sweating, had rolled off the top of the heap, obscenely alive.

Jaraffe slid behind the pile, leaving her in darkness. She heard him rattling among the bones, but she did not follow. Once, his light shot across the room, illuminating a skeleton sitting cross-legged against the wall, holding an urn between its knees. Inside the urn, besides beads and a few C.F.A. coins, there was a rusted can opener. She felt despair. What hand was cruel enough to create a human being, a sad fool who could see his end, and then smash him to dust? The light was dimming. "Jaraffe, don't burn out the batteries," she called softly, and the sound of her voice frightened her.

"*Oui, j'arrive!*" He rummaged noisily in the pile of skeletons, shaking the fingers on the hands, the toes on the feet, turning the heads this way and that. His hum was high, loud, and uncertain. At last he scurried back to her. "Come! Hurry!" He dropped down on all fours and sped out of the cavern and up the shaft. Darren followed, knocking her head against the ceiling, scraping her knees, senseless to the pain.

Outside, the sun fell in graceful surrender to the night, throwing out its last miracles, cloaking the jagged edge of the horizon in shadow. Birds sang unearthly notes, brazenly breaking the day's long silence. In the dying sun, Jaraffe's bare arms and legs turned gold, and as he stood on the ledge, holding the skeleton of a human hand like a scepter over the Dogon farmers in the fields below, he looked like a god. A few farmers still bent over their short, primitive hoes, but most of them had thrown the shafts over their shoulders and were walking toward the mountain. Their villages were built so cleverly into the sides of the cliffs that one could walk right by them and never spot a human dwelling. Like the birds, the farmers had begun to sing out to each other.

"Forgive me for calling you a liar this morning," Darren said. "I'm glad that you're my guide." Jaraffe turned his head to hide the frank pleasure on his face.

"This is the cave where we will sleep tonight," he said, motioning to an overhanging rock. "I hope it pleases you."

She crawled inside. The ceiling was so low that she couldn't stand up, but the floor was large enough for the two of them to stretch out when they slept. A hollow in the back wall led to other passages that were too dark to see.

"Jaraffe," she called, stepping out onto the ledge, "I think there are too many openings; something could come . . ." She stopped. He had opened her pack. The camera hung around his neck, and he was rubbing a stick of deodorant along his face. His nostrils flared delicately as he sniffed the scent.

She snatched the deodorant out of his hand. "You do not ever open my pack without my permission!"

He hunched his shoulders together and then lifted his chin. "I don't care. Mosquitoes don't bite Africans when they can bite white ladies."

"What?" She burst into laughter. "That's not mosquito repellent. That's deodorant; it goes under your arms. Oh, never mind." She pulled the camera off his neck and tried to take his picture, but he turned his back to her.

"You don't have anything good to eat in your pack," he said, grumbling. "The other Americans had chocolate, and macaroni-and-cheese. You don't even have a stove."

"You aren't required to eat with me." As she knelt beside him, putting the items back into the pack, she smelled the deodorant on his face and chuckled. "I'm sorry, Jaraffe. It's just that it's funny to Americans."

With her army knife, he cut a string from her roll of twine and tied the skeleton hand around his neck. "The other Americans had Kool-Aid as well. Grape." He held up the fruit she had bought in the market and looked at it with disgust before he cut off the top. "Beggar's food," he snorted, sliding two fingers inside the hard shell and popping a fleshy seed into his mouth. "Food for lepers."

"Where's the water?"

"Africans don't need water."

"Well, Americans do." She turned up the canteen he had nearly emptied.

"Americans carry extra batteries," he said. She tried to turn the flashlight on; the batteries were dead. He smiled and handed her the fruit. The sweet and sour seeds puckered her lips and burned her stomach, but the juice soothed her thirst. He laughed at her grimaces.

"Are you cold?" she asked.

"Africans don't get cold."

She tossed a sweater at his head and carried her own warm clothes toward the cave to change. When she looked back, he was smelling the sweater, running his fingers over the cashmere and sliding it along his cheek. Inside the cave, something rustled. Wind? She couldn't make herself crawl inside. With her back turned to Jaraffe, she changed her clothes and returned to sit beside him.

Black curls fell across his forehead, and his eyes gleamed yellow in the falling darkness. The sweater swallowed him. The cuffs flapped below his hands as he crossed his arms and commented, "Your body is very beautiful, but I find your derrière too small."

"Shut up, Jaraffe."

"I see that you are frightened to go in our cave, or perhaps you have fallen in love with me."

The muscles in her back tensed. "You? You are a child." His face stiffened in humiliation. He began to hum.

The stars came out in rapid succession, crowding the huge black sky until they nearly touched each other. She lay on her back looking up for Sirius, the great star of the Dogons.

When she gazed too long at the sky, she lost all sense of direction and had to press her hands flat against the cold, solid rock. Behind her the gaping mouth of the cave waited, and she dreaded it. The boy seemed a stranger to her now, chanting his lonely, foreign hymns, accompanying the one bird that remained awake. The birdcall was like nothing she had ever heard. It wasn't a screech or a caw or the notes of a song but something chilling and abrupt, like the scream of a woman.

"Jaraffe, what is that bird?"

"There is no bird."

"Yes, listen. It screams like a woman." It screamed then, louder than before. "That one."

"That's a hyena."

"Where is the hyena?"

"It's here." The scream came again, and her heart pounded. "She smells your fear," he added reproachfully.

"Aren't you afraid?"

"I am the son of a magician, do you forget so quickly? I went into the sacred Dogon grave and took my talisman." He rattled the fingers on the skeleton hand. "The hyena is afraid of me."

"What happens if the hyena comes into the cave while we are sleeping?"

She heard him yawn. A bank of clouds rolled across the sky, and the stars blinked out, one by one, like the lights going off in a house.

"You aren't earning your keep as a guide," she said.

"Ha! Ha, ha. I am a child, remember? I am a child when Madame decides that I am to be a child. Now Madame is afraid and needs a man. Am I to be a man now?"

He reached for her breast, laughing when she knocked his hand away. "A child, then. Well, the child is going to bed. Sweet dreams, Madame." He moved away.

She lay on her back looking up at the sky until the last star blinked out. Then it was terribly dark, and cold. Every sound—the rustle of weeds, the roll of gravel, the rasping of her own breath—was magnified until her nerves were taut with fear. She saw the empty stares of the skeletons. When the hyena screamed again, she jumped up and ran to the mouth of the cave.

"Jaraffe?" He did not answer. She leaned down and pushed her head through the opening, blinking in the darkness. "I'm not coming in until you answer me." Suddenly, something swished behind her. With a thud, the animal landed on her back. She screamed.

"Waa!" Jaraffe cried, rolling off her back, doubled over in laughter. He leaped about her, pulling at his hair, rolling his eyes, crying out in sharp female wails. "Waa!" he cried. "Oh, oh, help me! Where is my big, strong, handsome guide?"

With her heart still knocking in her chest, she swung her fist at him, but he ducked it like a boxer. "Damn you!" she yelled. He shrieked—a scared, mean laugh. She lunged for him and caught hold of his skinny arm, but he slipped out of her grasp. For a moment they stood facing each other in the dark, panting, and then she hissed, "I despise you." She began to sob in broken screams that scraped her throat raw, a horrible, lonely sound. She covered her mouth, choking in the effort to stop the noise. She felt his presence somewhere in front of her, small and no longer fierce, and she crawled into the cave. She made a thin pallet from the rest of the clothes in her pack and lay down, first on her back, then on her stomach. Then she rolled over on her back again. Each lump in the rock made a distinct stab into her flesh. She began to wonder about Jaraffe, and to want him with her, if only to slap him.

A few minutes later, he scooted into the cave. "And where is my bed?" he demanded. She remained silent. "You are angry with me." He stretched out beside her on the hard floor and pushed her arm. "Say something, Darren, my dear friend Darren." When she rolled away from him, he patted her head as if she were a baby. "You were crying, and I did not help you. Now I have scared you. You are so good to me, giving me food and water and this sweater. I do not even like grape Kool-Aid and macaroni-and-cheese and chocolate—well, maybe chocolate. I like the sweater, it keeps me warm and smells very nice." He gave a loud, appreciative sniff.

"You annoy me."

"This is true. I am annoying and rude and bad. I am ugly." He waited for her to contradict this last statement, and when she did not he continued. "Many people share your opinion. It is all true." He let his voice become pitiful. "Surely I will burn in hell. Or Allah will find some way to punish me, so that I never forget my sins against you and am always ashamed."

Despite herself, she spoke. "When I first met you, last night, I thought, Here is a boy different from all the other little bandits in Africa. Here is a serious boy. Now I see that I was mistaken. You are just like all the other scoundrels in the street."

"My remorse is more enormous than the sky."

"You are not sincere."

"This is true. I am sorry. Will you forgive me?"

She tossed him the roll of pants and shirts that had been her pillow and closed her eyes. Noisily, he made his bed beside her and went on with his apology. His voice purred against the cold, black walls. He spoke nonsense. At last, he lay down against her back, throwing an arm around her neck and sticking his cold feet between her calves.

"I don't like that, Jaraffe. Stop it."

"I don't have any socks. My feet are cold."

"You can take some socks out of my pack." She listened as he rummaged through her things, mumbling to himself in various tongues, and then she felt him once again press his small, hard body against her back. When his arm circled her neck, the skeleton hand, still tied around his neck, cut between her shoulder blades. "You will take me with you back to America, and I will go to medical school and become a great surgeon. . . ." he murmured sleepily in her ear. "We will get married . . . and have a big house in Dallas, Texas."

She fell into light sleep nettled with nightmares, and awoke strangling in his skinny arms, her face locked against his cheek. His breath shot out in hard, quick bursts, and his heart, racing against her own, knocked on her chest. Above them, the hyena's scream tangled with the anguished shrieking of another animal. The beasts thrashed and rolled on the roof of the cave, knocking pebbles and clumps of dirt from its ceiling. Jaraffe's arms gripped her like thin iron rods. His heart was banging so hard in his chest that she thought he would explode. She hugged the clinging boy tighter against her, hiding her face in his hair, her mind clamped tight on the will to live. For a long time, they lay in their rigid embrace, listening to the hyena chew its shrieking victim. The boy's glowing yellow eyes made the only light in the cave.

When Darren awoke, Jaraffe was gone. He had taken her camera and her hat with him. The leather purse hanging around her neck was flat and empty. Even her passport was gone. "Bastard!" she screamed out over the desert. "Thief!" She threw a rock over the side of the cliff, and then another, screaming as tears ran down her cheeks. Jaraffe had robbed her. She didn't want to climb back down into the world, not ever, but Jaraffe had drunk all of her water, and her tongue was swollen with thirst. She shouldered the pack and began to back slowly down the cliff.

By nightfall Darren was back at the Grand Hotel de Mali. Jaraffe's mother stood in the doorway of the bar, watching her stagger, hatless, dirty, ragged, across the courtyard. Silently, the hotelkeeper went behind the bar and handed Darren a beer. Then, without moving a muscle on her face, she wet a towel, and, leaning forward, roughly scrubbed Darren's face and hands. Darren stood still, in shock; then she sat down at the table and ate the plate of macaroni and tough, greasy meat the woman brought to her. When she pushed her plate back she saw the passport under it. "They're all cunning," she said softly, and pushed the small blue book into her bra. Then she waited for Jaraffe. While she waited she drank beer, arid each time she took a fresh bottle of Gazelle from Jaraffe's mother, she felt a new surge of power. I'll kill him, she thought.

Around ten o'clock Jaraffe sauntered into the bar, wearing a new white suit and a shirt the color of lemons. Darren's brown felt hat was tilted at a rakish angle on his head. A cigarette dangled from his lips. After a brief moment when it looked as though he might run back out the door, he flashed his best grin and said, "Darren, *ma chérie*, at last I find you, oh, at last." She waited. She let him swagger to her. As he bent down to touch his lips to her cheek in the French manner, she smelled alcohol and cheap perfume. He was saying, "Why did you worry me like this? I thought you were lost forever," and leaning forward to kiss her other cheek when she grabbed his neck. She pressed her fingers into the soft skin, digging them between the tendons, and shook him until her hat fell off his head. His strangled cries filled the room, "Mama!" he yelled. "Help me!"

His mother came and stood silently before them. "Help!" cried Jaraffe, and the gendarme ran out from the back room buckling his pants. Then the doorway filled with whores and men, shouting and pushing against each other to get into the room.

"He stole my money!" Darren yelled.

"I did not. This woman hired me to be her guide. I took her into the cliffs, as she asked me to, and then she paid me and told me to go. I gave the money to my mother, who needs it to take care of my poor father."

The crowd pressed noisily into the room and around Darren. One of the whores pushed her painted face down close and whispered, "He's a thief, that one." Darren felt the prostitute's long nails resting briefly on her arm. Jaraffe's mother stared straight at the wall.

The gendarme was looking into Darren's eyes. "I will help you," he said. He laid his broad hand on her shoulder. "Have confidence in me." His hand moved slowly upward until his fingers rested in her hair. She shook it off wearily. "You are an educated woman, eh? You know many things, some languages? You know perhaps how to drive a car? You know how to work a computer? Many, many things live in this head." He rolled his hand over her head as if it were a coconut. "Your head is no good here, eh?" He picked the hat off the floor and pushed it gently down over her ears, as if to stop her from thinking, and then snapped his fingers at Jaraffe's mother. The woman brought two beers; then, from inside her bra, she took a roll of soft bills and laid them silently before Darren. Jaraffe swaggered over and set down her camera. Darren waited a moment to see if the gendarme meant to demand her permit. The man grinned at her, then turned away and drank up, and she stuffed the camera into her bag.

In the morning, she took a jitney back to Bamako, and all along the way young boys begged to guide her.

Alice Walker

Alice Walker has been a leading voice among women writers in the last half of the twentieth century and into the twenty-first. She began as a writer of the civil rights movement in the American South in the 1960s and 1970s, gradually widening her interests until in recent years she has written about the sexual mutilation of African women, the World Trade Center bombings, and other issues of international significance. A native of Eatonton, Georgia, she attended Spelman College in Atlanta before transferring to Sarah Lawrence College in New York. She writes poetry, essays, and fiction, but she is best known for her widely acclaimed 1982 novel *The Color Purple,* about an oppressed young black woman's gradual struggle toward self-discovery. A best-seller, it won both the Pulitzer Prize and the American Book Award in 1982, and Steven Spielberg directed a film version of the novel in 1985. A sequel, *The Temple of My Familiar,* appeared in 1989. In her recent collection *The Way Forward Is with a Broken Heart* (2001), which includes the story "Blaze," she returns to the medium of short fiction in which she distinguished herself in the 1970s.

Blaze

Little Sister dreamed frequently of her lover's wife. "I dreamed," she said to Big Sister, as they lay drying off beside the lake, "that she, that is, her parents and she, had a maid when she was little. A black woman. I dreamed this woman spanked her, but also cared for her, as black maids do. And that that is why she is longing to reconnect with black women. She misses them."

"Them?"

"Well, the experience of them that could be embodied in one."

Little Sister remembered her own childhood and one of her best friends, a white girl named Blaze. Remembered the day her parents brought her to play with Blaze as usual, while her mother cleaned house for Blaze's mother, and Blaze's father had said: "Miss Blaze isn't here today. She'll be back . . . ." But she never came back for Little Sister or for her parents, who understood perfectly what they were being told: No more equality. No more friendship. "Miss" Blaze. And Blaze, like Little Sister, was only twelve years old.

For the life of her Little Sister couldn't recall anything she and Blaze had done together. They must have waded in the creek behind the house, caught tadpoles, made baskets out of willow rushes. Climbed trees. Played on the swing. She'd blocked the memories, of course. It was all, the experience of being demoted, turned away, blocked by rage. She had thought Blaze had decided it was time her friend called her "Miss" Blaze, but now that seemed unlikely. What child could have been perverse enough to think like that? At twelve or thirteen would it have seemed so important? It might. Because there had been white society, such as it was in those parts, to think of. Her white friends would have been her true peers. They would have been at an age to begin to understand it was possible that their mothers bought the friendliness and compliance of the black women who appeared magically at the back door of their invariably white houses each morning.

There was the rage, a shut door that seemed to be made of iron; but then way behind it, in the fields that encompassed her childhood, under a blue sky that was endless and magnificent, was the friendship, right in there with all the other good things of life. A time of mutual trust and happiness. And an unawareness of inequality, only the enjoyment of mutual sweetness. The barely worn dresses Blaze's mother, and Blaze herself, insisted she take for school, and the firewood, walnuts, handmade rocking chairs her parents gave to Blaze's family. But Little Sister refused to remember this emotionally. Refused to permit it any validation in her feelings. Because to do so, she felt, would be to become complicit in her own betrayal. And she felt she had been betrayed. No "good ole days" could ever exist for her, once she understood that even her happiest days rested on a foundation of inherited evil. An evil that said, when she least expected it: "Miss" Blaze. . . .

And yet.

Now she began to understand that the dream was about her own longings, not about her lover's wife's. For though she blocked any feelings except rage and contempt for Blaze, of course their friendship, or, rather, relationship, remained unresolved. Unfinished. It was as if they'd been playing an engrossing game of chess and someone unconnected to the game, they had thought, had suddenly snatched away the board. There they sat, startled, unprepared to continue without a structure, on opposite sides of an empty table. Nothing connected them anymore.

She would pretend later that her only girlfriends growing up were black. Blaze, no doubt, had pretended her only friends were white. And they had each gone to bed at night determined to forget and forget and forget. She had never set foot in Blaze's house again, after her father's comment. She wondered if anyone had explained to Blaze what had happened. Now she could imagine the cruelty of it, from Blaze's point of view. To return home, expecting to see the bright face of your friend, someone you loved, and to have that bright face, without explanation, never again appear.

What is not remembered emotionally, Little Sister had thought, is not remembered. But look at her adult friends. They were so often Blaze all over again. And in fact, it was through these white women who were her friends as an adult that she discovered what Blaze was like. She no longer remembered Blaze herself at all, but these women were invariably timid, sweet, docile, confused, morally lazy, loving and generous. They would not stand up for themselves, however, and she would soon feel the rage—because if they could not stand up for themselves, and they at least had the power of whiteness in a white supremacist society—they would certainly never stand up for her, or for real friendship or sisterhood with her. Yet, seeking to complete the "game" with Blaze, she picked these women again and again. Whereas her black women friends were chosen primarily for their challenging spirits, however envious, competitive, flighty, or, yes, confused and morally lazy they might be. The ones she really adored would stand toe to toe with the devil himself and yell Fuck you so loudly he'd cover up his ears.

Her mother, because she needed to work, was not able to escape "Miss"

Blaze, and called her that, always, even if there were no house guests or other young white people who'd come to call.

"No," she would say to Blaze who asked her to call her what she'd always called her, "your daddy says you're a young woman, and young women are called 'Miss.'" It was a wedge between them. Deliberate and effective.

Was that it? Was that the source of the rage? Not what was attempted against Little Sister, which her mother helped her to escape by not permitting her to return to Blaze's house, but what was forced on her mother, who could not escape? Little Sister had lived out her childhood at a time and in a place that permitted her to see both a remnant of slavery and a possibility of freedom. But the possibility of liberation was the gift she was unable to give her mother, just as the remnant of slavery, "Miss" Blaze, was the burden her mother refused to pass on to her.

Little Sister was unaware that her thoughts were causing her to glower. Or that she was staring at the surface of the lake as if a monster lurked just beneath. But she heard chuckling, and noticed Big Sister was looking at her.

"Stop frowning, you'll get wrinkles," she said. She sat on a blanket she'd brought from the backseat of the car, and sat oiling herself in the warmth of the afternoon sun.

"Changes, changes," said Little Sister, smiling briefly. "Does anything ever turn out the way you expect it to?"

"I don't think so," said Big Sister. "I never even thought it would be warm enough today to swim."

Little Sister nodded, and returned to her thoughts.

She thought about how hard it was to read the stories she sometimes received at the women's magazine where she worked because in them white women were talking about their closeness to the black women who had nurtured them. Each time she read such a story, she encountered her rage afresh. Embittered by the possibility, the probability, that their black servants *had* nurtured, *had* loved them, as one particularly sincere writer wrote, "unconditionally." It was a love compelled by forced circumstances and forced familiarity— similar to the forced affection one felt for certain likable white characters on TV. There they were, every Saturday night: Mary Tyler Moore, Bob Newhart, the *M*A*S*H* contingent; and they were silly and witty and bright. And you cared about them because they were there, and you liked television, and they were the best white folks to watch in a predominantly white medium.

Perhaps she was enraged because she had hoped love between maid and miss was impossible. That was obviously what every little girl whose mother was a maid hoped. For how could you compete with the little girl who had everything, could buy everything, including your mother? And had been buying your mother for centuries.

You could hate your mother for loving someone for whom she had to work. Perhaps. But how could you, since she worked for your benefit, because of you? The pain was because you felt she loved against her will. Because "If you can't be with the one you love," as the song went, "love the one you're with."

Now she felt the source of the tension she experienced, working at the modestly integrated, white women's magazine. She could not complain about the behavior of the women toward her. They went out of their way, for the most part, to welcome her, to support her, to assure her they recognized her value not only to them, but to the world. And yet, each time she walked into the office she had to seclude herself for several minutes in order to get hold of her breathing. And she was there by choice. But not totally.

The black woman who cleaned the office at night was there, like her mother, because she, doubtless, had children and herself to feed. She knew that that woman too had difficulty breathing, as surely as her own mother must have had. Or maybe not. Because cleaning an empty office was just a job. Working with the white women every day was somehow more, because you were drawn into relationship with them, and sometimes you genuinely cared. So perhaps the question was: Is not affection or love something pitiful, and degraded, when it is compelled by circumstances beyond your control? And when to choose not to love, or to feel affection, represents a greater danger to the soul than one's simple inability to do so?

She watched Big Sister floating on her back in the water, the oil she had slathered on earlier making a greasy circle around her. She thought of her lover, of their trips into the country. The way they would pick an especially hot day to go exploring the countryside in, and then swim in every lake, in every park, they came to. How they would lie on the grass, smoking grass. How she liked to sing with him. How he sang. And yet, no matter how happy they were, there was his wife, and the child, and Little Sister's obligatory worrying about them all. She was beginning to wonder how anyone ever had the strength to have affairs.

Lying on her back, watching the sun begin to sink behind the pines that ringed the lake, Big Sister began to feel like someone other than, different from, her usual oppressed self. She found herself immersed in a memory whose energy seemed about to suck her out, permanently, from her former life of gloom. This felt very strange. And yet, and this occurred to her for the first time: Something odd like this always happens to me when I spend time with Little Sister! She was remembering the day that she had had a different experience, from all the earlier ones, of Uncle Loaf and Auntie Putt-Putt.

She was eighteen, a young woman, and about to go off to school, several small towns over, to learn to be a veterinarian. She was dressed in a green plaid jumper, a crisp white blouse with a pointed collar, and her first pair of high-heel patent-leather slippers, which she wore with stylish Red Fox stockings. Her hair was waved away from her face and reached a kind of crest on top. She wore gold earrings and a necklace she'd received from her current boyfriend. The one she would have married if she'd had sense. She had liberally anointed herself with a cheap, bright-smelling perfume.

For years they had not really said much beyond "Howdy," or "How you?" To which the answer was, invariably, "Oh, tolerable. You?" They did not go beyond these preliminaries now. Big Sister settled herself, not behind Uncle Loaf's chair, as she'd done as a child, but beside him, in a chair identical to his own. He sat as usual, leaning backward against the wall in a wooden chair near the water shelf, which Big Sister noticed had recently been repaired. The last time she had visited, the nails had been coming loose, and the shelf, under its gallon bucket of water, sagged. She noticed that the railing of the porch had also been straightened where it bulged near the steps, and the steps themselves strengthened.

Auntie Putt-Putt came out of the kitchen, crossed the porch in front of them carrying a basket. She wore a large round straw hat, a faded yellow print dress made from feed sacks, and an ancient pair of sneakers without backs, so that her heels looked hard and gray as she walked down the steps and toward the garden.

Then, and Big Sister could not believe her eyes, Uncle Loaf brought his chair down onto the porch floor with a plop, went into his private room, the "front room," and returned wearing his own large straw hat, washed thin and very faded khaki shorts (for he had fought in World War I and returned home "shell-shocked," a word that everyone in the family used in discussing or describing him, but the meaning of which no one knew) and a soft white cotton shirt. On his arm he also carried a basket made of white oak strips, with a broad curved handle the color of his deep brown skin. He moved quietly and calmly down the steps toward the garden and his wife, Big Sister following, on her toes, protecting her shoes against the scraping rocks, wood chips and chicken doo-doo. Surprised. Flabbergasted. Wondering. Unbelieving. What was this? It was as if the quiet oak tree in the yard had suddenly shaken itself and begun to meander down the road.

Big Sister stood in the shade of the corncrib's overhang, watching. Auntie Putt-Putt did not seem to notice anything different. Nor did Uncle Loaf. Their goal was to collect the tomatoes that she sold to the local store, where they got their kerosene. Uncle Loaf started on a row next to Auntie Putt-Putt's but coming from the opposite direction. So that, as Big Sister watched in wonderment, forgotten by these two old people in their green universe hidden from the world, they met, but still did not acknowledge each other's presence, or the fact that a miracle had occurred. They stood a moment, swaying, their backs against their hands, shifted their baskets, and continued serenely along their separate rows.

When Big Sister was leaving them, they sent tomatoes to her family. Still Uncle Loaf said nothing, and, for once, Auntie Putt-Putt seemed out of ancient family gossip. Uncle Loaf went to his room and returned with a handful of silver dollars. He handed them to Big Sister. "Far away," he said. They did not kiss her. They had never kissed her. They were people of the hug. Their hug, reserved, as they were, was the circle of the world known so far, the rounded silence of their hidden universe. And she had walked out of their embrace, free at last.

Recalling this day now, as she lay once again beside Little Sister, who had fallen asleep, Big Sister began to feel health, balance of spirit and soul return to her. She saw that she too had been seen as someone deserving of getting away. Not Little Sister alone. She too had been supported. Not just frightened and burdened down with other people's children and horrible tales of woe. She too had been helped.

As she thought of this, and turned to Little Sister to tell her how that last day of her childhood had been, she noticed that though usually so cheery and confident, she had started, in her sleep, to weep.

"Ah, wake up, Little Sister, it's not as bad as all that!" Big Sister said gently, shaking her.

And true to her irritating self, Little Sister, tears still rolling off the side of her chin, opened her eyes and endeavored to smile.

"Oh, cut it out," said Big Sister. "I see those tears!"

"You do?" said Little Sister, surprised.

"Yes!" said Big Sister emphatically.

More tears appeared instantly in Little Sister's eyes. She began to sob, much as she had when she was a child. She cried, leaning against Big Sister's shoulder, until there were no tears left. And sure enough, soon she was smiling for real, because she was with her Big Sister, after all, and they were celebrating the close of a very happy day.

Bailey White

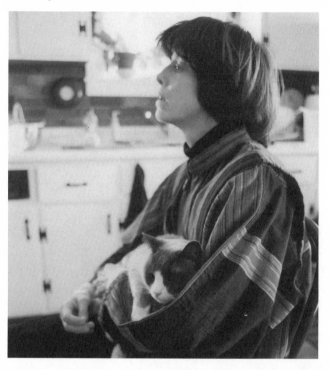

Before they ever read a word she had written, many readers
knew Bailey White as a gravelly southern drawl on National Public Radio,
recounting, with poignant whimsy, stories of her life and family in a small
south Georgia town. White was born in 1950 in Thomasville, Georgia,
and studied at Florida State University. Her first two books were collections of her radio commentaries: *Mama Makes Up Her Mind, and Other
Dangers of Southern Living* (1993) and *Sleeping at the Starlite Motel, and
Other Adventures on the Way Back Home* (1995). Her novel *Quite a Year for
Plums* appeared in 1998. "An Unsuitable Attachment," first published in
the *Oxford American,* is a nostalgic, comical story written in the tradition
of Eudora Welty. But it is clearly White's story, and no southern writer
has so skillfully woven monkeys, angry yellow jackets, and an estranged
brother and sister into the fabric of a single tale.

An Unsuitable Attachment

My father and his sister, my Aunt Araminta, were very close. They had identical well-bred ears, identical expressive noses, and identical old eyes that seemed to be looking out into the world from the same place. As children they had been inseparable, and as adults their attachment retained all the sweetness of a childhood friendship. He called her Ariloo, she called him Jaz.

Then, when she was in her late thirties, Araminta fell in love with a rich man my father disliked. My parents went up to New York for the wedding where my father gave away the bride with dignity and detachment and behaved like a perfect gentleman. On the train coming home, however, he became violently sick, threw up until he was so dehydrated and weak that he was put off the train and admitted to a hospital in North Carolina where my mother fed him diluted orange juice through a soda straw and rubbed him with rags dipped in iced water. After a week he was strong enough to come home.

Araminta stayed in New York. She wrote to my father faithfully once a week. He wrote less and less frequently. One day a letter came from Araminta: "Dearest Jaz," it read. "It has been several weeks since I have had word from you. Please write. I want the news of home." My father, preoccupied with farm matters, didn't write back.

Another letter came: "Dearest Jaz, If you don't write this time something dreadful will happen to you."

My father didn't write back.

The next month a wooden crate arrived in the mail. There were holes in the top, and faint scratching noises came from inside. My father set the crate down on the floor of the living room. He stood back and looked at it. He was very solemn. "It's from Araminta," he said.

We children stood quietly at the edge of the room near the doorway. My father's eyebrows were clenched over his stern, blue eyes, and the curve of his aquiline nose was more pronounced. When he got that look we knew to stay out of the way. "Papa's chewing his nose," we would whisper.

Finally, there was nothing to do but open the crate. "Get me a pry bar," my father said.

My little brother flew out of the room, returned with the pry bar, handed it to Papa, then raced back to take his place with my sister and me, out of bounds.

Papa went to work on the crate. He pried off one board from the top and stood back. A new sound came from inside. "Ech, ech, ech," it said.

Very slowly, a narrow little black hand came out through the hole. No one breathed. The little hand very delicately patted the top of the crate, all the way around, then withdrew. My father didn't move. He just stared at the crate, holding the pry bar loosely in his hand. Finally he spoke. "It's a monkey," he said. "Araminta has sent me a monkey."

"Oh, Jim," whispered my mother. "Not a monkey."

My father had a way with animals. By murmuring softly in their ears and gently nudging them between their front legs he could make wild horses lie down at his feet. Elephants at the circus would follow him around, offering him peanuts and nuzzling him with their trunks. Hens would sneak into the house to lay their eggs on his bed pillow, and squirrels made their nests in his coat pockets. He loved and understood animals, and treated them with tenderness and respect. But he hated monkeys. Some people have an unreasonable fear of rats or snakes; my father's loathing was for monkeys.

Now he stood back from the crate. He shifted the pry bar to the other hand. "Araminta has sent me a monkey," he said again.

Then he shivered all over, rubbed his forearms briskly, and knelt down and pried another board off the crate. The monkey jumped out. It was a small monkey, with long arms and legs and a long tail. It had scruffy light brown fur. It sat on top of the crate and stared into my father's face. "Ech, ech, ech," it said. Then it jumped into his lap. Without taking its eyes from his face, it began to play with the buttons on his shirt. My father sat very still. He began to sweat. My mother sat on the sofa with her hand over her mouth.

Finally, my father said, "Monkey, you put your hand under my shirt and I'll kill you." The monkey put its hand under my father's shirt and began patting his chest. My father sat very still. Then the monkey raced across the room and with one leap and a swing, as if it had been living in that house all its life, it jumped to the top of the grandfather clock. There it perched, looking down at us and saying, "Ech, ech, ech."

My father buttoned his shirt, and without a word he took the crate and the pry bar out into the yard. The monkey jumped down from the clock and, with a funny, sideways, three-legged gait, followed my father. We stared at each other. No one knew what to do. Even my mother just sat and gazed out the door.

"She has sent him a monkey. Araminta has sent him a monkey," she whispered. And that was the last we heard of Araminta for many years.

From that first day, the monkey followed Papa everywhere. When he went into the house she would wait on the steps for him to come out. When he went away in the car she would sit in the driveway and watch for the car to return. Papa never talked about her, never called her by name, never touched her. And always when she came too near he would shudder, hunch his shoulders, and rub his arms. But sometimes we would hear him in the barn talking to her in the quiet singing voice he used when he made horses lie down.

Papa built a wooden box with a tin bottom for the monkey in the limbs of a magnolia tree near the house. He put a few inches of sand in the box, and on cold nights he would light a kerosene lantern and hang it under the box to keep the monkey warm. Sometimes she would go inside the box. Other times she would sit and shiver in a tree outside the kitchen porch and look down haughtily at the people going and coming from the house. My father would stand under the tree and look up at the monkey. She would sit straight and still and look down at him. She would give a little shiver. Papa would go into the house and come out with a blanket which he would hand up to her. She would take it without a sound, and with a tired, graceful gesture she would draw the blanket around herself, daintily plucking at its folds and sighing with contentment.

My mother had no patience with the monkey when she did this. "He's got a house. Why doesn't he go into it?" she would ask. We had named the monkey Annabelle, but in all the years that she lived with us my mother never called her by name or acknowledged her gender. Likewise, when my mother would come near her, flouncing her skirts and making shooing sounds, the monkey would slowly turn her back and, tilting her head extravagantly, gaze with great absorption up into the sky.

Later, however, their dislike of each other became more outspoken and lost some of its elegance and grace. The monkey got into the habit of sneaking up on my mother as she came out of the hen house, snatching the egg basket from her, and climbing a tree, where she would sit, cradling the eggs in her lap and pelting them, one after the other, at my mother. My mother, in turn, took to saving pans of dishwater on the windowsill and dumping them with amazing accuracy onto the monkey as she strolled by the kitchen.

My little brother Ben was an exquisite child. There was an expression that was permissible in those days: "He's too pretty to be a boy." But the fact was, Ben was too pretty to be a human child. His golden hair lay on his head like feathers on a bird, his expressive, long-toed feet seemed meant for finer things than to carry him around our dusty yard, and he had a way of blinking his eyes where the top lids with their heavy lashes would come swooping down, ever so slowly, not quite meet the bottom lids, then swoop back up. They were deer's eyes, and in fact they shone in the dark like animal eyes. Papa called Ben his angel child. He was the first one of us the monkey bit.

It happened on a summer afternoon. Ben and Papa were in the barn making a set of shelves. Ben was sitting on the workbench handing Papa tools, telling stories, and making doodles in the sawdust. Papa had gone into the toolshed to get a level when he heard Ben say quietly, "Poppy? Poppy. Poppy? Poppy." Papa came out and saw the monkey crouched by Ben, hugging him tightly in her long arms. One whole side of his face was in her mouth. Her lips were peeled back so that Papa could see her yellow teeth pressing into Ben's cheek.

Her eyes gyrated wildly, and she looked at Papa and shot her eyebrows up and down. Every now and then she would make little hopping and thrusting movements with her body, but she kept her head still, her jaws exerting an even pressure on Ben's fat cheek.

Papa said, "Don't move, Ben. Just don't move." The monkey hopped and hopped. She made a little squealing sound. Ben watched Papa. His eyes didn't blink, but two big tears came drooling down his cheeks, leaving little tracks in the dust on his face. For ten minutes Papa stood and watched Ben and the monkey. He knew if he moved, or if Ben moved, the monkey would clamp down. Every few minutes Ben would say, "Poppy?" in a strangled little voice, and Papa would say, "Ben don't talk. Don't move." Finally, when she got good and ready, the monkey just turned Ben loose. She swung up into the rafters of the barn and began scratching herself. Papa scooped Ben up into his arms and paced up and down the courtyard of the barn hugging and kissing him and rubbing him all over. Finally, he set Ben down on the workbench and examined his cheek. Every tooth had left a deep dent, but not one had punctured the skin.

For the rest of the afternoon Papa took Ben with him everywhere, and everywhere they went the monkey followed silently, always keeping the same distance, always watching. Ben sat on Papa's lap on the tractor, sat in his little chair by Papa's chair at the supper table, and at bedtime Papa settled on the sofa and held Ben in his arms all night long.

This little adventure of Ben's inspired one of the most peculiar games I remember from my childhood. The game would start at the monkey's box. She would sit there and swish her tail, watching my sister and me. Then with a whoop we would swing down from the limbs of the magnolia tree, dash across the yard, climb to the top of the crepe myrtle, which would bend gently under our weight and set us lightly on the ground again. The monkey would be right behind us, baring her teeth, rolling her eyes, and screaming. From the crepe myrtle we would make the final dash to the safety of the screen porch, where we would collapse, breathless, and lie flat on our backs, tingling with the deliciousness of terror. The monkey would go back to her box and wait for us to be ready to play again. But at last the day came when the monkey skipped the crepe myrtle step and was waiting for us on the ground when we came swinging down. She grabbed us both in her stringy arms and bit us neatly and cleanly—me on the neck, my sister on the upper arm. Then she turned loose and went skittering across the yard, looking back over her shoulder and saying, "Ech, ech, ech." I'll never forget the feel of those stringy arms around my neck and the hot monkey breath in my face.

My mother was horrified. She washed the tooth punctures with alcohol, put my sister and me to bed, closed the curtains, and crept around in the darkened room fussing over us and worrying about strange tropical diseases.

"Something will have to be done about that monkey," she said grimly. And at the supper table that night she took it up with my father. We could see it coming. She sat up very straight, wiped the corners of her mouth with her napkin, settled it carefully back into her lap, and drew a deep breath. "Jim," she said, "something will have to be done about that monkey." She paused, but my father did not respond. She continued. "He throws hen eggs at me, and he has bitten *all* of the children." We, the bitten children, felt the weight of that "all" and squirmed in our seats.

My father did not look up. "I'll think about it, Eleanor," he said.

But the next morning our little wounds were healing nicely, my mother increased the ferocity of her skirt flapping and improved her marksmanship with the dishwater, and for ten more years the monkey lived with our family.

When my sister and I finished high school we were sent up to college in Virginia. It was the first time we had been away from home, and we were homesick. I used to lie awake at night and think up gruesome things that might be happening, at that very moment, to my parents. Fire, snakebite, lightning, falling trees, attacks by bulls—I thought of everything. On winter days when I would wake up before dawn in that strange place and look out at freezing rain falling in the darkness, it seemed very unlikely that at least one of those things had not happened since my last letter from home. So, I thought it only natural when we got a telegram from my mother: "HORSE FATHER MONKEY STUNG BY YELLOW JACKETS STOP COME HOME STOP LOVE MAMA STOP." It was typical of my mother's bewilderingly economical style, and we rode the train home in agonies of imagination.

It was late evening when we arrived. It was spring, and the air was thick with the smell of wisteria and honeysuckle. "How could a bad thing have happened here?" I wondered.

My mother greeted us at the door. She looked worn out but relieved. She hugged us and cried just a little. "He's better. He came out of it this afternoon.

The swelling's gone way down. He's been asking for Araminta. She's on her way down from New York. I haven't told him about the monkey."

Finally, we sat her down and got the whole story: My father had left his horse tied to an oak tree when he went to feed the hogs. When he came out of the hog pen, the horse had gone mad and was plunging wildly against the rope. My father got close enough to see that there was a cloud of yellow jackets swarming all over the horse. The harder the horse tried to get away, the tighter the knot drew against the oak tree. My father saw that he had only two choices—he could shoot the horse, or he could go into the swarm and cut the rope. His gun was in the house, so he opened his pocket knife and dove into the yellow jackets. The monkey, who had been watching from a distance, leapt onto my father's back and held him tight around the neck. My mother, hearing the screams of the monkey and the pounding of the horse's hooves, got there just in time to see my father stagger out, black with yellow jackets. She said the only part of his body that was not covered with stings was his back where the monkey had clung to him. My father had been in a coma for two days. The horse was alive, but would be a crazy, wild creature all its life. The monkey was dead.

We tiptoed up the stairs and peeked into the bedroom. My father was asleep. "Real sleep," my mother whispered. We sat beside the bed and listened to him breathing. Then we heard the door open and Araminta came into the room. She didn't look at us, but went straight to my father. She sat on the edge of the bed and took his hands in hers. He opened his eyes and looked at her.

"Ariloo," he said. "The monkey is dead."

"I know, Jaz," she whispered. "But it's all right. I've come home." And she bent down and gave him a little kiss on the cheek.

Lynna Williams

Lynna Williams was born in Texas. After studying journalism at the University of Missouri, Williams earned an M.F.A. in creative writing at George Mason University in 1990. She has taught creative writing at Emory University since then. Her book *Things Not Seen and Other Stories* was published in 1992. Cited as a New York Times Notable Book of the Year, the book earned Williams a Georgia Author of the Year Award. She has won the Loft-McKnight Prize for short fiction and a Loft Mentor Series Prize, and in 1994 she received a Dobie-Paisano Fellowship from the University of Texas and the Texas Institute of Letters. Describing her discomfort with the label of southern writer, Williams says, "I write about outsiders who are inside of a culture where people believe in God, but they themselves don't. . . . My stories are set in the South. But I have a hard time calling myself a Southern writer." Nonetheless, the dark humor in "Comparative Religion," exhibited through its focus on a fragmented family, puts Williams in the same company as Cynthia Shearer, Pam Durban, and others who write with as much disaffection as affection about the contemporary southern family.

Comparative Religion

When my father was away, what my mother did was drive. He was in San Antonio, preaching a three-day revival, and all day in Mrs. Richards's class I'd been picturing my mother closed up tight in our house, waiting until something told her to go get into the Lincoln. In world history, an hour before the last bell, I could feel my mother opening the car door in her navy-silk shirtwaist and spectator pumps, her dark hair feathering her ears. *Wait for me,* I thought. I didn't know I'd said it out loud until Patty Bailey leaned over her desk behind me. She said, "It's too late, Ellen. Columbus already sailed." I wanted to tell her to shut up—that her mother was safe inside their house, watching *The Price Is Right* on TV. I tried to imagine what I'd do if this time my mother didn't wait for me—if this time I went home and the car wasn't there.

I put my head down on the cool of the desktop, just for a second. Then I heard the stabbing sound Mrs. Richards's little heels made on the tile floor. I sat up, sure that she was coming to ask me what was wrong, but she was headed the other way, toward the door, where the principal stood with a girl I'd never seen before. The three of them talked, and then Mrs. Richards did her duck walk to the blackboard, bumping the girl along in front of her.

"Class, this is Hester Sarah Solomon," she said, and then waited for us to do our part, which was a big, phony "Hello, Hester Sarah." Half the class gave up in the middle, though, because the new girl so clearly didn't care. She had turned halfway to the window and was staring out at the empty playground as if it were the big screen at the Starlite Drive-In. The dress she had on was the color of applesauce, and so big that she had bunched the skirt in her fists to keep from tripping on the hem. Her hair was baby-fine and blonde, done up in an old-lady bun at the top of her head, and someone had jerked the hair back from her temples so tightly that her eyes looked almost Chinese.

Mrs. Richards wanted to get back to Christopher Columbus. She reached out to touch the new girl's shoulder, to make her face the class, and Hester Sarah swiveled her head around. When I saw her face, I forgot about the Starlite Drive-In; Hester Sarah looked as if she'd been startled awake and didn't like it, not one bit. That was how my mother looked when we had been driving a long time and a car coming at us honked because our lights weren't on. When my mother finally saw the nighttime, she always said, "I am the light of the world" as she felt for the switch at the side of the wheel. That was a Bible verse, but it sounded more like one when my father said it.

"Hester Sarah's family came to Abilene from Oklahoma City," Mrs. Richards said. "She has one brother in junior high and another in kindergarten, and her father is the new pastor of—" Mrs. Richards skittered to a stop.

"Gates of Grace Holy Apostolic Community," Hester Sarah said. She rolled the words out like a banner, and I knew exactly how she would sound quoting Scripture.

Mrs. Richards chipped in an "Oh, yes," but without conviction. Like me, she was used to churches with "First" in their names—churches like my father's, where she sang soprano in the choir. I said the name of the Reverend Solomon's church in my head; I knew that apostles were disciples, and that the gates of grace must be the way into heaven. But "Gates of Grace Holy Apostolic Community" used up too many words, the way Patty Bailey did when she brownnosed my father on Sunday mornings: "Oh, Reverend Whitmore, your sermon was just so holy, and righteous, and beautiful."

The other girls in the room were making little cawing sounds over Hester Sarah's dress, led by Patty, who now swung one leg out from under her desk and caught mine. "You can go to each other's church," she said, and snorted through her fingers. "Maybe she'll lend you something to wear." Patty said it loud enough for Mrs. Richards to hear, and Mrs. Richards charged halfway down the row to threaten her with study hall. Hester Sarah had heard too, but she went back to watching the playground. I'd gone a whole ten minutes without thinking about my mother, but suddenly I was sure she was still in our driveway. She'd have the nose of the Lincoln pointed toward Fitzgerald Street so that she could see me cut the corner at the top of the block.

Mrs. Richards finished with Patty and went back to the front of the class. She asked Hester Sarah to take a seat, and pointed to a desk at the end of my row. Hester Sarah started toward it, but when she was even with Patty Bailey's desk, she stopped. Just like that, she leaned over and put her face next to Patty's. She was staring at Patty's cheeks, which every girl in the room knew had been dabbed with Tangee Junior blush before the eight-thirty bell. "Whore of Babylon," Hester Sarah said, as if it were the answer to a question. Before Mrs. Richards could get to her, she said it again.

When I ran down Fitzgerald Street, the trees and the other houses seemed not to be there. All I could see was my mother's face inside the car. I ran harder, but she had seen me and was already pulling out of the driveway to come meet me. I stepped off the curb into the street, and my mother leaned over to throw open the passenger door. "Come on," she said, "I've been waiting," which was what she always said, as if I had deliberately held us up by going to grade school.

I threw my book bag into the back seat, and my mother took off before my right leg was all the way in the car. I didn't tell her how that felt, the sensation of my best penny loafer pulling along the street. I just lifted my foot into the car as fast as I could and tugged the door shut.

"Safest place to be is in a car," my mother said, and I nodded, because I knew she believed it. She drove slowly and carefully on the city streets, where someone my father knew might see us, but then we were out of Abilene and on the highway. I pushed myself up until I could see the buildings downtown shimmying in the rearview mirror, like a cartoon mirage. Just then my mother hit the brake, hard, to get off at the exit to Sweetwater, and I had to stretch my legs out to keep from falling. I knew we weren't going to Sweetwater. We weren't going anywhere; we were just driving around.

Sometimes when we were in the car together, my mother talked the whole time, not to me exactly but out loud. She usually talked about something she saw: a house with a fluttery windmill reminded her of flying in a plane; little kids stepping off a school bus made her wonder if the road was safe to cross. Other times she was quiet, and if I tried to talk, she shook her head no. This time she didn't say a word for hours. I didn't look at the clock—she didn't like that—but once or twice I saw the odometer turn over. We were going in a circle, I thought, and I was trying to imagine how Mrs. Richards could make this a story problem in math: Mrs. Whitmore leaves her house at 3:00 P.M. and drives a million miles. Why doesn't she just go home?

Then we turned off on a farm-to-market road, which looked like a skinny black line drawn through acres and acres of dried-out ranchland. On both sides of the road cattle bunched together at stock tanks, waiting their turn to drink. I was wishing I could draw a cow that didn't look like Lassie when my mother said, "Cattle." She did that sometimes, said what I was thinking, but I still jumped a little when it happened.

She slowed the car almost to a stop and watched the cows on her side of the road. "Look how close they are to each other," she said. "They don't like being alone; sometimes, in a storm, they crowd together so tight that one of them suffocates."

I must have made a sound, because my mother looked over at me. "We're safe, Ellen. We have room, and we can breathe, and nobody can get in unless we let them. And if they try, we'll just drive away."

Nobody had ever tried to get in the car, and we were still driving away. I didn't say that out loud, though; this wasn't school. At school, if I thought

Columbus was crazy to get in that dinky little ship, I said so to the whole class, and all that happened was that Mrs. Richards said, "What does the book say about your question, Ellen?"

My mother pressed down on the accelerator, and in a minute the cattle were behind us. After another mile she started to beat on the steering wheel rhythmically with the flat of her hand; she kept looking over at me, as if somehow I wasn't doing my part. As far as I knew, my part was to sit in the front seat and hope that my mother wouldn't drive us to the edge of the world. But things changed with her; that was the point. So I opened my mouth. What came out was how I'd missed "indefatigable" in the practice spelling bee, and about "Moira, My Darling," an Irish ballad that Mr. Pitts was teaching us in chorus.

It was almost dark, and I didn't know where we were anymore. My mother was still thumping the steering wheel, and I tried to think of something else. "We have a new girl in our class. Her father's the minister of a little church; it could be somewhere out here." I drew in my breath and let it out slowly. "It's called Gates of Grace Holy Apostolic Community." My eleventh birthday was four months away, but I'd started sixth grade that fall with kids who were already twelve. I was in the best reading group, the one named for a bird of prey. But "apostolic" still sounded wrong, not the way Hester Sarah had said it.

I said the church name again, but I didn't stop there. I knew I could tell my mother the rest of it, what Hester Sarah had said to Patty, and not just because "whore of Babylon" came from the Bible. Most of my friends' mothers had baby names for anything to do with people's bodies. Patty's mother was the worst: on our last choir trip Mrs. Bailey had gone up and down the line asking the girls if anyone needed to wee-wee before we left. At least when my mother talked to me, she called things by their right names. "Patty made fun of her," I said, "and the new girl called her a whore of Babylon."

My mother was so still that I looked to see if the car was moving in a straight line, afraid that somehow she had fallen asleep. I was half reaching for the wheel when she said, "Christ on the cross." I pulled my hand back and closed my eyes. Nobody's mother talked like that. The car filled up with the words, like a birthday balloon on a bicycle pump, and my mother's face expanded. She was looking at the road, but her right hand came off the wheel and floated near her mouth. "Gates of Grace," she said through her fingers. "Gates of Goddamned Grace."

The car skidded a little, and the driver of a pickup truck coming the other way leaned on his horn. My mother blew out her breath, and just as the pickup passed us, she jerked the Lincoln over to the shoulder and then straightened it again. I didn't try to stop myself from sliding off the seat. The dashboard was right there, and I pushed my forehead into it. I closed my eyes and thought of

Tweety Bird tricking Sylvester the Cat. Something else I'd learned about riding with my mother was that if I hurt myself, even a little, she'd stop the car.

She said "Ellen" once, and then again, and then "Jesus." But she wasn't saying a prayer. She pulled onto the shoulder, and when the car stopped, she jumped out and ran around to my door. I stayed where I was, not moving, and my mother opened the door. She sat sideways on the seat, her feet spraying gravel underneath, and pulled me up into her arms.

I let her push back my bangs and feel my forehead. After a minute she stopped saying my name, which worried me a little, and I opened one eye. I had to be careful: the point was to get us home, not to a hospital. At a hospital they'd see I wasn't hurt; I couldn't be sure what they'd see about my mother.

"Mama, what happened?" I tried to make my voice all puzzled and sweet.

"You threw yourself on the floor, that's what happened," my mother said, and she let go of me. She left the car and began to slide down the embankment. I waited for a minute, pinching my forehead a little because I wanted to, not because crying was going to get me anywhere. When my mother didn't come back, I got out of the car and started toward her. I kept one foot turned out, so I could run if I needed to.

I had almost reached her when she said, "You stay there, Ellen Ann. Stay there and think about what you did."

I said I was sorry, and I was. I was sorry that my father was in San Antonio. I was sorry that cars had been invented.

"You're all alike, you know that? You and your father and your little friend who calls people names. You won't let anyone alone. You won't let them be." She spoke breathlessly.

I moved my head, just a little, in case a nod was what she wanted.

"You could have told me you wanted to go home," she said. "But you didn't do that, did you? You pretended you were hurt to get your way, and you didn't care how you made me feel."

If I had said "I want to go home," we'd be in Mexico by now, but I didn't say so. Maybe she'd forgotten, but once she drove so far that we had to spend the night in Arkansas in a motel with a giant horse on the roof. I hadn't cried then, and I wasn't going to now. All I did was wait. The light was gone, and our bodies blended in the dark, ran together, until all our edges were gone. "We were having a nice drive, and you ruined it," my mother said. "Next time you can just stay home; what do you think about that?"

Now was the time to cry, to say how sorry I was, to swear that we could drive a million miles, a trillion, and go home only when she wanted. I was getting ready to, but a car passed by, and the headlights threw me off, pulled my eyes to the road. I wondered who was in that car, and then, even though she was one good reason I was standing in weeds, I thought of Hester Sarah Solomon. Hester Sarah's family would be singing, I thought, an old hymn like "Just As I Am" or "Abide With Me." Or maybe she and her brothers were counting stars, while her father told them about God's holy firmament. Maybe they were coming home from getting ice cream to celebrate Hester Sarah's first day in a new school. I almost smiled, but then my mother passed me on the way to the Lincoln. She was inside before I could climb up the embankment, and when I got to the top, the car was already rolling. I waited, counting the heartbeats under my hand, and when I got to five, I started to run.

First Baptist, my father's church, had a smooth green lawn, nineteen steps up to the sanctuary, eight ivory columns, and a stained-glass window for every disciple but Judas. Andrew fished from a little wooden boat, bobbing on a slash of blue; James and John mended their nets between two fig trees; Simon Peter, who was my favorite, had a two-part window, like an episode of *Bonanza* that began one week and ended the next. On top he sat at the Last Supper, elbows on the table, promising Jesus that he would never, ever betray him; below he denied to a mob of red and yellow dots that he had been a disciple at all. Bartholomew had a window, and Philip, and Thomas, and Matthew, and the other James, the other Simon, and Thaddaeus. Where Judas would have been, a lamb grazed at the foot of a cross. The cross was empty, because we were Southern Baptists, and our idea was that Jesus was up in heaven looking down. Never a moment passed when he wasn't watching over us, my father said every Sunday; the closeness of his watch was a measure of how much he loved us.

But inside our house on Fitzgerald Street, for every "In Jesus' name we pray, amen" that my father said out loud at meals, for every Bible verse, for every sermonette on God's love and God's law, exactly two commandments really mattered. The first, "Don't hurt your mother," was my father's. The second was "Don't tell on her," and that one was mine.

When I was little, my mother was crazy. She went into the hospital when I was three, and came out, and went back in. When she was out, she lived with my grandparents up in Kansas City. I was five and a half when she came home to Abilene. She had a special brass case for pill bottles, and an address book with nothing in it but doctors' names, and—I remembered this on my own—some missing hair in back, because apparently my grandmother's beautician had problems of her own. In all that time my father had prayed maybe a million prayers for her, and the Sunday after her return he told a packed church that Anna Starr Whitmore had been restored to us by the loving hand of God.

When my mother came home, the clean and quiet of her own house made her smile, and every day after breakfast she lingered in a different room, re-learning it, relearning us. She memorized my dolls' names, and brewed real tea for my tea parties on the screen porch. She came to every one of them dressed in her Sunday clothes. And she played with my father, too. Once, when the three of us sat down to breakfast, she looked right at me and said, "Herbert, pass Daddy the butter, please. You need a haircut, Herbert—how can you see with all that hair in your eyes?"

Across the table, my father began to fold his toast in half.

"I'm a girl," I said, because that was my only line.

"Herbert Ann, then; pass Daddy the butter," my mother said, and when my father raised his head, she started to laugh. He sailed the toast high over the table, and it touched down in her open hands.

After she came home, my mother was fine for a long time. If anybody wanted to ask me, she was still fine. The driving around had started in the summer, but I hadn't said a word to my father. I had thought and thought about it: I couldn't tell my father without hurting my mother. So when he left town, I ran all the way home after school, and when my mother pulled out of the driveway, I got into the car.

When my father was home, my mother did her best: she never missed a beauty-shop appointment or a Women's Missionary Union meeting at church, and when he held the passenger door open for her, she hopped right in. She wore hats on Sundays, pastel ovals outlined with lace, and as my father drove, she listened carefully to the sermon he was about to give. "Grace is never earned," he had said the week before, and my mother had said right back, "Then grace shouldn't work." He laughed and told her he'd change it to "A state of grace is never earned." My mother smiled, and for just that long I saw what my father saw.

But it wasn't always Sunday morning. And then one day I thought about my mother all the time. One day in school we did an experiment in science class. Mrs. Richards pumped air into a plastic bag, a little at a time, and we watched it swell and swell until finally the bag popped. Even though I'd known it was com-ing, I still jumped—and that was when I pictured my mother living in a see-through bag, watched by my father, and the choir, and the Dorcas Ladies Bible Class. The thing was, the car was bigger than a plastic bag. And in the car I was the only one watching her.

At times, when my father was home, when my mother was trying hard to be well, I thought it would all work out. My mother could stay with us, and my father could keep his miracle, and all I had to do was get in the car. But when I told my mother about Hester Sarah Solomon and the Gates of Grace Holy Apostolic Community, I saw her face. I heard what she said. And I knew why my father's prayers for my mother had stopped working. My mother didn't believe in God. I had thought I was the only one.

My report cards, every one of them all the way back to kindergarten, said I wasn't working up to my potential. But I had worked to believe in God. I tried much harder than I ever tried with fractions. When I was little, still expecting that one morning I'd wake up and be a Christian like everyone else, I was sure that believing was just a matter of time and effort. I mean, I took swimming lessons for years, and all that ever happened was I got wet. But one day I put my head under the water, I kicked out, and I could swim. Sooner or later, I believed, I'd bow my head one Sunday morning and be touched by the Holy Spirit, as my father always described it happening for him. I could close my eyes and, maybe, see Casper the Friendly Ghost, but that was it. I didn't stop trying, though. I never sat where I wanted to in church—in the last pew in the sanctuary, with the kids who chewed gum and wrote notes. I stayed up front, next to my mother, and I prayed. I gave my allowance to missionaries. I went to church camp. I sang hymns. Nothing happened.

So when I was eight, I went down the aisle one day at the close of the service and told my father I had accepted Jesus as my personal Lord and Savior. He kissed the top of my head, right there in church, and a week later he baptized me. I was sure that saying I believed, out loud in front of everyone, would somehow make it true. But all that happened was that I wasn't just a nonbeliever anymore. I was a nonbeliever and a big fat liar.

Hester Sarah Solomon believed. All you had to do was look at her to know that. And watching her, just for that minute when she said the name of her father's church in front of the class, I began to think about the possibility that nothing was wrong with my mother and me. Maybe something was wrong with our religion.

The morning after I bumped my head, the house was quiet when I got up for school. My mother wasn't downstairs, and I didn't know whether she was awake or not. I knew she had been up late after we got home, because she'd cooked a stack of waffles for me to warm up. They were in the refrigerator, with a note on church stationery that said she loved me, and that she'd see me later. The note was an old one; she kept it in the junk drawer to use after our drives.

I walked backward most of the way up Fitzgerald Street, watching the house, half expecting to see my mother come outside to get an early start on sitting in the car. For the first time, I wondered if part of what made her do it was how many Bibles my father owned, the framed pictures of his seminary classmates, the watercolor of the hills above Jerusalem that hung over the fireplace.

I was on the school's front steps when I heard the first bell ring, and I cut across the main hallway to get to class. As I passed the principal's office, I saw Hester Sarah Solomon with a man I was sure was her father. They were in the outer office, and I watched Mr. Shipp come out to take them inside. Hester Sarah's dress, the color of tuna salad, was worse than the one the day before, and the Reverend Solomon was turning a gray felt hat over and over in his hands. With every rotation, the shiny sleeves of his sport coat snaked above his wrists. I could see he was a preacher from Hester Sarah's face. The whole time he talked to Mr. Shipp, her eyes were fixed on his mouth, as if she could see every word, in capital letters, as it came out.

The tardy bell rang, and I had to get past the glass wall of the office before I could run. All through first period I waited for Hester Sarah to come back. Finally the door opened, and there she was, with Mr. Shipp, exactly like the day before. But this time, when she came to the blackboard, she looked out at the class.

She toed the tile with her right sneaker, and I heard Patty whisper, "Woolworth's. Two pair for two dollars." But she said it really low, and when Hester Sarah looked our way, Patty sucked in her breath so hard she whistled.

"I have to say I'm sorry," Hester Sarah said, and closed her mouth. Mrs. Richards sighed, a tiny sound like a dollhouse door shutting, and asked if Hester Sarah didn't have something more to say.

"I was wrong," Hester Sarah said, and as Mrs. Richards nodded, she added, "It's not up to me to say who's a whore of Babylon and who's not. That's up to God."

Hester Sarah lingered a little on "whore," but all Mrs. Richards did was flutter her hands. From the choked-off sounds behind me, I knew that Patty was about to cry, but she was quiet when Hester Sarah came down our row. The boys drew in their feet as she passed.

Mrs. Richards told us to get into our reading groups, and she put Hester Sarah in the lowest group, the one named for the state flower of Texas. I skipped my turn to read with the other Eagles so that I could listen to Hester Sarah, two rows over. She sounded out even baby words, like "farmer" and "weather." But I knew that the Ten Commandments were real to her. I knew that if I went up to her on the playground and said "Number eight," just like that the answer would come back: "Thou shalt not steal." I thought of her face when she looked at her father, and I thought that 99 percent of the Reverend Solomon's sermons were not about God's love, God's mercy, or God's eternal forgiveness. The Reverend Solomon would preach about sin, I thought—about casting out sin and demons, about escaping the flames of hell. The Reverend Solomon would preach about saving people, whether or not they wanted to be saved.

My father had been home from San Antonio only two weeks when he had to leave for Dallas. I got up early, took the chicken legs left over from Sunday lunch out of the fridge, and wrapped them in tinfoil. I usually took money to school for a hot lunch, but Hester Sarah brought her lunch, and in a paper bag, not a lunch box. She ate alone; Patty Bailey had made sure that the other girls wouldn't talk to her. But Hester Sarah acted as if she had arranged to be alone, for the greater glory of God.

My parents weren't downstairs yet. I unfolded a grocery bag and threw in the chicken, three oranges, a plastic container of French green beans, another of creamed corn, and a slab of red-velvet cake. We always had little cartons of milk around from choir suppers on Wednesday nights, and I put in half a dozen of those. I filled a Thermos with apple juice. I put in some paper plates and plastic forks. I was picturing myself laying down a trail of leftovers, leading Hester Sarah right to me. When I couldn't fit anything else into the bag, I lifted it into my book bag, heaved the book bag off the table with both arms, and called upstairs to say I was going. I was almost down the driveway when the screen door banged, and my father called for me to come back. He walked part of the way to meet me.

"You're going without saying good-bye?" he said. "You know I'm leaving today, and you just go sailing out the front door?" He was wearing the pants of his suit already, but with his blue-velour robe, the one my mother and I had given him for Christmas.

"I thought you were going next week." That was a lie. I had the dates for every revival meeting for a year marked off on the calendar in my room, but I knew he'd believe me. He'd believe anything.

"I'll only be gone for four days," he said. "The phone numbers are upstairs on my desk. You know you can call me, but I'll be home before you want to, probably."

We both knew what was next. "You and your mother take care of each other," he said, as if such a thing might actually happen. After a minute he reached out to hug me, and he felt the weight of the book bag on my shoulder. "Ellen Ann, what are you carrying around?"

I made my voice shake a little. "There's a new girl in my class who's hungry, I think. I'm taking some food so she'll have lunch with me." I tacked a little sob onto the end of the sentence.

My father leaned over to kiss my forehead. "You share your lunch every day if you want," he said. "When I get back, we'll see what else we can do." I let him knuckle-kiss my hand, a routine from my baby days, and then he stepped onto the porch. I hadn't even reached the sidewalk before I heard him call my mother's name, and I knew he'd gone back to watching her.

In the lunchroom I wrapped both arms around my grocery bag and followed Hester Sarah, ignoring Patty Bailey, who wanted to know where I thought I was going. Hester Sarah went to one end of a table in the far corner, and I dropped into a chair opposite her. At the other end two kids I knew from the playground picked up their trays and left. Hester Sarah unwrapped her sandwich, smelly pink meat on white bread, while I took out what I'd brought. I had covered half the table before I started pulling cartons of milk out of the bag.

"You got a tapeworm?" she said, and smiled. Mrs. Richards had shown us way too many color pictures of parasites in science the week before, but I hadn't thought that Hester Sarah was paying attention. She kept a Bible open on her desk, and every day a new pamphlet was stuck between pages of the Old Testament. Mrs. Richards had given up trying to stop her, and she played with the pamphlets all day, standing them at different angles so that none of us could miss the red headlines at the top. Today's pamphlet asked, "Will You Vacation Eternally in the Fiery Pit?" The illustration was of a terrified family of four, with matched luggage, falling through space.

"Will you help me eat all this?" I said. I hadn't said boo to Hester Sarah since she'd started school, and I thought I'd have to explain why I was all at once her friend. But she waved her hand at me, as if temporal matters didn't concern her. After a minute I understood: if I was sitting at her table, God had sent me. This close, her Chinese eyes were the color of tap water. I unwrapped the chicken legs, and Hester Sarah wadded up her sandwich without taking a bite.

"I haven't said the blessing yet," she said.

I nodded, careful not to turn my head to see if Patty Bailey was watching us. Hester Sarah put her hands together under her chin. "Heavenly Father, we thank thee for your bounty, and ask that you bless us this day, that all we do may be for thy glory. Keep us from Satan's path, O Lord, for truly we know his snares await even the most righteous. In Jesus' name we pray to be his apostles, forever and ever, amen." Her head stayed down, because I was late repeating the "amen." When I did, Hester Sarah opened her eyes and lifted a forkful of creamed corn to her mouth.

I was stalling now. I had imagined how this would go more than once, but Hester Sarah at the table was different from Hester Sarah in my head. A scary church was one thing that no one had tried with my mother and me. "I didn't see your brothers at recess," I said to Hester Sarah. "They're not sick, are they?"

"My brothers are doing mission work with our daddy over at Baird. When they grow up, the church'll be theirs."

"What do you get?" I felt my face go red, but she gave me that same never-mind wave of her hand.

"I get to love the Lord, and serve him all my days, and when I die, a place will be reserved for me among the ranks of righteous women."

I said "Oh," which was stupid but better than what I was actually thinking, which was "Big whoop." But Hester Sarah wasn't watching me. She had been alternating bites of green beans with chicken, her tongue flicking in and out of her mouth.

"Hester Sarah?" I said, as if she weren't right across the table, practically nose down in the red-velvet cake. "Can I talk to you about something?"

She bounced a little in her chair. "God's moving in your heart, isn't he? I've had a feeling all day that he was going to bless someone."

"All I know is I had to come talk to you." I crossed my fingers under the table. "There's this girl I know." I paused to see if Hester Sarah was buying that, but I didn't see any doubt on her face. Hester Sarah didn't have doubts—that was the point. "There's this girl I know, and she and someone else in her family—it's her aunt, I think—don't believe in God. I was wondering what would happen in your church about something like that. How you would help them, I mean." I'd meant to make my voice shake, but the shakiness started without me.

Hester Sarah was looking at me as though "whore of Babylon" would be a major compliment. "I know they didn't want to be this way," I said. "It's just something that happened."

She had put down her fork and was sitting with her head tilted back a little, as if she were God's vessel and I were pouring my story into her. "The devil isn't something that just happens to you," she began. At "you" I felt something give in my chest. Then I realized she didn't mean me in particular. "Salvation doesn't just happen either. If you want to be saved, you have to believe in the Lord God. Looking for shortcuts is blasphemy."

She didn't have a bit of trouble pronouncing "blasphemy." She was quoting her father, I was sure, and I tried to think of something my father said on Sunday mornings. "What about the healing power of God's love?" I said. Then I wished I hadn't. That was my father's big idea, and it wasn't working anymore.

"God heals those who bow before him, who worship his holy name."

I tried to imagine people lining up to join Hester Sarah's church. I spoke slowly, the way Mrs. Richards did when she taught long division. "What I asked you was how your church would help them believe. But it's okay if you don't know. I was just wondering."

I told myself that it was better this way. Hester Sarah ate with her mouth open, and my mother would die before she believed that that was God's will.

Hester Sarah's eyes were wet at the corners. She reached across the table, and her hand caught mine and held it. "Unbeliever," she said. I realized that I'd never before heard Hester Sarah give a right answer.

"Quit it," I said. "You're not making any sense."

"God makes sense," she said, and I had to catch my tongue sliding out of my mouth. My mother could drive me around until I went to college; college wasn't that far away.

A tiny wrinkle appeared between Hester Sarah's eyes, and she got up right there in the lunchroom and, still holding my hand, marched to my side of the table. She stood over me, and every time I shifted away from her, she moved in closer, until her mouth was hot against my ear. "If thou wilt not hearken unto the voice of the Lord thy God, the Lord shall smite thee with madness, and blindness, and astonishment of heart."

Hester Sarah was finished with me. She drew back her head and walked to her seat. She stacked the empty food containers and lifted them into my grocery bag. All I did was stare at her, as if no one in my whole life had preached to me. My mother is astonished of heart, I told myself. Just like that, there was one thing I believed.

A half hour before the last bell Hester Sarah was at the world map, sliding her finger up and down South America in search of Afghanistan. I tried not to look at her. I hadn't told on my mother, not exactly, but I had come closer than ever before. All I had to show for it was one "If thou wilt not hearken," which I didn't know for sure was a real Bible verse, and what felt like a whole chicken sideways in my throat.

I blinked. A watery Mrs. Richards was sending Hester Sarah back to her seat, but all at once Hester Sarah bent double, her hands on her knees, and started to cry. Some of her hair came loose, scattering bobby pins and streaming over her face. "It hurts," she said. "It really hurts." Mrs. Richards knelt by her, asking what was wrong, and then helped her into a chair. "Class, will someone please walk with Hester Sarah to the nurse's office?" she said.

No one volunteered, not even when Mrs. Richards asked a second time, but when Hester Sarah moaned, I couldn't stand it. I raised my hand and bounced my desk chair back onto Patty Bailey's foot, because she was the reason no one else had a hand up. When Patty yelled, I pulled the chair free without saying I was sorry. Mrs. Richards and I walked Hester Sarah to the door. "Feel better, dear," Mrs. Richards said, and her hand hovered over Hester Sarah's back without actually patting it.

In the hallway I told Hester Sarah to hold on to my arm, and tried to feel good that I was helping someone less fortunate. But all I managed was to not say what I was thinking, which was that the devil and I were as pleased as punch to be taking her to the nurse.

Hester Sarah put her arm in mine, and we started down the hall. But at the corner of the passage that led to the nurse's office she swatted my hand away. "Come on," she said, and when I didn't move, "Do you want to do this or not? Hurry up before someone sees us."

"Do what?" I said, but when Hester Sarah started to run, I followed her. She slammed through the big double doors at the front of the school and ran down the steps. On the sidewalk I grabbed for her arm again. "What are you doing?" I said. "Aren't you sick?"

Hester Sarah shook me off. "Which way is your house?"

"What are you talking about?" I said. "We're going to the nurse."

She made a small, exasperated sound. "It's more important to go to your house, Ellen. We can tell your mother I missed the bus and need a ride home, and when we get there, my father will pray with the two of you. In Oklahoma City he brought a family of five to the Lord, and not one of them had ever been inside a church, not once in their whole lives."

"My friend and her aunt go to church," I said, bearing down on "friend" and "aunt." "They go to a beautiful church."

I didn't know what my face looked like, but Hester Sarah could have been smelling her sandwich again; her nose was wrinkled, and she was breathing through her mouth. She held up two fingers. "Number one, my church is beautiful, because we believe in God. And number two, I know you're talking about your mother not believing in God, not anybody's aunt. I heard Patty Bailey saying that your mother was sick when you were little. She's sick again, isn't she? The devil's got hold of her, and she's sick."

I was pretty sure now that Hester Sarah was in the wrong reading group. "Since when do you listen to Patty?" I said. "You should hear what she says about you."

"I listen to God," she said. "He wants me to help bring your mother and you into his presence. I know he does."

"Do your ears work?" I sounded like a little kid whose nose was running, even though it wasn't. "I didn't say anything about my mother and me." The sunlight was so bright that I had to squint to see her, and when I did, she had captured her hair in her hands and was piling it on top of her head.

"I thought you wanted to do something to help her," she said. "God led you to talk to me, but now you're afraid. Don't be afraid."

My mother was afraid of everything, I thought, except this; she'd never been afraid I would tell. I wished for the nurse, Mrs. Richards, my father, for anybody but Jesus, to get me out of this. "I talked to you about my friend and her aunt, and that's the truth," I said carefully. "I mean it, Hester Sarah. I don't know what Patty said, but it doesn't matter, because tomorrow she'll tell people you made the whole thing up."

What was true was that I wasn't living up to my potential. I hadn't done my homework. I hadn't thought this through. At night when I had rolled my movie on the inside of my eyelids, my mother and Hester Sarah were barely in it. All I saw was me, the way it would be if my mother never stopped driving me around, if she never got better, if things were always the way they were now.

We hadn't gone beyond the sidewalk in front of the school, and I heard the last bell ring inside. I could feel the vibration all the way down my back. Any minute now kids from our class would storm out the doors and see us; Mrs. Richards would be right behind them. She would see us, and the principal would call my mother to come get me.

I turned back to Hester Sarah, who was trying to free the hem of her dress from between her sneakers. When she told her parents about this, both of them would be proud of her. Both of them would be at home until she grew up.

"Come on," I told her. "It's only five blocks."

She didn't think I meant it, but when I started down the sidewalk, she was right behind me, reciting one Bible verse and then beginning another, as if each were a point on a map. I didn't talk to her, or even turn around.

When we reached Fitzgerald Street, I knew before I looked that my mother was in the car. Hester Sarah had stopped, and I had to walk back to her. "These houses are huge," she said. "You live in one of these?"

I waited for the Bible verse about rich men and heaven, but it didn't come. What was coming toward us, right this minute, was my mother in the Lincoln. I left Hester Sarah on the sidewalk, yelling at me to stop, and I ran into the street. When my mother slowed down, I opened the door and threw myself inside. Hester Sarah was still yelling, but I knew my mother would think it had nothing to do with me.

We were almost at the end of the street before I raised myself up to look at Hester Sarah in the rearview mirror. I watched her getting smaller, but I didn't worry about her. She was standing in front of the Talliaferros' house, and the Talliaferros drank highballs in the back yard before dinner. Mrs. Talliaferro would call the Reverend Solomon to come get Hester Sarah, I was sure, and maybe he would save the whole family before he and Hester Sarah went home. Maybe next time she'd get her own mission trip to Baird.

I dropped back into the seat. When I looked over at my mother, I thought from her face that we might really be driving all the way to Mexico this time, and I closed my eyes. I pushed my head into the leather and imagined that it was night. My mother and I were safe in the car, riding and riding, and I asked her what she believed, what she held sacred, what women like us wanted most in all the world.

Philip Lee Williams

Philip Lee Williams is the author of eight novels and two works of creative nonfiction. His books have been translated into Swedish, French, German, and Japanese, and he has published poetry and short stories in magazines and journals around the country. His books include *In the Heart of a Distant Forest* (1984), *All the Western Stars* (1988), *The Song of Daniel* (1989), *The True and Authentic History of Jenny Dorset* (1997), and *Crossing Wildcat Ridge: A Memoir of Nature and Healing* (1999), an account of his experience with open heart surgery. Williams is a public information writer for the Franklin College of Arts and Sciences at the University of Georgia. Through shifting points of view in "An Early Snow," he contrasts the struggle of an old woman against encroaching senility with the unhappy marriage of her daughter, who is beginning to realize that her dreams of the future will never come true.

An Early Snow

Nana had wandered off before. Once Jane found her sitting by the pond at Memorial Park feeding Ritz Crackers to a one-eyed swan. Nana was repeating the words of Communion as the swan nabbed snatches of cracker from her bony fingers. They took Nana home and tucked her into bed.

"Nana, what were you looking for?" asked Jane the next afternoon.

"I don't know," said Nana, penitent.

Then it would start all over again. She would be standing by the stove thinking of cornbread and wondering about the temperature of things. One thought bled into another. If you cooked cornbread at four hundred, what was the temperature of the human body, and was it hot that spring when her daddy died in his easy chair? The next thing Nana knew, she would be picking black seeds from the lily pods two blocks away. At first, these travelings frightened her, but then she could not understand why Jane would be cross about it.

Jane and Andrew decided they'd have to put Nana in a home.

"Her house isn't up to code, we'd have to let them tear it down," said Andrew. He was a thick man. When Jane had married him, Andrew was trim and busy, but he'd grown thick, and he had no particular plans. Jane wanted him to be trim and to take her skiing in Vail. Her gynecologist, Dr. Whitman, was a runner and took his wife to Vail. Everyone adored him.

"Well, what else are we going to do?" asked Jane. She sipped her coffee. "Tie her to the bed? I wish I had some ideas, but if we don't do something, we'll find her dead on the railroad tracks." He looked for a long time into his coffee.

"Andrew?"

"As long as you understand about the house," he said. "It was a good house in its day."

"I don't feel anything for that house." Jane rose from the kitchen table and walked to the window and looked out. A light snow fell down the slope toward her now-fallow garden plot. "I wish I felt something for that house. When I was a little girl, it scared me. It was big and dark and drafty, and then Daddy died. I wanted to move to Los Angeles."

"Why Los Angeles." Behind her, not turning toward her, his voice, flat and barely interested. No question mark on the end.

"Because I could be a movie star," she said. "Then the whole world would love me. Don't you think that's why people become movie stars, because they can't get enough people to love them at home? Don't you think that's it? That's why I love Tom Cruise. Have you ever read about his life? He had a terrible life. He just needs somebody to love him, and I love him."

"You just love his picture," said Andrew. He was getting up but he wasn't coming toward Jane.

"That house breathed at night after Daddy died," said Jane. "I lay upstairs and prayed to God that He would lead us to a house with more light, but it never happened. We just stayed on and on, and then I left, but Nana didn't leave. She was never going to leave from the beginning, though she said she would leave. She wasn't going to and she knew it."

"I've never been that attached to a thing," Andrew said. "I've got to be getting back to work. You do what you think is best. I mean, I'll do it, you just decide. You want to move her here, we could fix up the basement. It needs it anyway."

Jane turned from the snow and looked at her husband. His belt was on the last hole, and his features, which she had hoped were loving and kind, seemed froggy and swollen. His mouth held open slightly. She tried to imagine their wedding picture, but that was another man, just as silent but with more hair and less waist and with promise.

"I don't want her here," said Jane. "I could not bear it if she were here."

Nana inhaled the savory spices and watched the snow lie softly across the small square of her back yard. Every day, she felt more distant from her body, as if she were separating from it slowly, like a dowdy, cast-off shadow. Then again, hadn't she felt that way since Hiram died in his easy chair? That night, she'd felt an evaporation come over her. She was sitting, crying, and then she was leaning against the mantel, watching the woman weeping and holding her two girls on the sofa. It was strange and comforting. You could look with interest at your own body and life without worrying about it. Of the girls, Janie took it worse. Then again, Mary Jean was two years older. She already had one foot out the door.

Nana held open small boxes of marjoram, cinnamon, clove, and nutmeg. She ran them back and forth beneath her lips like someone playing a harmonica. Each one reminded her of a different time, but they all blended together. This was an early snow. It would melt tomorrow. Sometimes, there was an early snow, a herald of something, but it brushed the earth white and then melted away into cold rainwater. Why didn't it just fall as rain in the first place? Seemed like a waste of time to Nana.

She set the spice boxes on the table of her small kitchen. A smear of nutmeg stayed on her right thumb, and she brought it to her nose and thought of Christmas. When she was a girl back in Hailey, she and her daddy would go into their woods, sometimes staying half the day to look for a Christmas tree, a tall cedar with limbs so aromatic and thick a clutch of birds might be hiding inside it. They'd whack down the perfect tree, and drag it back, sometimes taking more than an hour. Her daddy would stop to light a cigarette and tell her about the land, and how it had always been Indian country.

"Far as you can see, honey, the Indians owned all of this, and they'd never even imagined a man with white skin," he said. "Can you imagine that? Ain't a square foot of this land wasn't owned by the Indians. And they loved it all, but we came in and they had to leave. People don't seem to think much about it, but I never got over it. I cain't get over thinking about the Indians living in this land and then just getting run out. Lived here for generations upon generations, missy, and they's just one day over-run and run out."

"Where'd they go, Daddy?"

"Some went out to Oklahoma, and others, well you know they went up in the high mountains up near Cherokee," he said. "You know about that. I took you and your sister there two years ago. If I'd been one of them, I'd of died before I went to Oklahoma."

Nana walked through the house, still smelling nutmeg. That meant it was Christmas. In fact, tomorrow must be Christmas Day. She did not have her tree up. What had become of her memory? She would have to go cut a tree herself. Maybe her daddy was already in the woods waiting for her. Sometimes men took an early start on women. Hiram had taken an early start. Where *was* that man?

Nana put on her coat and took a hatchet from the closet beneath the stairs. The hatchet did not look like the right tool, so she put it back and retrieved a hammer, which in its swing and heft seemed about right. Her daddy was probably already out there with a saw. She came outside, leaving the front door open. Flakes had collected in the crannies of the window screens. Yes, she thought, the Indians would already be in the woods waiting for her. They were probably impatient to leave.

Jane pulled into her mother's driveway. She remembered her grandfather's car, a 1939 Oldsmobile, a green humpbacked thing. Or maybe it was something else. She could never remember the makes of cars. In those days, she mostly memorized car tags from across America, and when they'd go on vacation, she knew every one, calling it out from a hundred yards before anyone could read the name. That always amazed her daddy.

The snow fell steadily now, in huge clumpy and disorganized constellations. They had predicted two inches, but there was already more than that, and the radar showed more snow coming from the southwest. Jane remembered the snowman her daddy made, long before the neighborhood fell into ruin. Mrs. Hightower lived across the street, a dignified professional widow of a tent evangelist who claimed he had "saved ten thousand lives." When Jane was small, she wanted to save ten thousand lives, but for years she thought he'd led them out of a collapsing mine or something, some gallant and selfless effort requiring massive strength and courage. When she found out all those newly saved people had financial obligations to Rev. Hightower, she thought less of him. He retired from the ministry to live out his life in comfort and did that for exactly two weeks before he died in a car wreck that he caused. No other cars were involved. He had simply missed a curve and drove off the road into an oak tree.

"Why in the hell am I thinking of you?" she asked.

Jane went into the house. The front door was open, and she closed it, shaking her head and calling for her mama. The house was freezing cold and smelled of spices. Jane did not wish to think of the *Arabian Nights,* but the spices reminded her. Those tales were her favorite adventures as a girl, and she would act them out, and she and her sister were princesses, veiled in old handkerchiefs, waiting for princes to come galloping out of the desert to rescue them. She and Mary Jean would argue about which of them had the most handsome prince. Jane said Mary Jean's prince would have bad teeth and a wig.

"Mama!" Jane cried. "Where are you? Did you know the front door was standing wide open?"

She came through the living room and saw the hatchet lying on the floor, and for a long time, she could not attach it to a story, to the sense of anyone's life.

Nana walked for nearly a mile before she found some woods. They moved the woods back and forth all the time. They could do anything these days, put a man on the moon, invent new spices that smelled like a swirl of nutmeg and cinnamon, move entire forests. The woods were here now. At least she had found them. She walked up a long driveway and then off it and into the forest. The snow was so heavy that even the spaces in the forest were filling.

"Daddy!" she called softly. "Come on out where I can see you." No. He wouldn't be right here. He and the Indians would have gone far into the woods to find the perfect Christmas tree. Christmas must have been a special time of year for Indians. Didn't her daddy tell her that? Yes. The Indians built the shed where they laid the baby Jesus. She could remember that picture in her childhood Bible, of the Indians standing before the baby Jesus and holding gifts. Their huge headdresses trailed the ground, and a few of them knelt. One sat bareback on a white pony with black patches. Nana saw that her sneakers were untied, and she knelt to work on them but they were a new kind of string. They required secret knots. When she was young, her brother had taught her secret knots, named them all, but then he'd gone off and gotten killed in the South Pacific on the island of France. There was the broad-tailed knot, the granny knot, the singing knot. Perhaps shoestrings now must be tied with a singing knot. She failed to recall its shape. She made several cross-loops and snugged them. She felt a massive shudder shake her, bone to bone.

"Now my feet are wet," she said out loud. "Daddy, I didn't mean to wet my shoes."

Nana's teeth chattered. Two squirrels leapt from one limb to another, shaking off a curtain of dusty snow. She walked for a hundred feet and decided that the hammer was too heavy to carry, so she dropped it and went onward. This was how you found the perfect Christmas tree, walking all day and stopping to admire each branch, even if you did run out of breath going up and down hills. Yes, this was the rougher country she remembered. Something was missing, though. She stopped.

The wind drew a breath of ice. Nana closed her eyes and tried to think. Yes, the aroma of a lit match coming up to her father's cigarette, that rich smell. Except they found that cigarettes made you sick. Her daddy got sick. Then he died, not able to breathe. Nana remembered the funeral and how her mother wept. Nana opened her eyes and knew that her father was not here. No, she was here to leave with the Indians. They were being run off their land, and she would have to go with them to Oklahoma or was it California? All things being equal, she had rather go to California. She had always read stories about California to her little girls, about the movie stars, about how everybody was rich and it was never cold, and they all had swimming pools. Were any of those people Indians? They had to be. In fact, all of them must be Indians.

California could be over any ridge.

Andrew came home from work and calmed Jane down. He called emergency rescue, and nine men in trucks came, one man to a truck. Each truck had a fat-nosed winch on the front. Most were mud-caked. They covered the immediate area in twenty minutes, keeping in touch with walkie-talkies. Police came, and then two cars from the Sheriff's Department along with Lawrence Dome, head of the county emergency management agency. Jane stayed with Andrew, calling her mother over and over, but everything seemed heavy and muffled in the snow, and the cold was a sinking thing, sinking through bone and flesh and through the earth into stone. Jane decided her mother was dead. She did not want to think that her mother would be found alive. There would be terrible moaning, the funeral home's thin lamplight, and she explaining that she was one of the two girls, that she was Janie. Some of the older people coming from out of town would not recognize her.

I was Janie, the quiet one. I made doll clothes in the attic and read *National Velvet* and wanted a horse but we couldn't afford one, could we? I read movie magazines but I did not want to be a star. I wanted to be a star's helper, the one who made up the stories they acted upon. I was the quiet one who loved a rainy day and who could sit in a chair by the fire in winter watching my daddy smoke his pipe and sit without doing anything else and not mind. He did not need the world to whisper in his ear. He could sit for hours doing absolutely nothing, and that drove my mother crazy because she wanted to go dancing, to the VFW for bingo, to fly up to New York for a shopping spree, to load us all on a truck and drive to California. I was Janie, the quiet one. Thank you so much for coming tonight. Yes, of course I remember you. You played cards each Saturday night with Nana and Daddy until you moved away. Your husband was with the Farm Bureau. And no, I do not remember you, but I will pretend I do. See the handkerchief wrapped in my hand? That is for my grief. That is for my loss.

Jane slapped herself twice on the cheek.

"Are you all right?" asked Andrew.

"I'm cold," said Jane. "It's getting colder. Can't you feel that it's getting colder?"

"Early snow is always the coldest snow," said Andrew. "My granny told me that." He called Mama very loudly as they walked. Then, "Early snow is always the coldest snow."

Nana hooked up with the Indians near a cedar tree. They weren't visible, but she could feel their presence. They lived on stealth. She would go with her daddy to the barbershop when she was a girl, and there was a big picture from Anheuser Busch on the wall. It was called "Custer's Last fight," and Indians were about to kill the gallant general. He would be dead any minute. Nan would sit and look at the picture, at the dead men of two races, and think of death, and what it must have felt like. To be dead. It was not conceivable. Those Indians had strength, and they were half-naked because it was a hot day. Now, they wore moccasins, she presumed, because they made no sound at all as she walked through the woods at their sides. One of Nana's shoes came off. She could not stop to pick it up or she would get left.

"Please, Daddy," she said.

She walked on through the woods, and she felt herself falling behind. An enormous leafless oak scratched the snow clouds with its bony fingers. She stopped against it, breathing hard, wondering how far California might be through here. She gathered some strength and limped on until she found that the woods were thinning, and she was standing in the parking lot that surrounded a gas station. She could see her breath, and it was white as an eagle's feather. Some man was talking at her, but he was not an Indian, and he was not her father, and she could not understand his language, and then he was picking her up in his arms, and she knew that hot cocoa was next and a coal-grate fire and the sound of the wind outside. She would tell her granny about the Indians. Perhaps they were down the road in New Hope.

Jack Thompson came running up to Andrew and Jane, smiling and nodding at the same time.

"Jane, Mal Smith just called in, and they found your mama over on the highway at the Amoco," he said. "She's cold and missing a shoe, but she's apparently all right." He paused for a moment. "She's all right." Jack was nodding to emphasize the words.

"How in the world did she get over there?" asked Jane vaguely, thinking, *I am one of the girls, and when I was small, I would listen to the stories about all the wonderful places in the world, and I was sure I was going to live in Greece or France and that my husband would be a count or maybe I'd live in Hollywood and my husband would be a movie star.*

"Thank God," said Andrew. "They have her inside the Amoco?"

"Mal said he was bringing her back to your place, so you can just go on home," he said. "Looks like our job is done here. A good ending. You don't always get a good ending. Jane, your prayers have been answered."

"My prayers," said Jane, nodding and trying to smile.

There was a sudden brightness on the street, as if the clouds were thinning and the sun might come out, then a thickness sank upon them, and a shudder of coldness slipped upon Jane's shoulders as she headed for the car.

Shay Youngblood

Shay Youngblood's *Big Mama Stories,* first published in 1989, introduced her to the literary world as a writer with an ear for dialect and an eye for human character. After an undergraduate education at Atlanta University, she earned her M.F.A. in creative writing from Brown University. In the 1990s she turned to novels and to playwriting, where she has been especially successful. She won the Hollywood NAACP Theater Award for best playwright in 1991 for her play *Shakin' the Mess outta Misery;* the Lorraine Hansberry Playwriting Award in 1993 for *Talking Bones;* and the National Theatre Award from the Paul Green Foundation in 1995 for *Square Blues.* In 2002 she was visiting writer-in-residence at the University of Mississippi. Her story "Born with Religion" won the Pushcart Prize. Her most recent novels are *Soul Kiss* (1997) and *Black Girl in Paris* (2000). Like the other Big Mama stories, "An Independent Woman" celebrates the strong character of a woman whom Youngblood regards as a pillar of the African American community of her childhood.

An Independent Woman

For years Mr. Otis, Big Mama's good friend Miss Louise's brother-in-law, kept Aunt Mae company on Sunday afternoons in her upstairs bedroom. She and Mr. Otis kept the door closed and the gospel singing on the radio turned up loud. Once I asked her what they be doing in her room with the door closed.

"We be taking care of grown folks' business," was all she said. Her answer shut my mouth but not my mind to thinking that it must be more than listening to the radio they be doing all evening.

After the sun settled down and darkness fell gently round Aunt Mae's house, she could be found sitting like a queen at the head of her kitchen table pouring short glasses of Southern Comfort whiskey for women Big Mama said were loose and men she said were loud.

"That baby sister of mine, Mae Francis, always have been fast. She smart though, real independent. That woman could charm the skin off a snake," Big Mama would say.

Aunt Mae lived by herself in a big, old wooden house down the street from me and Big Mama in St. Pete's Alley, in back of the cotton mill. Before I was born, a man that was seeing Aunt Mae on the side left her the house and all but one hundred dollars of his money when he died. His wife had passed shortly before he did, and his grown children tried to take Aunt Mae to court over it. But they couldn't prove that he was crazy or that she was a operator. Aunt Mae said she gave him a shoulder to lean on, some understanding, and plenty of good whiskey.

"That ought to be worth something. A woman has got to look out for herself. When that old man was making me promises, I had him set em in ink at a lawyer's office. I'd done heard too many empty promises."

At a glance, Aunt Mae wasn't pretty like a movie star, but she had a special sideways look in her eyes and a way with her hands and hips that made her seem younger than most women in their sixties. She still kept her copper-and-silver hair parted down the middle and waved down each side to her shoulders. She wore her dresses short and bright. And didn't she love to dance.

When Big Mama had to go to work at night sitting with a rich, old white lady across the bridge in Prayerville, I was sent down the street to spend those evenings with Aunt Mae. She taught me some things bout being a woman.

"Don't you ever, long as grass is green, go nowhere with a man unless you got money in your pocket. If you with a man that don't mean you no good you can always tell him to go to the devil and take you a taxicab or a Greyhound home," she useta say.

Aunt Mae taught me some important things—like how to wear a tall hat on a windy day, how to walk in high heels, and how to dance with fat men. She knew so much bout dancing cause when she was fifteen, she left her home in rural Lee County to make her fortune in the nearest city. Her first job was working as a dance hall girl. She would waltz or jitterbug round the floor with customers for a dime a dance. Fat men, she useta say, were the worst.

"All they ever wanna do was hug up and grind, so I useta plump myself up with a pillow to keep em from getting too close to my privates."

Women, she said, were her best customers. Most were middle-aged women looking for a lil warm after losing a girlfriend. The ladies, she said, were polite, big tippers, and almost never asked her to go home with them. The men, on the other hand, wanted to take care of her, but she was suspicious.

"They was expecting a compromise on my part that I could not make. I always have been my own woman. I was too independent to take like that without giving. Even when you get married, if that's a load you wanna bear, have your own. The wine taste sweeter and the berries have more juice when you have your own. When you've earned it. Take marriage for a instance. Now that's a job, darling. I earned my way dollar for dollar. I put up with other women, drunks, and gamblers, but the one thing I would not tolerate was a liar. I throwed Willie Pew out of his own house two days after I married him for lying to me."

"Did you let him come back Aunt Mae?"

"No m'am, but he wasn't too proud to beg. I told him to get up off his knobby knees and out of my face. I didn't want to hear that mess. Wasn't no room in my life for liars and that's all there was to it."

"What did you do when he left?"

"You mean when I put him out? I tell you, the day I left home and the day I got my divorce, it was like the Fourth of July. After the smoke cleared I felt free."

"So why you get married in the first place?" I asked.

"Why anybody would—for security. You got to understand, at that time I was sixteen years old and didn't have nothing but a few dimes from my dance hall days and a whole lotta ideas bout starting a after-hours liquor business. Willie Pew was good looking, he had money and brains enough to know I was a good woman. But his lying took something outta me. I never took him back in my heart. We took to going our own ways and soon parted. Forever after I decided to take a friend on the side when I felt a need. Usually them kind was married."

One time Aunt Mae said she run off with another woman's husband and run back two months later by herself. She said love only last till the shine wear off.

Mr. Otis was married. He drove a green-and-white taxicab every day cept Sunday, when he would show up at Aunt Mae's and give me a dime to go catch the ice-cream truck, making me promise to eat the cone outside and play on the porch till the street lights began to flicker on hours later. Then Mr. Otis would come down the stairs all happy-faced, smelling like whiskey and walking funny. Soon he would go home to Miss Tweedie.

We all went to the same church. Mr. Otis was a deacon. Aunt Mae, Big Mama, Miss Tweedie, and her sister was all in the choir together. One time I heard Big Mama and her best friend, Miss Louise, talking bout how shameless it was that Mr. Otis didn't spend his only day off with his wife. I thought bout Aunt Mae. She only got him once a week. Poor Miss Tweedie got him the other six.

One Sunday Miss Tweedie come knocking on the front door. I peeped out at her from behind the screen door wondering why she come. She was a tall, skinny woman with a stiff neck and gray hair slicked back of her head in a bun. She held her head to one side like she was listening to something way off.

"Tell your Aunt Mae that Miss Tweedie want to talk to her for a minute," she said, wiping sweat off her neck with a pocket handkerchief.

By the time this happened my best friend Jeanette had told me, most probably, what Aunt Mae and Mr. Otis be doing behind them closed doors all Sunday afternoon. I got scared. She also said Miss Alice threw a knife at her husband Mr. Henry the time she caught him in the Club Three with just his arms round another woman. I ran up the stairs two at a time and knocked hard on Aunt Mae's bedroom door.

"Aunt Mae, Miss Tweedie at the door. She want to talk to you." I could smell Mr. Otis's cigar stinking up the hallway. I wondered if Miss Tweedie could smell it too.

After some time passed Aunt Mae said, "Tell her I be right there." I ran back downstairs to deliver the message, then kneeled behind a big chair in the living room with a view of the front door. Aunt Mae took her time coming down the steps. When she got to the door she was buttoning her new pink housedress up the front. I put my head in my hands and started praying.

"What you want, Tweedie?" Aunt Mae asked her, real casual.

"Want you to know you can have him," Miss Tweedie said, wiping her neck and looking down at the bottom of the screen door.

Aunt Mae looked right at her for a minute, real surprised, then throwed back her head and laughed loud like she do when she having a good time.

"I mean it, Mae Francis. Since Otis took up with you, all I had is trouble. Folks talk. Even the pastor know where Otis be on Sunday after church. I'm through," she said, staring straight as she could back at Aunt Mae, speaking a lil louder, looking a lil higher.

"You got the wrong idea, Tweedie. I don't need a husband. I ain't got time to take care a one. What I have is a liquor business."

Miss Tweedie almost threw her neck straight up and said, "Otis ain't bought groceries in over two years. Told me his mama in Ohio needed some operations. I found out she been dead ten years. Tell him his clothes be on the front porch this evening. G'night Mae Francis. See you in choir rehearsal." Then she turned and walked away.

Aunt Mae went back upstairs, and a few seconds later Mr. Otis run out the front door trying to catch his wife. Me and Aunt Mae watched them out the living room window, both of us laughing out loud at the sight of Mr. Otis running on drunk legs behind Miss Tweedie with his shirt tail flying in the wind. Aunt Mae poured herself a tall glass of Southern Comfort and two splashes in a dixie cup for me. We didn't say nothing, but we was both thinking bout poor Miss Tweedie.

Aunt Mae wouldn't let Mr. Otis come back no more. She told him to his face that he was a no-good, lying skunk butt and should be ashamed for having caused Miss Tweedie so much malicious misery. She and Miss Tweedie was almost friends after that.

"Women got to stick together. Men like that give me a bad name. I try to give married women a break. I don't want to be cause of no interference like that."

Aunt Mae didn't miss Mr. Otis none.

When the Sunday after-dark crowd came later that night, Aunt Mae was laughing loud, cussing, and pouring drinks like it was any other Sunday. I mixed my splash of whiskey with a can of gingerale and sat where I could see and hear everything. One of the regular ladies that came to Aunt Mae's on Sunday night, Miss Corine, was sitting next to me by the refrigerator. That night she turned to me and asked me what I wanted to be when I was grown.

"I wanna be like Aunt Mae," I said. "I wanna be independent so every day be like the Fourth of July."

Miss Corine smiled at me and said, "Amen, chile." She knew what I was talking about. She was an independent woman herself.

Notes

Page 1, "When I read . . . it can be literature?!": African American Publications: Biography Resource Collections. http://www.africanpubs.com/Apps/bios/0559AnsaTina.asp

Page 1, "Her other novels . . . *You Know Better* (2002).": http://www.africanpubs.com/Apps/bios/0559AnsaTina.asp; http://www.harpercollins.com/catalog/author_xml.asp?authorID'15404

Page 23, "an unusually literate writer . . . field or beyond.": *Contemporary Authors Online* (Gale Group, 2001).

Page 53, "After ten years . . . I found none.": *Contemporary Authors Online* (Gale Group, 2000).

Page 84, "most important event of [his] life": *Contemporary Authors Online* (Gale Group, 2001).

Page 164, "At the age of fourteen . . . for six years.": http://www.emory.edu/EMORY _MAGAZINE/spring98/hajin.html

Page 164, "If I am inspired . . . has hurt us most.": *Contemporary Authors Online* (Gale Group, 2002).

Page 189, "I tend to see . . . connectedness": http://www.southernscribe.com/zine/authors/Joseph_Sheri.htm

Page 221, "Her stories have been published . . . *Epoch*.": http://www.ugapress.org/books/shelf/0820317047.html

Page 284, "a social history . . . that bind them.": http://www.olemiss.edu/depts/english/news/newsletter/1997fall/shearer.html

Page 310, "Sumner's next book . . . a little too much.": http://www.npr.org/programs/morning/features/2001/aug/southern/010830.southern.sumner.html

Page 340, "I write about . . . calling myself a Southern writer.": Diane Winston, "Seeds of the Soul: New Southern Fiction Digs Deep into Chasms of Belief and Unbelief," *Dallas Morning News*, July 3, 1999.

Credits

"Willie Bea and Jaybird" by Tina McElroy Ansa is reprinted from *Callaloo* 14, no. 1 (1991), by permission of the author.

"Going Critical," from *Deep Sightings and Rescue Missions* by Toni Cade Bambara, copyright © 1996 by the Estate of Toni Cade Bambara. Used by permission of Pantheon Books, a division of Random House, Inc.

"The Road Leads Back," copyright 2003 by Michael Bishop, appears by permission of the author.

"Four from That Summer: Atlanta, 1981" by Pearl Cleage is reprinted from *The Brass Bed and Other Stories* (Chicago: Third World Press, 1991) by permission of the author.

"Nada" by Judith Ortiz Cofer was first published in *The Georgia Review* 46:4 (winter 1992). Reprinted from *The Latin Deli: Prose and Poetry* (Athens: University of Georgia Press, 1993) by permission of the University of Georgia Press.

"You're No Angel Yourself" by Janice Daugharty is reprinted from *Going through the Change* (Princeton: Ontario Review Press, 1994) by permission of the author.

"Soon" by Pam Durban. Copyright © 1996 by Pam Durban. Originally published in *The Southern Review*. Reprinted from *The Best American Short Stories, 1997* (New York: Houghton Mifflin, 1997) by permission of Brandt & Hochman Literary Agents, Inc. All rights reserved.

"The Lady of the Lake," copyright © 1992 by Scott Ely, was first published in *The Southern Review* 28:1 (winter 1992). Reprinted from *Overgrown with Love* (Fayetteville: University of Arkansas Press, 1993) by permission of the author.

"cv10" by Starkey Flythe is reprinted from *Lent: The Slow Fast* (Iowa City: University of Iowa Press, 1990) by permission of the University of Iowa Press.

"New Jerusalem," copyright © 1991 by Jim Grimsley, is reprinted from *64* by permission of the author. All rights reserved.

"Negro Progress" by Anthony Grooms was first published in *Callaloo* 17, no. 4 (fall 1994). Reprinted from *Trouble No More* (Palo Alto, Calif.: La Questa Press, 1995) by permission of the author.

"Rita's Mystery" by John Holman was first published in *The Oxford American*. Reprinted from *New Stories from the South: The Year's Best, 1998*, ed. Shannon Ravenel (Chapel Hill, N.C.: Algonquin Books, 1998), by permission of the author.

"An Early Snow" by Philip Lee Williams is reprinted from *The Chattahoochee Review* (spring 2000) by permission of the author.

"An Independent Woman" by Shay Youngblood is reprinted from *The Big Mama Stories* (Ann Arbor, Mich.: Firebrand Books, 1989) by permission of Firebrand Books. Copyright © 1989 by Shay Youngblood.

Photo Credits

Photograph of Tina McElroy Ansa by Jonée Ansa

Photograph of Toni Cade Bambara by Carlton Jones / W. E. B. Du Bois Film Project

Photograph of Michael Bishop by Beth Gwinn

Photograph of Judith Ortiz Cofer by John Cofer

Photograph of Pam Durban by Tom Meyer

Photograph of Jim Grimsley by Susan Yohann

Photograph of Anthony Grooms by J. D. Scott

Photograph of John Holman by Michael Romeo

Photograph of Charlotte Holmes by Will Brasfield

Photograph of Mary Hood by Charlotte Mealor

Photograph of Ha Jin by Lisha Bian

Photograph of Greg Johnson by Mimi Fittipaldi

Photograph of Sheri Joseph by Greg George

Photograph of Frank Manley by Bradd Shore

Photograph of Cynthia Shearer by Maude Schuyler Clay

Photograph of Charlie Smith © Star Black

Photograph of Melanie Sumner by Saskia Vanderlingen

Photograph of Philip Lee Williams by V. Jane Windsor

Photograph of Shay Youngblood by Rosalind Solomon